P9-CAO-437

Acclaim for

INNOCENT

"You'll hang on tight as the plot twists and swerves and keeps you guessing—and second-guessing...a nifty courtroom thriller."

—*St. Louis Post-Dispatch*

"Timely, pitch-perfect...another one of Turow's masterful and suspenseful murder trials...Turow turned a spellbinding page-turner into a work of art."

—Huffington Post

"Mesmerizing prose and intricate plotting lift Turow's superlative legal thriller, his best novel since his bestselling debut, *Presumed Innocent,* to which this is a sequel...Once again, Turow displays an uncanny ability for making the passions and contradictions of his main characters accessible and understandable."

—*Publishers Weekly*
(boxed and starred review)

"The writing is elegant, the characters lived-in, and the legal and trial details expertly rendered. It's the suspense, though, that will keep you reading."

—*Philadelphia Inquirer*

"An unusually introspective and elegiac book...With Barbara, Turow has created a great, terrifying character out of some Greek tragedy."

—*Entertainment Weekly*

"With all the plot twists and suspense of the first book."

—*New York Daily News*

"A beautifully written book with finely drawn characters and an intricate plot seamlessly weaving a troubled family story with a murder. Drawing the reader in and not letting go until the last page, Turow's legal thriller is a most worthy successor to *Presumed Innocent* and perhaps the author's finest work to date."

—*Library Journal* (starred review)

"Engrossing...As cleverly plotted and surprising as the original and even more cleverly narrated."

—*Chicago Tribune*

"It's a pleasure to return to the territory of *Presumed Innocent* even more for the complex characters than for the subtle and exciting courtroom scenes."

—Bloomberg.com

"Astute and affecting...Turow, as always, breathes realism as well as life into his characters...With smarts and compassion, Turow has again produced a novel that generates the thrills required by the genre and then transcends its limits." —*Richmond Times-Dispatch*

"Written in language that sparkles with clarity and resonates with honest character insight... I came away feeling amazed and fulfilled, as we only do when we read novelists at the height of their powers."

—Stephen King

"In INNOCENT, all Turow's writing skills and legal smarts are on display...the fine writing is enriched by his insights into the trial and criminal justice processes, and his insider views of lawyering." —*Washington Lawyer*

INNOCENT

ALSO BY SCOTT TUROW

SCOTT TUROW

INNOCENT

GRAND CENTRAL
PUBLISHING

NEW YORK   BOSTON

For Nina

———————

Copyright © 2010 by Scott Turow
Excerpt from *Testimony* copyright © 2017 by Scott Turow

Grand Central Publishing
Hachette Book Group
1290 Avenue of the Americas, New York, NY 10104
grandcentralpublishing.com
twitter.com/grandcentralpub

Originally published in hardcover by Grand Central Publishing in 2010.
First oversize mass market edition: January 2012
Reissued: May 2017

Grand Central Publishing is a division of Hachette Book Group, Inc. The Grand Central Publishing name and logo is a trademark of Hachette Book Group, Inc.

The publisher is not responsible for websites (or their content) that are not owned by the publisher.

ISBNs: 978-1-4789-4847-6 (oversize mass market reissue), 978-1-4789-4846-9 (trade paperback reissue), 978-0-446-56821-0 (ebook)

Printed in the United States of America

OPM

10 9 8 7 6 5 4 3 2 1

PROLOGUE

Nat, September 30, 2008

A man is sitting on a bed. He is my father.

The body of a woman is beneath the covers. She was my mother.

This is not really where the story starts. Or how it ends. But it is the moment my mind returns to, the way I always see them.

According to what my father will soon tell me, he has been there, in that room, for nearly twenty-three hours, except for bathroom breaks. Yesterday, he awoke, as he does most weekdays, at half past six and could see the mortal change as soon as he glanced back at my mother, just as his feet had found his slippers. He rocked her shoulder, touched her lips. He pumped the heel of his palm against her sternum a few times, but her skin was cool as clay. Her limbs were already moving in a piece, like a mannequin's.

He will tell me he sat then, in a chair across from her. He never cried. He thought, he will say. He does not know how long, except that the sun had moved all the way across the room, when he finally stood again and began to tidy obsessively.

He will say he put the three or four books she was always reading back on the shelf. He hung up the clothes she had a habit of piling on the chaise in front of her dressing mirror, then made the bed around her, pulling the sheets tight, folding the spread down evenly, before laying her hands out like a doll's on the satin binding of the blanket. He threw out two of the flowers that had wilted in the vase on her night table and straightened the papers and magazines on her desk.

He will tell me he called no one, not even the paramedics because he was certain she was dead, and sent only a one-line e-mail to his assistant to say he would not be at work. He did not answer the phone, although it rang several times. Almost an entire day will have passed before he realizes he must contact me.

But how can she be dead? I will ask. She was fine two nights ago when we were together. After a freighted second, I will tell my father, She didn't kill herself.

No, he will agree at once.

She wasn't in that kind of mood.

It was her heart, he will say then. It had to be her heart. And her blood pressure. Your grandfather died the same way.

Are you going to call the police?

The police, he will say after a time. Why would I call the police?

Well, Christ, Dad. You're a judge. Isn't that what you do when someone dies suddenly? I was crying by now. I didn't know when I had started.

I was going to phone the funeral home, he will tell me, but I realized you might want to see her before I did that.

Well, shit, well, yes, I want to see her.

As it happens, the funeral home will tell us to call our family doctor, and he in turn will summon the coroner, who will send the police. It will become a long morning, and then a longer afternoon, with dozens of people moving in and out of the house. The coroner will not arrive for nearly six hours. He will be alone with my mom's body for only a minute before asking my dad's permission to make an index of all the medications she took. An hour later, I will pass my parents' bathroom and see a cop standing slack-jawed before the open medicine cabinet, a pen and pad in hand.

Jesus, he will declare.

Bipolar disorder, I will tell him when he finally notices me. She had to take a lot of pills. In time, he will simply sweep the shelves clean and go off with a garbage bag containing all the bottles.

In the meanwhile, every so often another police officer will arrive and ask my father about what happened. He tells the story again and again, always the same way.

What was there to think about all that time? one cop will say.

My dad can have a hard way with his blue eyes, something he probably learned from his own father, a man he despised.

Officer, are you married?

I am, Judge.

Then you know what there was to think about. Life, he will answer. Marriage. Her.

The police will make him go through his account three or four more times—how he sat there and why. His response will never vary. He will answer every question in his usual contained manner, the stolid man of law who looks out on life as an endless sea.

He will tell them how he moved each item.

He will tell them where he spent each hour.

But he will not tell anybody about the girl.

PART ONE

I.

Chapter 1

Rusty, March 19, 2007, Eighteen Months Earlier

From the elevated walnut bench a dozen feet above the lawyers' podium, I bang the gavel and call the last case of the morning for oral argument.

"*People versus John Harnason,*" I say, "fifteen minutes each side."

The stately appellate courtroom, with its oxblood pillars rising two stories to a ceiling decorated with rococo gildings, is largely empty of spectators, save for Molly Singh, the *Tribune*'s courthouse reporter, and several young deputy PAs, drawn by a difficult case and the fact that their boss, the acting prosecuting attorney, Tommy Molto, will be making a rare appearance up here to argue in behalf of the State. A ravaged-looking warhorse, Molto sits with two of his deputies at one of the lustrous walnut tables in front of the bench. On the other side, the defendant, John Harnason, convicted of the fatal poisoning of his roommate and lover, waits to hear his fate debated, while his lawyer, Mel Tooley, advances toward the podium. Along the far wall, several law clerks are seated, including Anna Vostic, my senior clerk, who will leave the job on Friday. At my nodding direction, Anna will ignite the tiny lights atop counsel's podium, green, yellow, and red, to indicate the same things they do in traffic.

"May it please the Court," says Mel, the time-ingrained salutation of lawyers to appellate judges. At least seventy pounds overweight these days, Mel still insists on wearing bold pin-striped suits as snug as sausage casings—enough to instill vertigo—and the same lousy rug, which looks as though he skinned a poodle. He begins with an oily grin, as if he and I, and the two judges who flank me on the three-judge panel that will decide the appeal, Marvina Hamlin and George Mason, are all the best of friends. I have never cared for Mel, a bigger snake than usual in the nest of serpents that is the criminal defense bar.

"First," says Mel, "I can't start without briefly wishing Chief Judge Sabich a happy birthday on this personal milestone."

I am sixty years old today, an occasion I have approached with gloom. Mel undoubtedly gleaned this tidbit from the gossip column on page two of today's *Trib*, a daily drumbeat of innuendo and leaks. It concludes routinely with birthday greetings to a variety of celebrities and local notables, which this morning included me: **"Rusty Sabich, Chief Judge of the State Court of Appeals for the Third Appellate District and candidate for the state Supreme Court, 60."** Seeing it in boldface was like taking a bullet.

"I hoped no one had noticed, Mr. Tooley," I say. Everyone in the courtroom laughs. As I discovered long ago, being a judge somehow makes your every joke, even the lamest, side splitting. I beckon Tooley to proceed.

The work of the appellate court in its simplest terms is to make sure that the person appealing got a fair trial. Our docket reflects justice in the American style, divided evenly between the rich, who are usually contesting expensive civil cases, and the poor, who make up most of the criminal appellants and face significant prison terms. Because the state supreme court reviews very few matters, nine times out of ten the court of appeals holds the final word on a case.

The issue today is well-defined: Did the State offer enough evidence to justify the jury's murder verdict against Harnason? Appellate courts rarely reverse on this ground; the rule is that the jury's decision stands unless it is literally irrational. But this was a very close case. Ricardo Millan, Harnason's roommate and business partner in a travel-packaging enterprise, died at the age of thirty-nine of a mysterious progressive illness that the coroner took for an undiagnosed intestinal infection or parasite. There things might have ended were it not for the doggedness of Ricardo's mother, who made several trips here from Puerto Rico. She used all her savings to hire a private detective and a toxicologist at the U who persuaded the police to exhume Ricardo's body. Hair specimens showed lethal levels of arsenic.

Poisoning is murder for the underhanded. No knife, no gun. No Nietzschean moment when you confront the victim and feel the elemental thrill of exerting your will. It involves fraud far more than violence. And it's hard not to believe that what sunk Harnason before the

jury is simply that he looks the part. He appears vaguely
familiar, but that must be from seeing his picture in
the paper, because I would recall somebody so self-
consciously odd. He is wearing a garish copper-colored
suit. On the hand with which he is furiously scribbling
notes, his nails are so long that they have begun to curl
under like some Chinese emperor's, and an abundance
of unmanageable orangey knots covers his scalp. In
fact, there is too much reddish hair all over his head.
His overgrown eyebrows make him resemble a beaver,
and a gingery mustache droops over his mouth. I have
always been baffled by folks like this. Is he demanding attention or does he simply think the rest of us are
boring?

Aside from his looks, the actual evidence that Harnason murdered Ricardo is spotty. Neighbors reported
a recent episode in which a drunken Harnason bran-
dished a kitchen knife on the street, screaming at
Ricardo about his visits with a younger man. The State
also emphasized that Harnason went to court to prevent exhuming Ricardo's body, where he maintained
that Ricky's mother was a kook who'd stick Harnason
with the bill for another burial. Probably the only piece
of substantial proof is that the detectives found micro-
scopic traces of arsenic oxide ant poison in the shed
behind the house that Harnason inherited from his
mother. The product had not been manufactured for
at least a decade, leading the defense to maintain that
the infinitesimal granules were merely a degraded left-
over from the mother's time, whereas the real perpe-
trator could have purchased a more reliably lethal form
of arsenic oxide from several vendors on the Internet.

Despite the familiarity of arsenic as a classic poison, such deaths are a rarity these days, and thus arsenic is not covered in routine toxicological screenings performed in connection with autopsies, which is why the coroner initially missed the cause of death.

All in all, the evidence is so evenly balanced that as chief judge, I decided to order Harnason freed on bail pending his appeal. That does not happen often after a defendant is convicted, but it seemed unfair for Harnason to start doing time in this razor-thin case before we passed on the matter.

My order accounts, in turn, for the appearance today by Tommy Molto, the acting PA. Molto is a skillful appellate advocate, but as head of his office, he rarely has the time to argue appeals these days. He is handling this case because the prosecutors clearly read the bail ruling as an indication Harnason's murder conviction might be reversed. Molto's presence is meant to emphasize how strongly his office stands by its evidence. I give Tommy his wish, as it were, and question him closely once he takes his turn at the podium.

"Mr. Molto," I say, "correct me, but as I read the record, there is no proof at all how Mr. Harnason would know that arsenic would not be detected by a routine toxicological screening, and thus that he could pass off Mr. Millan's death as one by natural causes. That isn't public information, is it, about what's covered on an autopsy tox screen?"

"It's not a state secret, Your Honor, but no, it's not publicized, no."

"And secret or not, there was no proof that Harnason would know, was there?"

"That is correct, Chief Judge," says Molto.

One of Tommy's strengths up here is that he is unfailingly polite and direct, but he cannot keep a familiar shadow of brooding discontent from darkening his face in response to my interrogation. The two of us have a complicated history. Molto was the junior prosecutor in the event twenty-one years ago that still divides my life as neatly as a stripe down the center of a road, when I was tried and then exonerated of the murder of another deputy prosecuting attorney.

"And in fact, Mr. Molto, there wasn't even clear evidence how Mr. Harnason could have poisoned Mr. Millan, was there? Didn't several of their friends testify that Mr. Millan cooked all the meals?"

"Yes, but Mr. Harnason usually poured the drinks."

"But the defense chemist said arsenic oxide is too bitter to be concealed even in something like a martini or a glass of wine, didn't he? The prosecution didn't really refute that testimony, did you?"

"There was no rebuttal on that point, that is true, Your Honor. But these men shared most of their meals. That certainly gave Harnason plenty of opportunity to commit the crime the jury convicted him of."

Around the courthouse these days, people speak regularly of how different Tommy seems, married for the first time late in life and ensconced by luck in a job he plainly longed for. Tommy's recent good fortune has done little to rescue him from his lifetime standing among the physically unblessed. His face looks time-worn, verging on elderly. The little bit of hair left on his head has gone entirely white, and there are pouches of flesh beneath his eyes like used teabags. Yet there is no denying a subtle improvement. Tommy has lost weight and bought suits that no longer look as if he'd slept in them, and he often sports an expression of peace and, even, cheerfulness. But not now. Not with me. When it comes to me, despite the years, Tommy still regards me as an enduring enemy, and judging by his look as he heads back to his seat, he takes my doubts today as further proof.

As soon as the argument is over, the other two judges and I adjourn without our clerks to a conference room adjoining the courtroom, where we will discuss the morning's cases and decide their outcome, including which of the three of us will write each opinion for the court. This is an elegant chamber that looks like the dining room in a men's club, right down to the crystal chandelier. A vast Chippendale table holds enough high-backed leather chairs to seat all eighteen judges of the court on the rare occasion that we sit together—en banc, as it is known—to decide a case.

"Affirm," says Marvina Hamlin, as if there is no point for discussion, once we get to *Harnason*. Marvina is your average tough black lady with plenty of reason to be that way. She was ghetto raised, had a son at sixteen, and still worked her way through school, starting as a legal secretary and ending up as a lawyer—and a good one, too. She tried two cases in front of me when I was a trial judge years ago. On the other hand, after sitting with Marvina for a decade, I know she will not change her mind. She has not heard another human being say anything worth considering since her mother told her at a very early age that she had to watch out for herself. "Who else could have done it?" demands Marvina.

"Does your assistant bring you coffee, Marvina?" I ask.

"I fetch for myself, thank you," she answers.

"You know what I mean. What proof was there that it wasn't someone at work?"

"The prosecutors don't have to chase rabbits down every hole," she answers. "And neither do we."

She's right about that, but fortified by this exchange, I tell my colleagues I'm going to vote to reverse. Thus we each turn to George Mason, who will functionally decide the case. A mannerly Virginian, George still retains soft traces of his native accent and is blessed with the white coif central casting would order for a judge. George is my best friend on the court and will succeed me as chief judge if, as widely anticipated, I win both the primary and the general election next year and move up to the state supreme court.

"I think it's just inside the boundary," he says.

"George!" I protest. George Mason and I have been at each other's throats as lawyers since he showed up thirty years ago as the newly minted state defender assigned to the courtroom where I was the lead prosecutor. Early experience is formative in the law like everything else, and George sides with defendants more often than I do. But not today.

"I admit it would have been an NG if it was tried as a bench in front of me," he says, "but we're on appeal and I don't get to substitute my judgment for the jury's."

This little tweak is aimed at me. I would never say it aloud, but I sense that Molto's appearance, and the importance the PA places on the case, has moved the needle just enough with both of my colleagues. Yet the point is I've lost. That too is part of the job, accepting the law's ambiguities. I ask Marvina to draft the opinion for the court. Still a little hot, she exits, leaving George and me to ourselves.

"Tough case," he says. It's an axiom of this life that, like a husband and wife who do not go to bed angry, judges of a court of review leave their disagreements in the impressions conference. I shrug in response, but he can tell I remain unsettled. "Why don't you draft a dissent?" he suggests, meaning my own opinion, explaining why I think the other two got it wrong. "I promise I'll look at the matter fresh when it's on paper."

I rarely dissent, since it's one of my primary responsibilities as chief judge to promote harmony on the court, but I decide to take him up on his offer, and I head down to my chambers to begin the process with my law clerks. As chief, I occupy a suite the size of a small house. Off a large anteroom occupied by my assistant and my courtroom staff are two compact offices for my law clerks and, on the other side, my own vast work space, thirty-by-thirty and a story and a half high, with wainscoting of ancient varnished oak that lends my inside chambers the dark air of a castle.

When I push open the door to the large room, I find a crowd of forty or so people who immediately shrill out, "Surprise!" I am surprised all right, but principally by how morbid I find the recollection of my birthday. Nonetheless, I pretend to be delighted as I circle the room, greeting persons whose long-standing presence in my life makes them, in my current mood, as bleakly poignant as the messages on tombstones.

Both my son, Nat, now twenty-eight, too lean but

hauntingly handsome amid his torrents of jet hair, and Barbara, my wife of thirty-six years, are here, and so are all but two of the other seventeen judges on the court. George Mason has arrived now and manages a hug, a gesture of the times with which neither of us is fully comfortable, as he hands me a box on behalf of all my colleagues.

Also present are a few key administrators on the court staff and several friends who remain practicing lawyers. My former attorney, Sandy Stern, round and robust but bothered by a summer cough, is here with his daughter and law partner, Marta, and so is the man who more than twenty-five years ago made me his chief deputy, former prosecuting attorney Raymond Horgan. Ray evolved from friend to enemy and back again in the space of a single year, when he testified against me at my trial and then, after my acquittal, put in motion the process that made me acting PA. Raymond again is playing a large role in my life as the chair of my supreme court campaign. He strategizes and shakes the money tree at the big firms, leaving the operational details to two she-wolves, thirty-one and thirty-three, whose commitment to my election seems about as deep as a hit man's.

Most of the guests are or were trial lawyers, an amiable group by nature, and there is great bonhomie and laughter. Nat will graduate from law school in June and, after the bar, begin a clerkship on the state supreme court, where I, too, was once a law clerk. Nat remains himself, uncomfortable in conversation, and Barbara and I, by long habit, drift near from time to time to protect him. My own two law clerks, who do a similar job to the one Nat will be taking, assisting me in researching and writing my opinions for this court, have assumed less distinguished duty today as waiters. Because Barbara is perpetually ill at ease in the world beyond our house, especially in larger social gatherings, Anna Vostic, my senior clerk, serves more or less as hostess, pouring a dribble of champagne into the bottom of the plastic glasses that are soon raised for a lusty singing of "Happy Birthday." Everyone cheers when it turns out I still am full of enough hot air to extinguish the forest fire of candles on the four-tier carrot cake Anna baked.

The invitation said no presents, but there are a couple of gags—George found a card that reads, "Congratulations, man, you're 60 and you know what that means." Inside: "No more khakis!" Below, George has inscribed by hand, "P.S. Now you know why judges wear robes." In the box he handed over, there is a new death-black gown with braided golden drum major epaulets fixed at the shoulder. The mock finery for the chief inspires broad guffaws when I display it to the assembled guests.

After another ten minutes of mingling, the group begins to disperse.

"News," Ray Horgan says in a voice delicate enough for a pixie as he edges past on his way out. A grin creases his wide pink face, but partisan talk about my candidacy is forbidden on public property, and as chief judge, I am ever mindful of the burden of being an example. Instead, I agree to come by his office in half an hour.

After everyone else is gone, Nat and Barbara and I

and the members of my staff gather up the paper plates and glasses. I thank them all.

"Anna was wonderful," says Barbara, then adds, in one of those bursts of candor my odd duck of a wife will never understand is not required, "This whole party was her idea." Barbara is especially fond of my senior law clerk and often expresses dismay that Anna is just a little too old for Nat, who has recently parted with his long-term girlfriend. I join the compliments for Anna's baking, which is locally famous in the court of appeals. Emboldened by the presence of my family, which can only mark her gesture as innocuous, Anna advances to embrace me while I pat her back in comradely fashion.

"Happy birthday, Judge," she declares. "You rock!" With that, she's gone, while I do my best to banish the startling sensation of Anna full against me from my mind, or at least my expression.

I firm up dinner plans with my wife and son. Barbara predictably prefers to eat at home rather than at a restaurant. They depart while the odors of cake and champagne linger sadly in the newly silent room. Sixty years along, I am, as ever, alone to deal with myself.

I have never been what anybody would call a cheerful sort. I'm well aware that I've had more than my fair share of good fortune. I love my son. I relish my work. I climbed back to the heights of respectability after tumbling into a valley of shame and scandal. I have a middle-aged marriage that survived a crisis beyond easy imagining and is often peaceful, if never fully connected. But I was raised in a troubled home by a timid and distracted mother and a father who felt no shame about being a son of a bitch. I was not happy as a child, and thus it seemed very much the nature of things that I would never come of age contented.

But even by the standards of somebody whose emotional temperature usually ranges from blah to blue, I've been in a bad way awaiting today. The march to mortality occurs every second, but we all suffer certain signposts. Forty hit me like a ton of bricks: the onset of middle age. And with sixty, I know full well that the curtain is rising on the final act. There is no avoiding the signs: Statins to lower my cholesterol. Flomax to downsize my prostate. And four Advil with dinner every night, because a day of sitting, an occupational hazard, does a number on my lower back.

The prospect of decline adds a special dread of the future and, particularly, my campaign for the supreme court, because when I take the oath twenty months from now, I will have gone as far as ambition can propel me. And I know there will still be a nagging whisper from my heart. It's not enough, the voice will say. Not yet. All this done, all this accomplished. And yet, at the heart of my heart, I will still not have the unnameable piece of happiness that has eluded me for sixty years.

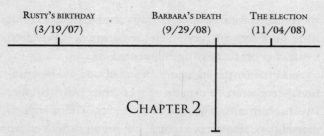

RUSTY'S BIRTHDAY
(3/19/07)

BARBARA'S DEATH
(9/29/08)

THE ELECTION
(11/04/08)

CHAPTER 2

Tommy Molto, September 30, 2008

Tomassino Molto III, acting prosecuting attorney for Kindle County, was behind the PA's desk, big and heavy as a '60s Cadillac, wondering how different he was, when his chief deputy, Jim Brand, struck a single knuckle on the door frame.

"Deep thoughts?" asked Brand.

Tommy smiled, making the best efforts of a chronically blunt personality to be elusive. The question of how much he had changed in the last two years arrived in Tommy's brain like a drip from an eave once or twice every hour. People said he was dramatically altered, joking all the time about where he hid the genie and the magic lamp. But Tommy was in his second stint as acting prosecutor and he'd learned to recognize the flattery people always paid to power. How much could anybody change, after all? he wondered. Was he really different? Or was he simply who he had always known he was at the core?

"State copper from Nearing just called in," said Brand once he entered. "They found Barbara Sabich dead in her bed. The chief judge's wife?"

Tommy loved Jim Brand. He was a fine lawyer and
loyal in a way few people were these days. But even
so, Molto bridled at the suggestion he had a peculiar
interest in Rusty Sabich. He did, of course. Twenty-
two years later, the name of the chief judge of the
court of appeals, who Tommy had unsuccessfully prosecuted for murdering a female colleague of theirs, still
coursed through him like current after the insertion of
a plug. But what he did not care for was the insinuation he had carried a long grudge against Sabich. A
grudge was a badge of the dishonest, who could not
face the truth, including a truth that was unflattering
to them. Tommy had long accepted the outcome of
that case. A trial was a dogfight, and Rusty and his dog
had won.

"So?" asked Tommy. "Is the office sending flowers?"

Brand, tall and solid in a white shirt starched stiff as
a priest's collar, smiled, revealing good teeth. Tommy
did not respond, because he had actually meant it. This
had happened to Tommy his entire life, when his own
internal logic, so clear and unfaltering, led to a remark
that everybody else took for blatant comedy.

"No, it's strange," said Brand. "That's why the lieutenant called it in. It's like, 'What's up with this?' The
wife croaks and the husband doesn't even dial 911.
Who appointed Rusty Sabich coroner?"

Tommy beckoned for more details. The judge,
Brand said, had not told a soul, not even his son, for
nearly twenty-four hours. Instead, he had arranged the
corpse like a mortician, as if they would be waking her
right there. Sabich attributed his actions to shock, to
grief. He had wanted it all to be just so before he shared

the news. Tommy supposed he could understand that. Twenty-two months ago, at the age of fifty-seven, after a life in which poignant longing seemed as inevitable as breathing, Tommy had fallen in love with Dominga Cortina, a shy but lovely administrator in the Clerk of Court's office. Falling in love was nothing new for Tommy. Every couple of years throughout his life some woman appeared at work, in the pews at church, in his high-rise, for whom he developed a fascination and a desire that ran over him like an oncoming train. The interest, inevitably, was never returned, so Dominga's averted eyes whenever Tommy was near her seemed to be more of the same, surely understandable since she was only thirty-one. But one of her friends had noticed Tommy's pining glances and whispered he should ask her out. They were married nine weeks later. Eleven months after that Tomaso was born. Now if Dominga died, the earth would collapse the same way as a dead star, all matter reduced to an atom. For Tommy was different, he always decided, in one fundamental way: He had felt joy. At long last. And at an age when most people, even those who'd enjoyed large helpings, gave up the hope of having more.

"Thirty-five years married or whatever," Tommy said now. "Jesus. A guy could act strange. He's a strange guy anyway."

"That's what they say," answered Brand. Jim did not know Sabich really. To him, the chief judge was a remote personage. Brand did not recall the days when Rusty roamed the halls here in the PA's office with a scowl seemingly aimed principally at himself. Brand was forty-two. Forty-two was a grown-up. Old enough to be president or to run this office. But it was a different grown-up from Tommy's. What was life to Tommy was history to Brand.

"The copper's whiskers are twitching," said Brand.

Cops were always hinky. Every good guy was really a bad guy in drag.

"What does he think happened?" Molto asked. "Any sign of violence?"

"Well, they'll wait for the coroner, but no blood or anything. No bruises."

"So?"

"Well, I don't know, Boss—but twenty-four hours? You could hide a lot of stuff. Something in the blood-stream could dissipate."

"Like what?"

"Shit, Tom, I'm spitballing. But the coppers think they should do something. That's why I'm coming to you."

Whenever Tommy thought back to the Sabich trial twenty-two years ago, what echoed through time was the teeming emotions. Deputy Prosecuting Attorney Carolyn Polhemus, who'd been a friend of Tommy's, one of those women he couldn't help longing for, had been found dead and naked in her apartment. With the crime falling in the midst of a brutal campaign for prosecuting attorney between Ray Horgan, the incumbent, and Tommy's lifelong friend Nico Della Guardia, the murder investigation was charged from the start. Ray assigned it to Rusty, his chief deputy, who never mentioned that he'd had a secret fling with Carolyn that had ended badly months before. Then Rusty dogged the case and conveniently failed to collect a variety of proof—phone records, fingerprint analyses—that pointed straight at him.

Sabich's guilt had seemed so plain when they charged him after Nico won the election. But the case fell apart at trial. Evidence disappeared, and the police pathologist, who'd identified Rusty's blood type in the semen specimen recovered from Carolyn, had forgotten the victim had her tubes tied and couldn't explain on the stand why she'd used a common spermicide as well. Rusty's lawyer, Sandy Stern, lit up each crack in the prosecution facade and attributed every failure— the missing evidence, the possible contamination of the specimen—to Tommy, to a self-conscious effort to frame Sabich. And it worked. Rusty walked, Nico was recalled by the voters, and to add insult to injury, Sabich was appointed acting PA.

Over the years since, Tommy had tried to make an even assessment of the possibility that Rusty was not guilty. As a matter of reason, it could have been true. And that was his public posture. Tommy never talked to anyone about the case without saying, Who knows? The system worked. The judge went free. Move on. Tommy didn't understand how time began or what had happened to Jimmy Hoffa or why the Trappers lost year after year. And he had no idea who killed Carolyn Polhemus.

But his heart did not really follow the path of reason. There it was scorched on the walls the way people blackened their initials with a torch on the interior of a cave: Sabich did it. A year-long investigation eventually proved that Tommy had committed almost none of the breaches he'd been slyly accused of in the courtroom.

Not that Tommy hadn't made mistakes. He'd leaked confidential information to Nico during the campaign, but every deputy PA talked out of school. Yet Tommy hadn't hidden evidence or suborned perjury. Tommy was innocent, and because he knew he was innocent, it seemed a matter of equal logic that Sabich was guilty. But he shared the truth only with himself, not even Dominga, who almost never asked him about work.

"I can't go near this," he told Brand. "Too much history."

Brand hitched a shoulder. He was a big guy, walked on at the U, and ended up an all-conference outside linebacker. That was twenty years ago. He had a huge head and not much hair left on it. And he was shaking it slowly.

"You can't get off a case whenever a defendant comes bobbing by on the merry-go-round for a second time. You want me to go through the files and see how many indictments you've signed already on guys who beat their first beef?"

"Any of them about to be elected to the state supreme court? Rusty casts a big shadow, Jimmy."

"I'm just saying," said Brand.

"Let's get the autopsy results. But until then, nothing else. No nosy coppers trying to sniff Rusty's behind. And no involvement by this office. No grand jury subpoenas or anything unless and until something substantial turns on the post. Which ain't gonna happen. We can all think whatever we wanna think about Rusty Sabich. But he's a smart guy. Really smart. Let the Nearing coppers go play in their sandbox until we hear from the coroner. That's all."

Brand didn't like it, Tommy could tell. But he'd been a marine and understood the chain of command. He departed with the faint damning that always went with it when he declared, "Whatever you say, Boss."

Alone, Tommy spent a second thinking about Barbara Sabich. She had been a babe as a young woman, with tight dark curls and a killer bod and a tough look that said that no guy could really have her. Tommy had barely seen her in the last couple of decades. She did not share the same responsibilities as her husband and had probably avoided Molto. During Sabich's trial years ago, she sat in court every day, sizzling Tommy with a furious look whenever he glanced her way. What makes you so sure? he sometimes wanted to ask her. The answer was gone to the grave with her now. As he had since his days as an altar boy, Tommy moved himself to a brief prayer for the dead. Commit, dear Lord, the soul of Barbara Sabich to Your eternal embrace. She was Jewish, as Molto remembered, and wouldn't care for his prayers, and even before Rusty's indictment had never much cared for Tommy, either. The same welling hurt Tommy had felt his whole life in the face of frequent scorn rose up in him, and he fought it off, another ingrained habit. He would pray for her anyway. It was inclinations like these that Dominga had recognized and that eventually won her. She knew the good in Tommy's heart, far more than any human being save his mother, who passed five years ago.

With the image of his young wife, slightly plump, bountiful in the right places, Tommy for a moment was overcome with longing. He felt himself swelling below.

It was no sin, he had decided, to lust after your own wife. Rusty had probably once yearned for Barbara that way. Now she was gone. Take her, God, he thought again. Then he looked around the room, trying once more to decide how different he was.

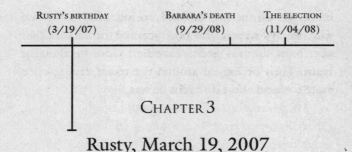

RUSTY'S BIRTHDAY
(3/19/07)

BARBARA'S DEATH
(9/29/08)

THE ELECTION
(11/04/08)

CHAPTER 3

Rusty, March 19, 2007

The State Court of Appeals for the Third Appellate District now resides in the seventy-year-old Central Branch Courthouse, a white-columned redbrick structure that was remodeled in the 1980s with federal crime-fighting money. Most of the funds were spent refurbishing the criminal courtrooms on the lower floors, but a fair chunk also went to create a new home for the court of appeals on the top floor. The millions were invested in the hope that this area, beyond Center City and the canyon created by I-843, would revive, but the defense lawyers depart in their luxury cars as soon as court is over, and few merchants have been inclined to take a stake in a neighborhood in which the largest number of daily visitors are accused criminals. The concrete square between here and the County Building across the street, a bland piece of public architecture, has proved most useful as a place to stage demonstrations.

I am no more than two hundred feet outside the courthouse door, on my way to meet Raymond and learn his news about my campaign, when I hear my name and turn to find John Harnason standing behind me. He now wears a straw porkpie hat, his reddish hair protruding a little bit like Bozo's. I sense at once that he has been lurking, waiting for me to emerge.

"So, may I ask. How am I doing, Judge?"

"Mr. Harnason, you and I should not be speaking, especially when your case is under consideration." No judge can meet with a party outside the company of the other side.

Harnason touches a stout finger to his lips. "Not a word about that, Your Honor. Just wanted to join in the birthday wishes and say thanks personally for my bail. Mel told me it would take a judge who was swinging titanium ornaments to grant bond. Not that I wasn't entitled. But he said nobody gets applause for setting convicted murderers on the loose. Of course, you know a little of what it's like to be in this kind of spot."

By long practice, I show no reaction. At this stage of my life, months pass without people making any reference to my indictment and trial. Instead, I start to turn away, but Harnason holds up a hand with those strangely long nails.

"Have to say I was curious whether you remembered me, Judge. I've been a bit of a bad penny in your life."

"We've met?"

"I used to be a lawyer, Your Honor. Long ago. Until you prosecuted me."

In all, I spent nearly fifteen years in the prosecuting attorney's office, more than twelve as a deputy and two, like Tommy Molto, as the court-appointed acting PA, before I was elected to the bench. Even then, there was no chance I could remember every case I handled, and by now it's hopeless. But we charged very few lawyers in those days. We did not prosecute priests or doctors or executives, either. Punishment, back then, was reserved largely for the poor.

"Wasn't called John," he says. "That was my dad. Used to go as J. Robert."

"J. Robert Harnason," I say. The name is like an incantation, and I let slip a tiny sound. No wonder Harnason looked familiar.

"Now you've placed me." He seems pleased the case came to mind so quickly, although I doubt he feels anything but pique. Harnason was a knockabout neighborhood lawyer, scuffling for a living, who eventually hit on a familiar strategy to improve his lifestyle. He settled personal injury cases, and instead of paying out the share of the insurance proceeds due his clients, he kept it until he stilled one client's repeated complaints by repaying him with the settlement money due somebody else. Hundreds of other attorneys in the Tri-Cities committed the same big-time no-no every year, dipping into their clients' funds to make rent or pay taxes or their kids' tuition. The worst cases led to disbarment, and Harnason probably would have gotten away with only that, but for one fact: He had a lengthy arrest record for public indecency, as a denizen of the gay shadow world of those years, where bars were alternately raided and shaken down by cops.

His lawyer, Thorsen Skoglund, a taciturn Finn now long gone, didn't bother pulling punches when he came to argue my decision to charge Harnason with a felony.

'You're prosecuting him for being queer.'

'So?' I answered. I frequently recall the conversation—if not who it concerned—because even when I said that, it felt as if a hand had started waving near my heart, asking for more attention. One of the harshest realities of the jobs I've had, as a prosecutor and a judge, is that I have done a lot in the name of the law that history—and I—have come to regret.

"You changed my life, Judge." There is nothing unpleasant in his tone, but prison was a hard place for a punk in those days. Very hard. He had been a handsome young man as I remember him, a bit soft-looking, with slicked-back auburn hair, nervous, but far more self-possessed than the oddball who has come to accost me.

"That doesn't sound like a thank-you to me, Mr. Harnason."

"No. No, I wouldn't have offered any thanks at the time. But frankly, Judge, I'm a realist. I truly am. Even twenty-five years ago, shoe could have been on the other foot, you know. I applied twice to the prosecuting attorney's office and nearly got hired as a deputy PA. I could have been the one trying to send you away because of who you slept with. That's what they prosecuted you for, really, right? If my memory's good, there wasn't much proof besides you had your finger in the pudding?"

The facts are close enough. I've got Harnason's message: He sank, I floated. And it's hard, at least for him, to see why.

"This is not a fruitful conversation, Mr. Harnason. Or an appropriate one." I turn, but he reaches after me again.

"No harm meant, Judge. Just wanted to say hello. And thanks. You've had my life in your hands twice, Your Honor. You did me better this time than the first—at least so far." He smiles a little at the caveat, but with that thought his look grows more solemn. "Do I have a chance, at least, Judge?" Uttering the question, he suddenly seems as pathetic as an orphaned child.

"John," I say, then stop. 'John'? But there is something about the fact that Harnason and I met decades ago, and the harm I did him, that demands a less imperial pose. And I can hardly retrieve his first name now that it's come out of my mouth. "As you could tell from the argument, your points aren't falling entirely on deaf ears, John. The discussion isn't over."

"Still hope, then?"

I shake my head to indicate no more, but he thanks me nonetheless, bowing slightly in utter obsequiousness.

"Happy birthday," he calls again when I've finally turned my back on him. I walk off, fully haunted.

When I return to the building, following a mildly disturbing campaign meeting with Raymond, it is after five, the witching hour after which the public employees disappear as if sucked out by a Hoover. Anna, the hardest-working clerk I've ever had by a long measure, is here, as she often is, toiling alone. Shoeless, she wanders behind me into my inner chambers, where the rows of leather-spined legal volumes that are basically ornamental in the computer era repose on the bookshelves along with photos and mementos of family and career.

"Getting ready to go?" I ask her. We will celebrate

Anna's last day with me on Friday with a dinner in her honor, something I do for all departing law clerks. The following Monday, Anna will join the litigation department in Ray Horgan's firm. She will have a higher salary than I do and a long-delayed start on Real Life. In the last twelve years, she has been an EMT, an advertising writer, a business school student, a marketing executive, and now a lawyer. Like Nat, Anna is part of a generation that often seem frozen in place by their unrelenting sense of irony. Virtually everything people believe in can be exposed as possessing laughable inconsistencies. And so they laugh. And stand still.

"I suppose," she says, then brightens. "I have a birthday card."

"After everything else?" I answer, but I accept the envelope.

"You're SIXTY," it reads. There is a picture of a knockout blonde in a tight sweater. "Too old not to know better." Overleaf: "Or to care." The card adds, "Enjoy it all!" Below, she has written simply, "Love, Anna."

'Not to care.' Were it only so. Is it just my imagination that the buxom girl on the front even looks faintly like her?

"Cute," I say.

"It was too perfect," she answers. "I couldn't pass it up."

I say nothing for a second as we stare at each other.

"Go," I finally tell her. "Work." She is, alas, very cute, green-eyed and dishwater blond, ruddy, sturdily built. She is pretty and, if not quite in the drop-dead category, full of earthy appeal. She sashays off in her straight skirt with a little extra hip roll of a broad but nicely turned behind and looks back to measure the effect. I flip my hand to tell her to keep moving.

Anna has worked for me for almost two and a half years now, longer than any other clerk I've employed. A canny lawyer with an obvious gift for this profession, she also has a sunny, eager nature. She is open with almost everyone and is frequently blazingly funny, which delights no one more than her. On top of all that, she is tirelessly kind. Because her computer skills exceed those of most of the IT staff, she is always giving up her lunch hour to fix a problem in another chambers. She bakes for my staff, remembers birthdays and the details of everybody's families. She is, in other words, a human being engaged by human beings and is beloved around the building.

But she is happier about the lives of others than she is about her own. Love, in particular, is a preoccupation. She is full of yearning—and despair. She has brought to chambers a stream of self-help titles, which she often trades with Joyce, my courtroom bailiff. *Loved the Way You Want to Be. How to Know If You Are Loved Enough.* When she reads at lunch, you can see her bright exterior peeled away.

Anna's lengthy stint with me, which was extended when the successor I'd hired, Kumari Bata, ended up unexpectedly pregnant and on total bed rest, has led to an inevitable familiarity. For some time now, when we work together a couple nights a week to clear up administrative orders, she allows herself a free-form confessional that often touches on her romantic misfortunes.

'I've been dating around, trying not to take

anything too seriously so I don't get my hopes up,' she told me once. 'That's worked in a way. I have no hope at all.' She smiled, as she does, enjoying the humor more than the bitterness. 'You know, I was married for a nanosecond when I was twenty-two, and once it was over, I never worried I wouldn't find anybody special. I thought I was too young. But the men still are! I'm thirty-four. The last guy I went out with was forty. And he was a boy. A *baby*! He hadn't learned to pick up his laundry off the floor. I need a man, a real grown-up.'

All of this seemed innocent enough until a few months ago, when I began to sense that the grown-up she had in mind was me.

'Why is it so hard to get laid?' she asked me one night in December as she was describing another unrewarding first date.

'I can't believe that,' I finally said, when I could breathe.

'Not by anyone I really care about,' she answered, and abjectly shook her midlength, many-toned hairdo. 'You know, I'm really starting to say, What the hell? I'll try anything. Not *any*thing. Not midgets and horses. But maybe I should go to one of those places I never considered. Or that I actually considered and laughed off. Because trying to do what's "normal" hasn't produced such especially good results. So maybe I should be bad. Have you been bad, Judge?' she asked me suddenly, her dark green eyes like radar.

'We've all been bad,' I said quietly.

That was a pivot point. By now, her approaches whenever we are alone are unabashed and direct—cheap double entendres, winks, everything short of a

FOR SALE sign. A few nights back, she suddenly stood and laid her hand on her midriff to tighten her blouse as she stood at profile.

'Do you think I'm top-heavy?' she asked.

I took too long enjoying the sight before I answered in as neutral a tone as I could muster that she looked fine.

My excuses for tolerating this are twofold. First, at thirty-four, Anna is a little long in the tooth for judicial clerks and well beyond any developmental stage that would mark her behavior as part of childhood. Second, she will not be around here much longer. Kumari, now a healthy mom, started last week, and Anna has stayed a few final days to train her. For me, Anna's departure will be both a genuine tragedy and a considerable relief.

But since the mere passage of time is going to solve my problems, the one thing I have not done is what good judgment really requires—sit Anna down and tell her no. Gently. Kindly. With openhearted tribute to the flattery I'm being paid. But nohow, no way. I have prepared the speech several times but cannot bring myself to deliver it. For one thing, I could end up badly embarrassed. Anna's sense of humor, which could be called "male" in this Mars and Venus era, veers often to the risqué. I still fear she would say this was all a joke, the kinds of cracks ventured, as we all do now and then, to be sure you don't really mean them. A sorer truth is that I am reluctant to stop drinking in the sheer aqua vitae that springs from the purported sexual willingness, even in jest, of a good-looking woman more than twenty-five years my junior.

But I have recognized all along I will turn away. I

don't know what percentage of attractions are consigned to mere flirtation and never pass the best controlled of all borders, the one between imagining and actual events, but surely it's most. In thirty-six years of marriage, I have had one affair, not counting a drunken tossing in the back of a station wagon when I was in basic training for the National Guard, and that lone mad, compulsive detour into the pure excesses of pleasure led directly to me standing trial for murder. If I'm not the poster boy for Twice Wise, nobody will ever be.

I work in my chambers for no more than half an hour when Anna sticks her head in again.

"I think you're late." She's right. I have my birthday dinner.

"Crap," I answer. "I'm an airhead."

She has the flash drive she prepares each night with draft opinions I will review at home, and she helps me into my suit coat, settling it in on my shoulder.

"Happy birthday again, Judge," she says, and lays one finger on the middle button. "I hope whatever you wish for comes true." She gives me an utterly naked look and rises in her stocking feet to her toes. It's one of those moments so corny and obvious that it seems it could not quite happen, but her lips are set on mine, if only for a second. As ever, I do nothing to resist. I light up from root to stem but say no word, not even goodbye, as I go out the door.

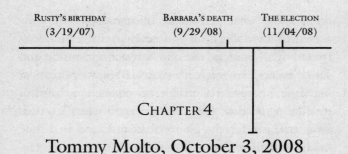

RUSTY'S BIRTHDAY
(3/19/07)

BARBARA'S DEATH
(9/29/08)

THE ELECTION
(11/04/08)

CHAPTER 4

Tommy Molto, October 3, 2008

Jim Brand knocked on Tommy's door but remained on the threshold, waiting for the PA to motion him in. During Tommy's first brief term as PA in 2006, he had felt a lack of regard. After more than thirty years in this office, he had such a defined reputation as a stolid warrior, here from eight a.m. to ten p.m. each day, it seemed hard for other deputy PAs to treat him with the deference due the office's ultimate authority. As chief deputy, Brand had changed that. His respect and affection for Molto were obvious, and it was natural for him to make the kinds of small formal gestures—knocking on the door—that by now had led most of the deputies to greet Tommy as "Boss."

"Okay," says Brand. "So we got a little update on Rusty Sabich. An initial path report on the wife."

"And?"

"And it's interesting. Ready?"

That actually was a question worth asking. Was Tommy ready? Going around again with Rusty Sabich could kill him. In terms of common understanding these days, the kind that floated around the courthouse like the fluoride in the tap water from the river Kindle, the Sabich case had been a rush to judgment by Nico. Tommy was along for the ride, but not responsible for the ultimate decisions, which were inept but not made with true malice. This interpretation suited everybody. After being recalled as prosecuting attorney, Nico had moved to Florida, where he had made several gazillion dollars in the tobacco litigation. He owned an island in the Keys, to which he invited Tommy, and now Dominga, at least twice a year.

As for Tommy and Sabich, both had crawled to shore in the aftermath of a personal disaster and resumed their lives. It was actually Rusty, then acting PA, who'd given Tommy his job back, a silent acknowledgment that all that frame-up stuff was horse-hockey. When the two were together these days, as occurred frequently, they managed a strained cordiality, not only as a matter of professional necessity but perhaps because they had overcome the same cataclysm together. They were like two brothers who would never get along but were scarred and shaped by the same upbringing.

"Cause of death heart failure, as the result of arrhythmia and a possible hypertensive reaction," said Brand.

"That's interesting?"

"Well, that's what Sabich said. That she had a skippy heart and high blood pressure. He told the cops that. How does somebody just guess?"

"Come on, Jim. There was probably a family history."

"That's what he said. That her old man died that way. But maybe her aorta blew out. Maybe she had a stroke. But no—he says, boom, 'heart failure.'"

"Let me see," said Molto. He extended his hand for the report and in the process decided it was a good idea to close the door. From the threshold, he looked out beyond the anteroom, where his two secretaries worked, to the dark corridors. He had to do something about these offices; that was another thing Tommy thought each day. The PA had been housed in the dismal County Building, where the light had the quality of old shellac, throughout Tommy's three-decade career here and for at least a quarter century before that. The place was a hazard, with the wires in plastic casings running across the floors like sausages escaped from the butcher's and the rattling window units that were still the only means of air-conditioning.

After returning to his chair, he read the autopsy notes. It was right there: "Hypertensive heart failure." She had a high bp, a family with hearts as fragile as a racehorse's ankles, and had died in her sleep, probably with a fever as the result of a sudden flu. The coroner had recommended a conclusion of death by natural causes, consistent with her known medical history. Tommy just kept shaking his head.

"This woman," said Brand, "was a hundred and nine pounds and five foot three. She worked out every day. She looked half her age."

"Jimmy, I got ten bucks that says she worked out every day because nobody in her family lived past sixty-five. You can't beat the genes. What's the blood chemistry?"

"Well, they did an immunoassay. Routine tox screen."

"Anything show up?"

"A lot showed up. This lady had a medicine cabinet the size of a steamer trunk. But no positives on anything she didn't have a prescription for. Sleeping pill, which she took every night, lots of crap for manic-depression."

Molto gave his chief deputy a look. "Which crap can cause heart failure, right?"

"Not in clinical doses. I mean, not usually. It's hard to measure the levels on that stuff postmortem."

"You got a consistent medical history. And if she didn't die of natural causes—which is maybe one chance in fifty—it's because she accidentally took an overdose of her meds."

Brand rumpled up his lips. He had nothing to say, but he wasn't satisfied.

"What's with the guy sitting there for twenty-four hours?" asked Brand. A good prosecutor, like a good cop, could sometimes make a case out of one fact. Maybe Brand was right. But he had no evidence.

"We have nothing to investigate," Tommy told him. "With a guy who's going to be sitting on the state supreme court in a little more than three months and potentially voting yea or nay on every conviction this office gets. If Rusty Sabich wants to make our lives miserable, he'll have ten years to do it."

Even as he argued with his chief deputy, it was slowly coming to Tommy what was going on here. Rusty Sabich was nobody to Brand. It was who he was to Tommy that was driving this. In order to get his job back when Rusty was acting PA two decades ago, Tommy had to admit that he had violated office protocols for the handling of evidence in connection with Sabich's trial.

Molto's punishment was minimal, giving up any claim for back pay over the year he had been suspended during the post-trial investigation.

But as time passed, Tommy's admission of wrongdoing had become a dead weight. More than half the judges of the Kindle County Superior Court these days were former deputy PAs who had worked with Tommy. They knew who he was—solid, experienced and predictable, if dull—and had been happy to appoint him the office's temporary leader when the elected PA, Moses Appleby, had resigned with an inoperable brain tumor only ten days after taking the oath of office. But the Democratic-Farmers-Labor Party Central Committee, where every dirty secret was always known, was unwilling to slate Tommy for this job—or even a judgeship, the position Tommy actually coveted because it offered more long-term security for a man with a young family. Voters did not understand nuance, and the entire ticket might be compromised when an election opponent unearthed Tommy's admission and started acting as if he had confessed to a felony. Maybe if he had the somber star power of somebody like Rusty, he could overcome that. But all in all he had been happy to leave that dark note in his biography largely unknown by all but a few insiders. No doubt Brand was right. Proving Sabich was actually a bad guy could rinse away the stain. Even if everybody knew everything, no one would care then if Tommy had overstepped.

But that kind of long shot was not worth the risks. Holding this job had seemed for years to be another of Tommy's futile yearnings, and he felt the sweet power of pride in doing it well. More to the point, he had the opportunity to repair much of the lingering damage to his reputation from the accusations at Rusty's trial, so that when a new PA was elected in two years, Tommy could reclaim the mantle of white knight and exit to a big boy's salary doing in-house investigations for some corporation. That would never happen if people thought he'd used this position to pursue a vendetta.

"Jimmy, let's be straight, okay? No way I can fuck around with Rusty Sabich again. I got a one-year-old. Other guys my age, they're thinking about hanging it up. I gotta consider the future. I can't afford to wear the black hat again." Tommy was regularly befuddled by where he stood now on the life chain. He had not meant to butt in line or take another turn, only to have a bit of what he'd so far missed. He had never been one of those guys with an ego so big that he thought he could brazen even time.

But Brand's look said it all: That was not Tommy Molto. What he'd just heard—the self-interest, the caution—that was not the prosecutor he knew. Tommy felt his heart constrict in the face of Brand's disappointment.

"Fuck," said Molto. "Whatta you want?"

"Let me dig," said Brand. "On my own. Really careful. But let me be sure this really is nothing."

"Anything leaks, Jimmy, especially before the election, and we've turned nothing, you can just write my obit. You understand that? You're fucking around with the rest of my life."

"Quiet as Little Bo Peep." He lifted his large square hand and put a finger to his lips.

"Fuck," said Tommy again.

RUSTY'S BIRTHDAY
(3/19/07)

BARBARA'S DEATH
(9/29/08)

THE ELECTION
(11/04/08)

CHAPTER 5

Rusty, March 19, 2007

When I depart the bus in Nearing, the former ferry port along the river that turned into a suburb not long before we moved here in 1977, I stop at the chain pharmacy across the way to pick up Barbara's prescriptions. A few months after my trial ended twenty-one years ago, for reasons fully understood only by the two of us, Barbara and I separated. We might have gone on to divorce had she not been diagnosed in the wake of an aborted suicide attempt with bipolar disorder. For me, that ended up being excuse enough to reconsider. Past the trial, past the months of climbing down, branch by branch, and still never feeling I had reached the ground, past the nights of furious recriminations at the colleagues and friends who had turned on me or not done enough—after all that receded, I wanted what I had wanted from the time the nightmare began: the life I had before. I did not have the strength, if the truth be told, to start again. Or to see my son, a fragile creature, become the final victim of the entire tragedy. Nat and Barbara moved back from Detroit, where she had been teaching mathematics at Wayne State, subject to only one condition: Barbara's vow to adhere scrupulously to her drug regimen.

Her moods are not stabilized easily. When things were going well, especially in the first few years after Nat and she came back home, I found her far less cantankerous and often fun to live with. But she missed her manic side. She no longer had the will or energy for those twenty-four-hour computer sessions when she pursued some elusive mathematical theory like a panting dog determined to run a fox to ground. In time, she gave up her career, which brought more frequent gloom. These days Barbara refers to herself as a lab rat, willing to try anything her psychopharmacologist suggests to get a better grip. There is a handful of pills at the best of times: Tegretol. Seroquel. Lamictal. Topamax. When she gets the blues—which in her case ought to be called the blacks—she reaches deeper into the medicine cabinet for tricyclic drugs, like Asendin or Tofranil, which can leave her sleepy and looking as if holes had been drilled into the pupils, requiring her to walk around inside the house in dark glasses. At the worst moments, she will go to phenelzine, an antipsychotic that she and her doctor have discovered will reliably pull her back from the brink, making it worth its many risks. At this stage, she has prescriptions for fifteen to twenty drugs, including the sleeping pills she takes every night and the meds that counter her chronic high blood pressure and occasional heart arrhythmia. She orders refills on the Internet, and I pick them up for her two or three times a week.

Birthday dinner at home is a desultory affair. My wife is a fine cook and has grilled three filets, each the size of Paul Bunyan's fist, but somehow all of us have exhausted our quota of good cheer at the celebration in chambers. Nat, who at one point seemed as if he would never leave the family house, returns reluctantly these days and is characteristically quiet throughout the meal. It is clear almost from the start that our main goal is to get it over with, to say we dined together on a momentous day and return to the internal world of signs and symbols with which each one of us is peculiarly preoccupied. Nat will go home to read for tomorrow's law classes, Barbara will retreat to her study and the Internet, and I, birthday or no, will put the flash drive in my computer and review draft opinions.

In the meantime, as often happens with my family, I carry the conversation. My encounter with Harnason, if nothing else, is odd enough to be worth sharing.

"The poisoner?" asks Barbara when I first mention his name. She rarely listens if I discuss work, but you can never tell what Barbara Bernstein Sabich will know. At this stage, she is a frightening replica, with far better style, of my own slightly loony mother, whose mania late in life, after my father left her, was organizing her thoughts on hundreds of note cards that were stacked on our old dining room table. Rigidly agoraphobic, she found a way to reach beyond her small apartment as a regular caller on radio talk shows.

My wife too hates to leave home. A born computer geek, she cruises the Net four to six hours a day, indulging every curiosity—recipes, our stock portfolio, the latest mathematical papers, newspapers, consumer purchases, and a few games. Nothing in life steadies her so much as having a universe of information at hand.

"It turns out I prosecuted the guy. He was a lawyer who was living off his clients' money. Gay."

"And what does he expect from you now?" Barbara asks.

I shrug, but somehow in retelling the story, I confront something that has grown on me over the hours, which I am reluctant to acknowledge, even to my wife and son: I am sorely guilty that I sent a man to the penitentiary for the sake of prejudices I'm now ashamed I had. And in that light I recognize what Harnason was slyly trying to suggest: If I hadn't prosecuted him for the wrong reasons, stripped him of his profession, and hurled him into the pit of shame, his life would have turned out entirely differently; he would have had the self-respect and self-restraint not to have murdered his partner. I started the cascade. Contemplating the moral force of the point, I go silent.

"You'll recuse now, won't you?" Nat asks, meaning I'll remove myself from the case. When Nat lived at home after college, it was rare for him to intervene directly in the substance of our conversations. Usually, he assumed a role more or less like a color commentator, interrupting only for remarks about the way his mother or I had expressed ourselves—'Nice, Dad,' or 'Tell us how you really feel, Mom.'—clearly intended to prevent either of us from upending the precarious balance between us. I have long feared that mediating between his parents is one more thing that has made the path rougher for Nat. But these days, Nat will actively engage me on legal issues, providing a rare avenue into the mind of my dark, isolated son.

"No point," I say. "I already voted. The only doubt

on the case, and there's not much, is about George
Mason. And Harnason really didn't try to talk about
the merits of his appeal anyway." The other problem,
were I to unseat myself now, is that most of my colleagues on the court would suspect I was doing it for
the sake of my campaign, trying to avoid recording my
vote to reverse a murder conviction, an act that seldom
pleases the public.

"So you had an eventful afternoon," says Barbara.

"And there was more," I say. The declaration
brings Anna's kiss back to mind, and fearing I may
have flushed, I go on quickly to recount my meeting
with Raymond. "Koll has offered to drop out of the
primary."

Koll is N. J. Koll, both a legal genius and a vain-
glorious meathead, who once sat with me on the court
of appeals. N.J. is the only opposition I expect in the
primary early next year. Having the party's endorse-
ment, I am sure to clobber Koll. But it will take a considerable investment of time and money. Because the
Republicans so far have not even fielded a candidate in
this one-party town, N.J.'s withdrawal would be tan-
tamount to my winning what even the newspapers
openly refer to as the "white man's seat" on the state
supreme court, in distinction from the two other Kindle County seats customarily occupied by a female and
an African-American.

"That's great!" says my wife. "What a nice birthday
present."

"Too good to be true. He'll only drop out if I support his reappointment to the court of appeals as chief
judge."

"So?" asks Barbara.

"I can't do that to George. Or the court." When I arrived on the appellate court, it was a retirement home for party loyalists who too often appeared amenable to the wrong kinds of suggestions. Now, after my twelve years as chief, the State Court of Appeals for the Third Appellate District boasts a distinguished membership whose opinions appear in law school texts from time to time and are cited by other courts around the country. Koll, with his zany egocentricities, would destroy everything I've accomplished in no time.

"George understands politics," says Barbara. "And he's your friend."

"What George understands," I counter, "is that he deserves to be chief. If I helped put Koll in his place, all the judges would feel I stabbed them in the back."

My son had Koll in class at Easton Law School, where N.J. is a revered professor, and reached the standard conclusion.

"Koll's a fucking nut-job," Nat says.

"Please," says Barbara, who still prefers decorum at the dinner table.

N.J., a person of little subtlety, backed up his offer with a threat. If I don't accede, he'll change parties and become the Republican candidate in the general election in November '08. His chances will be no better, but he will increase the wear and tear on me and exact maximum punishment for not making him chief.

"So there's a campaign?" Barbara asks, somewhat incredulous when I explain all this.

"If Koll wasn't bluffing. He might decide it's a waste of time and money."

She shakes her head. "He's spiteful. He'll run for spite." From the lofty distance she maintains on my universe, Barbara sees deeply, like a kingfisher, and I know instantly she's right, which brings the conversation to a dead end.

Barbara has brought home the remains of Anna's carrot cake, but we are all still recovering from the sugar coma it nearly induced. Instead we clear and wash. My son and I spend another twenty minutes watching the Trappers boot away a spring training game. The only time I ever spent with my father, outside the family bakery, where I worked from the age of six, was moments once or twice a week when he would allow me to sit beside him on the divan while he drank his beer and watched baseball, a game for which he had an unaccountable fascination as an immigrant. It was more precious than treasure when, a couple times a night, he would venture a comment to me. A fine player in high school, Nat seemed to abandon any interest in baseball when he lost his starting position junior year. But by whatever transitivity there is across the generations, he will almost always spend a few minutes beside me in front of the TV.

Aside from our expressions of anguish about the ever-hapless team, or conversations about law, Nat and I do not tend to talk. This is in deliberate contrast to Barbara, who beleaguers our son with a daily call, which he generally limits to less than a minute. Yet it would violate some essential compact if I did not probe his current state now, even knowing he is going to deflect my questions.

"How's your note coming?" Nat, who aspires to be

a law professor, is going to publish a student article in the *Easton Law Review* about psycholinguistics and jury instructions. I have read two drafts and cannot even pretend to understand it.

"Just about done. In type this month."

"Exciting."

He nods several times as a way to avoid more words. "Okay if I go up to the cabin this weekend?" he asks, referring to the family place in Skageon. "I want to get away to look over the note one more time." It is not my place to ask, but it's nearly certain Nat will go only with his favorite companion—himself.

With two gone in the ninth, Nat has finally had enough. He calls out his good-byes to his mother, who by now is zoned in to the Net and does not answer. I close the door behind him and go to find my briefcase. Barbara and I have resumed our normal mode. There is no sound, no TV, no dishwasher rumbling. The silence is the absence of any connection. She's in her world, I'm in mine. Not even the radio waves that come out of deep space could be detected. Yet this is what I chose and more often still believe I want.

In my little study, I download from my flash drive and mark up draft opinions, then check my personal e-mail, where I find several birthday greetings. Around eleven, I creep to the bedroom and discover that Barbara unexpectedly has remained awake. It is, after all, my birthday. And I guess I am going to be the birthday boy.

I suspect that sexual practices in long marriages are far more varied—and thus, in an abstract way, interesting—than among the couples who hook up in singles bars. From some friends our age, I hear occasional comments suggesting that sex is largely passé in their relationships. But Barbara and I have maintained a robust sex life, probably as a way to make up for the other deficits in our marriage. My wife has always been a great-looking woman and is even more striking now, when so many of her peers have been laid low by the years. Still a 1960s girl, she has allowed her tight natural curls to gray, and goes largely without makeup despite the pallor of age. But she remains a beauty, with precise features. She works out for two hours five times a week on the equipment in our basement, a routine that both counters the ailments that run in her family and keeps her girlishly shaped. I always feel the surge of male pride that comes from escorting a very attractive woman when I enter a room with her, and I still enjoy the sight of her in bed, where we find ourselves making love two or three times a week. We remember. We coalesce. It's prosaic most often, but so is much of life at its best—with the family around the table, with buddies at a bar.

Not that there will be any of that tonight. Once I'm in our bedroom, I realize I have entirely misread the meaning of Barbara waiting up. Steel hardens her face when she is upset—the jaw, the eyes—and right now, it's all iron.

I ask the simple yet eternally dangerous question: "What's the matter?"

She frumps around beneath the covers. "I just think you could've talked to me first," she says. The remark is incomprehensible until she adds, "About Koll."

My jaw actually hangs. "Koll?"

"You think this doesn't affect me, too? You made a decision, Rusty, to put me through months of campaigning, without even speaking to me. You think I'll be able to go to the grocery store after a workout with my hair plastered to my cheek and smelling like a gym sock?"

The truth is that Barbara orders most of our groceries online, but I skip the debater's point and ask simply why not.

"Because my husband would be pissed off. Especially if somebody sticks a microphone in front of my face. Or takes a picture."

"Nobody is going to take a picture of you, Barbara."

"If your ads are on TV, everybody will be watching me. Wife of a candidate for supreme court justice? It's like being a minister's spouse. It's bad enough as it is with you as chief judge. But now I'm really going to have to play the part."

There is no talking her out of this vague paranoia; I have tried for decades. Instead, I am struck by her remark about playing a part. We do not often get to this point, where the terms under which our marriage resumed are forced into the open. Nat was our mutual priority. After that, I have been entitled to remake my life as best I can with no deference to her. But because I accept that order as morally correct, I do not think often of how that must feel to Barbara—an unending penance as a drug-controlled Stepford wife.

"I'm sorry," I say. "You're right. I should have talked to you."

"But you wouldn't have thought about it, would you?"

"I just apologized, Barbara."

"No, no matter what it means to me, you really wouldn't have thought about letting N.J. become chief."

"Barbara, I can't consider whether or not my wife is"—I visibly reach for words, so we both know what has been rejected: 'mentally unbalanced,' 'bipolar,' 'nuts'—"publicity shy in making professional decisions. N.J. would damage the court enormously as chief. I put my own self-interest aside. I can hardly place more weight on yours."

"Because you're Rusty the paragon. Saint Rusty. You always need to run a steeplechase before you can let yourself have what you want. I'm sick of this."

You're sick, I nearly say. But I stop myself. I always stop myself. She will rage now, and I will just absorb it, thinking as a mantra, She's crazy, you know she's crazy, let her be crazy.

And so it goes. She works herself into a greater fury with each moment. I take a chair and say next to nothing except to repeat her name from time to time. She leaves the bed and resembles a boxer, pacing as if she were in the ring, fists clenched but hurling invective instead of punches. I am thoughtless, cold, self-absorbed, and unconcerned about her. In time, I go to the medicine cabinet to locate the Stelazine. I show her the pill and wait to see if she will take it before she enters the final, destructive phase in which she will lay ruin to something more or less precious to me. In the past, right in front of me, she has smashed the crystal bookends I was given by the bar association when I was elevated to chief judge; immolated my tuxedo trousers with the fire flick we use to light the barbecue; and thrown into the toilet two Cubans I had been given by Judge Doyle. Tonight, she finds the box George gave me, removes my gift, and right in front of me scissors the epaulets off the shoulders of the robe.

"Barbara!" I scream, yet do not stand to stop her. My outburst, or her act, is enough to reel her back a bit, and she snatches the pill off her bedside table and downs it. In half an hour, she will be in a druggy coma that will cause her to sleep most of tomorrow. There will be no apology. A day or two from now, we will be back to where we started. Distant. Careful. Disconnected. With months of peace ahead before the next eruption.

I find my way to the sofa in my study outside the bedroom. A pillow, sheet, and blanket are stored there for these occasions. Barbara's rages always shake me, since sooner or later I look down through a tunnel in time to the crime twenty-one years ago, wondering what madness made me think we could go on.

I have a Scotch in the kitchen. When I became a lawyer, I had no use for alcohol. At this age, I drink too much, rarely to excess but seldom heading off to bed without first administering some liquid anesthesia. In the john, I empty my bladder for the last time and hold there. At certain times of year, the moon shines directly through this bathroom skylight. As I stand in the magic glow, the memory of Anna's physical presence returns, potent as the melody of a favorite song. I recall my wife's remark about my difficulties in letting myself have what I want, and almost in reprisal I release myself to the sensation, not merely the movie of Anna and me locked in embrace, but the languor and exhilaration of escaping the restraint on which I've staked my life for decades.

I linger there, until, with time, I recede to the present, until my mind takes over from my senses and begins a lawyerly interrogation of myself. The Declaration of Independence said we have a right to pursue happiness—but not to find it. Children die in Darfur. In America, men dig ditches. I have power, meaningful work, a son who loves me, three squares every day, and a house with air-conditioning. Why am I entitled to more?

I return to the kitchen for another drink, then make my bed on the leather sofa. The liquor has done its job, and I am drifting into the dust of sleep. And so concludes the day commemorating my sixty years on earth, with the feeling of Anna's lips lightly on mine and my brain cycling through the eternal questions. Can I ever be happy? Can I truly lie down to die without trying to find out?

The role of judge and clerk is largely unique in contemporary professional life, because a law clerk is basically engaged in an apprenticeship. They come to me brilliant but unmolded, and I spend two years showing them nothing less than how to reason about legal problems. I was a clerk myself thirty-five years ago, to the chief justice of the state supreme court, Philip Goldenstein. Like most law clerks, I still worship my judge. Phil Goldenstein was one of those people called to public life by his passionate faith in humanity, believing that good lurked in every soul and that his job as a politician or a judge was merely to help let it out. That is the sentimental faith of another era and certainly, if I have to be blunt, not one I ever took up. But my clerkship was a glorious experience nonetheless, because Phil became the first person to see great things for me as an attorney. I viewed the law as a palace of light, whose radiance would erase the mean and crabbed darkness of my parents' home. Being accepted in that realm meant my soul had exceeded the tiny boundaries for which I had always feared I was destined.

I'm not sure I've been able to follow the justice's generous example with my clerks. My father never gave me a model of gentle authority, and I probably draw back too often and come off as officious and self-impressed. But a judge's clerks are his heirs in the law, and I have a special attachment to many of them. The seven former clerks who attend Anna's party Friday night are among my favorites, all of them notable successes in the profession. They join the rest of my staff to make a jolly table of fifteen in a dark back room at the Matchbook. We all drink too much wine and gently roast Anna, who is ribbed about her constant dieting, her laments over single life, her sneaking of occasional cigarettes, and the way she turns a suit into casual attire. One person has bought her bedroom slippers to wear in the office.

When the event is over, Anna drives me back to the courthouse, as we planned. I'm going to get my briefcase, and she will box up the last of her belongings, then drop me at the Nearing bus. Instead, it turns out that each of us has bought the other a small gift. I sit on my old sofa, whose cracked leather inevitably reminds me a little of my own face, in order to open the box. It holds a miniature scale of justice, which Anna has had engraved: "To the Chief—Love and gratitude forever, Anna"

"Lovely," I say, then she sets herself down beside me with the small package I have given her.

Distance. Closeness. The words are not merely metaphors. We walk down the street nearer to the persons with whom we are connected. And in the last months of Anna's clerkship, a professional distance has largely vanished between us. When we get into an elevator, she inevitably crowds right in front of me. 'Oops,' she will say as she wedges her rump against me, looking over her shoulder to laugh. And of course, now she sits flank to flank, shoulder to shoulder, not an angstrom between us. The sight of my present—a pen set for her desk and a note invoking Phil Goldenstein, telling her she is destined for great things—brings her to tears. "You mean so much to me, Judge," she says.

And so, as if it signifies nothing at all, she drops her head against my chest and I eventually wrap my arm around her. We say nothing, not a word, for minutes, but we do not change positions, my hand now tight on her firm shoulder and her fine hair, sweet with the applications of conditioners and shampoo, resting right above my heart. There is no need to voice what is being debated. The longing and the attachment are fierce. But the perils and the pointlessness are plain. We are curled together, each trying to determine which loss would be worse—going forward or turning away. I still have no idea what will happen. But in this moment I learn one thing: I have been lying to myself for months. Because I am fully willing.

And so I sit there thinking, Will it happen, will it actually happen, how can it, how can it not, how can it? It is like the moment when the jury foreman stands with the folded verdict form in his hand. Life will change. Life will be different. The words cannot be spoken quickly enough.

In my moments given to this fantasy, I have promised myself the decision will be only hers. I will not ask or make advances. And so I hold her to me now, but do no more. The feeling of her solid form arouses me naturally, but I merely wait, and the time goes on and on, perhaps twenty minutes in total, until eventually I feel her face turn up to me from within the crook of my arm and the warmth of her breath on my neck. Now, she is waiting. Poised. I feel her there. I do not think No or even Wait. Instead, this is my thought: Never again. If not now, then never again. Never again the chance to embrace the most fundamental excitement in life.

And so I look down to her. Our lips meet, our tongues. I groan out loud, and she whispers, "Rusty, oh, Rusty." I find the exquisite softness of the breast that I have imagined in my hand a thousand times. She pulls away to see me, and I view her, beautiful, serene, and utterly without a second thought. And then she speaks the words that elevate my soul. This daring, gorgeous young woman says, "Kiss me again."

Afterward, she drives me to the bus and near the station veers into an alley so we can kiss good-bye.

Me! my heart screams, Chief Sabich, smooching like a seventeen-year-old in the shadows beyond the cone of light from the streetlamp.

"When will I see you?" she asks.

"Oh, Anna."

"Please," she says. "Not just once. I would feel so slutty." She stops. "Sluttier."

I know there will never be a sweeter moment than the one we had just had. Less inept, but never more exultant.

"All affairs end badly," I say. I am perhaps the world's leading exhibit. Tried for murder. "We both should think about this."

"We both have," she answers. "I could see you thinking every time you looked at me for months. Please. So we can talk, if nothing else?"

We both know that the only talk will occur between the acts, but I nod and then alight after kissing her deeply again. Her car, an aged Subaru, goes off with the phlegmy sound of a failing muffler. I walk slowly to the bus. How, my heart shrieks, *how* can I be doing this again? How can any human being make another time the same mistake that all but ruined his life? Knowing the likelihood of one more catastrophe? I ask myself these questions with every step. But the answer is always the same: Because what has lain between then and now—because that time is not fully deserving of being called living.

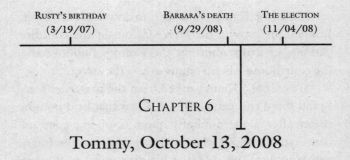

RUSTY'S BIRTHDAY
(3/19/07)

BARBARA'S DEATH
(9/29/08)

THE ELECTION
(11/04/08)

CHAPTER 6

Tommy, October 13, 2008

Jim Brand applied to the PA's office out of the bottom of his night law school class and received a form rejection. But he showed up in the reception area to beg for an interview, and Tommy, passing by, liked what he saw. It was Tommy who pushed Brand through the hiring committee, taught him how to write a decent brief, made Jim the puppy lawyer on a number of big cases. And Brand, in time, proved out. He had a natural feeling for the courtroom, with the instincts of a jock who knew when there was trouble on his blind side. Defense lawyers lamented his smash-mouth style, but they said that about Tommy, too.

But unlike most people you do a favor, Jim Brand never forgot who he owed. Tommy was his big brother. They had been best men at each other's weddings. Even now, once a month, at least, Tommy and Brand had lunch by themselves, both as a way to keep up with each other and to noodle on the office's recurring problems, which were otherwise easily ignored in the onrush of emergencies. Usually they had a quick sandwich nearby, but today Brand left a message with the secretaries for Tommy to meet him downstairs at noon. Jim was just nosing his Mercedes out of the concrete parking structure abutting the County Building and the courthouse when Tommy got to the street.

"Where to?" Tommy asked from the passenger seat. Brand loved this car, a 2006 E-Class that he'd bought cheap after a three-month quest involving constant conversations about what he'd turned up on the Internet or in want ads. He and his girls polished it every Sunday, and he'd found a leather cleaner that gave the vehicle that new-car smell. The auto was so pristine, Tommy was not comfortable even crossing his legs, for fear his shoes might leave dust on the seat cushion. About the happiest day of Brand's life came when he was pulling out one evening and some toothless wino teetered by and said, 'Hey, man, that's some slick sled.' Brand still repeated the line all the time.

"I was thinking Giaccolone's," said Brand.

"Oh, God." At Giaccolone's they stuck an entire veal cutlet in an Italian roll and buried it in marinara. As a young PA, Tommy would take the dicks who'd worked on a case over there whenever a jury went out, but these days one sandwich was an entire week's calorie count. "I'm gonna feel like a boa constrictor trying to digest a horse."

"You're going to enjoy lunch," said Brand, which was the first clue Tommy had that something was up.

Giaccolone's was not very far from the U, and the famine appetites of undergraduates had sustained the place years ago, when it required youthful bravado or armed companions to enter the neighborhood. Back then it was a mess around here. The playground across the street was a weed-choked empty lot, with purple thistles growing beside refuse dumped in the middle of the night—worn wheel drums and chunks of stressed concrete with the rusty rebar sticking out. Now there were sleek town houses over there, and Tony Giaccolone, the third generation in the business, had done the unthinkable and added salads to the huge menu that hung over the counter. The U Medical Center, whose free-form architectural style resembled a bunch of Tomaso's blocks dumped on the floor, had crept within a few hundred yards, morphing and expanding like one of the cancers they were famous for treating there.

Around the back of Giaccolone's there were concrete picnic tables. With their sandwiches, each dense as a brick, Brand and Tommy headed that way. A copper-colored Buddha in a suit sprang to his feet as they approached.

"Hey there," said Brand. "Boss, you remember Marco Cantu, right? Marco, you know the PA."

"Hey, Tom." Cantu wound up and smashed his hand into Tommy's. In Marco's days on the force, he had been known as No Cantu, smart enough but legendary lazy, the kind of cop who proved they shouldn't have put air-conditioning in the cruisers, because in the summer Marco wouldn't get out even to stop a murder. He had landed on his feet somewhere, though. Tommy remembered that much. Put in his twenty, then rode the diversity wave into paradise.

"Veep for security at the Gresham," said Cantu when Tommy asked what he was up to these days. The Gresham was a classic hotel, built around a magnificent lobby where the marble pillars rose tall as sequoias.

Tommy was over there now and then for bar association functions, but you needed a corporate expense account to pay for the rooms.

"That must be a tough gig," said Molto. "Once a month, you go into crisis mode when you need to whisper to some drunken executive that it's time to leave the bar."

"Actually," said Marco, "I got a staff of four to do that. I just listen in on my earpiece." Cantu had the device in his pocket and held it up for a second for laughs.

"What about celebrities?" asked Brand, who was always starstruck. "You must get a few."

"Oh, yeah," said Marco. "And they can be a handful." He told the story of a nineteen-year-old rock star who clubbed his way around town one night and decided when he returned at three a.m., utterly toasted, that it was a good idea to remove every stitch of clothing in the lobby. "I didn't know what to do first," said Marco, "block the paparazzi or turn up the heat to keep the kid from catching cold. What a little twerp."

"You get some local celebrities, too," said Brand. "Didn't you tell me you were running into the chief judge of the appellate court all the time over there spring before last?"

"Truly," said Marco. "Seemed like whenever I seen him, there was this *chiquita* on his arm."

Brand's dark eyes found Tommy's. Molto knew now why they were here.

"How young?" asked Tommy.

"Past voting age. I don't know. Thirty? Good-looking, with a great set of headlights. First time, I seen him just sittin around in the lobby. That don't make sense, right? Chief judge gotta be a busy fella. I went over to gab. But I could see his eyes rolling sideways, looking somebody off. I bent down to straighten my trouser cuff and could make this chick pedaling backward, headed for the elevator.

"Then a couple of weeks later, I'm up on one of the floors, checking out some jet-lagged Asian businessman who didn't answer his wake-up call, and as the elevator doors open, I can see this couple breaking apart, scurrying to their corners. Judge and her. She was literally sticking her blouse back in her skirt, and old chiefy, he's got that look, you know, Bladder, don't fail me now. Couple weeks later, I catch sight of him marchin into the lobby, and when he sees me, he literally makes like a ballerina and whirls full around and goes back out the revolving doors. The chick, though—she's at reception."

"What time of day was this happening?" Tommy asked, making a wary survey of the customers around them. At the next table there was a group from the hospital, all in their long white coats with their instruments in the breast pockets. They were teasing one another, laughing it up, and took no account of the PA within ten feet of them.

"Lunch twice. Last time was right after work."

"The judge is catching a nooner?"

"How it looked to me," said Marco.

Tommy took his time with his warring judgments. It didn't surprise him Rusty was a hypocrite, that he'd run for supreme court and fuck around at the same time. Some guys were like that, little head first and only. The idea of cheating on his wife was incomprehensible to

Tommy, literally beyond the compass of any desire. Why? What could be more precious than a wife's love? Overall, this whole story merely confirmed his judgment that Rusty Sabich was an asshole.

"Seems to me," said Tommy, "I've been to bar association luncheons in that hotel?"

"Sure. All the time."

"Conference rooms always full, night and day?"

"Back then, yeah. Right now business could use a little boost."

"Okay," said Tommy, "but there are a lot of reasons for this young woman and him to be roaming around there. Any chance you took a peek at your registration records, Marco, to see if the judge actually checked in?"

"Yeah. But like I said, it was the girl at the desk."

"That mean there's no record?"

"No record."

Tommy looked at Brand, who was happy enough with the way things were going to resume an eager assault on his sandwich. Even at this age, Jimmy was always famished. Molto had a lot to say, but not in front of Marco. They talked about the U's football team, until Cantu folded up the waxed paper and what little was left of the bun. Ready to go, Marco rested his hands on his wide thighs.

"You know, I never liked the way Rusty fucked with you at that trial," said Cantu. "So I didn't mind telling a couple of guys this story with a cold one in my hand."

"I appreciate it," said Tommy, although the machinery inside him was going tilt. He figured Cantu was just putting a spit polish on his own grudge with Sabich.

"But the hotel," Marco said. "'The privacy of our

guests.'" With his thick fingers, Cantu danced the quotation marks in the air. "Super-duper big deal. Like it's some goddamn Swiss bank or something. So, anything ever hits the fan, I didn't tell you. You need this on paper, send a dick around, and I'll go run to my boss so he can run to his boss. Comes out same in the wash, but you know how it goes."

"Got it," said Molto, and watched Marco walk off in his nice suit.

Tommy threw away the rest of his sandwich and motioned Brand back to his car. Jim had parked the Mercedes across the street in a NO-PARKING zone, where he could watch it. Getting in, Brand scraped up the placard he'd thrown on the dash—KINDLE COUNTY UNIFIED POLICE—OFFICIAL BUSINESS—and slipped it back behind his visor.

"You know, that guy was no kind of cop when he was on the street," Tommy told him.

"I'd say a sack of dung," said Brand, "only the dung might complain."

"And there's some bad mojo between Rusty and him, right?"

"That's my read. The first time we talked it through, Marco let on about Sabich calling him out on a motion to suppress when Rusty was a trial judge."

"Okay, so maybe No Cantu is seeing a little more than meets another guy's eye."

"Maybe, maybe not. But you know, if he's right, it's a motive to *adios* Mrs. Judge."

"Whatever you call it, it was a year and a half ago. And that's not much of a motive for murder. Ever hear of divorce?"

"Not with my wife," said Brand. "She'd kick my ass." Jody, a former deputy PA, was a hard case. "Maybe Rusty thought a divorce would disagree with his campaign."

"So he could wait six weeks."

"Maybe he couldn't. Maybe the young lady's with child and starting to show."

"Lot of maybes here, Jimmy."

They were on Madison now, right across from the main doors of U Hospital. There was a crowd on the corner waiting for the light, docs and patients and workers by the looks of them, and every single person, eight when Molto counted, was talking on a cell phone. Whatever happened to the here and now?

"Boss," said Brand, "Rusty's not gonna get executed at midnight on this. But you said, Bring me somethin. And this is something. We got a guy here with a track record for murder. Now his wife dies all of a sudden and he lets the body cool an entire day for no good reason. And turns out, he was getting some play on the side. So maybe he wanted an easy trade-in. I don't know. But we gotta look. That's all I'm saying. We got a job to do and we gotta look."

Tommy gazed down the broad avenue canopied by the solid old trees that rose in the parkway on either side. It just would have been worlds easier if it were somebody else.

"How'd this information come to you, anyway?" he asked. "Who pointed you at Marco?"

"One of the Nearing cops shoots pool with Cantu every Tuesday night."

Tommy didn't like that part. "I hope they're all

talking in their quiet voices. I don't want half the Nearing station bopping around, asking every second person they see if they got any reason to think Rusty Sabich cooled his wife."

Brand promised he had the lid screwed down tight. The best Tommy could tell himself was that it hadn't hit the press yet. He asked Brand what he wanted to do.

"I say it's time to pull his bank records, his phone records," said Jim. "Let's see if there really is a mystery girl and whether they're still making time. We can put a ninety-day letter on everybody, keep them from telling Rusty until after the election." Under the state version of the Patriot Act, the PAs had the right to subpoena documents and order the person providing them to tell no one but a lawyer for ninety days. It was a pale version of what the feds could do—they had the right to keep the subpoenas secret forever—but the local criminal defense lawyers had raised hell, as usual, up at the capital.

Tommy groaned and quoted Machiavelli, an Italian who knew what was what. "If you shoot at the king, you better kill the king."

But Brand was shaking his big bald head.

"Assume the worst, Boss, assume it's a dry hole. Rusty'll be pissed when he finds out, maybe he pokes us in the eye now and then, but he's not going anywhere to complain. He's on the supreme court, he didn't get hurt, and he's not advertising that once upon a time, while his missus was still breathing, he had a girlfriend. He'll just hate your guts a little more than he hates your guts already."

"Great."

"We got a job, Boss. We got some information."

"Half-ass information."

"Half-ass or not, we have to run it out. You want some Nearing copper crying in a reporter's beer six months from now about how they turned up some good shit on the new justice before he got elected and you needed a heart transplant because you didn't want big bad Rusty to paddle your ass again? That's not good either."

Brand was right. They had a job to do. But it was a peril. The joke was thinking you were ever really in charge of your life. You pressed your oar down into the water to direct the canoe, but it was the current that shot you through the rapids. You just hung on and hoped not to hit a rock or a whirlpool.

Tommy waited all the way back to the courthouse before he gave Brand permission to proceed.

RUSTY'S BIRTHDAY
(3/19/07)

BARBARA'S DEATH
(9/29/08)

THE ELECTION
(11/04/08)

CHAPTER 7

Rusty, March–April 2007

Four days after becoming lovers, Anna and I meet again at the Hotel Gresham. Her place is out. Her roommate, Stiles, arrives unpredictably. More to the point, her East Bank development of redbrick midrises is only two blocks from the state supreme court, where Nat is already putting in a few hours each week.

Appearances being paramount, we have agreed through several cryptic e-mails that she will put her credit card down for the hotel room. I sit in the lobby, pretending I am awaiting someone else. When the registration clerk turns away, Anna's eyes find mine. I slip my hand inside my jacket and touch my heart.

When you have looked at a woman for months with the imagination's desiring eye, a part of you cannot accept that it's really her naked in your arms. And to some extent, it isn't. Her waist is narrower than I'd realized, the thighs a trifle heavier. Yet the essence of the thrill is having jumped the wall into my fantasies, an experience as otherworldly as crawling between the bars and romping with the jungle animals in the zoo. At last, I think, when I touch her. At last.

Afterward, as she works the tail of her blouse back into her skirt, I say, "So this actually happened."

Her smile is blissful, innocent. When Anna enjoys something, she feels no self-consciousness.

"You didn't want to, did you? I could feel you weighing this every time I stepped into the room. And deciding not to."

"I didn't want to," I say. "But I'm here."

"I only think about something once," she tells me. "And then I decide. It's a gift. About three months ago I realized I wanted to sleep with you."

"And you're like the Mounties, right? Always get your man?"

She smiles, smiles for all the world. "I'm like the Mounties," she says.

In my chambers, at campaign events, as I walk down the street or ride the bus, I go through the gestures of a normal life, but inwardly I've moved to a new location. I think of Anna constantly, obsessively reviewing the incremental steps we took over the months on our way to becoming lovers, still stunned to have escaped the hard limits I'd fixed on my existence. At home, I have no impulse to sleep, not merely because I am reluctant to lie down beside Barbara, but because more vitality has entered my body in the last week than I have experienced in decades. And without the display case glass behind which every female but my wife has reposed safely for a generation, there is a tactile thrill in the presence of virtually any woman.

Yet I know at all moments that what I am doing is in every colloquial sense insane. Powerful middle-aged

man, beautiful younger woman. The plot scores zero
for originality and is deservedly the object of universal
scorn, including my own. My first affair—twenty-plus
years ago—left me so racked by conflict that I started
seeing a shrink. But I have no thought now of finding another therapist, which has been a loose agenda
item for years, because I don't need someone else's
advice to know this is simply crazy, hedonistic, nihil-
istic, and that most important "istic"—unreal. It must
stop.

For Anna, discovery would be nowhere as cataclysmic as for me. It would make for an embarrassing start
to her career. But she would never shoulder most of the
blame. She has no wife to whom she's vowed fidelity,
no continuing public responsibilities. At the court, the
fact that we restrained ourselves until she was no longer
employed might save my position, but N. J. Koll would
become the instant favorite in our contest.

And those would be the least of the costs. Barbara's
rage is lethal and at this stage is most likely to make her
a danger to herself. But by far the worst would be facing Nat and his new look, empty of any respect.

One revelation of my first affair was that I carry
around a lot of baggage from the dark, unhappy home
in which I was raised. Until then, I had naively thought
I was Joe College or Beaver Cleaver, someone who had
been able to convert himself, the son of a sadistic war
survivor and an eccentric recluse, into a better-than-
average normal American guy. I still yearn in some ways
to be a paragon, master of an elusive regularity. But I
am haunted by the shadow who knows I am not. No
one is. I know that, too. But I am far more concerned

by my shortcomings than anybody else's. Vice has that attraction. It means embracing who I am.

Anna is like many people I knew in law school, not intellectual but brilliant, so agile with the lawyer's tasks of mating fact and law that it is as thrilling as watching a great athlete on the playing field. Now suddenly peer to peer, I find her brightness engaging at an elemental level. But our conversations involve little sweetness or murmuring. It is lawyer to lawyer, almost always a debate, half-amused, but never without an edge. And what we debate is a truth that had to be clear to both of us from the start: This cannot possibly end well. She will meet someone better suited to her. Or we will be discovered and my life again will lie in smoking ruins. Either way, there is no future.

"Why not?" she asks when I say that casually on the second afternoon.

"I can't leave Barbara. For one thing, my son would never forgive me. And for the second, it's unfair." I explain some of the history, even detailing the pharmacopeia in Barbara's medicine cabinet as a way to make a point: My wife is damaged goods. I took her back knowing that.

Anna's look flutters somewhere between sullen and hurt, and she flushes.

"Anna, you understood this. You had to understand this."

"I don't know what I understood. I just needed to be with you." Tears are crawling down her bright cheeks.

"Here's the problem," I say to her. "There is a fundamental difference between us."

"Age, you mean? You're a man. And I'm a woman. I don't think about age."

"You're supposed to. You're starting and I'm ending. Have you noticed that men my age lose their hair. And that it starts growing from their ears. That their guts soften. What do you think that's about?"

She made a face. "Hormones?"

"No, what would Darwin say? Why is it advantageous for the old men to look different from the young men? So the fertile young women can see who they should be mating with. So some lounge lizard my age can't get away with telling you he's twenty years younger."

"You're not a lounge lizard. And I'm not a bimbo." Offended, she throws back the covers and stalks, in naked glory, to the desk for a cigarette. I had never seen her light up before and was a trifle taken aback that she booked a smoking room. I kicked the habit when I left the reserves, but I have never stopped finding in the smell of a burning cigarette the aroma of blind indulgence. "What do you think?" she asks. "This is just an experience for me?"

"That's what it will end up being. Something crazy you once did so you could learn better."

"Don't tell me I'm young."

"Neither of us would be here if you weren't young. We would hold far less fascination for each other."

Standing behind, I turn her to me and run my hands the full length of her torso. Physically, she is glorious, a power Anna enjoys and works hard to hold on to—manicures and pedicures, hair appointments, facials, 'routine maintenance,' as she calls it. Her breasts are perfect, large, beautifully belled, with a broad, dark aureole and long nipples. And I am fascinated by her female parts, where her youth somehow seems centered. She's waxed there, 'a full Brazilian,' is her term. It's a first for me, and the smooth feel provokes my lust like a lightning bolt. I worship, drink, and take my time as she alternately moans and whispers directions.

In this state of amazement, life goes on. I do my job, write opinions, issue orders, meet with bar association groups and committees, settle the ongoing bureaucratic combat within the court, but Anna, in various sultry poses, is always warring for my attention. Koll's change of parties, which he made within a week of my birthday, has sucked the urgency out of my campaign for the moment, although Raymond continues to schedule fund-raising events.

Anna and I talk several times a day. I call only from work, wary of the detailed cell bills that are mailed to my house. Alone in my chambers, I will phone Anna's private line at the firm, or she will dial my inside number. They are hushed conversations, always too quick, an odd mix of banalities and proclamations of desire: "Guerner put me on this bitch of a document case. I'll have to work all weekend." "I miss you." "I need you."

One day on the phone, Anna asks me, "What happened with *Harnason*?" Anna's last official act as law clerk was to draft my dissent, and she is concerned about the case, as well as many others she worked on. I have largely forgotten about *Harnason*, like so much else in my life, but I summon Kumari once I put down the receiver. Responding to my dissent, George gallantly exercised the right of every judge of my court, circulating

Marvina's feisty opinion and my draft to all chambers, asking if the case seemed appropriate for en banc review, in which all eighteen judges would decide the case. Several of my colleagues, reluctant about offending the chief, have chosen the diplomatic alternative of not responding at all. I set a deadline of a week and end up thumped roundly, 13 to 5—counting Marvina, George, and me—in favor of affirming the conviction. This all but guarantees that the supreme court will also refuse to hear the case, on the theory that eighteen judges can't be wrong. Relishing victory, Marvina asks to rework the opinion one more time, but in no more than a month John Harnason will be returning to the penitentiary.

My mind is on Barbara almost as often as Anna. At home, I am entirely beyond suspicion. The nights before Anna and I are to meet next, I scrutinize my naked bulk in the full light of the bathroom. I am old, lumpy, bulging. I trim my pubic hair with a nose hair clipper, eliminating the long, unruly wires of gray. I should worry that Barbara might notice, but the truth is that she does not remark on my trips to the barber or serious razor burns. After thirty-six years, she is attached to my presence much more than my form.

When I had been with Carolyn, decades before, I was impossibly distracted. But Anna has made me more appreciative and patient with Barbara. Escaping to pleasure has emptied that bitter storehouse of resentments I keep. Which is not to say it is easy to carry on with the deception. It undermines every moment at home. Taking out the trash, or having sex, which I cannot entirely avoid, seems to be enacted by a second self.

The falseness is not simply about where I was or the highlights of my day. The lie is about who, in my heart of hearts, I really am.

My impossible desire to be loyal to two women takes me repeatedly to the highest pinnacles of absurdity. For example, I insist on repaying Anna in cash for the hotel rooms. She laughs it off—her salary is higher than mine, and with a raise of 400 percent over her clerkship, she feels as if she is under a waterfall of money—but an old-fashioned chivalry, if you can call it that, is offended to think I can sleep with a woman twenty-six years my junior and have her pay for the privilege.

But raising the money is more daunting than I had first considered. Barbara is paymaster in our house and, as a PhD in mathematics, takes numbers as the principal relationship in life; she could tell you without so much as blinking the exact amount of last June's electric bill. While I can pass off a couple extra trips to the ATM as losses at the judges' poker game, raising several hundred dollars extra every week seems impossible, until almost by divine intervention a cost of living adjustment for all the judges in the state, long held up by litigation, suddenly comes through. I stop the direct deposit of my pay on April 17 and instead bring my check to the bank, where I deposit the same amount that used to appear electronically, while taking back the COLA in cash. That includes the two-and-a-half-year backlog, nearly four thousand dollars, that comes with the first check.

"I'm glad this is a secret," I tell Anna as we lie in bed one early afternoon. We meet now two or three times a week, at lunch or after work, when I can claim I am at a campaign event. "Because that way you won't hear from millions of people telling you you're crazy."

"Why am I crazy? Because of the age thing?"

"No," I say, "that's only normally crazy. Or abnormally. I'm referring to the fact that the last woman I had an affair with ended up dead."

I've caught her attention. The green eyes are still, and the cigarette has stopped midway to her lips.

"Should I be afraid you'll kill me?"

"Some people would point out the historical pattern." She still hasn't moved. "I didn't do it," I tell her. She probably has no clue, but this is the greatest intimacy I've allowed her. For more than two decades, as a matter of principle, I have never bothered with any reassurance even to the closest friends. If they harbor suspicions, despite knowing me well, those will never be allayed by my denials.

"You know," she says, "I remember a lot about that case. That was the first time I thought about becoming a lawyer. I read about the trial every day in the paper."

"And how old were you? Ten?"

"Thirteen."

"Thirteen," I say, heavy-hearted. I am beginning to realize I will never get used to my monumental stupidity. "So you have me to blame for the fact that you became a lawyer, too? Now people will really say I corrupted you."

She whacks me with the pillow. "So who do you think did it?" she asks.

I shake my head.

"You don't know?" she asks. "Or you won't answer? I have a theory. Do you want to hear it?"

"We're done with this subject."

"Even though you just told me I'm in mortal danger?"

"Let's get dressed," I say, making no effort to hide the fact I'm annoyed.

"I'm sorry. I didn't mean to push buttons."

"I don't talk about it. Veterans don't talk about wars. They just get over them. It's the same thing. Not that you haven't made me wonder."

"Who did it?"

"Why are you here? Given my dangerous history."

She has put on her undergarments but now removes her bra with the flourish of a stripper, hurling it toward the walls.

"Love," she says, falling into my arms, "makes you do crazy things." We are both late, but this attitude of abandon parches me yet again with longing, and we fit together once more.

Afterward she says, "I don't believe it. I just don't."

"Thank you," I say quietly. "I'm glad it didn't stop you."

She shrugs. "Maybe the other way."

I peer curiously.

"I mean, you're still kind of a legend," she says. "Not just for lawyers. Why do you think nobody sane wants to run against you for the supreme court?"

The supreme court. My heart flips around several times. In the meantime, she looks off, not fully here.

"You know," Anna says then, "sometimes you do things you don't really understand. You just have to do them. Sense or no sense—it doesn't matter much."

This conversation intensifies a question I already

ask myself all the time. What is wrong with a young woman, whom in almost every other regard I know to be gifted and refreshingly sane, that she would be interested in someone nearly twice her age, let alone somebody married? I have no illusion she would be drawn to me if every lawyer, judge, and flunky did not address me as "Chief" whenever I walk into the Central Branch Courthouse. But what does it mean to her to be sleeping with the chief? Something. I realize that. But I will probably never understand the secret part of her she hopes I might fill in. Who she wants to be in the law? Who she wishes her father was? The man she craves to be in her secret dreams? I don't know—nor, probably, does she. I sense only that she needs to get as close as possible, since whatever it is she seeks can only be absorbed skin to skin.

Here is what I have forgotten: the pain. I forgot that an affair is constant torment. Over the falseness at home. Over the anxiety we will be discovered. Over the suffering I know is coming at the inevitable end. Over the agony of waiting to be with her next. Over the fact that I am truly myself only for a few hours every several days in a hotel room, when those sweet moments, as close to heaven as we know on this earth, seem to make all the other anguish worthwhile.

I rarely sleep through the night and am up at three or four a.m. with a glass of brandy. I tell Barbara it is the court and the campaign that concern me. I sit in the dark and bargain with myself. I will meet Anna two more times. Then stop. But if I am going to stop, then why not stop now? Because I cannot. Because the day I give her up is the day I accept that this will never happen again. That I have, in a few words, begun to die.

Despite habitual precautions, I find myself growing somewhat cavalier about the dangers. They are ever-present, but when you go undetected two times, then four, then five, part of the extraordinary thrill becomes beating the odds. One day when Anna and I are meeting at the Gresham, Marco Cantu, a former copper I'd known when he was on the street, sees me sitting in the lobby with no apparent purpose and comes by to say hello. He now heads the hotel's security operation. Something about the way I tell him I am meeting a friend for lunch sounds wrong even to me. I therefore feel half electrocuted by panic a week later when, as we are headed down, the elevator doors open on an intervening floor to disclose Marco, who has the stature of a miniature sumo wrestler. It is a bad moment, Anna and I still nuzzling and splitting as the car stops, our movement surely visible to Marco.

"Chief! We're seein lots of you."

I do not introduce Anna and can feel Marco looking straight through me. The next week, I spot him as I'm coming into the hotel and pirouette to go back through the doors until he's vacated the lobby.

"Time to change the scene of the crime," I tell her as soon as I am safely in the room. "Marco was on the street a long time. He was lazy, but he had a great sense of smell."

Anna has undressed by now. She is in the fluffy hotel robe but has closed it not with the belt, but with a thick red satin ribbon tied in an elaborate gift bow.

"Is that how you think of it? A crime?"

"Anything that feels this good has to be wrong," I answer. I have hung up my jacket and am on the bed slipping off my shoes before I recognize that I was far too flip. She is staring.

"You could at least pretend to think about being with me."

"Anna—" But we both know she is close to the truth. I have spent no nights with her. On Friday of the third week, I told Barbara I was going to a bar function and dared to come home at one-thirty, even then having left the hotel with Anna begging me to stay. She talks often about somehow getting away for a weekend, waking up with each other and walking together in the open air. But I don't freely imagine us at large. I am fiercely attached, but to me our relationship belongs in the captive space of a rented room, where we can shed our clothes and grasp the different things we are each so desperate to obtain.

"Seriously. You'd never marry me, would you?"

"I'm taken."

"Duh. No. If Barbara wasn't in the picture? If she dropped dead. Or ran away?"

Why is my first instinct evasion? "I'm too poor for a trophy wife."

"There's a compliment."

"Anna, people would laugh in my face."

"And that's why? Because people will laugh?"

"Because there's a reason to laugh. A man married to a woman young enough to be his daughter is flying too close to the sun."

"I'd say that's my problem, wouldn't you? If I want

to push you around in a wheelchair at high school graduation—"

"And change my Depends?"

"Whatever. Why can't I make those choices?"

"Because people usually have a hard time keeping deals where all the benefits are on the front end. They end up feeling sharp resentments later on."

She turns away. These conversations always bring her to tears. We are in a room today almost entirely consumed by the king bed. It looks out on the air shaft from which the clatter of the hotel kitchen rises.

"Anna, there is someone out there who will die to marry you."

"Well, he hasn't shown up yet. And don't tell me about somebody else. I don't want a consolation prize."

"I won't lie to you, Anna. I can't. I'm lying everywhere else. I have to tell *you* the truth. There's no reality to this. Am I supposed to change my campaign slogan? 'Vote for Sabich. He's on top of his staff.'"

She laughs out loud. Blessedly, her sense of humor never fails her. But her back is still to me.

"Anna, I would marry you if I was forty. I'm sixty."

"Stop telling me I'm young."

"I'm telling you I'm old."

"They're both pretty annoying. Look, you're not here by accident. You fuck me, then give me these speeches that imply you can't really take this seriously."

I turn her to me, bending very slightly so we are entirely eye to eye.

"Does that make sense to you? What you just said? That I don't take this seriously? I've risked everything to be with you," I say. "My career. My marriage. The respect of my son."

She breaks from my grasp, then abruptly faces me again, the green eyes intense.

"Do you love me, Rusty?"

It's the first time she's dared to ask, but I have known all along the question was coming.

"Yes," I say. From my lips, it feels very much like the truth.

She wipes an eye. And beams.

After the last encounter with Marco Cantu, our meeting places are governed by the whims of hotelrooms .com, where it always turns out one of several Center City establishments has space at the last minute at rock-bottom prices. Anna handles the bookings and e-mails me the locale, then arrives ten minutes before me to register, sending the room number to my handheld. We depart at the same ten-minute intervals.

And so I am on my way out of the Renaissance on a splendid spring day, with a clean sky and the smell of everything opening, when I hear a voice, more or less familiar.

"Ah, Judge," it says. When I pivot, Harnason is there. It is an awful moment. I realize at once he followed me here two hours ago and has been waiting like a faithful dog tethered to a lamppost. How much does he know? How many times has he trailed me? As happens so often these days, I am nearly knocked to my knees by the magnitude of my stupidity.

"Imagine meeting you," he says without a hint of sincerity, so I know my guess is right. I beg my heart to settle down while I calculate what he could have possibly observed. He knows I go to hotels at lunchtime, that I sometimes stay too long for a normal midday meal. But that's all he's seen. If he was on my heels, he would not have caught sight of Anna arriving ten minutes before me.

"Imagine," I finally answer. Harnason is not above blackmail, and I await his threat. It will be pointless. There is not a thing I can do to change the outcome in his case. But instead, as we stand about ten feet apart, Harnason's red face darkens to a sunset shade.

"I can't stand it, Judge," he says. "Not knowing. When I got bail, I was ecstatic, but it's not like being free. It's like walking along, waiting for a trapdoor to spring open under me right here in the sidewalk."

I look at Harnason, whom I condemned once for the wrong reasons, and whose fight I've fought, out of his sight.

"The opinion won't be much longer," I say, and turn away. At once, I feel his hand on my sleeve.

"Please, Judge. What's the difference? If it's decided, what does it hurt to tell me? It's terrible, Judge. I just want to know."

It's wrong. That's the correct answer. But some faint scent of Anna's perfume pervades my skin, and I still have the drained, fucked-out stardust feeling emanating upward from my dick. Who am I today to cling to principle? Or more important, to deny him now the compassion I owed him thirty years ago?

"You should prepare yourself for bad news, John."

"Ah." It is a sound from the gut. "No hope?"

"Not really. You're at the end of the road. I'm sorry."

"Ah," he repeats. "I really didn't want to go back. I'm too old."

Standing here on the street, with the shoppers and business folk swirling around us, many electronically transported to their own universes by their cell phones or iPods, I have a hard time with my feelings. I am strangely sympathetic to Harnason but also impatient with the way he's preyed on me and wheedled information, and I know I need to draw a hard line to prevent further intimidations. Most of all, in the moment I'm a bit galled by his self-pity. As a prosecutor, I always had some respect for the guys who went off without batting an eye, who lived by the watchword 'Don't do the crime if you can't do the time.'

"John, let's face facts. You did it, didn't you?"

He does not take an instant to answer. "So did you, Judge. And you're here."

No, I am about to say, violating my longtime scruple against answering.

"I was acquitted," I reply. "As I deserved to be."

"I deserved it, too," he says. He has his handkerchief out and blows his nose. He is blubbering freely now, crying like a child. A few of the people brushing past us to get into the hotel turn as they go, but Harnason doesn't care. He is who he is.

"But not because you didn't do it," I say. "How was that, John? The month you knew you were killing that man?" I'm not sure what I mean to accomplish by confronting him this way. I suppose I am asking this question: Where is the line? How does one stop? Once I've fucked my clerk and betrayed my wife, once I've thrown everything I've ever accomplished to the wind, where is the point of restraint?

"Do you really need to ask, Judge?"

"I do."

"It was hard, Judge. I hated him. He was going to leave me. I was old and he wasn't. I'd been his meal ticket and he was grateful at first, but now he was tired of me. I'm too old to find somebody else, somebody like that. You understand that much, right?"

I wonder again how much he knows about Anna, as I nod.

"But I didn't actually believe I was doing it at first," says Harnason. "I'd thought about it. I admit that. I went to the library, did some research. There's an appellate court case. Did you know that? From Pennsylvania. It talks about arsenic not being screened." He laughs a little bitterly. "The prosecutors never seemed to remember I was trained as a lawyer."

"And where was the arsenic? In the drinks?"

"I baked." Harnason chuckles the same way, at his accusers' expense. Prosecutors are historians, engaged in a reconstruction of the past with all of history's perils. They never get it completely right, because the witnesses are biased, or blame shifting, or wrong, or because, as in this case, the investigators never asked the right questions or put together what they already knew. "All those people who testified I never cooked were right. When Ricky was home, the kitchen was his. But I baked. And Ricky had a sweet tooth. The first few times, I told myself it was just for fun, just to see if he would notice or how I would feel, if I could do what I'd read about. I may have done it five times and still thought it wasn't for real, that I was going to stop. You know, I've told myself that a lot," Harnason says suddenly. "That I was going to stop." His wizened eyes go off to many other places. "But I never do," he says morosely. "I didn't stop. Somewhere, day seven or eight, I realized I wasn't going to. I hated him. I hated myself. I was going to do it anyway. And you, Judge. How did it feel when you killed that prosecutor? Act of passion?"

"I didn't do it."

"I see." His look is cold. He got gulled and beaten on this deal. "You're better than me."

"I would never say that, John. Maybe I got better breaks. Nobody is good by himself. We all need help. I got more than you did."

"And who's helping you now?" he asks. He chucks his pink face toward the hotel. Here we are, sinner to sinner. I feel belittled by my own predictability.

There has been too much truth told in this conversation for me to lie. I just shake my head yet again and turn away.

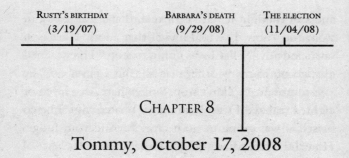

RUSTY'S BIRTHDAY
(3/19/07)

BARBARA'S DEATH
(9/29/08)

THE ELECTION
(11/04/08)

CHAPTER 8

Tommy, October 17, 2008

Rory Gissling was the daughter of a copper, Shane Gissling, a detective sergeant for the long end of his career. As a girl, Rory had it all, smarts, looks, a cheerleader's personality; Shane wanted what dads wanted for daughters in those days, learn how to make a living and marry well enough that you never needed to do it. He had no thought about his daughter on the force, where shit floated. She made straight A's at the U in accounting, passed the CPA exam on the first try, and got off to a rocket start at one of the big accounting firms. All well, except she felt as if she were serving a sentence. Four years along, she chucked it and applied to the academy without a word to her parents. The storytellers said Shane had cried his eyes out in misery when he got the news.

Rory went to Financial Crimes after two years on a beat and had been a star ever since. When she walked in with Jim Brand, Tommy was a little disappointed to see she had sort of gone to seed since their last meeting a few years ago. As someone whose appearance was always against him, who struggled to keep himself looking merely out of shape, he did not quite understand how a woman like Rory, who once could turn traffic, just let it go, put on forty pounds in all the wrong places. Not fifty yet, she was still blond and pretty and nicely turned out, which maybe meant she'd battled the weight thing and lost, probably hated mirrors, and worried some what Phil, her husband, a lieutenant in Traffic, thought about it all.

"What are the happy returns?" Tommy asked. Tommy and Brand had decided Rory would be the best bet on the force to serve the documents subpoenas. She had enough rank that they could ask her without checking in with a commander and the brains to figure out whatever came back with no need for assistance. And she was one of the few cops actually proud to keep a secret.

"*No sé*," said Rory. "I don't know what you guys had to start." She gave the PA a stiff look as she and Brand settled in the wooden armchairs in front of Tommy's desk. Tommy had instructed Brand not to explain anything about the investigation, and Rory, typical of all cops, hated working blind. Police officers always wanted to know everything, mostly because that was one of the principal delights of being a cop, feeling you sort of had the drop on everyone. From cop to cop it varied, whether the information made them feel superior or just not so bad. "This is like working with the Feebies. 'Just do what I say.'"

Nothing against Rory, but Tommy knew there was exactly one way to keep the fact that Rusty was under the microscope on murder from hitting the street, and that was to trust no one.

"You know who the subject is, right?" Tommy asked, as if the name alone were explanation enough.

"When you serve four SDTs"—subpoenas duces tecum, subpoenas for documents—"with the same guy's name on them, yeah, you kind of catch on. I'm figuring the judge has got something going on the side. Last time I checked, screwing wasn't a crime. Even for a candidate for the supreme court. And you're being way too quiet for this to be some kind of payback thing, just to rat him out to the press. So there's something big here. That the dish?"

Brand looked at Tommy, who didn't answer. He was thinking through what Rory had said. The documents she'd unearthed somehow confirmed Cantu, and showed Rusty had been stepping out.

"I gotta ask this much," said Rory. "We talkin a boy or a girl?"

Tommy felt his face drop. He said, "Female," eventually.

"Shit," said Rory, who apparently thought this was really going to be fun.

"We're hearing she's a lot younger, though," said Brand. "How's that?"

"Not the same," Rory answered.

"You know why he's doing a woman thirty years younger than him?" Brand asked Rory.

"Because he's lucky," she answered with a sick smile. She thought he was messing with her, talking to her as if she were a guy, the cop version of equal opportunity. Brand, however, was serious.

"Because anybody his age would know better. I don't think you score a lot of coffee dates off eHarmony

.com when you say in your profile, 'Once accused of murdering my mistress.'"

"I think that would turn some women on," said Rory.

"Why is it," Brand asked, "I never met those kind of women?"

"Anybody working here?" Tommy said. "Rory, how's it figure that Rusty's getting some? What came back on the subpoenas?"

"Actually, not much," said Rory. "We picked up his bank account number from his county payroll records. That was the best thing I got, his bank account."

Tommy asked if the bank had received the ninety-day letter ordering them not to talk. Rory gave him that look, I'm not stupid, then opened her file folder. Class began. She handed out copies of Rusty's statements.

What Rory showed them over the next few minutes was that last April, Rusty had stopped the automatic deposit of his county check at his bank. That was just when a cost of living adjustment for the state judges had finally come through, after being held up more than two years by some cock-and-bull litigation by a taxpayers group. Instead of the electronic deposit, Rusty walked into the bank every two weeks with his paper check and deposited the same amount to the penny that had been going in before the COLA. He pinched off the remainder in cash, including more than four grand for the backlog paid to start.

Tommy wasn't getting the point.

"It means he wants some money the missus don't know nothing about," Rory said. Now and then she talked just like her old man, bad grammar and everything, as if she were sorry she'd been a Phi Beta Kappa.

Brand pointed at Molto. "Told you," said Jim. "The girl is good."

"No, I told you," said Tommy. "Only I'm not seeing how dollars equals dollies. Maybe the judge likes the ponies."

"Or crack," said Rory. "That was my first guess," she said, "since I'm just guessing." She gave Tommy another dark look. She was not letting him off easy. "Most of the cash, naturally, I can't tell you where it went. But I got a pretty good idea. Sometimes he'd come into the bank, make the deposit, and use the cash he was getting back, plus some extra he had in his sock, to buy cashier's checks."

"Nice get," said Tommy.

"Better lucky than good. The bank just coughed up the cashier's checks with the rest of the records. I never thought to ask. Usually with all the financial privacy laws, you gotta beat them like a drum just to get what you're entitled to. But they had it all in a package in less than a day. Probably the ninety-day letter gave them all a jolt. I don't think they see many of those out in Nearing."

She passed the first cashier's check around, dated May 14, 2007, for $250. It was made payable to a company called STDTC.

"Stands for?" asked Tommy.

"Sexually Transmitted Disease Testing Corporation."

"Whoa."

"Yeah, whoa," she said.

"Why's he got a dirty dick?" asked Tommy.

"Boy," said Rory, "I can give you a lot of theories. All of them fun. You already shot down the first one. Maybe he forgot his raincoat. Maybe the girlfriend and him wanted to go naked and were holding hands in the waiting room while they tested together. Obviously, though, if he brought something home, he wouldn't get too far with the missus telling her he got it off a toilet seat."

"Can we get the results?" Tommy asked Brand.

"Only if we ask the feds. Under the Patriot Act, they can get your medical info without you knowing. But the state assembly nixed that on the local version."

The feds would steal the case if they could. Chief judge. Supreme court. They always wanted everything that would make headlines above the fold. But Tommy didn't really need them. The bare fact that Rusty tested meant he'd been roving.

Tommy looked at Brand. "Maybe Rusty's girl's a pro?"

Brand waggled his head. It was a theory.

"Maybe he got some names from Eliot Spitzer," Jim said. They all laughed, but Rory wasn't buying that, because hookers were usually a habit, and Rusty had started depositing his whole paycheck, including the COLA, as of June 15 last year.

"How'd he explain that to the old lady?" Brand asked her.

"Tells her the COLA finally came through."

Brand nodded. So did Tommy.

"Assuming he wanted the cash to keep some girl,

that must have stopped," Rory said. "At least for a while."

"Why only for a while?" asked Brand.

"Here's cashier's check number two."

The check, dated September 12, only a little more than a month ago, was made payable to Dana Mann for $800. The memo on it said, "9/4/08 Consultation." Prima Dana, as he was known, was the king of the high-end divorce bar, representing the rich and the richer. The street rap made him a preening jerk, cagier than he was smart, whose main skill was doing the United We Stand routine with grieving divorcées, but there were also some who credited his tact and judgment, and Rusty apparently was one of them.

"So how are you figuring this?" Tommy asked her.

"You mean why did he pay for a consultation?"

"No," said Tommy. He could explain that much. Prima Dana was up in the court of appeals all the time. If Rusty was sticking with Barbara and not becoming Dana's client, then as long as Rusty had settled Dana's bill, the judge didn't have to take himself off Dana's future cases, a move that otherwise would be as good as a public announcement that he had been thinking about divorce at some point.

"Divorce would be a little tough in the middle of a campaign," Brand said.

"Especially if there was another woman," said Tommy.

"Can we get Prima Dana's records?" Rory asked.

Tommy and Brand both shook their heads.

"Nothing but the bill and the payment," Tommy answered. "He'd never tell us what they discussed. It's privileged. Not that it's worth the bother. How many times in the last decade has Prima Dana filed an appearance in anything but a divorce case?"

Brand went to Tommy's computer. Jim was one of those guys who understood computers as though he'd been born inside the machine and could seemingly extract information by touching a couple of keys, all in the time it took Tommy to remember how to open his e-mail program.

"'Practice limited to matrimonial law,'" Brand read off Prima Dana's website.

Rory had another cashier's check to Prima Dana in July 2007 with a similar notation. So apparently Rusty had been lingering with the idea of divorce for a while. The earlier occasion correlated pretty well to the times he'd been seen traipsing around with his young honey.

"So how are you putting this together?" Tommy asked Rory.

Rory shrugged. "My way back machine got broke. Could be a lot of things, but you know, pretty for sure he had a girl. After that, we can just spitball. We all know the usual: She told him to cut the missus loose or the store was closed, he wouldn't, they split, and by this September he was having second thoughts. He was getting ready to bail. Then," said Rory with a little dramatic trill, "Mrs. Judge very conveniently passed away instead." She looked at Tommy, then Brand. Of course she'd figured it out. Of course. This girl was good. Rusty's second check to Prima Dana was less than three weeks before Barbara had died.

"Nothing," said Tommy, pointing at her. "Not even to Phil."

Over her lips, she did a lightning version of the lock and tossed key.

Tommy weighed it out. There could be a lot of other explanations, but that one was pretty good.

"Do we know who this girl is?" he asked.

Rory took a beat. "I was thinking maybe the big boys had a clue."

"We're SOL on that," said Tommy.

Rory was, too. Records of the landline phones were sixed by now, and the cell phone detail showed a few calls every day, but almost all to his house or his son or the drugstore in town.

She smiled. "We could subpoena the court's telephone records. But it kind of seems like the ninety-day letter has got to go to the chief judge. And the detail, a year and a half later, has got to be trashed now, too, just like the other phones."

"E-mail?" asked Brand.

"These days every provider purges their server after thirty days. That doesn't mean he don't have messages on his own hard drives. I think it'd be especially interesting to take a look at his computer at home. Or at work."

"We're not going there right now," Tommy said. "Not before the election. And not without more than we have."

Tommy thanked Rory, laying it on thick about the kind of job she'd done.

"I'm on this?" she asked from the door, meaning she would be the cop who got the collar, if there ever was one.

"You're on it," said Tommy. "Wouldn't want nobody else. We'll call you."

Brand and Tommy sat alone. You could hear the phones chirping and deputies yelling at one another in the hall.

"We got something, Boss. The STD test—that's not for the happily monogamous. And we know he's talking about ending the marriage just a few weeks before she checks out."

Tommy thought. "Maybe Barbara was having the affair," he said. "Maybe he's paying a PI with the COLA and it's the investigator he's meeting in the hotel, who by the way is a young woman, which is damn good cover for a PI. Maybe he tests to be sure his wife hadn't brought home the nasty. Over time he can't forgive her, so he goes to commune with Prima Dana."

Brand ripped out a wild laugh. "You really missed your calling, you know. You'd have been a whiz on the other side, Boss. You have the head for it."

"But not the stomach," answered Tommy. "Look, Jimmy. The coroner says Barbara died of natural causes."

"Because the bad judge sat for twenty-four hours to wait for whatever really killed her to dissolve in her gut." Brand came around Tommy's desk. "We gotta surface, Boss." Brand had a whole long list of things to do. Get Rusty's computers. Do interviews to see how Rusty and Barbara were getting along, and develop a minute-by-minute timeline on what happened the night before Barbara died. Talk to the Sabiches' kid.

"Not yet," Tommy answered. "It hits the press, Rusty loses the election. Rusty loses the election and we made his defense, no matter what kind of evidence we come up with eventually. You know this song, every word: 'Acting PA wants revenge for old case, keeps Sabich off court.' We take our time, we don't have to listen to that."

"They serve ten-year terms on the supreme court," said Brand.

"Not with a murder conviction," Tommy answered.

"And what if we come up short?" asked Brand. "We get close but not close enough. This guy not only strolls on murder again, but is up there beating on us."

Tommy knew all along that Brand would get to this: Let it leak and put Rusty's lights out. Do a little justice instead of none at all. In the heat of the moment, Brand was still inclined to cut corners now and then. Tommy had probably been the same way, if he was going to be honest, and without the same excuse. Brand's father keeled over dead at his desk at National Can when Brand was eight. There were five other kids. The mom did what she could, became a teacher's aide, but they were trapped in a strange existence, residing in a nice suburban house paid off by the dad's mortgage insurance, in a town where they couldn't afford to live. Brand went through school with everybody around him having more—better clothes, vacations, cars, meals. These days, Brand did a lot of gourmet cooking—he and Jody got together every month with three other couples and tried their hand at stuff they'd seen on *Iron Chef*. A few years ago, Tommy asked Jim offhandedly what got him interested in food.

'Being hungry,' Brand answered. He wasn't talking about mealtimes these days, Tommy realized. The

Brand family wanted in a community where nobody even understood the concept. Stuck in the middle, Brand always felt nobody in his house had time for him. His mom had twins, five years younger than Jim, to concentrate on. His older brothers were both doing what they could to hold things together for the rest of the brood.

In high school, Brand was in trouble all the time— cutting school, hanging out at poker parlors, where he started playing on the sly when he was fifteen. They'd have tossed him out if it hadn't been for football. Brand was a savage on the field. But their savage. He probably ended the seasons of four or five teammates during practice and twice the number of opponents, but he was all-conference and rarely missed a tackle in the open field. They told him he wasn't big enough to play linebacker in Division I, but he changed their minds when he got to the U. He made it the same way he did here, when Tommy got him the chance, on sheer will. That in turn was why Brand loved Tommy: because Tom was the first person in Jim's life who he felt cut him a real break without something to gain for himself. But when you turned up the heat at moments, particularly at trial, the hungry, pissed-off kid was still there, who didn't like playing by the rules because he thought they were made by people who didn't give a fig about the likes of him. Sooner or later, the grown-up took over. Brand always came back to himself, but sometimes you had to kick him in the ass. And Tommy did that now.

"No," said Tommy to the idea of a leak, with just enough irritation to make the point. He had learned this lesson the hard way years ago with the first Sabich case. You're here to prosecute crimes, not decide elections. Just do the job. Investigate. Build a case. Try it. The fallout was not your concern. "No choice. Nothing public before the election."

Brand didn't like it. "Besides," he said.

There was always a "besides" with Jimmy. He thought long and hard before he saw the boss.

"We got another way to deal with all of this," Brand said. "Punch a hole in that vendetta defense."

"Which is?"

"Prove he got away with murder twenty years ago. The PA isn't looking for revenge. He's looking for justice. The blood standards and the sperm fraction from the old case have still got to be in the police pathologist's deep freeze, don't they?"

Tommy knew where this was going because he had considered the possibility a couple of times a year for the past decade, once he realized that DNA would provide a definitive answer about whether Sabich was guilty of Carolyn Polhemus's murder. Of course, he'd never had a decent reason to do the tests.

"Not yet," he said.

"We could go in for an ex parte court order. Say it's part of a grand jury investigation."

"You pull that evidence out of the deep freeze at McGrath," he said, referring to police headquarters, where no secret was safe, "especially with a grand jury court order, and every cop in town will know in two hours, and every reporter about five minutes after that. When it's time, there may be a way without a court order."

Brand stared. This was the first time Tommy

actually betrayed himself, showed how much thought he'd given to Rusty—and the DNA.

"Not yet," said Tommy. "After the election we can look at all of this again."

Brand was frowning.

"Not yet," Tommy repeated.

CHAPTER 9

Rusty, May 2007

What is great sex? Does it have to be prolonged? Or inventive? Are circus maneuvers required? Or merely intensity? By whatever measure, my bouts with Anna are not the greatest of my life—that title will forever rest with Carolyn Polhemus, for whom sex on each occasion was a shameless conquest of the most extreme altitudes of physical pleasure and lack of inhibition.

Anna is of a generation for many of whom sex is first and foremost fun. When I knock on the hotel room door ten minutes behind her, there is often an amusing surprise: A nurse in six-inch come-fuck-me heels. Her torso wrapped in Saran. A green arrow in body paint that plunges between her breasts and joins a V immediately above the female cleft. The gift bow tying her robe, beneath which she was naked. But the humor sometimes implies a lack of consequence I never feel.

She is, of course, far more experienced than I. Anna is the fourth woman I have slept with in the last forty years. Her "number," as she blithely refers to it, is never disclosed, but she mentions enough in passing that

I know my predecessors are many. I am concerned, therefore, when it develops that she has trouble reaching climax. With apologies to Tolstoy, I would say that all men come alike, but each woman arrives at orgasm her own way—and Anna's way often eludes me. There are days when I have my own problems, finally leading me to call on my doctor for the little blue pill he's often offered.

But for all that might, at moments, seem to make Anna and me candidates for an instructional video, there is an inescapable and wondrous tenderness every time we are together. I touch her the way you would a holy relic—adoringly, lingering with the certainty that my yearning and my gratitude are radiating from my skin. And we have the one thing that great lovemaking always requires—in our best moments, nothing else exists. My shame or anxiety, the cases that vex me, my concerns about the court and the campaign—she is the only thing in the known universe. It is a beautiful, perfect oblivion.

No matter how much Anna insists that we should not consider our ages, the difference is there constantly, especially in the gap it creates in our communications. I have never held an iPod, and I do not know whether it is good or bad when she says that something "kills." And she has no clue about the world that made me, no memories of Kennedy's assassination or life under Eisenhower—not to mention the sixties. The great fusion of love, the sense that she is I and I she, is sometimes subject to question.

It also means that I talk too often about Nat. I

cannot resist asking Anna's assistance, as someone who is far closer to him in life.

"You worry too much about him," she tells me one night as we are lying in each other's arms between bouts. Room service will knock soon with dinner. "I know a lot of people who went to law school with him at Easton and they all say he's brilliant—you know, one of those people who talk in class only once a month and then say something even the professor never thought of."

"He's had a hard time. There's a lot going on with Nat," I say.

Because you love your children, and make their contentment the principal object of your existence, it's something of a downer to see them turn out not much happier than you. Nathaniel Sabich was a good kid by most common measures. He paid attention in grade school, he dissed his parents with relative infrequency. But he had an uncommonly hard time growing up. He was a rambunctious little boy, who had trouble sitting still and paged ahead to see the end when I was reading him a story. As he grew older, it became plain that all the random motion had its source in a kind of worry he took deeper and deeper into himself.

The therapists have had no end of theories why. He is the only child of two only children and came up in a hothouse of parental attention that may well prove there is such a thing as loving a child too much. Then there was the trauma of my indictment and trial, when no matter how we pretended, our family dangled like a movie character clinging to a broken bridge.

The explanation I go to most often is the one that leaves me least to blame: He inherited some of his mother's depressive disorder. By the time he had reached adolescence, I could see the familiar black funk descend on him, marked by the same brooding and isolation. We went through all the stuff you would expect. Report cards marked by A pluses and F's. Drugs. It was perhaps the most shamed day of my life when my pal Dan Lipranzer, a detective who was on the eve of his retirement to Arizona, popped into my chambers unexpectedly a decade ago. 'Drug Task Force picked up a drippy-nosed kid who goes to Nearing High yesterday and he says he's buying his poppers from the son of a judge.'

The good news was that this development allowed us to leverage Nat back into psychotherapy. When he began on SSRIs near the end of college, it was as if he had left a cave and come into the light. He started grad school in philosophy, finally moving out of the house for good, and then, with no discussion with us, made the change to law school. My son has been the living receptacle of so much anxiety and longing for both Barbara and me that we each seem startled at times that he is finally making his way on his own, but that probably has to do with the uneasiness of being left face-to-face with each other.

"Were you happy he went to law school?" Anna asks.

"Relieved in a way. I didn't mind grad school in philosophy. I thought it was a worthy enterprise. But I didn't know where it was going to lead. Not that law school made it much better. He talks about being a law professor, but it's going to be hard for him to do that straight from a clerkship, and he doesn't seem to have other ideas."

"How about a J. Crew model? You realize the guy's gorgeous, don't you?"

Nat is lucky enough to resemble his mother, yet the truth, which only I seem to recognize, is that the piercing quality to his handsomeness, the acute blue eyes and the universe of somber mystery, comes straight from my father. Young women are drawn like a beacon by Nat's exceptional good looks, but he has always been unnaturally slow to form a bond and has entered yet another remote phase as the result of a disastrous breakup with Kat, the girl he saw the last four years.

"They offered him a job. Somebody from an agency saw him on the street. But he's always hated people talking about his looks. It's not the basis he wants to be judged on. Besides, there's a better career if he wants to make easy money."

"What's that?"

"Everybody your age. You can all be rich beyond your wildest dreams."

"How?"

"Learn to remove tattoos."

She laughs as Anna laughs, as if laughing is all there is to life. She squirms and giggles. But the talk of Nat has left something lingering with her, and she rises to an elbow a few minutes later to see me.

"Did you ever want a daughter?" she asks.

I stare for quite some time. "I think that's the kind of remark that Nat would have called 'deliberately transgressive' in his grad school days."

"You mean out of bounds?"

"I think that's what he means."

"I don't think boundaries cut a lot of ice around here," she says, and nods to the walls of the hotel room. "Did you? Want a daughter?"

"I wanted to have more children. Barbara had all kinds of excuses: She could never love another child as much as Nat. Stuff like that. In retrospect, I think she knew she was sick. And fragile."

"But did you want a daughter?"

"I already had a son."

"So yes?"

I try to cast my mind back to the yearnings of those years. I wanted children, to be a father, to do better than was done to me—it was a dominating passion.

"I suppose," I answer.

She stands and slowly sheds the robe she has put on for warmth, letting it fall from her shoulders as she fixes me with a longing gaze I used to see in her last days working in my chambers.

"That's what I thought," she says, and lies down beside me.

Leaving Anna, when we meet at night, remains difficult. She begs me not to go and is not above the tactics of a jezebel. Tonight she dresses reluctantly, and as we approach the door, she places both hands on it and gyrates her back end at me like a pole dancer.

"You're making it hard to leave."

"That's the idea."

She keeps up this lewd little shimmy, and I plant myself against her and join the motion, until I am fully aroused. I abruptly raise her skirt, pull aside her underpants, and push myself inside. No rubber: a daring act by our terms. Even the first time, Anna had condoms in her purse.

"Oh, Jesus," she says. "Rusty."

But neither of us stops. Her hands are braced against the door. Every bit of the desperation and insanity of our relationship is here for both of us. And when I finally release, it seems to be the truest moment we've had.

Afterward, we are both a bit shaken and re-dress in chagrined silence.

"Teach me to shake my ass at you," she says as I leave first.

Guilt is a commando who arrives in stealth and then sabotages everything. After that brief moment of abandon, I am visited perpetually by obvious fears. I nearly weep late at night when I receive one of Anna's cryptic e-mails. "Visitor arrived," it says, using the quaint Victorian slang for menstruation. But even after that, there is an acronym that feels like a frozen hand squeezing my heart, whenever it comes to mind: STD. What if Anna, who is well traveled, is unknowingly afflicted with something I could pass on? I repeatedly envision Barbara's face when she comes home from the gynecologist.

I know this concern is largely irrational. But the what-ifs are each like nails driven into my brain. There is so much torment already that I simply cannot cope with yet another random worry. So one day in my chambers, I put the search term—"STD"—in my computer and find myself at a site. I make the 800 call from a pay phone in the bus station, with my back turned so nobody can hear.

The young woman at the other end is patient, consoling. She explains the testing protocol and then says she can charge my credit card. The initials that would appear on the bill would be innocuous, but it is the kind of detail that would never sink below Barbara's attention; she always asks whether any unexplained expense is deductible.

My silence says it all. The polite young woman then adds, "Or if you'd rather, you may pay with a postal money order or a cashier's check." She gives me a PIN that will supplant my name in all my dealings with the company.

I buy the cashier's check the next day when I am at the bank, making one of my jiggered deposits. "Should I list you as remitter?" the teller asks.

"No," I say, with embarrassing speed.

I go straight from there to the thirtieth-floor office in a Center City building where I have been told to drop the check. I find myself at the door of an import/export concern. I peek in, then back out to reexamine the address in my pocket. When I enter again, the receptionist, a middle-aged Russian woman, eyes me with an imperial look and asks in a strong accent, "Are you here to give me money?" It makes sense, I realize, this front. Even if a sleuth has followed me here, he'd miss my purpose. She takes my check and throws it unceremoniously into a drawer and goes back to work. What a menagerie of the unfaithful this woman must have met. Gay men by the dozens. A mom with two kids in the stroller who's gotten pumped by the guy next door, at home these days while he's looking for work. And probably lots of fellows like me, graying and in middle years, rattled by fears about the three-hundred-dollar hooker they passed some time with. Weakness and folly are her business.

The actual test is uneventful by comparison. I am in a medical office across from University Hospital, where I sign in only with my number. The woman who draws the blood never bothers with a smile. After all, every patient is a potential peril to her. She gives me no warning that the needle may hurt.

Four days later, a counselor informs me I'm clean. I tell Anna the next time I'm with her. I debated saying anything but realize that hard science is better than my word about my personal history.

"I wasn't worried," she answers. She peers under her full brows. "Were you?"

I'm sitting on the bed. It is noontime, and down the hall I can hear the minibar porter knocking on doors so he can come in and check—a great pose for a PI, I think in my current state of disquiet.

"A lot of questions I didn't want to ask." Because I cannot promise not to sleep with Barbara, I have realized that I am in no position to ask fidelity from Anna. I still do not know whether she is seeing other men, but I seldom get responses to the brief e-mails I dare to send her on the weekends. Oddly, I am not jealous. I repeatedly imagine the moment when she will tell me she is moving on, that she's gotten what she can from this experience and is going to resume her progress toward a normal life.

"There isn't anyone but you right now, Rusty." 'Right now,' I think. "And I've always been safe. I'm sorry I freaked. But I'd never have an abortion."

"I shouldn't have done it."

"I loved it," she says quietly, and sits beside me. "We could do it that way. Now that we know. I have a diaphragm."

"And what happens when you meet somebody else?"

"I told you. I'm always safe. I mean," she says and stops.

"What?"

"There doesn't have to be anyone. If you tell me you're thinking about leaving Barbara."

I sigh. "Anna, we can't keep having this conversation. If we have only two hours together, we can't spend half of it fighting."

Now I've hurt her. It's always easy to read when Anna is angry. The hardest piece of her, the one engaged by the cruel mechanics of the law, takes over and her face becomes rigid.

Sorely tried, I sprawl on the bed and put a pillow on my face. She will recover in time and settle beside me. But for now, I am alone and in a kind of meditation where I test myself with the question she has often asked. Would I marry Anna if some freak circumstance somehow made it possible? She is howlingly funny, a pleasure to look at, and a person I savor, dear to me as breath. But I have already been thirty-four. I doubt I could rejoin her on the other side of a bridge I've already crossed.

Yet something else is as suddenly clear as the solution to a math problem I formerly could not solve. I see now what I have come together with Anna to recognize: I erred. I blundered. She may not be the right alternative. But that doesn't mean there never was one.

Twenty years ago, I thought I was making the best of many bad choices, and I was wrong. Wrong. I could have done something else, found someone else. Worse. I should have. I should not have returned to Barbara. I should not have sold my happiness for Nat's. It was the wrong choice for all three of us. It left Nat growing up in a dungeon of voiceless suffering. And yoked Barbara to the daily evidence of what anybody, in a righter mind, would prefer to forget. My heart right now is like some overloaded man-of-war toppled by a light wind, sinking into the waters it was meant to sail. And it will not do to blame anybody but myself.

When I return to chambers, there is an urgent message from George Mason on my desk. Three, in fact. Life in the court of appeals moves at the pace of suspended animation. Even so-called emergency motions can be resolved in a day or two, not an hour. When I look up, George is on the threshold. He has come down in person in the hope I have returned. He is in shirtsleeves, stroking his striped tie as a way to soothe himself.

"What?" I ask.

He closes the door behind him. "We issued the opinion in *Harnason* Monday."

"I saw that."

"I bumped into Grin Brieson on the way to lunch today. She called Mel Tooley to arrange for Harnason's surrender and never heard back. Finally, after the third call, Mel admitted he thinks the guy is in the wind. The coppers went out this morning. Harnason's been gone at least two weeks."

"He jumped bail?" I ask. "He fled?"

Harnason went to a riverboat casino and used a high-limit credit card to buy twenty-five thousand dollars in chips, which he promptly cashed to grubstake his flight. With a two-week head start, he is probably far outside the country.

"The papers don't have it yet," George tells me. "But they will soon. I wanted you to be prepared when the reporters call." The public doesn't know a thing about what supreme court justices do. But they will understand I let a convicted murderer loose who will now be at large forever, one more bogeyman to dread. Koll will bludgeon me with Harnason's name. I wonder vaguely if I have actually given the jerk a chance.

But that is not what paralyzes me when George finally leaves me alone behind my large desk. I have known for the seven weeks I have seen Anna that disaster was looming. But I hadn't seen its shape. I was willing to chance hurting the people closest to me. But no matter how ironic, I am stunned to realize that I have assisted in a serious violation of the law. Harnason played me so well. The election is the least of my concerns. With the wrong prosecutor—and Tommy Molto is certainly the wrong prosecutor—I could end up in jail.

I need a lawyer. I am too disoriented and full of self-reproaches to figure any of this out myself. There is only one choice: Sandy Stern, who represented me twenty-one years ago.

"Oh, Judge," says Vondra, Sandy's assistant. "He's been out of the office, a little under the weather, but I know he would want to talk to you. Let me see if he can take the call."

It is several minutes before he is on the line.

"Rusty." His voice is frayed and weak, alarmingly so. When I ask what's wrong, he says, "A bad laryngitis," and turns the conversation back to me. I do not bother with pleasantries.

"Sandy, I need help. I'm ashamed to say I've done something stupid."

I await the ocean of rebukes. Stern is fully entitled: After I gave you another chance, another life.

"Ah, Rusty," he says. His breath seems labored. "That is what keeps me in business."

Stern's doctor has ordered him not to talk for two weeks and thus not to come into the office. I prefer to wait for him rather than seek advice from anyone I would trust even a fraction less. After forty-eight hours pass, I recover my balance somewhat. The news of Harnason's flight has broken. The police have run all leads and found no trace of his whereabouts. Koll has howled about my misjudgments, but the controversy is relegated to a two-inch item at the bottom of the local news page because the general election is so far away. Ironically, Koll would have scored far larger if he'd remained in the primary.

I have no idea how the mess with Harnason will play out, if Sandy will advise me to make a clean breast of the matter with the court or keep my peace. But my soul is at rest on one thing: I must stop seeing Anna. Having had a taste of ruin again, I cannot tolerate any more danger.

Three days later, I arrive early in the lobby of the Hotel Dulcimer, to be sure I intercept her before she goes up to the room. From my untimely appearance, she knows something is awry, but I draw her toward one of the columns and whisper, "We have to stop, Anna."

I watch her face crumple. "Let's go upstairs," she says impatiently. If I say no, I know she will be unable to keep herself from making a scene here.

She cries bitterly as soon as the door is closed and takes a seat on an armchair, still in the light raincoat she wore in today's storm.

"I've tried to imagine," she says. "I've tried to imagine this so many times. What was I going to feel like when you said this? And I just couldn't. I just couldn't, and I can't believe it now."

I have decided in advance not to explain about Harnason. I said nothing at the time of the incident, and no matter how paradoxical, I'm certain the same woman who encouraged my illicit passions would be crushed to think I could behave as a judge with such blatant impropriety. Instead, I say simply, "It's time. I know it's time. It's only going to get harder."

"Rusty," she says.

"I'm right, Anna. You know that."

To my surprise, she nods. She herself has been coming to terms. Eight weeks, I think. That will be the final duration of my flight from sanity.

"You have to hold me again," she says.

She is in my arms for a long time as we stand just inside the door. It is a bookend of our first moments together. But we hardly need the reminder. The bodies have their own momentum. We are both quick to finish, knowing perhaps we are on stolen time.

Dressed again and at the door, she clings to me once. "Do we have to stop seeing each other?"

"No," I say. "But let's give it a little while."

Once she's gone, I lie there a long, long time. More than an hour. The rest of my life, dark and doomed, has started.

I would say there is no coping with the loss, but that is untrue. I walk through my life like an amputee who feels the phantom pain of the missing limb, my heart bursting with longing and my mind telling me, in perhaps the saddest note of all, this too will pass. Never again, I think. The curse has now come true. Never again.

After a week, it's better. I miss her. I mourn her. But some peace has returned. She had been so unattainable—so young, so much a citizen of a different era—that it is hard to feel fully deprived. And no matter what the course with Harnason, this part of the tale will remain untold. Barbara will not know. Nat will not know. I have avoided the worst.

I wonder all the time. Is it Anna I miss? Or love?

Two weeks after our last meeting at the Dulcimer, Anna shows up in chambers. I recognize her voice from my desk, where I am working, and hear her tell my secretary that she was in the building to file a brief and just wanted to drop by. She lights up when she sees me in my doorway and breezes into the inner chambers uninvited, just another former clerk who's happened by to pay respects, something that occurs all the time.

She is gay, joking loudly with Joyce about the fact

they are each wearing the same boots, until I close the door. Then she slumps and drops her face into her hands.

I can feel my heart thumping. She is so lovely. She's in a gray suit, nicely tailored, whose feel I recall as clearly as if my hand were on it now.

"I've met somebody," she says quietly once she looks up. "He actually lives in my building. I've seen him a hundred times and just started talking to him ten days ago."

"Lawyer?" My voice too is very low.

"No." She gives her head a determined shake, as if to suggest she'd never be that stupid. "He's in business. Investments. Divorced. A little older. I like him. I slept with him last night."

I manage not to flinch.

"I hated it," she says. "Hated myself. I mean, I tell myself there are people like you and me in everybody's life, people who can't stay forever but who matter immensely at the moment. I think if you've led an open and honest life, there will be those people. Don't you think that?"

I have friends who believe all relationships really fall under this heading—good only for a while. But I nod solemnly.

"I'm trying everything, Rusty."

"We each need time," I say.

She shakes her lovely hair about. It's been cut in the last two weeks, turned under a bit.

"I'll always be waiting for you to say you want me back."

"I'll always want you back," I answer. "But you'll

never hear me say it." She smiles a trifle as she gathers in the deliberate absurdity of my last remark.

"Why are you so determined?" she asks.

"Because we reached the logical conclusion. There is no happy ending. Nothing happier. And I'm beginning to come to terms."

"And what terms are those, Rusty?"

"That I don't have the right to live twice. Nobody does. I made my choices. It would disrespect the life I've lived to throw all that over. And I have to show some gratitude to whatever force allowed me to skate across the thinnest ice and make it. I mean, I've told you over and over, Barbara cannot know. Cannot."

Anna looks at me in a hard way, an expression I've seen occasionally and that will greet hundreds of witnesses on cross-examination in the next decades.

"Do you love Barbara?"

There's a question. Oddly, she has never asked until now.

"How many hours do you have?" I ask.

"A lifetime if you want it."

I smile thinly. "I think I could have done better."

"Then why not leave?"

"I might." I have never said this aloud.

"But not for someone younger? Not for a former clerk. Because you care about what people would say?"

I do not answer. I have already explained. She continues to apply that cool, objective eye.

"It's because you're running, isn't it," she says then. "You're picking the supreme court over me."

I see it instantly: I must lie. "I am," I say.

She emits a derisive little snort, then lifts her face

again to continue her frigid assessment. She sees me now, all my weakness, all my vanity. I've lied, but she still has glimpsed the truth.

Yet I have accomplished one thing.

We are done.

My relationship with Sandy Stern is intense and sui generis. He is the only lawyer who appears in the court of appeals from whose cases I inalterably recuse myself. Even my former clerks come before me five years after they've left. But Stern and I are not intimates. In fact, I did not speak to him for nearly two years after my trial, until gratitude overwhelmed other feelings I had about what had gone on in my case. By now, we have an appreciative rapport and eat lunch on occasion. But I hear none of his secrets. Yet his role in my life was so epochal that I could never pretend he is just another advocate. His defense of me was masterful, with every word spoken in court as significant as each note in Mozart. I owe him my life.

We chat in his office about his kids and grandkids. His youngest, Kate, has three children. She divorced two years ago but has remarried. His son, Peter, moved off to San Francisco with his partner, another physician. Clearly the most content is Marta, his daughter who practices with him. She married Solomon, a management consultant, twelve years ago, with whom she has three kids and a full life.

Sandy looks himself, if rounder, all of that obscured by perfect tailoring. One advantage of appearing middle-aged as a younger person is that at this stage you seem immune to time.

"You look like you recovered well from your laryngitis," I tell him.

"Not quite, Rusty. I had a bronchoscopy the day before you called me. I shall be having surgery for lung cancer later this week."

I am devastated for both our sakes. His damn cigars. They are ever-present, and when deep in thought, Stern seldom remembers not to inhale. The smoke pours out of his nose like a dragon's.

"Oh, Sandy."

"They tell me it is good they can operate. There are worse scenarios with this sort of thing. They will remove a lobe, then wait and watch."

I ask about his wife, and he describes Helen, whom he married as a widower, as herself, brave and funny. As always, she has been just what he needs.

"But," he says, enjoying the joke, "enough about me." I wonder if I was truly doomed, if my hours were dwindling, I would choose to ascend the bench. It is a tribute to what Stern has done that he feels these remain his best moments.

I tell him my story in bare strokes, relating the minimum he needs to know: that I was seeing someone, was followed by Harnason, who caught me unaware and left me unsettled—angry, intimidated, guilty. The story draws Stern's complex Latin expression, all his features briefly mobilized while he embraces the elusive categories of life.

The two weeks I have waited to see Sandy have not done much to clarify my thinking about my predicament with Harnason. I want Stern's advice concerning what the law and ethics require me to do. Must I tell the truth to my fellow judges or the police? And what will happen to me as a result? Listening, Stern reaches out reflexively for his cigar and stops. Instead, he rubs his temples as he thinks. He takes quite some time.

"A case like this, Rusty, a man like that—" Stern does not complete the sentence, but his manner suggests that he has fully grasped Harnason's strangeness. "He bankrolled his flight very cleverly, and I suspect he has made equally careful plans to hide himself. I doubt he will be seen again.

"If he is apprehended, then of course—" Sandy's hand drifts off. "It would be problematic. One might hope the fellow would keep your confidence out of gratitude, but it would be unwise to expect that. As a criminal matter, however, it seems to me a very difficult prosecution— a twice convicted felon, whom you initially sent to the penitentiary? Not much of a witness. And that assumes Molto could gin up some imagined crime. But if Harnason is the only witness the state has—and it's difficult to see how there could be another—it will be a meager case.

"As a disciplinary matter for the Courts Commission, that is another thing. Unlike the criminal inquiry, you will be required to testify eventually, and no matter how confused you found yourself, we both know your conduct ran afoul of several canons of judicial conduct. But as long as the prospect of criminal prosecution is not ephemeral—and it surely is not with Tommy Molto sitting in the PA's chair—you need say nothing to your colleagues. I rarely make a record of my exchanges with clients, but in this case, I will do a memo to the file, in case you ever want to substantiate that you received this advice from me."

He speaks offhandedly, but of course he is referring to the likelihood he will be dead by the time any occasion arises for me to explain my silence.

In the elevator down, I try to absorb Stern's assessment, which is largely the same as my own. Understanding the realities, I am likely to get away with all of it. Harnason is gone for good. Barbara and Nat will remain unknowing about Anna. I will ascend to the supreme court and will forget in time a brief era of incredible folly. I will obtain what I've wanted, if not fully deserved, and, having risked it all, may enjoy my life more than I might have otherwise. The train of reason seems inexorable but is of little comfort. A sickness swims through my center.

I emerge from the gauntlet of revolving doors into a radiant day, with the first full heat of summer. The street is thronged with lunchgoers and shoppers, who walk with their wraps across their arms. Out in the street, roadworkers are repairing winter-made potholes, heating tar whose fulsome aroma seems oddly intoxicating. The trees in the park across the way wear new green, finally in full leaf, and the steely smell of the river is on the wind. Life seems pure. My way is set. And thus there is no hiding from the truth, which nearly brings me to my knees.

I love Anna. What can I possibly do?

RUSTY'S BIRTHDAY
(3/19/07)

BARBARA'S DEATH
(9/29/08)

THE ELECTION
(11/04/08)

CHAPTER 10

Tommy, October 23, 2008

Tommy Molto did not like the jail. It was three stories high, but dim as a dungeon, even in daytime,
because in 1906 they prevented escapes by building
windows that were only six inches wide. There was also
something unsettling about the sound, the anguished
din arising from three thousand captured souls. And
none of that was to talk about the odor. No matter how
strict the sanitation, so many men in quarters this close,
with a coverless stainless-steel toilet between every two
of them, filled the entire structure with a swampy, fetid
smell. It wasn't the Four Seasons. Nor was it meant to
be. But you would think after thirty years of visiting the
place to talk to witnesses, to try to roll defendants,
Tommy would be used to it. But his gut still clutched.
Some of it came down to the ugly reality of what he did.
Tommy tended to think of his job as being about right
and wrong and just deserts. The fact that his work cul-
minated in a stark captivity that he himself always
doubted he could survive remained even now an unwel-
come reality.

"Why are we talking to this bird now?" Tommy

asked Brand as they waited in the gate room. It was
nine p.m. Tommy had been at home when Brand
reached him. Tomaso has just gone down, and Dominga was in the kitchen, cleaning up. The house still
smelled of spice and diapers. These were the precious
hours in Tommy's day, feeling the rhythm of his family, the sweet order arriving out of the relative chaos of
the rest of his life. But Brand wouldn't have asked the
boss to come out unless it was something that really
couldn't wait, and he'd gone and put his suit back on.
He was the PA. Wherever he went, he had to look the
part, and as it turned out, both the warden and the
captain of the COs had skedaddled in from home once
they heard he was coming, so they could shake hands
and pass some gas together. It was only a second ago
they had departed, leaving Tommy to get a briefing at
last from his chief deputy.

"Because Mel Tooley said it would be worth the
trip. Really, really worth the trip. He's got something
the PA has to hear in person. And nine p.m. with no
reporters within a mile, that's the best time."

"Jimmy, I got a wife and a kid."

"I got a wife and two kids," Brand answered. He
was smiling, though. He thought it was cute, the way
Tommy sometimes acted as though he'd invented having a family. Brand had more faith in Mel Tooley than
most people because Mel shared office space with one
of Brand's older brothers.

"So background me," Tommy said. "This guy, the
poisoner, what's his name again? Harnason?" Eighteen
months ago, the head of the appellate section in the
office, Grin Brieson, had begged Tommy to argue the

case. He recalled that much and, naturally, that he had won despite Sabich's dissent. But the other details were gone in the wash of time.

"Right. He's been in the breeze for a year and a half now."

"I remember," said Tommy. "Sabich gave him bail." Last month, N. J. Koll had been running commercials calling Rusty out, ballyhooing the fact that the PAs had opposed bond for Harnason. Once Barbara croaked, N.J. had to take the high road and pull his stuff off the air, a relief to Molto. Tommy didn't like having his office in the middle of an election fight, especially that one.

"They grabbed Harnason yesterday in Coalville, burg three hundred miles south, on the other side of the state line, population twenty grand. That was Harnason's new homestead. He hung out a shingle as a lawyer, practicing under the name of Thorsen Skoglund."

"Asshole," said Molto. Tommy took a second to remember Thorsen, long gone now, an honorable man.

"So he's practicing law and on the side, get this, he's working as a children's party clown. You just can't make this stuff up. He was bringing in more as a clown than a lawyer, which may tell you something, but it was all going pretty good until his drinking problem got the better of him and he caught a DUI. The print comparison came back from the FBI about two hours after he had bonded out. Harnason apparently thought it was still the old days when it would have taken weeks. He was at home packing when the local sheriff came for him with a SWAT team."

Mel Tooley had waived extradition and the sheriff

in Coalville had driven Harnason back to the Tri-Cities himself. Not a lot of bail-jumping murder fugitives were picked up in Coalville. The sheriff would be talking about Harnason the rest of his life. So far, Harnason had not been to court, and the press had no idea he was in custody again, but the story would probably get out. All in all, that would be good news for Rusty. When Koll's ads went up again, he wouldn't be able to wave his arms around about the madman Sabich had set free, who was still on the loose.

By now, Tommy and Brand had been buzzed through the two sets of massive iron bars, a sort of air lock between captivity and freedom, and were escorted by a corrections officer named Sullivan back to the interview rooms. Sullivan knocked on a white door and Tooley came out into the narrow corridor. Mel, usually a bulbous fashion plate, was in civvies. He'd been gardening, apparently, when Harnason had hit town about five p.m. There was dirt under Mel's polished fingernails and on his jeans. It took Tommy a second to realize that in the rush, Tooley had forgotten his toup. The truth was he looked better without it, but Tommy decided to spare Mel that opinion.

Tooley did the usual bowing and scraping because the almighty PA had come out at night.

"I love you, too, Mel," said Tommy. "What's the scoop?"

"Okay, this is strictly hypothetical," said Mel, lowering his voice. In the jail, you never knew what side anybody was playing on. Some of the COs worked for the gangs, some were on a reporter's pad. Tooley crept close enough that you would think he was cozying up for a kiss. "But if you were to ask Mr. Harnason why he decided to make a run for it, he would tell you he had advance word of the appellate court's decision."

"How?"

"That's the good part," said Mel. "The chief judge told him."

Tommy felt as though he'd been hit in the head with a board. He couldn't imagine this. Rusty had a very hard stick up his ass as a judge.

"Sabich?" Tommy asked.

"Yep."

"Why?"

"It's a pretty strange conversation. You'll want to hear it yourself. There's some juice here. I mean," said Mel, "at a minimum you're going to bounce him off the supreme court with this. At a minimum. You may even make him an aider and abettor on the bond jump. And criminal contempt. For violating the rules of his own court."

Mel was like everyone else who thought Tommy would give up a nut to get Rusty again. The PA laughed out loud instead.

"With Harnason as the only witness? A one-on-one between a convicted murderer and the chief judge of the court of appeals? And me as the prosecutor?" Worse, the way this tale would dovetail with Koll's commercials, everyone would ridicule Tommy as N.J.'s gullible stooge.

Mel had meaty cheeks on which the acne scars caught the shadows.

"There's another witness," Tooley said quietly. "He told somebody about the conversation at the time."

"Who?"

Mel smiled in his lopsided way. He had never been able to raise the right side of his face.

"I'll have to assert the attorney-client privilege at the moment."

There's a dream team, Tommy thought. A scumbag murderer and a scumbag lawyer. Tooley was probably dirty on this whole thing and had helped Harnason light out for the wilderness. But Mel was Mel. He'd make sure Harnason forgot about that part, and Tooley would clean up fine on the stand. He knew how to fool a jury. He'd been doing it for close to forty years.

"We gotta hear this from your guy," Tommy told him. "No front-side deal. We like what he's saying, we can talk. Call it a proffer. Hypothetical. Whatever the frig you wanna call it, so we can't use it against him."

After a second with his client, Tooley waved Brand and Molto into the attorney room. It was no more than eight-by-ten, whitewashed, although black streaks appeared irregularly up the wall. Molto preferred not to think about how the heel marks got there. As for the prisoner, John Harnason did not look particularly well. He'd shaved his mustache and let his hair go gray when he skipped, and he'd picked up weight. He sat in his optic orange jumpsuit, his hands manacled and his legs in irons, both sets of restraints chained to a steel loop embedded in the floor. The pale shadow of the watch they had taken from him when he was captured was still visible amid the strawberry blond thatch on his forearm, and he looked around anxiously, pivoting his head the full 180 every few seconds. He'd been in the county jail only a few hours but was already habitually on the lookout for whatever might be coming from behind. Screw all that stuff with waterboarding and foreign rendition, Tommy thought. They should just dump al-Qaeda in the Kindle County Jail overnight. You'd know where Osama was in the morning.

Tommy decided to question Harnason himself. He started by asking when he'd begun planning to run.

"I just couldn't face going back, once I knew I was going to lose the appeal. Before that, I was really thinking we would win. That's what Mel thought."

Tooley did not quite dare raise his eyes to Tommy's. Winning appeals was a rarity for a defense lawyer. Tooley had been setting up his client for another ten grand for a cert petition to the state supreme court.

"And how did you know you were going back?"

"I thought Mel told you," said Harnason.

"Well, you tell us," said Tommy.

Harnason took some time to study his pudgy folded hands.

"You know, I've known the man forever. Sabich. Professionally. If that's what you call this." Harnason ran his hand between Molto and him. Tommy shrugged: close enough. "And after he gave me bond, I just started to wonder about him. I thought, Maybe he feels bad. About sending me away to start. He should, Lord knows."

Neither Tommy nor Brand knew that part, and Harnason explained his first encounters with Rusty long ago. Tommy could still remember the queer busts Ray Horgan used to stage right before elections, out in the public forest and in the Center City Library men's room and at various bars, herding the arrestees onto school buses in front of the cameras. Times change,

Tommy thought. He still wasn't sure how he felt about gays marrying or raising kids, but God didn't put an entire community on earth unless they were part of His plan. Live and let live, was what he felt now. But back in the day, he knew he would have handled Harnason's case the same way Rusty did.

Confused about whether Sabich actually remembered him, Harnason on impulse had decided to pay him a visit after the oral argument, just a hello and happy birthday and thanks for the bail ruling. Tommy took a second to wonder what part Harnason's visit had played in Sabich's dissent in the case.

"Mel chewed me out for that," Harnason said. "The last thing I wanted was for Sabich to get off the case. But there was something strange when I saw him."

"Meaning?" Tommy asked.

"A connection. Sort of—" Harnason took a great deal of time, and his soft face, with islands of pink color, moved several times around the words he was thinking of. "Peas in a pod," he said.

Tommy got it. Lawyers. Fuck-arounds. And murderers. Tommy couldn't help it. He was starting to like Harnason.

Brand was beside Tommy, making notes on a yellow pad now and then but mostly watching Harnason closely, clearly trying to make up his own mind. Harnason was speaking most of the time with his head down, his sparse gray hair and his bald spot all you saw of his face, as if the memory of all of this weighed about eighty pounds. Tommy realized the problem. Harnason appreciated what Sabich had done for him. He didn't enjoy peeing on the guy.

"Sabich had said something vague, they heard my arguments, something, it sounded a little hopeful, but it wore on me," said Harnason, "the not knowing, waiting for the decision. Sometimes you can't take any more. So I figured, Well, he talked once, maybe he'll tell me at least what's going to happen. So I followed him a couple of times. I waited for him to go out to lunch and I followed him."

The first time, Rusty went to the Grand Atheneum. It was interesting that it was not the Hotel Gresham, where Marco Cantu got paid for doing nothing. Apparently Rusty had been on a bed tour, probably because he'd seen too much of Marco while he was boinking his sweet young thing over there. But Harnason didn't know about Marco or the STD test. So his story was checking out so far.

"Was Sabich with anybody?"

"I assume." Harnason smiled. "Not that I saw her. I watched him head straight to the elevator. He was gone a long while. Longer than I could wait. It started pouring. So I beat it and followed him again the next week. Same deal, except a different hotel. But straight to the elevator and upstairs forever." Harnason had forgotten the name of the hotel, but from the location it had to be the Renaissance. "I was outside over three hours. But there he comes. A little skip in his walk. Soon as I saw that, I knew for sure he'd been getting it on."

"Anybody with him this time?"

"Negative. But the look on his face when he saw me— You know, that pie-eyed, 'oh shit' kind of look. Instead of pissed off. I mean, maybe that's why he talked. He tried to blow me off. But I asked him, just as a mercy, really, Tell me. Am I going back or not? And he did. Get ready for bad news. You're at the end of the road. I just blubbered like a little girl."

"And all this while you're standing there on the street? You and the chief judge, and the chief judge tells you your case is going to be affirmed?" The whole thing was crazy. Lunchtime on Market Street, a hundred people must have seen them, and Rusty is blabbing ex parte? A defense lawyer—Sandy Stern was who Rusty would get if he wasn't dead—would fillet Harnason. But the standard rebuttal made sense. If Harnason was going to make something up, it would have come without bumps and blemishes like that. Often they spit out stories like this, too strange not to be true. "And you told Mel about that?"

Harnason looked at Mel, who beckoned with his hand. Harnason said he'd called him that day.

The four men sat there in silence, while Tommy played it all out. Tooley was right. They were going to scuttle Rusty Sabich's ship with this. The best part was it wouldn't be Tommy's case. The way Harnason told the story, Sabich had not committed a crime. Tommy would just pass the information to the Courts Commission. They in turn would pay Rusty a visit, and he'd probably end up resigning quietly, take his pension, and go into practice rather than endure a public hearing where the stuff about the chick in the hotel was likely to come out.

Tommy looked over at Jim to see if he had anything else. Brand asked Harnason if he'd repeated the whole conversation with the chief judge.

"That was the important part as far as I was

concerned," Harnason said quietly, smiling a trifle at his own expense. "There was a little more back-and-forth."

"Well, let's hear it."

Harnason took his time. It seemed like he was trying to understand the part coming next himself.

"Well, you know I'm carrying on, and he says to me, basically, Come on, cut it out, you killed him, didn't you?"

"Did you?" Brand asked.

Mel interrupted—he didn't want Harnason confessing—but Tommy said there could be no holdbacks. Brand asked again if Harnason killed Ricky.

"Yeah." Harnason thought about that and nodded. "Yeah, I did. And that's what I told Sabich, I did. But, I said, you got away with murder yourself, and he looks at me and he says, The difference is I didn't do it."

Molto cut in. "That's what he told you? You were talking about twenty years ago?"

"Absolutely. He said he didn't do it. And he was looking me in the eye, too."

"You believed him?"

Harnason considered that. "I think I did."

This back-and-forth dizzied Tommy for a second. But he didn't miss the point in the present. Harnason was savvy enough to know what Tommy wanted to hear, yet he wasn't going to say it. The man was one of those weird cons, one with principles. There was not the remotest chance he wasn't speaking the truth.

"Anything else?" asked Brand.

Harnason tried to scratch his ear and realized the manacles wouldn't let him reach that far. "I asked him who he was with in the hotel."

"Did he answer that?"

"Just turned his back on me. That was the end of the conversation."

Brand said, "He didn't deny that part? He just turned away?"

"Right."

"Any more? Anything else between you and the chief judge?"

"That's pretty much it."

"Not pretty much," said Brand. "Everything. You remember anything else?"

Harnason looked up to recall. He made a face.

"Well, one other thing was a little weird. When I told him I killed Ricky, he asked me what it was like to poison somebody."

Tommy could tell from the way Tooley jolted, he hadn't heard that before. Brand was too cool even to quiver, but sitting next to him, Tommy could already sense the uptick in Jimmy's pulse.

"He asked you what it was like to poison somebody?" Brand repeated.

"Right. How did I feel? Day after day? What was it like?"

"And why did he want to know that?" asked Brand.

"I guess he was curious. We were already pretty far off the reservation. That's when I said to him, You know what it's like to kill somebody, and he said he hadn't done it."

Brand went through it with Harnason a few more times, trying to get the conversation in sequence, pressing Harnason to be more precise. Then the two prosecutors departed, telling Tooley they'd evaluate and be back in touch. They were careful to say nothing else to each other until they were a block from the jail. It was a strange neighborhood here, the buildings marked by gang signs and the bangers themselves often lingering near the jail, as if it gave them some kind of peace of mind to be near their homeboys inside. The toughs on the street might enjoy rousting the PA if they recognized him, and Brand and Tommy walked quickly back to the parking structure beside the County Building. As they passed, there was a heavyset woman at a bus stop, listening to a little boom box and practicing her Jazzercise moves, right out there in the open at eleven at night, as if she were at home naked in front of the mirror.

"Okay," said Brand, "you know what I'm thinking."

"I know what you're thinking."

"I'm thinking," said Brand, "that's why the chief judge ponied up the info on the appeal. Because he's got a hot thing on the side and he's already considering maybe cooling the old lady. Because a candidate for the supreme court doesn't want an ugly divorce in the middle of the campaign, especially not if it involves putting his hotdog in the wrong bun. And he wants to do a little field research, figure out if he can actually do the deed."

Tommy wagged his head back and forth. It sounded like *Law & Order*. A little too tidy.

"It'd be a better theory, Jimmy, if we had any evidence that Barbara died from some kind of overdose, instead of heart failure."

"Maybe we just haven't found it yet," said Brand.

Tommy gave Jim a look. That was the biggest mistake a prosecutor could make, hoping for proof that didn't exist. Cops and witnesses could hear that the wrong way and make your dreams come true. Tommy could see their breath in the evening air. He wasn't ready for fall yet and had forgotten a topcoat. But it wasn't just the cold that bothered him. He was still reeling from the part where Harnason said Rusty told him he didn't kill Carolyn. Tommy admittedly had his own stake, but it was a problem for Brand's theory. Either Sabich was a killer or he wasn't. It was both women or none; that was what experience would tell you.

"The part about the first murder still throws me," Tommy said.

"Sabich was lying," answered Brand. "Just because he got dirty with the guy on one thing doesn't mean he'd give himself up as a killer. Besides, there's a way to deal with that and be sure."

He was talking again about the DNA.

"Not yet," Tommy said. It was still too soon. "So remind me again. How was it this weirdo almost got away with it?"

"Which weirdo, Boss? Our cup runneth over."

"Harnason. He poisoned the boyfriend with arsenic, right?"

"Right. But it's not a common poison these days. It's hard to get, and it doesn't show up on a routine tox screen."

Tommy stopped walking. Brand had gone only one more step.

"You think?" Brand asked.

"Sabich was one of the judges on the case, right? He knows all of this. About what is and isn't on a routine tox screen?"

"Definitely part of the record."

Careful, Tommy told himself. Careful. This was the Temple of Doom. He knew it, and he was still blundering right down the path.

"Full mass spectrometer on Barbara's blood?" asked Brand.

"Talk to the toxicologist."

"Full mass," said Brand. "We have to do that. We have to. Strange behavior after the death. A little thing on the side. Questions about poisoning somebody. We're just doing our job, Boss. We have to do that."

It sounded right. But Tommy was still unsettled by all of it, the jail, and Harnason, who was just one of those weird guys, and the troubling idea that he was actually hard on Sabich's trail.

He and Jim talked about how to get the full mass quietly, then parted for the night. Tommy walked down the third floor of the parking structure toward his car. The garage at this hour was a dangerous place, worse than the streets. One of the judges had been mugged here several years ago, but there was still no security. The shadows were deep where the vehicles were parked during the daytime, and Tommy stayed in the center of the floor. But the Halloween atmosphere set off something in him, an idea that floated up and in which he could feel for the first time the thrill as well as the peril.

What if, Tommy suddenly thought. What if Rusty really did it?

II.

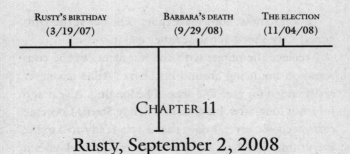

RUSTY'S BIRTHDAY
(3/19/07)

BARBARA'S DEATH
(9/29/08)

THE ELECTION
(11/04/08)

CHAPTER 11

Rusty, September 2, 2008

The inside line in my chambers rings, and when I hear her voice, just the first word, it is nearly enough to bring me to my knees. It has been a good six months since the last time I saw her, when she came by to have lunch with my assistant, and well more than a year since we brought things to a close.

"Oh," she says. "I didn't really expect you. I thought you'd be out campaigning."

"Are you disappointed?" I ask. She laughs as she always does, in full grasp of life's delights.

"It's Anna," she says.

"I know," I say. I'll always know, but there is no point in making this any harder for either of us.

"I need to see you. Today, if possible."

"Something important?"

"To me? Yes."

"Are you okay?"

"I think so."

"Sounds a little mysterious."

"This will be better in person."

"Where do you want to meet?"

"I don't know. Someplace quiet. The bar at the Dulcimer? City View? Whatever they call it."

I replace the phone with the fragments of the conversation bouncing around inside me. Anna has never really ended for me. The ache. The longing. A year ago July, not long after I had visited Sandy Stern, I became convinced for several days that I was ready to forsake everything and beg Anna to take me back. I visited Dana Mann, an old friend, who is the king of high-end divorce in this town. I didn't intend to tell him about Anna, just that I was thinking about bringing my marriage to an end and had some questions about how quietly I could do that, assuming Barbara agreed. But Dana's strength as a lawyer is for the weak joints in the masonry, and with five or so questions he had the outline of the entire story.

'I don't think you came here for political advice,' he said. 'But if you want this to stay off the front pages during the campaign, you'd be better advised to do nothing.'

'I've been unhappy for a long time. Until I got involved with this woman, I didn't realize quite how desperate I am. But now I'm not sure if I can do nothing. I was better off before, just for that reason.'

'"The precise character of despair is that it does not realize it is despair,"' said Dana.

'Who is that?'

'Kierkegaard.' Dana laughed off my look of total disbelief. I've known Dana since law school, and he wasn't quoting philosophers then. 'I represented a professor at the U last year who taught me that. Same kind of situation.'

'What did he do?'

'He left. She was his grad student.'

"How badly did it cost him?'

'It cost him. The U rapped his knuckles pretty hard. He'd gotten her grants. He had to take a year's leave without pay.'

'Is he happy anyway?'

'So far. I think so. They just had a baby.'

'Our age?' I was incredulous. Somehow, Dana's story was enough to prove it was all impossible. I could never try to cheat nature that way. Or brook the thought of what a divorce could do to Barbara, how savagely she might suffer. I told Dana before I left that I did not expect to come back.

Yet there are still nights, while Barbara sleeps, when I am consumed by pining and regret. I never had the heart to delete from my home computer the parade of e-mails Anna sent me back then. Most were one-line messages about where we would meet next. Instead, I've gathered them all into a subfolder I titled Court Affairs, which once every month or so, I open in the still house like a treasure chest. I do not read the actual messages. That would be too painful, and the contents were too brief to mean much. Instead, I simply study her name echoing down the page, the dates, the headings. 'Today,' most were called, or 'Tomorrow.' I linger with memory and wish for a different life.

Now, in the wake of Anna's call, I consider her urgent tone. It could be anything, even a professional problem. But I heard the strain of a personal lament. And what will I do if she has come to tell me that she cannot go on without reuniting? What if she feels as

I have felt so long? The Dulcimer was the last of the places we met. Would she have chosen it if passion was not her purpose? I hover then, above myself, my soul looking down on my hungry heart. How can longing unfulfilled seem to be the only meaningful emotion in life? But it does. And I realize I will not say no to her, just as I could not say no when she turned her face to me on the sofa in my chambers. If she is willing to leap, I will follow her. I will leave behind what I've had. I stare at the pictures arrayed on my desk, of Nat at various ages, of Barbara, always beautiful. It's pointless to try to fathom the full consequences of what I'm about to do. They are so many and so varied that not even a Russian chess master or a computer would be able to play out every step. But I will do this. I will try to have at last the life I want. I will, finally, be brave.

CHAPTER 12

Tommy, October 27, 2008

Pathologists, toxicologists, the whole bunch weren't really wired like everybody else. But what would you expect when it was the dead who rocked their world? Tommy always figured part of the thrill for these guys was realizing the stiff was gone and they were still here. It was an idea, anyway.

The toxicologist who had come in with Brand looked okay. Nenny Strack. She was a little brown-eyed redhead, mid-thirties, attractive enough to be wearing a short skirt. She was over at the U Med School and worked for the county on a contract basis. Brand had gone directly to the police pathologist to get the work done quickly, and he in turn had leaned on American Medical Service, the Ohio outfit that was the reference laboratory for half of U.S. law enforcement. Tommy had feared these maneuvers would send up flares when the blood draws from Barbara's autopsy came back out of the coroner's refrigerator, but nobody noticed.

"So?" Molto asked the two of them.

"Long story or short?" Brand asked.

"Short to start," said Tommy, and Brand opened his hand to Strack. She had a file folder in her lap.

"The sampling of cardiac blood shows a toxic level of an antidepressant compound called phenelzine," she said.

Brand was looking down at his lap, maybe to keep from smiling. It was nothing to smile about, really.

"She didn't die of natural causes?" Tommy asked. He heard the shrill note in his own voice.

"Not to be difficult," said Dr. Strack, "but it's not my job to render an opinion on the cause of death. I can tell you that the symptoms reported— death by arrhythmia, with a possible hypertensive reaction—are classically associated with an overdose of that drug."

Dr. Strack took a minute to describe phenelzine, which was used to treat atypical depression, often in conjunction with other compounds. It worked by inhibiting production of an enzyme called MAO that broke down various mood-altering neurotransmitters. The effect on the brain often improved emotional states, but limiting the enzyme could have fatal side effects in other parts of the body, especially when foods or drugs containing a substance called tyramine were ingested.

"There's a whole list of things you shouldn't eat when you're being treated with phenelzine," Strack said. "Red wines. Aged cheeses. Beer. Yogurt. Pickled meat or fish. Any kind of dry sausage. They all increase the drug's toxicity."

"Where would she have gotten this stuff?"

"It was in her medicine cabinet. If it wasn't,

American Medical would never have identified it." Dr. Strack explained how the mass spectrograph on the blood sample worked. Initially, it produced a virtual forest of color bars. All the spectrographic patterns for the one hundred or so drugs surveyed as part of a routine tox screen were then eliminated, because they had already been covered. The small number of remaining colors could represent thousands of ions. So the lab referred to the inventory of Barbara's medicine cabinet, matching against those knowns. Phenelzine was identified almost at once.

"So this could have been an accidental overdose?" asked Molto.

"Well, if you just look at the blood levels, you'd have to say probably not. The concentration is about four times a normal dose. Assuming that's a true result, then you'd ask if she could have forgotten and taken a pill twice. I suppose. Four times? That would be unusual. Patients who take this stuff are usually warned up and down about how dangerous this drug can be."

"So it wasn't accidental?"

"I'd say no, offhand, but there's a phenomenon called 'postmortem redistribution' that causes certain antidepressants to migrate to the heart after death, giving you inflated concentrations in cardiac blood. That's particularly true of tricyclics. Whether MAO inhibitors act the same way hasn't been defined in the literature. I don't know if phenelzine migrates, and neither does anybody else, not for sure. If we'd realized what we were looking for at the time of the autopsy, we could have done a blood draw from the femoral artery, because there's no postmortem redistribution that far from the heart, but a femoral draw's not standard practice in this county, and obviously, we can't do that now. So no toxicologist will be able to say for sure that the high concentration of phenelzine in her blood means she actually ingested a lethal dose of the drug, as opposed to it being a redistributive effect after her death."

Brand would never say I told you so, but Tommy realized that if he had let Jim treat this as a murder investigation from the jump, they might have those answers. Lost in himself for a second, Molto felt a sigh escape. Sometimes when Tomaso roused them in the middle of the night and Tommy rocked his son back to sleep, he would try to figure out which of a day's decisions was going to come back to bite him. He always went back to bed thinking, You can only do your best. Making mistakes was part of being in charge. You could only hope they turned out to be small.

He looked back at Dr. Strack. "So this redistribution thing means maybe she didn't get an overdose? Maybe she just took a pill and cheated a little and had a pepperoni pizza?"

"That could have happened."

"And what about suicide? Is this one of those drugs that has a tendency to make depressives even more suicidal?"

"That's what the literature says."

"No note," said Brand, trying to discount the possibility Barbara killed herself. "Cops didn't find a note."

Tommy raised a hand. He didn't want a debate right now.

"So maybe it's suicide. Maybe it's murder. Maybe it's an accident. That's all you can say?" Molto asked her.

"Assuming phenelzine caused the death. You'll need the pathologist to say that definitively."

This Dr. Strack looked okay, but by now Tommy had a feel for her. She'd gotten bumped around on cross-examination often enough that she'd rather not go to court at all. He thought science was about investigating the unknown, but experts like Strack seemed to prefer that the unknown remain that way. He really didn't get it.

In the wooden-armed chair next to Strack, Brand was easy to read. His chin was lowered and he was making a face like he was biting back on heartburn. Tommy could see that Dr. Strack had spun Jim, gone soft when she sat down to talk to the PA himself. Jim wouldn't have trotted her in here unless she'd been a lot more positive with him in his office. In the unlikely event this case went to trial, they'd have to insert a steel bar in her spine or find another expert.

"What about time?" Brand asked. "If you let a day pass after the death, what impact would that have on identifying the phenelzine overdose in the autopsy?"

Dr. Strack touched her face while she considered her words. She was wearing a wedding ring with a diamond chip the size of a bread crumb, the kind of ring that said 'I married my high school sweetheart when we had next to nothing but big love.' It made Tommy feel a little better about her.

"Probably quite a bit," she said. "The quicker the autopsy was done, the easier it would be to rule out postmortem redistribution. And of course, analysis of the stomach contents gets more difficult, because the gastric juices continue to erode what's there. It'd be harder to find a pill, or to identify the phenelzine or even what she ate, including products that contain tyramine. But again, a pathologist could give you a better answer."

Brand cut in. "Okay, but if somebody fed her a lot of cheese and then gave her a couple of pills, and then let the body cool for a day—that would make the phenelzine poisoning harder to establish reliably."

"Theoretically," said Dr. Strack, in character.

Tommy ran the whole thing back in his mind. "And we missed this initially because—?"

"Because MAO inhibitors aren't covered on a routine tox screen."

"And which of the pills in her medicine cabinet, at least the ones with a known toxicity—which of them aren't covered on a routine tox screen?" Brand asked.

Dr. Strack checked her file. "This is the only one. The sedatives, the antianxiety drugs, the antidepressants. They're all regularly screened. With her medical history, the phenelzine wouldn't stand out. If you didn't have toxic levels of anything else, you wouldn't expect it with that, either."

Molto asked some more questions, but the little doctor was gone in a minute.

"Fuckin little squirrel," Brand said as soon as he had closed the door behind her.

"Better to know now," Molto told him. "Did you check the transcript in *Harnason*?"

Brand nodded. Tooley had talked about phenelzine, among dozens of compounds, when he'd crossed Dr.

Strack at trial. Mel had been attempting to show that not even an experienced toxicologist knew which drugs were included on the regular screening, let alone poor Harnason. Tooley's cross-examination, including his mention of phenelzine, had been summarized in the Statement of Facts in Harnason's brief to the court of appeals. So Rusty knew. They'd have no trouble proving that.

Tommy had felt his adrenaline rising throughout the conversation, and now he sat back in the PA's big chair with the aim of calming himself and thinking more carefully.

"This is great stuff, Jimmy," he finally said, "but no matter who our toxicologist is, we'll never prove the cause of death."

Brand argued the case. A girlfriend. Visiting Prima Dana. Asking Harnason what it felt like to poison somebody. Letting the body cool a day so the phenelzine and everything else would rot in her gut.

"You can't make him for murder, Jim, without proving beyond a reasonable doubt that she was killed intentionally." This was the problem he'd predicted to Brand from the outset. If you assume somebody as smart and experienced as Rusty Sabich did a thing like this, then you had to realize he'd make himself bulletproof. The reality that Sabich might have killed Barbara and would beat it anyway took Tommy down like a stone.

Brand wasn't ready to quit.

"I want to put a subpoena and a ninety-day letter on the pharmacy. See if Rusty connects to the phenelzine at all."

Tommy waved a hand, giving Jimmy carte blanche.

"We're this close." Brand's thumb and index finger were nearly touching.

The acting PA just shook his head and smiled at him sadly.

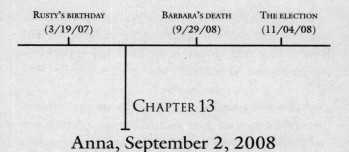

RUSTY'S BIRTHDAY
(3/19/07)

BARBARA'S DEATH
(9/29/08)

THE ELECTION
(11/04/08)

CHAPTER 13

Anna, September 2, 2008

All my life, I've seemed to have a talent for catastrophic blunders, errors that have set me back years at a time. I started at least two careers—in advertising and then, after my MBA, in marketing—that never suited me, and I've always fallen for the wrong guys. When I was twenty-two, I married a man who just really wasn't very interesting—we stayed together all of seventy-two days—and I've made worse mistakes than that, especially a couple of wild affairs with married guys where the tragic outcome was as clear as if somebody had written me the message that appeared in Daniel's cave.

Like everybody else, I'm inclined to blame my failings on my parents, a father who skipped at the age of six and hasn't been much more than a Christmas card since and a mom who, while loving, often seemed to expect me to raise her. I was eight years old and setting an alarm so I could get her up to go to work. Somehow I grew up inclined to think that anything she might not approve of was worth a second look.

But what I'm about to do is staggering even measured against my own history. After hanging up with
Rusty, I look at the phone in my hand and wonder how
dangerous and crazy I really am.

One of my law school profs liked to say that most of
the world's troubles start with real estate, which is certainly true here. Last June, I decided to buy a condo. I
loved the idea of finally having something of my own,
but from the instant I signed the contract, the globe
seemed to descend into economic panic. Within a week,
my roommate, who had agreed to take over the lease on
my current apartment, got laid off and decided to move
in instead with his boyfriend. At work there were suddenly whispers about falling revenues and axing associ-
ates and even partners. I could see myself at Christmas,
with no job but suddenly getting all kinds of experience
in court, because I would be defending myself in foreclosure, eviction, and bankruptcy proceedings.

Right after the Fourth of July, I sent out an e-mail
blast and posted my apartment for sublease everywhere I could think of, including, with the help of
a young partner's wife, on the internal website of
the state supreme court. My place is less than two
blocks from the court and would be perfect for an
incoming law clerk. I got back this e-mail the same
afternoon:

FROM: NatchReally1@clearcast.net
TO: AnnaC402@gmail.com
Sent: Wednesday, 7/9/08 12:09 pm
Subject: Re: My Apartment

Hey Anna—

I saw your post. Very cool to know you
are doing well. I can't even imagine
owning a condo, frankly. A galaxy far far
away.

Anyway, how much of a pain would it be if
I took a quick peek at your place next
weekend? I have been living with three of
my friends in a house in Kehwahnee, but
the show is over in September, since two
of them are getting married. I still have
not decided what I am doing when my
clerkship ends—I know, I'm about eight
months late—but I am still considering an
offer from a firm, and if I do that, I can
probably afford my own apartment. I
haven't really looked, but seeing a
familiar name made me think I should. If I
love your place, that could help me decide
on a job. I know that is totally backward,
but I've gotten nowhere trying to make
decisions like a normal person. And even
if I don't take it, I can rave about it to
the new clerks who are still looking.

Let me know if you'll have time.

                                    Nat Sabich

   I had some second thoughts about this, but desperation has its own logic and I couldn't figure out a good

excuse to tell him no. He came through the door at eleven the next Sunday morning in jeans and a T-shirt, a good three to four inches taller than his dad, lean and shockingly beautiful, with the scads of black hair and Aegean blue eyes and a cute little flavor saver under his lip. He cruised through, telling me how great the place was, even though I knew he'd be saying that if there were bats hanging from the ceiling, and finally had a cup of coffee with me out on my little balcony, where I was able to show him how to lean the right way to get a great view of the Center City and the river.

'Sweet,' he declared, and took off his shoes and wiggled his bare toes on the rail.

I have always liked Nat, who I got to know when he visited his dad. He's so gorgeous, you sometimes feel half-afraid to look at him for fear your jaw will drop, but he's too awkward and self-conscious ever to be called cool. He's guileless in an appealing way. You meet so few people who actually seem sincere instead of acting the part.

It was a great day, the air full and the tugs booming out on the river, and we chilled, having a nice talk, not an easy thing to do with Nat. He speaks like he's on tape delay, as if what he means to say has to pool somewhere inside him for brief inspection before he lets it go. It can be challenging, even for somebody like me who is accustomed to getting most of the airtime in any conversation.

We both had gone to law school after other stuff and swapped our stories.

'I always thought about becoming a shrink,' he said, 'because I've seen so many of them, but, like since I was little, I've viewed everybody as sort of locked inside their own story of the world, and I was never sure I'd ever really know how someone else felt. Which is kind of why I started grad school in philosophy. But law at least is sort of the story people can agree on.'

I laughed at the description. When I told him how proud his dad seemed of everything he accomplished in law school, he stared as if I'd come off the alien pod.

'Whoever knows what my dad is thinking?' he finally asked. 'He's never said a word to me about any of it— law school, law review, the clerkship—even though I've gone every step of the way in his footsteps. It's like he's afraid if he says something, I might notice.'

I looked into my coffee. 'How is your dad?' I asked.

'Pretty focused on the election. Koll has been pounding away about this guy Harnason who skipped town after my dad gave him bail, and my dad's just beside himself.' He repeated some of the campaign advice his father was getting from Ray Horgan, then stopped himself to ask if I knew Ray. I gave him a long look because I was sure at first he was kidding.

'I work for Ray,' I finally said.

'I'm an idiot.' Nat socked himself in the head. 'I'm surprised you haven't been talking to my dad yourself. He usually stays in touch with his ex-clerks, and he always talked about you like you were the coolest thing since Pop-Tarts.'

'Did he? Really?' Even then I felt my heart surge with the compliment. 'I'm just working so hard I'm basically a hermit.'

That led to a long discussion of being a young associate in a law firm. I told Nat the truth. It's either a very crass deal—you're there to pay off your student loans or put together a down payment—or an act of blind hope, because you think being a lawyer is really interesting, if only you could get to the interesting parts. Which I haven't done yet.

'The big worry,' I said, 'is that while you're figuring that out, you'll get hooked on the money.'

'Like by buying a condo?' he asked with a cute little smile I'd seen a couple times already.

'Right. Or renting a really nice apartment by yourself.'

We laughed at each other, but that was pretty much that. As we headed inside, I asked what else he might do.

'I worked as a sub at Nearing High odd days while I was in law school, and I could go back to it. What I'd really love is to teach law,' he said, 'but you have to publish to get hired anywhere decent. I did a note, but I need more. I was supposed to spend this year writing this off-the-grid law review article about neuroscience and the law, but I broke up with my girlfriend the semester before I graduated, and I'm still so bummed about it I can't concentrate on stuff like that when I come home from work. Maybe I can do it next year while I sub.'

'Sorry about the breakup,' I said.

'Oh, I can totally see how it was for the best, I really can, but the whole process kills me. One day you're in the middle of somebody's life, and the next you're handing back the key, and even her dog won't pee on your foot.'

I laughed pretty hard, even though I was caught up in the melancholy of his observation.

'Been there, done that.' I heaved a sigh. 'Doing,

actually.' I didn't quite have the stuff to look him in the eye and moved toward the door.

'I don't usually talk this much,' he said when he got there. 'I must feel like I know you better than I actually do.' I had no idea how to answer a remark so odd, and we stood in silence another second.

When he'd left, my heart was rocking and rolling in my chest. Nat had inevitably dragged his father into my apartment with him. In the time since Rusty and I came to the end, I tried not to think about him much, but when I did, it was with terrible pity for myself—for being so crazy and vulnerable and stupid, for wanting something I so clearly was never really going to have. Dennis, the therapist I see, calls love the only legally accepted form of psychosis. But I guess that's why love is wonderful, as well as dangerous, because it can make you so different. Some of the books I've read say that love in the end is about change. I'm still not sure.

Nat wrote back within two hours to say what I thought was already established, namely, that he would not take the place.

After listening to you, I realized I must be brain-dead to think I could work in a law firm. I will email all the incoming clerks at the Supreme Court who may still be looking and say how awesome your place is and such a steal that whoever rents it should just about get indicted.

I need to apologize a little, since I know I came off as some kind of psycho

weirdo half mental patient, babbling
about my shrinks, but it was really cool
to talk to you, and I was thinking maybe
we could even have coffee in a couple of
weeks, so I could bounce any new job
developments off you.

The other thing is that when I went over
the whole conversation in my head, I
thought it was kind of a hoot that we
each were asking the other one what
my dad really thinks. That is SO my
dad.

Talk soon.

                                    Nat

I read this e-mail over several times, especially the
part about having coffee. Is this guy a little into you? I
wondered. I worked for half an hour on a response that
would hit the right notes.

Nat—

I completely understand. And thanks so
much for your help inside the Court. I'll
keep my fingers crossed.

And no, you did not come off as some kind
of "psycho weirdo." On the DL, I just
started doing therapy about a year ago,
after a really really bad breakup, and I

truly feel sometimes like I was wasting
my life up until then. I'm still a little
embarrassed about it—both because I
need it, and I like it so much. But
that's the only time I'm taking for myself
these days. I hate making coffee dates
because I always end up breaking them.
But please send an email now and
then and let me know how things are
going.

   As soon as I hit send, I was drilled by a truth I seldom care to recognize: I'm lonely. I have made so many changes in the last decade, it's been hard to hold tight to friends, especially since most are married now with kids. I'm happy for them, but they've come to terms and aren't interested in putting a lot of stuff under the microscope. You can't sit there pouring your heart out to somebody who isn't going to reciprocate. I have single girlfriends, but nine times out of ten we end up talking about men, which doesn't work right now. In the year-plus I've spent getting over Rusty, I've isolated myself behind a wall of work. Most weekend evenings, it's been TV and Lean Cuisine.

   So that was that with Nat until a guy named Micah Corfling contacted me about ten days later. He was going to clerk for Justice Tompkins and had gotten an e-mail from Nat raving about my place and ended up renting it from a few pics I sent. When I wrote Nat to say I owed him, he sent this message back:

FROM: NatchReally1@clearcast.net
TO: AnnaC402@gmail.com
Sent: Friday, 7/25/08 4:20 pm

Cool!!! So if you owe me, how about lunch
or something tomorrow? It doesn't have to
be anyplace nice, because except for my
suits I really don't own any clothes
without holes.

FROM: AnnaC402@gmail.com
TO: NatchReally1@clearcast.net
Sent: Friday, 7/25/08 4:34 pm

Sorry, Nat. It's like I told you. Work
work work. I'll be in the office all day.
Rain check?

FROM: NatchReally1@clearcast.net
TO: AnnaC402@gmail.com
Sent: Friday, 7/25/08 4:40 pm

I have to do a couple things over at the
Court. I'll meet you near your building.

FROM: AnnaC402@gmail.com
TO: NatchReally1@clearcast.net
Sent: Friday, 7/25/08 5:06 pm

I have a draft due on a brief. I'll be
frantic and lousy company. Another time?

FROM: NatchReally1@clearcast.net
TO: AnnaC402@gmail.com
Sent: Friday, 7/25/08 5:18 pm

Come on! It's Saturday! And you sublet
your place thanks to me. (Sorta kinda.)

By then, I was feeling like a pretty big ingrate, so
I agreed to meet for something superquick at Wally's,
realizing I should take the opportunity to cool him
out. As I was leaving to meet him on Saturday, I asked
Meetra Billings, the pool secretary who was typing
the brief for me, to call in twenty minutes and pretend
the partner wanted to see me.

Wally's is a takeout deli with a few tables. During the
week, it's all bang and bustle in there. The patrons and
employees shout at top volume, and the rusted window
unit in the transom bangs as though there's a jack-
hammer inside, while Wally, an immigrant from somewhere east of Paris, yells, 'Closs door, closs door!' to
the people in the queue to get in. But on Saturday you
can actually hear the voices of the countermen gruffly
demanding, 'Next!' out of habit. Nat was already there.
There were two coffees on the table, one with cream
and two yellow packets resting on the lid, which is how
I take mine, a nice touch. His cell phone was also on
the Formica, and I asked if he was expecting a call.

'From you,' he answered. 'I figured you'd cancel at
the last minute.'

Nailed, I made a face. 'I don't have your number.'

'Clever of me,' he said. 'So, I mean can I ask—what's
that about?'

I took a seat at the table, trying to come up with a reasonable excuse.

'I just feel like it would be weird if we started hanging out. With my having worked for your dad and all?' It sounded ridiculously lame, even to me.

'I'm thinking there's something else,' he said. 'Jealous boyfriend, maybe, who wants to lock you in a closet?'

'No.' I actually laughed. 'No relationship. I'm taking kind of a time-out from men.'

'Because of that breakup? What happened?'

I missed a breath before I finally shook my head. 'I can't talk about that, Nat. It's too raw. And too embarrassing. But I need to be surer of who I am, and what I want, before I get involved again. I haven't gone this long without a date since seventh grade. But I do feel more virtuous. Except when the batteries drain on my Rabbit.'

I guess I was trying to forestall more questions about my broken heart, but I still couldn't believe that had sailed out of my mouth. Yet I'd already found we shared a pretty outrageous sense of humor, and Nat roared. His laughter seems to come from some hidden part of him.

'That sounds like a therapist's idea,' he said. 'The time-out?'

It was, of course, and we ended up in this pretty deep conversation about therapy. He'd done tons but had quit because he was afraid he was turning into one of those people who lived just so they could talk to their shrink about it. I hadn't ever really discussed seeing Dennis, and I was actually disappointed when

Meetra called. I also felt like a terrible goof because we hadn't even ordered lunch yet. I apologized like mad but still got up to leave.

'And when's moving day?' he asked.

'Sunday, August 3. I hired professionals for the first time in my life. I've hit up my friends so often I didn't have the courage to ask again. All I have to handle is the stuff I'm afraid the movers will break. It'll be a pain, but less.'

'I could help. Strong like ox,' he said in an accent. 'And I work really cheap.'

'I couldn't ask.'

'Why not?'

My mouth moved a little while I groped for the words, and he finally cut in.

'Hey, okay, so let's get it out there. "Just friends." You're on a time-out and I'm too young for you anyway. Your thing is older guys, right?'

'Yeah, father runs. It's pretty predictable I've been into older guys.'

'So okay,' he said. 'I don't feel like I've been voted off the island. Just name the day.'

I couldn't pretend I didn't need the help, especially somebody strong enough to handle my new TV, which I was afraid to hand over to the movers. One thing I'd realized in my two meetings with Nat was that I was starved for male company. I've always had close friends who are guys, sharing certain common ground— sports, gross jokes, dark movies. As I've gotten into my thirties, when almost everyone else is paired up, opposite-sex friendships have seemed tougher to maintain. Wives get jealous, and the borders are better patrolled.

It was hard not to welcome Nat on these terms. Especially since his roommate had an SUV he could borrow.

And so, on Saturday, August 2, Nat was at my door again. It was a horrible day to move, close to a hundred. The sun was so intense that you felt as if you were being hunted, and the air was as close as a glove. I'd been up all night packing. Once I got started, I just kept going, and when we carted everything down to the dock, it turned out I'd boxed too much for a single load.

By noon, we had the first run up in the new place. It's on the sixth floor of an old building along the river, with lots of period detail—dentil moldings at the ceiling and beautiful oak and gumwood, including the window frames, which have never been painted. I had bought it out of a foreclosure and hadn't realized that the bank had turned off the electric. There was no AC and we were both dripping. He had completely sweated through his sleeveless tee, and I looked even worse with my seventy-dollar haircut licked to my face.

We decided Nat would return for the remaining boxes while I went out to buy us lunch. It took me longer than I expected to navigate my new neighborhood, and when I got back he was already upstairs, standing out on my back porch. He was naked to the waist while he wrung out his T-shirt and looked awfully goddamn good doing it, lean but ripped with muscles, and I felt the effect in my whole lower body. I turned away just before he could catch me gawking.

'Ready to eat?' I showed him the bag when he came back inside.

'Not an air lunch like last time?'

I poked him in reprisal. There was no table, and

while I tried to figure out where we could sit, he pointed to one of the last boxes he'd brought in. It was stacked with various framed photos I've stored for years, all too precious to toss and too embarrassing to display.

'I couldn't help noticing,' he said, and pulled out a blowup of an old snapshot taken when I was no more than five, of my mother, my father, and me. It was Christmas, and the snow was piled high in front of our bungalow. Wearing a felt hat and overcoat, my dad looked fairly dashing as he held me. I was dressed in a little kilted outfit complete with tam, and my mom smiled beside us. And even so, there was a certain visible discontent among the three of us, as if we all knew the cheerful pose was just that.

'That's one of the only pictures I have of the three of us,' I told Nat. 'My aunt basically hid it. After my dad split, my mom went through every family photograph and cut him out. Literally. With a scissors. Which never made complete sense to me. He was playing around, but from the little hints I've picked up over the years, I think she may have been doing the same thing. I've never really been sure. It's weird.'

'I know what that's like,' he said. 'I think my dad had an affair when I was a kid. It had something to do with his trial, but you know, neither he or my mom was ever willing to talk about any of that, so I still don't know exactly what went down.'

Neither of us seemed to know what more to say. Nat looked back to the box and pulled out another picture, which turned out to be my bridal photo.

'Wow!' he said. The truth, which I wasn't about to

admit, was that I looked so great that day, I have never been willing to throw away the picture.

'That photograph,' I said, 'is literally the only good thing I got out of my marriage. You think, someone like me, no kids and not much money, back to zero will be no biggie. But it is. Marrying anybody is such an act of hope. And when it craters—it takes a long time to regather yourself.'

The next picture he pulled out stopped him cold.

'Get outta here,' he said. 'Is that Storm?'

In the picture, the famous rocker is in a studded leather jacket, with his arms around me and my best friend, Dede Wirklich, both of us fourteen at the time. I'd won a drawing from a local radio station, two concert tickets and the chance to meet Storm backstage, and naturally I chose Dede to go with. When I'd discovered her in second grade, I'd felt as though I had found a missing piece of myself. Her father had taken off, too, and we seemed to understand each other in a way that did not require speaking.

She was kind of a cutup, and got in a lot of trouble as the years went on. Very often we were in these pranks together—we once stole into the principal's office and hid a noisy cricket, which took him days to find—but the teachers were more reluctant to blame me because I tended to be the best student in the class. We started drinking together at eleven when we smuggled shots of gin and vodka from her mother's stash, replacing them with water every day until both bottles tasted exactly like the tap.

By high school, Dede had gone totally Goth, right down to the black fingernails and white eye shadow, and it was pretty clear she was always going to be in trouble. Her boyfriends were all loners and misfits, guys with biker tatts and cigarettes drooping from the corners of their mouths, who were never good to her. Senior year, she got pregnant by one of these characters and had Jessie.

Nat asked if I still saw her, and I told him we came to an ugly end.

'I actually moved in with her after my marriage broke up, but it was a bad scene. I got stuck with all the housework, including making Jessie's school lunch. Dede resented me, because even though my life was no bowl of cherries, it was still going to end up better than hers, and for my part, I got fed up lending her money I was never going to see again, and worn out by Jessie, who was an incurably needy, whiny little girl. It all led to this unreal moment which I'd rather not talk about.'

Looking down again to the photograph, Nat changed the subject by asking what Storm was like.

'Truth?' I answered. 'I was so incredibly nervous that if it weren't for the picture, I wouldn't even remember it happened.'

'Storm's a good show,' Nat said. 'I saw him three times. That's all I did when I was in college—go to concerts and get stoned. Unlike now, when I go to work and get stoned.'

He was in a bantering mode, but I stared.

'Nat, you're not really going to the supreme court with reefer in your pocket?'

He was sheepish and muttered something about it being a hard year.

'Nat, if you ever got caught, you'd be prosecuted. Your dad's way too prominent for you to catch a break. They'll suspend your law license, and nobody will let you near a high school, either.'

My lecture embarrassed him, naturally, and we ended up in silence, as we sat on the floor to eat. Down low, with our backs against the plaster, it turned out to be the coolest place in the apartment. Nat was still sunk into himself. He'd told me when we had lunch that his former girlfriends all described him as dark and remote. I hadn't seen what they were talking about until now.

'Hey,' I said. 'We all do stupid stuff. Just ask me. I'm the world leader.'

He looked straight at me for a second. 'So tell me about that breakup,' he said.

'Oh, Nat. I don't think I could.'

His look lingered only a second, then he shrugged and went back to his sandwich with no more to say. I saw how completely you could lose connection with him, especially when he feels bad about himself.

'No questions,' I said. I had closed my eyes to figure out exactly how I could do this, but even so, I sensed him turning my way. 'Right after I stopped working for your dad, I began seeing a much older guy. Very, very successful, very prominent, somebody I'd known and looked up to for a long time. It was pretty wild. But also purely nuts. He was married and was never going to leave his wife.'

'Ray, right? Ray Horgan. That's why you gave me that goofy look when I mentioned his name at your apartment.'

I opened my eyes and stared hard. I can do that when I have to.

'Okay,' he said. 'No questions. What do you say in court? "Withdrawn." Sorry. Sorry, sorry.'

I told him the rest of the story in a few words: a great guy who had always told me it was crazy and finally broke it off. You could hear the faint burble of the TV in the apartment next door after I finished.

'So I bet you're going to go looking through these boxes for my scarlet letter,' I finally said.

'Hey,' he answered. 'Like you said, we all do dumb things.' He took some time then to tell me the long story of the affair he'd had with the mother of one of his closest friends during his senior year in high school. In the circumstances, it was a kind thing for him to share.

'You're a good guy, Nat.'

'I try,' he answered. Our heads had ended up lolled against the wall as he had quietly described the way he'd blundered into that woman's bed, and our faces by now were not very far apart. His eyes were full on mine, and there wasn't any missing the meaning of his look. I could feel everything, my loneliness and longing, and could have done something incredibly, unbelievably stupid at that moment, the same way I always have. But you have to learn something from living. I ruffled his wet hair instead and got back to my feet.

He was visibly chafed, and a few minutes later said he had to jet, although he made a halfhearted offer to drive me home that I declined. When I got back eventually, I e-mailed profuse thanks and promised to invite him to my first dinner party.

He didn't answer for two days, and I knew I was
in trouble the way something popped in my chest the
instant I saw his name in my in-box and read the subject line.

FROM: NatchReally1@clearcast.net
TO: AnnaC402@gmail.com
Sent: Monday, 8/4/08 5:45 pm
Subject: My Heart

Anna—

Sorry I've been AFK but I've been
thinking. A lot. Always dangerous.

I completely understand where you're at.
But I am starting to have feelings here,
which you probably realize. And I need to
watch out for myself. I can go along
really well and then something seems to
knock me off balance, and I start to
sink. And I can go pretty low. But we do
seem to have connected here, really
really connected, and I'm just wondering
if I can maybe talk you into reconsider-
ing. I mean, older guys haven't worked
out, so maybe a younger guy is what
you've needed all along. And I mean,
what's the difference really, we're both
pretty much at the same point on the Man-
dala? Anyway, I think you get what I'm
trying to say because you seem to get me.

It was so sweet, I got a little teary reading, but there was no point. And even so, I actually hesitated to write back until late the next evening.

FROM: AnnaC402@gmail.com
TO: NatchReally1@clearcast.net
Sent: Tuesday, 8/5/08 10:38 pm
Subject: Re: My Heart

I think I get you too, Nat. And I think
you get me. And it probably would be nice
to spend some time and see what happens,
if what went on in my life hadn't gone
down, but it did. This would be a really
bad idea for a lot of the reasons I've
already explained and one or two I don't
want to go into, even with you. I actually talked to Dennis about it this
afternoon after I got your last message.
I am not the kind who would give my
shrink a veto over my life. And frankly,
he's not that kind of shrink. But we can
both see how this is so not a good idea
at all. And I just can't keep getting
into relationships that are really just
deck chairs on the Titanic. I don't know
what else to say except I am so so so
sorry.

I was not sure he would even bother to respond, but he did late the next day, although just to say good-bye.

Anna—

I think I have to stop this cold. Like
not hang out or communicate or anything.
There's something about the way we've
clicked that seems to me to lead only one
place. And I'm actually walking around
moping and heartbroken. And then going
home to reread your emails. Which, to say
the least, is a dangerous cycle.

You have not said a word yet that really
makes me understand it. Age? Working for
my father? Your own breakup? We could
blow through those issues in no time. But
the one word I do understand is no. You
have your reasons. But I realize I'm just
going to make myself crazier by keeping
this up.

I think you are completely great.

    I didn't answer. There was no more to say. But he
sent another message that night.

Anna—

I have just reread your last message and
I finally got it. I mean I'm stoned, so I
know this won't make any sense in the
morning. But right now, I need to ask you
a question about my father that is so far

out and so Soap Opera you're going to be
sure I am totally wigged-out.

I've been thinking about the fact you
thought it would be strange to hang with
me because of my dad. And the way you got
silent about him maybe having an affair.
And that stuff about your mom stepping
out. So here's the question.

Are you my sister? Or my half-sister? I
know this only makes sense because I am
completely toasted. But still. So if you
don't mind answering one more email, that
would be great.

FROM: AnnaC402@gmail.com
TO: NatchReally1@clearcast.net
Sent: Thursday, 8/7/08 12:38 am
Subject: Re: My Heart

Oh Nat. I'm laughing and also crying a
little. I would even like to answer yes
bc it would finally put your mind at ease.
And I think it's a pretty brilliant sideways guess. But the answer to your question is no. No.

You are right. This shouldn't continue.
I think you are beyond great. You are
perfect. But let me tell you what I tell
myself. If we could connect like this,

then it can happen somewhere else. Too
often I've wanted the dynamos, the Some-
bodys I'd like to be, instead of a guy
who will make me feel good enough to be
that Somebody myself. So you've given me
a wonderful gift, and I will never be
able to thank you enough.

                    Your loving friend, Anna

CHAPTER 14

Tommy, October 29, 2008

I know you got something," Tommy Molto told Brand when he met him outside the Central Branch Courthouse. Jim was on trial, dressed in a nifty glen plaid, a better suit than any prosecutor really could afford. Molto sometimes told Brand that he must have secretly been born Italian. The case he was trying was a triple murder in which one of the victims was the niece of the movie star Wanda Pike. Gorgeous and mournful, Wanda was in court along with her posse every day. Knowing that would occur, Brand had decided to keep the case rather than letting somebody more junior from the Homicide Division handle it. Jimmy had never been confused about the fact he liked seeing himself on TV. The trial was on lunch recess, and Brand had come outside to meet the boss. He was going to be cold. It was a brisk day with a sabering wind and scuffy, ugly clouds.

"How's that?" asked Brand.

"How's what?"

"How you know I got something?"

"Because you wouldn't haul my ass out across the

street, or take time for lunch meetings in the middle of trial, unless you did."

"Maybe I think you need exercise. Maybe I like to see you busting down the street like a pigeon." Brand actually thrust out his belly and walked a few steps in imitation. Jimmy was way too cheerful. This was going to be good. Tommy gestured him inside, but they were waiting for Rory Gissling, who came along in a minute bundled in a heavy coat and bright scarf. She had a manila envelope under her arm.

They reentered the courthouse and went upstairs to find someplace to talk. Judge Wallach's courtroom was open, and they huddled together on the corner of one of the plush benches, Rory between the two prosecutors.

"Show him," Brand told her.

"So we subpoenaed Barbara's pharmacy for all the receipts, refills, all the records in the month before she died," Rory said. She took a quarter inch of paper out of her envelope.

"Show him the receipt for the phenelzine," said Brand.

Rory thumbed through the pages, then handed a copy of a charge slip to the PA. Paying for the purchase of the phenelzine, it was dated September 25, last month, and plainly showed Rusty Sabich's signature. Brand was grinning like a kid at Christmas.

"You mind?" Tommy said, and took the rest of the papers from Rory. He flipped through the stack. "Rusty picks up all the prescriptions," he said. "That's what it looks like."

"Eighty, ninety percent," Rory answered.

"So?" Tommy asked.

"He picked up the *phenelzine*," Brand said.

"So?" Tommy asked again.

"Show him the stuff for the day before she died," said Brand.

Rory pulled several sheets from the ones in Tommy's hand. Rusty had signed the charge slip for the purchase on a renewal of Barbara's sleeping pills on September 28.

"I thought we were looking at a phenelzine overdose," Molto said.

"Look at the dupe of the register tape," said Brand. "The back page there. It's the other stuff he bought you need to see."

Tommy took a second to decode the abbreviations, but the tape appeared to reflect a bottle of Rioja, pickled herring, Genoa salami, and some aged cheddar, as well as a quart of plain yogurt. The PA needed a little more time before it clicked.

"That stuff all reacts with the drug, right?" he asked. "It's got whoesy whatsit in it, all of it?"

"Tyramine. All of it." Brand bobbed his head. "He literally bought the entire no-no food group. Could turn a normal dose of phenelzine lethal. And a quadruple dose into a sure thing. I'd say the judge was preparing a different kind of Last Supper."

Tommy looked at the slip again. The time of purchase was 5:32 p.m.

"They're having cocktails," he said.

"What?" Brand slid over. "Where do you get that from?"

"He went to the store at dinnertime. He bought a bottle of wine and some appetizers. They're having cocktails, Jim."

"Yogurt?" asked Brand.

"For the dip," Tommy said.

"Dip?" asked Brand.

"Yeah, if you're being healthy, you use yogurt instead of sour cream. And speaking of dips," said Tommy to Brand, "with your dad's history, you oughta know stuff like that. You ever hear of cholesterol?" Tommy spelled it for him, and Brand waved him off. Rory added some sage words about her dad, who'd just had a bypass. Brand ignored them and stuck to the case.

"We got him, don't we?" he asked. "It's right there, isn't it?"

Tommy could feel the weight as his chief deputy and the detective watched him. Brand had been sold for a long time, but that wasn't the point. The call on this case was going to be Tommy's entirely. The risks were all on his tab, and he was the one who had to be satisfied. And when he added it up, he still wasn't. Rusty's grocery list looked pretty damning, but they were still trying to make a lot out of stuff a defense lawyer would call coincidental.

"We're closer," Tommy said quietly.

"Boss!" Brand protested. He began to go through all the evidence, and Tommy had to warn him to keep his voice down. The last thing they needed was a reporter walking into the courtroom and overhearing all this.

"Jimmy, you two have tumbled to some amazing stuff. But it's all circumstantial. You don't need me to tell you the way somebody like Sandy Stern will pick this case apart. 'Who has not gone to the store to pick up groceries, a prescription, ladies and gentlemen?'"

Tommy did a better imitation than he expected of Stern's mild accent. "You've seen Stern sell snake oil. And the biggest problem is never going away. Our own expert will get up on the witness stand and admit on cross-examination she has no way to exclude sixteen other causes of death besides murder. It's light. The case is too light. We need something else."

"Where the fuck do I get something else?" Brand demanded. That was the point, of course. "How about the DNA?" he asked after a second.

Tommy had been thinking a lot about that lately, when he was up with Tomaso in the middle of the night, and he'd realized the DNA was not the answer. But he didn't want to get into that in front of Rory and simply said what he'd been saying for weeks: "Not yet."

Brand looked at his watch. He had to get back to court. He stood up and backpedaled as he headed out.

"I'm not giving up, Boss."

Tommy laughed out loud. "I wasn't worried about that."

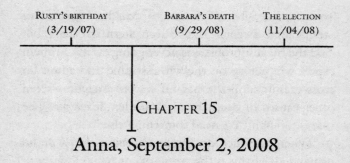

RUSTY'S BIRTHDAY
(3/19/07)

BARBARA'S DEATH
(9/29/08)

THE ELECTION
(11/04/08)

CHAPTER 15

Anna, September 2, 2008

After my marriage ended and I moved in with Dede, the same question obsessed me. I would lie in bed in the mornings and wonder for an hour, Was I ever in love with Paul? I thought I had been, but now I had my doubts. Yet how could I, or anybody, ever make such a fundamental mistake? How would I ever know the real deal?

Man by man, relationship by relationship, those issues have perplexed me and left me feeling each time that something was missing. I have been fascinated by some men and in other cases—none more than Rusty—virtually obsessed, gripped by a fierce hunger. But could anything so fraught be grown-up lasting love? Could it have led to that? I have awaited the Day I Know I Am Really in Love the way some people anticipate the Rapture.

I was gloomy the first weeks of August and was reluctant initially to believe it had anything to do with Nat. In time, I faced the fact that I missed him or, more honestly, the chance I'd seen in him, an opportunity to have something different, which felt both new and right. This realization hit me harder than I might have anticipated. It brought up a lot of stuff about Rusty, which I didn't expect, especially anger. Late at night, there were moments when I couldn't understand my own reasoning. What taboo was I violating, whose feelings was I trying to spare? If the father didn't want me, why couldn't I be with the son? Wouldn't that mean things had worked out for everyone? When I reconsidered all of this in the morning, it felt as though all the ground I'd gained in the last fifteen months had washed away beneath my feet.

But I thought I was getting over it. It felt as though I had put this disappointment on the shelf beside many prior ones. And then this morning, I was in the supreme court hearing room to assist Miles Kritzler, who was arguing a futile mandamus petition for an important client. He got oral argument by rule, but the justices were not happy he was taking their time, and they sat up there, all seven of them, with these looks that said, Just kill me. His red light was going to come on any second, and just then somebody scampered up onto the bench to deliver a brief to Justice Guinari, and when I looked over, Nat was already facing me, so thin and haunted and impossibly beautiful, those sea blue eyes full of an amazing beseeching look. I was afraid the poor man was going to start weeping and that if he did, I would cry, too.

When I got back to the office, there was a message from him in my voice mail:

"When I leave work around six, I'm going straight to your apartment. I'm going to ring the bell, and if you're not home, then I'm going to sit on the front step until you come home. So if you've gotten a grip again and still don't want this, then you better go sleep at one of your girlfriends', because I'm going to be sitting there all night. You're going to have to tell me no to my face this time. And unless I understand you a lot less than I think I do, I don't think that will happen."

I knew then that for all the hesitation and reluctance, all the telling myself, 'No, this is insane,' all the warnings of incredible peril, that despite all of that, my heart had a plan and I was going to have to follow it. As the songs say, I would give everything for love. This is a greater, deeper truth about me than any of the admonitions and lessons I have been trying so hard to take in. And I have always known it.

In the last few months I lived with Dede, I was dating a cop named Lance Corley, who had been a student in an econ class I took at night to finish college. He was a sweet man, big and handsome, and when he came by he spent a lot of time with Jessie. He had a daughter of his own he didn't see much. I could tell that Dede had a crush on him almost from the start and that it was only getting worse as time went on. She was completely transparent. She'd ask me several times a day when I thought he might show up. In the end, Lance decided he was going to try to reconcile with his ex, mostly because seeing Jessie had made him realize how desperately he missed his own daughter.

When I explained all that to Dede, she was sure it was a lie, that I was not letting Lance come to the apartment because I didn't want him to fall for her. It got so bad that I finally asked Lance to call and explain, but that was a mistake. The utter humiliation of Lance knowing she harbored this flaky hangup with him infuriated her.

I woke up about six the last morning I lived there, and Dede was standing over my bed with a pair of kitchen scissors between her hands, extended in my direction. I could see she was completely smashed, shaking as if there were a motor in her chest, her face blotchy and her nose running as she stood there crying, toying with the idea of killing me. I jumped up and screamed at her. I slapped her and cursed her and took away the scissors while she crumpled in a heap in the corner of my room so that someone happening by might even have mistaken her for a pile of dirty laundry.

Now I listened to Nat's voice message six or seven times and then picked up the phone to call Rusty. I said I had to talk to him, even though I couldn't imagine what I would say. But crazy things happen in life all the time when people fall in love. I have a friend who got divorced and married her ex's brother. I heard about a lawyer in Manhattan, one of the senior partners in his firm, who at the age of fifty fell in love with a boy working in the mailroom and changed genders so the young man would have him, which actually worked out for a while. Love is supreme. It has its own quantum mechanics, its own rules. When love is involved, you can give only so much ground to propriety or even wisdom. If you love somebody badly enough, then realize that is who you are and try to have him.

That day at Dede's, while I packed, she went on crying and saying, 'I wasn't going to do it, I wasn't going to do it. I was pretending or something, but I wasn't going to do it.'

She said that a thousand times, and finally I was completely fed up. I zipped my last bag and slung it across my back. 'And that's what's wrong with you,' I answered.

Those were the last words I ever spoke to her.

CHAPTER 16

Rusty, September 2, 2008

Anna is already there when I arrive at the Dulcimer. She is nervous, fingering a highball glass full of bubbles, but beautiful. Her life in private practice has given her a sleeker look, a better coif and nicer clothes. I sit beside her on a tufted banquette in the bar.

"Cut your hair?"

"Less to take care of. More time to work." She laughs. "Confessions of a high-priced slave."

"It's very becoming."

My compliment leaves her briefly silent until she mutters, "Thanks."

"What are you drinking?" I ask.

"Fizzy water. I have something I need to finish at work."

My heart sags: She is going back to work. I say nothing. She moves her purse so it's in the open space between us.

"Rusty, I don't know how to say this. So I think I just have to come out with it. I'll try to explain. But the point is that I've started seeing Nat. I mean, I haven't, but I'm going to. I'm going to see him today. And

I don't know where it will go, but it's pretty serious already. It's very serious already."

"My Nat?" I actually blurt. For an instant I can feel nothing inside myself. And then what surges forth is rage. It storms out of my heart. "This is insane."

Looking at me, Anna's green eyes are welling.

"Rusty, I can't describe how hard I tried to avoid this."

"Oh, for Chrissake. What are you going to tell me about now? Fate? Destiny? You're a grown-up human being. You make choices."

"Rusty, I think I'm in love with him. And that he's in love with me."

"Oh, my God!"

She is crying by now as she holds the cool glass to her cheek.

"Look, Anna, I know you want to get back at me. I know I disappointed you. I know all is fair in love and war. I've heard every crappy expression. But this is impossible. And you have to stop."

"Oh, Rusty," she says, sobbing. "Rusty, I did everything the right way. I was so good. I wish you understood. I tried so hard to make this not happen."

I want to think. But the dimension of this is unimaginable. And I can feel my arms and hands shaking in fury.

"Does he know? About us?"

"Of course not. And he never will. Never. Rusty, I know this is crazy and difficult, but you know, I have to try, I really have to try. I don't know if I can handle this or you can handle this, but I have to try, I know I have to try."

I rear back in the chair. I am continuing to experience difficulty catching my breath.

"Do you know how often I've longed for you and

stopped?" I ask her. "*Made* myself stop? And now, what? I'm supposed to watch you parade around my house? This is sick. How could you do this to me? To him? For God's sake."

"Rusty, you don't want me."

"Don't tell me what I want." I remain angry enough to slap her. "I know how this adds up, Anna. Don't preach sincerity to me. You're tightening the screws in the shittiest way imaginable. So what's my choice? Get rid of Barbara now, right now. Is that it? Get rid of her or you'll literally destroy my home?"

"Rusty, no. It's not about you. It's about him. That's the whole point of what I'm trying to tell you. It's about him. Rusty, Rusty—" Then she stops. "Rusty, I never felt like this about"—she stumbles—"about anyone. I mean, maybe I should be a case study in some psychiatric journal. Because I'm not sure if this would have happened without it. Without us. But it's different, Rusty. It really is. Rusty, please let us be."

"Go fuck yourself. You're crazy, Anna. You don't know what you want. Or who you want. Psychiatric journal is right."

I throw money on the table and hear her muffled outcry behind me as I bang out of the hotel, striding in outrage down the street. I seethe in the oldest, most elemental way. I go several blocks. Then stop suddenly.

Because one thing is clear. No matter how angry I am, I must do something. I must. There is no clear path. I will think and think and nothing will be right. But I must do something. And the mystery of that seems as large a thought as God.

What will I do?

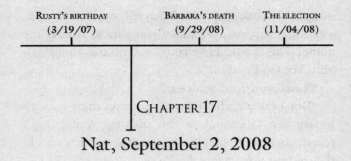
CHAPTER 17

Nat, September 2, 2008

How I see it is that we're all pretty much cruising along, like a bunch of people on the highway. Everybody's in his space and headed to his own destination, listening to the music they like, or different radio stations, or talking on the phone, and otherwise just trying to stay out of one another's way. And then every once in a while, you're ready to stop and welcome a passenger. And who knows why?

I'm still not sure when I got so into Anna. I thought she was cool as soon as I met her after she went to work for my dad, but I was with Kat then, and once we broke up, my mom got completely in the way by asking once or twice if Anna really was too old for me, which pretty much iced the whole thing. And then one day this summer, I was at work and saw Anna's name on this post about her apartment, and I thought, Yeah, go check this out. And sitting out on her balcony, I couldn't quite believe how totally freaking cool she was, brainy and beautiful and funny and tuned in. Not that it was mutual at first. I hung myself way out there. And she said no. Sweet and kind and all of that. But, no.

So now it's about a month later, I'm at work and I'm still a mess over Anna. I'm less of a mess, because I just couldn't stay as much of a mess as I was the first two weeks. When it goes bad, I have this thing where I just can't hit reset. I go down and stay down. I rewind. And replay. And cry. Totally unboy. I'd get up from my desk at the court and go into a stall in the john and cry about four times a day. Then I began to ration myself. One cry in the morning and one in the afternoon. Then once at work. And once at home. Somehow, it was worse than my breakups with Paloma and Kat. And I knew I'd built this whole thing up inside my head to be the Perfect Relationship only because it didn't happen. It's a platonic ideal. I am completely in love, even though I know it's more with the idea of love than anything else. But maybe that *is* worse. Real or not. Hope is an amazing thing. Hope is maybe the most essential thing in life. You go on with hope. And without it, you are flattened.

That's still the mood today when I walk into the supreme court hearing room to deliver a brief that the law clerk on the case, Max Handley, forgot to take up to the courtroom. And there she is. For a month I have imagined a couple times a day that I am seeing her on the street, but that's only a blink, before I realize, No, too bad, no. But this time, even from the rear, even though she's changed her hair, even though I catch no sight of her face, I know it's Anna. She's sitting at the appellant's table, writing notes as fast as she can while one of the older partners from her firm is giving an oral argument that frankly has left every justice cold. This guy, the partner, is going to get flushed, maybe even before he leaves the courtroom. And when I see her, I

stop so fast that half the figures on the bench, eager for
distraction, stare at me. I am so fucking up!

So I crawl up to Justice Guinari and hand off the brief.
I am trying to figure out how I'm going to be able to
walk out now without repeating the same stupid performance. Eyes forward, shoulders straight. But of course,
I'm too broken up and hungry for her not to peek. And
then, when I turn, I see, thank God—I see, thank God,
there is a God, something I have always believed—her
eyes are fixed on me. The partner is still droning. But
Anna has stopped writing. She is not doing anything but
watching me. She is not blinking. She cannot turn away.
And I know everything—it's in that look. She's been as
burned as me. And she is giving up. Whatever it was that
made her say no, she can't say it anymore. She's giving
up. She's giving in. To love. It's the movies! It's the movies from the forties! It's kismet. Fate. Dharma.

I stumble out of the courtroom and go back to my
desk to use my cell phone. I leave a voice mail and tell
her after work I am going straight to her apartment and
that I'm going to sit there all night if I have to, until she
tells me what she wants face-to-face.

And that is what I do.

When she gets home, I am sitting on the single step
outside the old greystone. I really would have sat there
the rest of the night, but in fact I've been there only
fifteen minutes. And she sits next to me, she puts her
arm on mine, she puts her head on my shoulder, and
we cry, we both cry, and then we go inside. And it's just
this simple. Take it from a former grad student in philosophy. This is what every human longs to say: It's the
happiest moment of my life.

CHAPTER 18

Tommy, October 31, 2008

McGrath Hall had been the police headquarters since 1921. The redstone heap might have passed for a medieval fortress, with stone arches over the massive planked oaken doors and notched battlements on the roof.

Brand, who was still on trial, had sent a message across the street from the courtroom asking if Tommy could meet him outside the County Building at twelve thirty, and the Mercedes had slid to the curb and taken off again so quickly that it looked like a getaway. Brand zagged through the lunch-hour traffic as if he were hopped up. Tommy got a call from the FBI, and he and Brand had gone past the security gate and parked behind the Hall before he was free again to talk to his chief deputy.

"So what are we doing here?" he asked.

"I don't know," said Brand. "Not for sure. But the day Rusty called in Barbara's death, the Nearing coppers took all the bottles in Barbara's medicine cabinet and swept them into a plastic bag, instead of doing an inventory there. So I had Rory ship every vial over here on Wednesday to see if Dickerman could turn anything from them."

"Okay. Good thinking," Tommy said.

"Rory's idea, actually."

"Still good thinking. And what did Dickerman come up with?"

"You ask all the tough questions. Mo left a message that he had some interesting results. He wouldn't say it was 'interesting' if it was a zero, but I couldn't connect because I've been in court all day. Still, I didn't want him to put it on paper. Around here that would leak in about thirty seconds."

"Also good thinking," said Molto.

Brand explained that they had come to the Hall because Mo had had knee replacement surgery last week and wasn't getting out. Jim figured it was better if Tommy was here to ask whatever questions he wanted to. That wasn't bad thinking either.

They found one of Mo's assistants holding open a fire exit in the basement. She was wearing a crepe witch's hat and a black fright wig.

"Trick or treat," she said.

"Indeed, indeed," said Brand. "I wake up every day thinking that very thing."

Together, the three moved down the dark halls into the realm that Mo Dickerman ruled. Mo Dickerman, aka Fingerprint God, was at age seventy-two the oldest employee of the Kindle County Unified Police Force and without doubt its most esteemed. He was the foremost fingerprint expert in the Midwest, author of the leading texts on several techniques, and a frequent lecturer at police academies around the world. Now that forensic science was hot stuff on TV, you could barely hit the clicker without seeing Mo poking his heavy black-framed glasses back up on his nose on one true crime show or another. In a department that like most urban police forces was always mired in controversy and, not infrequently, scandal, Mo was probably the lone emblem of unimpeached respectability.

He was also frequently a pain in the ass. The nickname of Fingerprint God had not been applied entirely in admiration. Mo regarded his opinions as akin to scripture and would not brook even so much as an interruption. If you made the mistake of cutting in, he would simply wait you out and then go back to the beginning. He was often a difficult witness, refusing to acknowledge seemingly obvious conclusions. And he was wildly unpopular with the brass on the force because of the way he leveraged his public standing with threats to quit unless his lab in the McGrath Hall basement was equipped with the latest innovations, money that sometimes might have been better spent on bulletproof vests or overtime.

Mo hobbled forth on sticks to greet them.

"Ready for the twist contest?" Brand asked.

An angular New Yorker whose thick hair was only beginning to show some gray, Mo bent both elbows and rocked a few inches each way. Brand offered an earnest thank-you for Mo's quick turnaround on their request, and Dickerman clicked his way into the lab, a dim warren of crowded cubicles and pillared boxes and several clear arenas for Mo's high-priced machines.

He stopped in front of his current favorite piece of equipment, a vacuum metal deposition unit. The top commanders had held out against it for several years because they feared explaining to the county board or the public why they needed a machine that literally developed latent fingerprints in gold.

When Tommy was a line prosecutor, fingerprints were nothing more than patterned sweat revealed by ninhydrin or other powders. If the print had dried up, you were generally cooked. But starting in the 1980s, experts like Mo had figured out how to expose the amino acids sweat left behind. These days if you developed a latent print, there was sometimes the possibility of extracting DNA from it as well.

Mo's VMD machine was a horizontal steel chamber about three feet by two. Everything inside it cost a fortune—molybdenum evaporation dishes; combination rotary and diffusion pumps that produced a vacuum in less than two minutes; a polycold fast-cycle cryochiller to speed the process by removing moisture; and a computer that controlled it all.

After an object for examination was placed inside the VMD, a few milligrams of gold were poured into the evaporation dishes. The pumps then created the vacuum, and a high current was passed through the dishes, evaporating the gold. It was absorbed by the fingerprint residue. Zinc was evaporated next, which for chemical reasons adhered only to the valleys between the ridges and whorls of the fingerprint. The high-definition photographs of the resulting golden fingerprints always wowed juries.

Mo, being Mo, insisted on explaining the whole process again, even though both Tommy and Brand had received the tutorial several times. What Mo had placed in the VMD yesterday was the plastic vial from the phenelzine scrip Rusty had picked up. He had four clear prints, one toward the top, three on the bottom. The brown plastic pill bottle, now dusted in gold, was in a sealed plastic envelope on a table beside the machine.

"Whose?" asked Tommy.

Mo lifted a finger. He was going to answer in his own time.

"We compared them with the decedent's. With predictable problems. I've been talking to the guys in the pathologist's office for twenty years, but they still print the dead like they're mopping the floor. They don't roll the fingers, they drag them." Dickerman displayed the ten-cards the techs had prepared as part of the autopsy. "There's nothing resembling an identifiable print on either the middle finger right hand or the right little finger." Within each of the squares Mo pointed to, there was no more than an inky smudge. Dickerman shook his long face in mild despair.

"At any rate, I can tell you categorically that the four prints on the vial you wanted me to examine were not made by eight of ten of Mrs. Sabich's fingers."

"So they could be Barbara's?" asked Brand.

"Not this one," said Mo, pointing to the largest print in the photographs at the bottom, "because that's clearly a thumb. But at that point, I couldn't tell whether either of the remaining prints came from Barbara's middle finger, or even conceivably the pinky."

"And now?" asked Tommy. Brand took a step back behind Dickerman and rotated his eyes skyward. He had no use for Mo's fan dance.

"So the next step was to see if we could identify whose prints these were. I assumed you guys had a guess, but Jim and Rory didn't want to name names. So we ran the prints through AFIS," said Mo, referring to the automated computer identification system that contained images of all the prints from the county for the past several decades. "And we matched impressions on two different print cards." Mo laid down the ten-cards that had been culled out of his own archives. One contained the prints Rusty Sabich had given when he'd begun county employment thirty-five years ago. The others had been taken when Sabich was indicted. "All four prints on that vial are his." Mo touched the cards as if each was a fetish. "I always liked Rusty," he added, as though he were speaking of the dead.

Jim had a small, settled smile. He'd always known. Tommy would have to give him that whenever they talked about the case in the years to come.

"And how do we know Sabich didn't just take the bottle out of the packaging to help his wife?" Tommy asked.

Brand answered that. He had the papers Rory was carrying the other day in Wallach's courtroom.

"The scrip was for ten pills. But when the cops inventoried the bottle, there were only six in there." He picked up the plastic envelope containing the bottle that was next to Mo's precious machine and showed Tom the six orange tablets on the bottom of the vial. "So somebody took four of them out," he said, "and what I'm hearing is that the only person whose prints are here are the judge's."

"Could she have touched the bottle without leaving prints?" Molto asked.

Dickerman smiled. "You know the answer to that, Tom. Sure. But VMD is the most discriminating method we have of identifying any prints that were ever here. And if I'm following what Jim just said, Mrs. Sabich would have to have touched the bottle four times without leaving prints. We've got other bottles from the medicine cabinet that we've started processing. So far we have her prints on eight of the nine we've tested. On the ninth the impressions are smudged."

"Could be hers?"

"Could be. There are points of comparison, but it looks like somebody else touched it, too, which may make DNA hard, distinguishing the alleles and getting enough to test."

"That would be a tough argument for a defense lawyer," said Brand, "saying she got anywhere near the phenelzine, if her prints show up on every other bottle and not this one."

Brand and Molto headed back to the same rear exit through which they'd come in. Tommy still didn't want to encounter the dozens of cops he knew who would be coursing around upstairs and would ask why the PA was down here off Mt. Olympus. At the door, Brand took a moment to thank Dickerman again and discuss the next round of examinations, while Tommy went out into the slashing wind to think over what he'd just heard. The steely sky that would prevail in Kindle County for the next six months, as if the Tri-Cities had fallen under a cast-iron pot lid, was closing around them.

He did it again. The words, the idea, stretched out through Tommy like a piano key with the damper pedal compressed. Rusty did it again. The son of a bitch did it again. No "once burned, twice wise" for him. Standing here, Tommy felt so many things that he was having difficulty sorting them out. He was enraged, of course. Rage had always come easily to Tommy, although less so as the years passed. Yet it remained a familiar, even essential, place to him, like a firefighter who was most himself as he entered a burning house. But he also lingered with the thought of vindication. He had waited. And Rusty had shown his true colors. When it was all proved in court, what would people say to Tommy, the people who for decades had looked down on him as some law enforcement rogue who'd gotten off easy the way bad cops so often do?

But the strangest part, amid all these predictable responses, was that as Tommy stamped his feet in the cold, he suddenly understood. If he could not have been with Dominga, what would he have done? Would he have murdered? There was nothing people wanted more in life than love. The wind came up and went through Tommy with the icy directness of a pitchfork. But he understood: Rusty must have loved that girl.

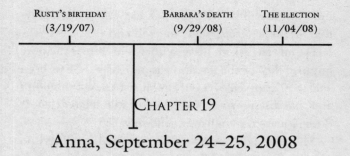

RUSTY'S BIRTHDAY   BARBARA'S DEATH   THE ELECTION
(3/19/07)   (9/29/08)   (11/04/08)

CHAPTER 19

Anna, September 24–25, 2008

I love Nat. I Am Really in Love. Finally. Fully. So often before I thought I was on the brink, but now every morning I get up amazed by the unearthly wonder of it. We have been Velcroed to each other since the day he appeared in the supreme court, and we have spent every night together, except for a single trip I had to make to Houston. The New Depression, which has pushed the law biz off a cliff and in sober moments makes me worry about my job, has been a blessing for now, because I can depart work most nights at five. We cook. We love. And we talk for hours and hours. Everything Nat says pleases me. Or touches me. Or makes me laugh. We do not fall asleep until two or three a.m., and in the morning we can barely drag ourselves out of bed to get to work. Before he leaves, I look at him sternly and say, 'We can't keep doing this, we have to sleep tonight.' 'Right,' he says. I ache all day until I can return to him, when the whole blissful sleepless cycle starts again.

Nat moved in the first week, and there really was no discussion about where he will live at the end of the month. He will be with me. It's like everybody always told me: When it happens, you will know.

Dennis has asked, because that is his job, if the pure impossibility of the situation is part of it, if I've been able to give myself over only because I know I shouldn't and that disaster somehow lurks. I can't answer that. It doesn't matter. I am happy. And so is Nat.

My plan, as far as Rusty is concerned, has been no plan at all, except to allow him a warning. As he sat on that banquette in the Dulcimer, he grew lethally angry. I was unsurprised, not because I was hoping for that result, as he claimed, but because I always sensed there is a molten core behind that taciturn exterior. But in time, we will both get accustomed to the bizarre way this has turned out. We have one essential thing in common. We love Nat.

In the meanwhile, I have resolved to stay away from Rusty, which is not as easy as I might have hoped. Barbara calls Nat every day. He generally picks up and then tells her as little as possible. The conversations are brief and often practical—specials he might be interested in at a local grocery chain, news of family and the campaign, questions about his job search or his expected living arrangements at the end of the month. The last of those inquiries has meant that sooner or later he had to tell her about me. He warned me there was no choice because his mother seemed to be nurturing a hope he might move back home. Even so, I begged him to hold off.

'Why?'

'God, Nat. Doesn't that seem like a lot to tell her in one breath, we're dating and then that we're living together? It will sound crazy. Can't you just tell her you're going to share space with a friend?'

'You don't know my mother. "Who's the friend? What's he do? Where was he raised? Where did he go to school? What kind of music does he listen to? Does he have a girlfriend?" I mean, I wouldn't get away with that for a minute.'

So we agreed that he would tell her. I insisted on standing by so I could hear his end of the conversation, but I buried my head in one of my sofa pillows when he described himself as 'a love zombie.'

'She's thrilled,' he said when he hung up. 'Completely thrilled. She wants us to come for dinner.'

'God, Nat. Please no.'

I could tell from the way his brows narrowed that he was beginning to find my vehemence about his parents odd.

'It's not like you don't know them.'

'It would be weird, Nat. Now. With us so new. Don't you think we should socialize with some normal people first? I'm not ready for that.'

'I think we should get it over with. She'll ask me every day. You watch.'

She did. He begged off, using standard excuses, his work or mine. But day by day I am beginning to understand more about the weird symbiosis between Nat and his mom. Barbara hovers over his life like some demanding ghost without an earthly presence of her own. And he feels a need to satisfy her. She wants to see us together, but finds it trying to leave her home. So we must come to her.

'You could just say no to her,' I told him last week.

He smiled. 'You try it,' he answered, and indeed the next night, he lifted his cell in my direction. 'She wants to talk to you.'

Fuck, I mouthed. It was a quick conversation. Barbara gushed about how exciting this was, how pleased Rusty and she were that Nat and I seemed to mean so much to each other. Wouldn't we come and let the two of them share our happiness for just an evening? Like a lot of brilliant people with problems, Barbara is great at putting you in the corner. The easiest thing was to agree to a week from Sunday.

I held my head in my hands afterward.

'I don't understand this,' he said. 'You're one of the cool kids. Little Miss Social Skills. My mom has been telling me for a year and a half to ask you out. You're the first girlfriend I've had she approves of. She thought Kat was weird and that Paloma was a bad influence.'

'But how's your dad with this, Nat? Don't you think this will be strange for him?'

'My mom says he's completely cool and totally thrilled.'

'Have you actually talked to him?'

'He'll be fine. Take it from me. He'll be fine.'

But I cannot imagine that Barbara's enthusiasm about Nat and me, or the prospect of seeing us together, can do anything but set Rusty spinning. And as I fear, today at work, when I slip in to check my personal e-mail, my heart jumps to see two in my in-box from Rusty's account. When I open the messages, they weirdly turn out to be read receipts on e-mails I sent in May 2007, sixteen months ago.

It takes me a while to piece things together. During

my time with Rusty, I was the one who booked the hotel rooms, since he couldn't use his credit card. I would forward the online confirmation to him, receipt requested so I knew he'd gotten word and did not have to bother to reply. I often dispatched these messages in a series—the initial confirmation, a reminder that morning, and then a last e-mail giving the room number once I had checked in. Because I was getting the acknowledgments, I realized that often the only message he was opening was the last one, which he looked at on his handheld on the way over, without having to chance reviewing the other e-mails with somebody around.

The two read receipts that arrived today are from those e-mails that went unopened last year. At first, I take this as a kind of perverse stalking, an effort to remind me where the two of us were not all that long ago. But with another hour's thought I realize he may not even know the messages are coming to me. When you open an e-mail on which the sender's requested a receipt, a little pop-up appears, warning you that the notification will be sent. The pop-up also contains a little box to check that reads, 'Don't show this message again for this sender.' He probably chose that option long ago. By the end of the day, I decide there may be a positive spin here: Rusty is finally doing what he should have done sixteen months before and deleting all my messages. It's a sign he's moving on, that he is happy to let Nat and me be.

The next morning by ten, there are three more. Far worse, I realize that deleting the messages wouldn't trigger the receipts. The point is to show the e-mail was read. It is a disturbing, even sickening, image, of Rusty in his chambers, reliving these details. Feeling there is little choice but to have it out with him, I pick up the phone and dial his inside line. It rings through and is answered instead by his assistant, Pat.

"Anna!" she cries out when I say hello. "How *are* you? You don't come around enough."

After a minute of pleasantries, I tell her I have a question for the judge about one of our cases and ask to speak to him.

"Oh, he's been on the bench all morning, honey. He went up more than an hour ago. They have arguments back to back. I won't see him until half past twelve."

I have the self-possession to say to Pat that I will call Wilton, my coclerk, for the information I need, but when I put the phone down, I am too panicked and disoriented even to take my hand off the receiver. I tell myself I have gotten this wrong, that there must be another explanation. On my screen, I examine the read receipts again, but all three were sent from Rusty's account less than half an hour ago, when Pat says he was on the bench and nowhere near his PC.

And then it comes, the dreadful realization. The catastrophe that was always in the offing has happened now: It's someone else. Somebody is systematically reviewing the record of my meetings with Rusty. The hotels. The dates. For a breathless second, I fear the very worst and wonder if it's Nat. But he was himself last night, gentle and utterly adoring, and he is too guileless to keep this kind of discovery to himself. Given his nature, he would just be gone.

But my relief lasts no more than a second. Then I

know the answer with an absolute certainty that turns my heart to stone. There's one person with the savvy to invade Rusty's e-mail account, and the time to be making this painstaking inspection.

She knows.

Barbara knows.

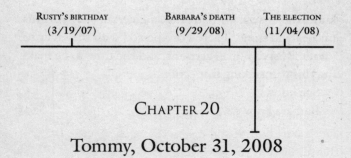

CHAPTER 20

Tommy, October 31, 2008

After their meeting with Dickerman in McGrath Hall, Tommy and Brand did not speak a word until they were in the Mercedes.

"We need his computer at home," Brand said then. "It's the only real chance we have to find the girl. I want to issue a search warrant today. And we need to interview the son pronto to see what he has to say about what was cooking between Mom and Dad."

"That's page one, Jimmy. He'll lose the election."

"So what? Just doing our jobs," said Brand.

"No, damn it," said Tommy. He stopped to gather himself. Brand had done great work here; he'd been right when Tommy was wrong. There was no reason to get angry at him for charging ahead. "I know you think this is a really bad, pathological, fucked-up guy, a serial killer who's sitting on his throne at the right hand of God, and I get it, but think. Think. You blow Rusty off the court and you're just feeding the theory of defense."

"The vengeful prosecutor crap? I told you how to deal with that."

He was referring to the DNA, testing the sperm fraction from the first trial.

"That's what we do next," said Tommy.

"I thought you don't want to get a court order."

"We don't need a court order," Tommy said.

Brand looked at the boss narrowly, then pushed the auto's start button and began easing the Mercedes into the traffic. On the street near police headquarters, six kids were being herded back to grade school after lunch by a couple of moms. Everybody was in costume. Two of the little boys were in suits and ties, wearing masks of Barack Obama.

Tommy had first thought of what he was about to explain to Brand a decade ago. In those days, he had moved back in with his mom to take care of her in the last years of her life. Her noises—the coughing from the emphysema, most often—would wake him on the cot he slept on in the dining room. Once she was settled, Tommy would think about everything that had gone wrong in his life, probably as a way to convince himself he'd be able to withstand this loss, too. He'd ponder the thousand slights and undeserved injuries he'd borne, and so he would think now and then about the Sabich trial. He knew that DNA testing would answer to everybody's satisfaction whether Rusty had been tooled or literally gotten away with murder. And he'd tempt himself with the thought of how it could be done. But in the daylight, he would warn himself off. Curiosity killed the cat. Adam, Eve, apples. Some stuff you were not meant to find out. But now he could know. Finally. He rolled out the plan again in his head one last time, then detailed it for Brand.

This state, like most states, had a law mandating the assembly of a DNA database. Genetic materials collected in any case where evidence was offered of a sexual offense were supposed to be added and profiled. Rusty had been accused only of murder, not rape, but the state's theory allowed that Carolyn might have been violated as part of the crime. The state police, without a court order or any other form of permission, could withdraw the blood standards and sperm fraction from Rusty's first trial from the police pathologist's massive refrigerator and test them tomorrow. Of course, in the real world the cops had too much trouble keeping up with the evidence being gathered today to bother going back to cases dismissed two decades ago. But the fact that the law was there and applied without time limit meant that Rusty had no legitimate expectation of privacy in the old samples. He could hoot and holler at trial if the results implicated him, but he'd get nowhere. To give them some cover, Brand could tell the evidence techs to forward all specimens from before 1988 to the state police, explaining that they wanted the oldest first to prevent further degradation.

Brand loved it. "We can do it now," he said. "Tomorrow. We can have results in a few days." He thought it through. "That's great," he said. "And if he shows up dirty, we can go for the full download, right? Search warrant for his computer? Interviews? Right? We can roll by the end of the week. We have to, right? Nobody will ever be able to say boo? That's great," said Brand. "That's *great*!" He threw his heavy arm around Molto and gave him a shake as he drove.

"You got it wrong, Jimmy," Tommy said quietly. "That'll be the bad news."

The chief deputy drew back. This was what Tommy had been up thinking about for several nights in the past week.

"Jimmy, we got bad news and worse news here. If," said Tommy, "if we don't match, we're screwed. Screwed. Case closed. Right?"

Brand looked at Molto without overt expression but seemed to know he was playing from behind.

"It's too thin, Jimmy. Not with the history. I just want you to understand before we go running down to the lab that it's make or break."

"Christ," said Brand. He went through all the evidence again, until Tommy interrupted.

"Jimmy, you were right all along. He's a wrong guy. But if we basically prove he didn't commit the first murder, we can't indict now. We'd just be a bunch of vengeful shits trying to recast a truth we don't like. Everything inside the courtroom and outside would be about my grand obsession. This case is paper thin. And if we have to throw in the fact that Rusty was falsely accused once before by the same office, combined with him being the chief judge of the court of appeals with everybody but God testifying as a character witness, we will never get a conviction. So we need to know what the DNA shows now. Because if it exonerates him on the first case, we're stone-cold end of the road."

Brand stared into the traffic, thickening as they passed closer to Center City. Today, Kindle County was halfway to Mardi Gras. The office workers were out for lunch in all kinds of getups. Five guys were walking along with burgers in their hands, each one dressed like a different member of the Village People.

"How's he get good DNA results into evidence?" Brand asked. "Even if the DNA cleans him up twenty years ago, so what? Okay, so we're sore losers. The prosecutors' motives are irrelevant."

"But the defendant's motives aren't. You want to put on a circumstantial case and argue the guy would risk cooling his wife? You think he's not entitled to show that he was once prosecuted for a murder he didn't commit? Doesn't that make it far less likely that he would take that kind of chance now?"

"Fuck, I don't know with this creep. Maybe it makes it more likely. Here's a guy who understands the system completely. Maybe he's clever enough to think that we can never go on him because of the first case. Maybe he thinks that DNA gives him a free shot this time."

"And he'd be right," Tommy said to Brand. At a light, they stared at each other until Brand finally broke it off to look at his watch. He swore because he was late. Molto thought of offering to park the Mercedes for him, but Jim was too upset now for jokes.

"We're gonna make him on the first case," said Brand. "I got fifty that says we make him."

"That'd be the worse news," Tommy answered. "The best thing that could happen to us would be having an excuse to walk away from this case. The really bad news will be if it turns out to be Rusty's spunk twenty years ago. Because if he was the doer, this isn't a go case. It's a gotta-go case. We can't let him sit on the supreme court knowing he's a two-time killer. We can't."

"That's what I'm telling you. But everybody will understand. They'll know we're not chasing ghosts."

"But we'll *lose*. That's the really, really bad news. We have a case we gotta bring that we're going to lose. Because the DNA never comes in for the prosecution. Never. It's a one-way street. He was acquitted. We can't use the old evidence against him now. It wouldn't make sense without retrying the old case, and no judge will allow that. And besides, there were so many questions about the specimen by the end of that trial, nine judges out of ten wouldn't admit it now anyway. If the DNA is good for Rusty, it sails in. And if it makes him a killer, it's out. So we've got the same thin case, even with the DNA, where we're going to have our fingers crossed that we don't get directed out on corpus delicti, because we don't have enough proof to show murder."

"No." Brand shook his head hard on his thick neck. "No way. You're laying a mattress, Boss. We all do it."

"No, Jimmy. You said it before. This guy is smart. Way smart. The bad news is that if he killed her, he thought it all through. And he figured out how to do it and walk again. And he will."

They were at the courthouse. Brand finally looked at Tommy and said, "That would be really bad news."

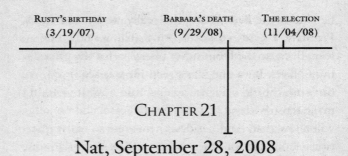

RUSTY'S BIRTHDAY
(3/19/07)

BARBARA'S DEATH
(9/29/08)

THE ELECTION
(11/04/08)

CHAPTER 21

Nat, September 28, 2008

You're not really in a relationship until you see each other's stuff—the way I sometimes can't talk for an entire hour after dealing with my parents or how she goes off completely if I so much as mention Ray Horgan, the geezy guy she had a thing with. Sometimes it takes a while to get a peek into the little corners of craziness every person tries to hide. I had been going out with Kat nearly a year and sometimes worried she was just too normal for me, until she got out of bed one morning, complaining about her knee. When I asked how she hurt it, she looked at me, no trace of humor, and said, 'I got hit with a mace when I was a Crusader in one of my prior lives.' At that point, it's all about how well your junk fits with hers. Can you still take each other seriously despite it and stay in tune?

My life with Anna has been, no lie, pretty much paradise, but the one thing that has made her a total whack-job all month has been my parents. I think the way my mom sometimes overwhelms me tends to bug Anna as much as me, and she also seems unsure about her relationship with my dad, convinced, perhaps, that he'll never get beyond seeing her as one of his minions. Privately, I've also wondered if her fling with Ray has something to do with it. My guess is that she assumes my father knows and she's even more embarrassed to be around him, since he would have expected her to exhibit better sense.

But because of all of that, Anna pretty much had a cow when I told her I was going to have to out us to my mom, who was relentless about asking where I would be living at the end of the month. And I really wondered for a second if I would need to dial 911 after I told Anna my mom had invited us to dinner. In the end, my mom, who can be the irresistible force, got on the phone with Anna and cornered her the same way she corners me. But even after Anna said yes the prospect has seemed to make her unbelievably tense.

I came back from school last Thursday night, only a few days before our date with my parents, and found her home already, sitting in the dark and crying, with a pack of cigarettes beside her and at least eight butts in an ashtray. It's a no-smoking building, too.

'What?' I asked, and received no answer. She was frozen at the kitchen table. When I took the chair beside her, she reached for both my hands.

'I love you so much,' she said. She could barely choke out the words.

'I love you, too,' I answered. 'What is this about?'

She gave me this disbelieving look, searching my face for a long time, the tears welling over her green eyes like jewels. 'I so, so, so don't want this to get fucked up,' she said. 'I would do anything to keep that from happening.'

'It's not happening,' I told her, which didn't seem to do much good. She seemed to get a grip for a couple days, but today when we get ready to go to my parents', she's in a state again.

As we cross the Nearing Bridge on the way, Anna says, "I may be sick." The suspension structure is known to boogie in heavy winds, but it's a great day, still more summer than fall, and the late sun has thrown a gold net on the water. We barely make it to the other side before Anna pulls her new Prius into the public forest and dashes from the car. I get there in time to hold her from behind while she vomits into a rusted oil drum used as a garbage can.

I ask, knowing better, if it's something she ate.

"It's this whole fucking thing, Nat," she answers.

"We can cancel," I say. "Tell them you're sick."

She's still gripping the can but shakes her head vehemently. "Let's get it over with. Let's just get it over with."

When she feels good enough to take a few steps, we move to a decrepit picnic table with a squeaky bench, the surface decorated with spray-painted slogans and hunks of bird shit.

"Oh, gross!" she says.

"What?"

"I puked in my hair." She is inspecting the blondish strands with obvious pain.

From the car, I bring a half-drunk bottle of water and a couple of old napkins preserved from fast-food meals, and she does her best to clean up.

"Just tell your parents you found me under a viaduct."

I say she looks great. She doesn't. She's lost all color, and a team of rodents might have held a track meet in her hair. I have given up consoling her or asking why.

She asks me to drive, which means she must assume my role as guardian of the cupcakes. Anna volunteered to bring dessert and has baked four giant cupcakes, each of our individual favorites with our names frosted on top. My dad will get the carrot cake he adores, and my mother a kind of blueberry muffin made from soy flour. For herself and me, she prepared something far more decadent, these giant killer double chocolate chip balls. She grips the plate from both sides in her lap and positions the quart of ice cream she bought for à la mode between her feet.

"Can I beg one thing," she says as I'm about to trigger the ignition. "Don't leave me alone with either one of them. Okay? I'm not in the mood for any heart-to-hearts. Just tell me to go upstairs and look at your room. Something like that to get me out of the way. Okay?"

"Okay." She has actually made this request several times before.

In a few minutes, we are at the house in which I grew up. These days, every time I arrive it looks different to me—smaller, quainter, a little like something from a fairy tale. It's an odd structure to start, the kind of thing my mom would pick, with weeping mortar and this supersteep roof, a style that doesn't seem to match the abundant flowers that remain in bloom in urns and pots in front. All the time I was growing up, my mom said she couldn't wait to move back to the city, but when my dad proposed it a couple years ago, she'd changed her mind. The fact they're still here reflects the enduring stalemate between them. She wins. He resents it.

My mom sweeps the door open before we even set foot on the stoop. She's wearing a little makeup and one of these waffle-fabric athletic suits, which is pretty much dressed up for her when she's at home. She hugs me and then raves about the baked goods as she accepts the plate from Anna, kissing her cheek breezily in the process. She apologizes as soon as we are through the door. My dad and she have been working in the garden all day, and they are running behind.

"I sent your father to the store, Nat. He'll be right back. Come in. Anna, can I get you anything to drink?"

I've told Anna that my mom likes red wine, and she bought a fancy bottle, but my mom decides to save it for dinner. Anna and I each take a beer from the fridge for now.

My mom's moods are so unpredictable that often when I'm headed out here to visit, I will call my dad's cell to discuss her as if she is a weather balloon. 'Bad day,' my dad will warn me. 'Lower than catfish crap.' But she is rarely as visibly excited as she seems tonight, dashing around the kitchen. Hyper is not usually in her emotional range.

Anna has never been here before. My mom really doesn't open the house to anyone but family, and I show Anna the living and family rooms, identifying all my now dead grandparents and my cousins in their photographs and letting her poke me about all my little-kid pictures. Eventually, we rejoin my mom in the kitchen.

"It's simple," my mom says about dinner, "just like I

promised. Steak. Corn. Salad. Anna's cupcakes. Maybe with a little ice cream." She smiles, a cholesterol nut relishing the thought of being evil.

Together Anna and I take on the salad. A knockout cook, Anna has started on a dressing, using olive oil and lemon, when my dad comes in with several plastic bags bearing the orange logo of Mega-Drugs. He thunks them down on the counter, extends his hand to Anna, and then gives me a quick hug.

"I never would have predicted this," he says, motioning to the two of us. "It makes too much sense."

We all laugh, then my mom makes my dad look at the stuff Anna baked. He chips a tiny bit of frosting off her muffin. Anna and my mom both cry out at once.

"Hey, that's mine," my mother tells him.

"You have the longest name," my father points out.

My dad is limping as he moves around the kitchen, and I ask how his back is.

"Rotten at the moment. Your mother had me digging for her new rhododendron all afternoon."

"Here," my mother answers. "Take your Advil and stop complaining. The exercise is good for you. Between the campaign and George Mason's rotator cuff, I don't think you've had any kind of workout all month." My dad normally plays handball a couple times a week with Judge Mason, and he does look a little softer than usual. He puts the pills my mom hands him on the counter, then disappears into the family room and comes back with a glass of wine for her.

"Did you remember the appetizers?" she asks as he's in the fridge, taking a beer for himself.

"Yes, horse deserves," he declares, a rotten joke he

has made since I was a boy. He bought aged cheddar and Genoa salami, family favorites, although my mom will not eat much of that. She loves the pickled herring he brought home, but she'll have only a piece or two because the salt is bad for her blood pressure, so my dad has also come back with yogurt, which he mixes with onion soup to make a dip, while Anna and I set out the carrots and celery that were already in the refrigerator, as well as the other items my father got.

As we are all toiling, my mom questions Anna about work and then with no apparent segue about her family.

"Only child," she explains.

"Like Nat. That's probably an important thing to have in common."

Anna is chopping onion for the salad, which has brought a dribble from her eyes, and she makes a joke of it.

"It wasn't that bad of a childhood," she says.

The three of us laugh uproariously at the remark. Now that it's actually happening, Anna seems to be doing fine. I understand. Every spring for more years than I could count, I was convinced I would never remember how to hit a baseball and found myself amazed the first time I felt the buzz of solid contact and heard the ringing of the bat.

Anna diverts further inquiries by asking my father about the campaign.

Cutting more salami, he says, "I'm pretty sick of hearing about John Harnason."

My mom turns from the counter to shoot my dad a look. "We should never have had to go through any of this," she says. "*Never.*"

I catch Anna's eye to warn her, as I should have before, about this subject.

My dad says, "It'll be over soon, Barbara."

"Not soon enough. Your father hasn't slept through the night all month."

She enjoys this role, telling on my dad, and he turns away, knowing better than to risk further comment. I thought my father's nights as an insomniac were long past. When I was a boy, there were periods when he was up, roaming the house. I would sometimes hear him and was actually comforted to know he was awake, able to dispel the nighttime spooks and demons I feared. Listening, watching now, I can feel that the weight of the household is different in some minute way. The campaign seems to have brought the usual silent conflicts between my parents more into the open.

Accustomed to my mother's criticisms, my father offers her the appetizer platter, which he and Anna and I seem to be doing a good job of hogging down. Then my dad takes the steaks out of the fridge and begins to season them. He needs more garlic powder, he says, and heads down to the basement to bring it up.

"Boys cook?" my dad asks me when he's ready to face the fire.

"Mom, you mind if Anna looks around upstairs while we're out there? I wanted her to see my room."

"Anything you like up there, Anna, feel free. Nat won't let me throw away a thing. Don't you think a shelf full of baseball trophies is just what your new place needs?"

We all laugh again. It's hard to tell if this jolliness is nerves or actual enjoyment, but it's uncharacteristic for

the home in which I was raised. Out of sight of anybody else, Anna rolls her eyes at me from the staircase,
while I follow my dad out to the porch. The sun is setting, falling into the river in a vivid display of colors,
and there is a little fall coolness to the air.

My dad and I play with the knobs until the barbecue is ignited, and we stand there watching the flames
spread between the burners as if it were a religious rite.
When I was a child, my mom always surrounded me
in a way that didn't seem to require words, and maybe
as a result I have never gotten the knack of talking to
my dad. Of course, I didn't really talk all that much
to anybody before Anna, which must mean something,
I guess. Naturally, my dad and I have conversations,
but they are usually to the point, unless we are talking about law or the Trappers, the two subjects where
we are liable to become animated together. Usually my
principal communion with my father comes, like now,
from coexistence, breathing the same air, firing off
occasional comments about the flames or the way the
meat is sizzling.

In my junior year of high school, I realized I did
not especially like baseball as a sport. At that point, I
was the starting center fielder on the Nearing team,
although I was sure to lose the spot to a terrific fresh-
man, Josey Higgins, who unlike me had no trouble hitting breaking pitches and was even faster in the field.
He went on to a full ride at Wisconsin State, where he
was All Mid-Ten. What came to me almost in a single
moment as I was trained on a fly arcing its way to me
was that I had watched baseball on TV and trotted onto
the field every summer since I was six years old only so

I could talk about it with my father. I was not especially resentful, just unwilling to continue doing that once I understood. When I quit, I heard little complaint from the coach, who was plainly relieved not to have to deliver the inevitable speech about the good of the team. Everyone—including my dad—always thought I dropped out rather than warm the bench, and I have been just as happy to leave it that way.

When we have been standing there some time, he asks what I am going to be doing next week when my clerkship is over. I've decided to go back to subbing while I work on my law review article, on which I've recently made some progress. He nods as if to say it's a reasonable plan.

"So overall?" he asks as he's ducking left and right around the smoke.

"I'm really happy, Dad."

When I turn, he's stopped to look at me intently with a largely unfathomable expression, while he allows the billows to surround him. I realize it's been a long time since I answered either of my parents that way. Over the years, I far more often have fended off their questions about my state of being by describing myself simply as 'okay.'

To evade my dad's attention now, I take a long draft of my beer and look into the small yard where I played as a child. It once looked as big as the prairie. Now the little continuous space has been broken by the new rhodie, three feet high if that, with its glossy leaves and the fresh earth surrounding it my father turned today. Things change, and sometimes for the better. I am proud Anna is here with me, pleased with myself for realizing how good she'd be for me and pursuing her and making her love me, and I'm happy I have brought her together with these other people I love. It's one of those moments I hope I will always remember: That day I was so happy.

RUSTY'S BIRTHDAY
(3/19/07)

BARBARA'S DEATH
(9/29/08)

THE ELECTION
(11/04/08)

CHAPTER 22

Tommy, November 4, 2008

O ver the years, the PA's office, like any other institution, had developed its own odd protocol. The boss stayed put. The prosecuting attorney walked into his office in the morning with his briefcase under his arm and never left, except for lunch and court. It was nominally a sign of respect. Everyone who needed to speak to him came to the mountain. But the practice actually protected the freewheeling demeanor within the PA's office. Guys could stand in the hallways sixty feet apart and talk over a case while they tossed a softball. People could say "fuck" as loud as they wanted to. Deputies could bad-mouth judges, and cops could spout. Within his inner sanctum, the PA conducted himself with a dignity the everyday life of his office would never really reflect.

As a result, Tommy often felt as if he were in jail. He had to intercom or phone everybody. For more than thirty years, he had cruised the hallways, popping in and out of offices to gossip about cases and the kids at home. And right now, he was sick of waiting. First thing this morning Brand had gone to a meeting at the crime lab, where they were going to brief him on the DNA results on the two-decade-old sperm fraction from the first Sabich trial. Tommy had left his office six times by now to see if Brand was back.

In the moment, the fact that these results would force Tommy's hand one way or the other, leave him caught between bad news and worse, seemed to matter less. Nor did he really care about the notion Brand was suddenly promoting, that after they convicted Rusty Sabich, Tommy could run for PA next year. The truth was that if that happened and a judgeship opened up, Tommy would probably toss the mantle to Brand. But anytime Brand speculated that way out loud, Tommy hushed him. Politics would never be his passion. What Tommy Molto really cared about was the same thing he had cared about for decades as a prosecutor. Justice. About whether something was right or whether it was wrong.

So if twenty years ago they'd gone on an innocent guy, he'd be the first to tell Rusty he was sorry. And if it was the other way, if it was Rusty who did Carolyn, then—then what? But he knew instantly. It would be like his marriage. It would be like finding Dominga and falling in love with her. And having Tomaso. The one lingering blot on his career would be lifted. But most important, Tommy himself would know. The guilt that still nagged at him from that time, for having stupidly talked out of school to Nico, would be dissolved. He would have been right, in his own eyes more than anyone else's. He would be fifty-nine years old. And thoroughly reborn. Only God could remake a life so completely. Tommy knew that. He took an instant to offer prayerful thanks in advance.

Then he heard Brand bang into his office next door and Tommy stepped in immediately. Jim still had his briefcase in his hand and his overcoat half off and was surprised to see Tommy on his threshold. Master in the servant's quarters. He stared a minute. Then he smiled. He said what Tommy had always known someone would say eventually.

Brand said, "It's him."

PART TWO

III.

CHAPTER 23

Nat, June 22, 2009

State your name, please, and spell your last name for the record." From his seat at the walnut defense table, Sandy Stern clears his throat. It is a reflex these days both before and after he speaks, a phlegmy little rattle that never sounds quite normal.

"Rozat K. Sabich. S, A, B, I, C, H."

"Are you known by any other name?"

"Rusty."

On the witness stand, my father in his pressed blue suit maintains perfect posture and an unruffled demeanor. In his place, I would be a mess, but in the last few months my dad has taken on the distant air of a mystic. For the most part, he seems to have stopped believing in cause and effect. Things happen. Period.

"And may we call you Rusty?" Stern asks, lifting the back of his hand gallantly, as if he might be imposing. After my father agrees, Stern asks him to tell the jury how he is employed.

"I was elected to the state supreme court last November, but I have not yet taken the oath of office."

"And why, sir, is that?"

"Because I was indicted on these charges, and felt it was fairer to all concerned to await the outcome of this trial. In the interval, I remain the chief judge of the State Court of Appeals for the Third Appellate District here in Kindle County, although I have taken administrative leave."

Stern brings out that both the supreme and appellate courts are what lawyers call courts of review, meaning basically that they hear appeals.

"And tell us, please, what it means to be a judge on a court of review."

My dad details the duties. Across the courtroom, Tommy Molto stands to object as my dad begins to explain that the appeal in a criminal case ordinarily does not give the judges any right to overrule a jury's factual decision.

Judge Basil Yee visibly weighs the issue, wagging his gray head from one side to the other. From downstate Ware, Judge Yee was specially assigned by the state supreme court to preside over this case after all the judges in the Kindle County Superior Court, whose decisions my father has routinely reviewed for well more than a decade, recused themselves together. He is a Taiwanese immigrant who came to Ware, a town of no more than ten thousand, at age eleven, when his parents took over the local Chinese restaurant. Judge Yee writes flawless English but still speaks it as a second tongue, with a strong accent that includes high Asian pitches, and at times he ignores some of the connective tissue of language—articles, prepositions, state-of-being verbs. His regular court reporter did not accompany him upstate and the annoying way Jenny

Tilden is constantly interrupting to tell the judge to spell what he has just said has made him a man of even fewer words.

Judge Yee rules for my dad, who lays it on pretty thick, just as Molto feared, making sure the jury knows they will have the last word on his innocence or guilt.

"Very well," says Stern. He coughs and grips the table to struggle to his feet. Sandy has received Judge Yee's permission to question witnesses while seated whenever he likes. In one of those can-you-believe-it consequences that medicine may not comprehend for aeons, his brand of non-small-cell lung cancer is known to cause arthritis in one knee, which has left him hobbling. Beside him, Marta, his daughter and law partner, reflexively puts her left hand with its bright manicure on her father's elbow to lend a subtle boost. I have heard about Sandy Stern's magnetism in a courtroom since I was a boy. Like a lot of things in life, it's pretty much beyond anybody's ability to explain. He is short—barely five feet six, if that—and to be honest, pretty dumpy. You would walk past Sandy Stern on the street a thousand times. But when he stands up in court, it is as if someone lit a beacon. Even though he is worn out by cancer, there is a precision to every word and movement that makes it impossible to remove your eyes.

"Now tell us if you would, Rusty, a bit about your background." Stern runs my father down his résumé. Son of an immigrant. College on a scholarship. Law school while working two jobs.

"And after law school and your clerkship?" Stern asks.

"I was hired as a deputy prosecuting attorney in Kindle County."

"That is the office Mr. Molto now heads?"

"Correct. Mr. Molto and I started there within a couple years of one another."

"Objection," Molto says quietly. He has not looked up from the legal pad on which he is writing, but the strain shows in his chin. He sees just what my dad and Stern are up to, trying to remind the jury that my father and Tommy have a history, something they probably already know from the papers that replay the details of the first trial daily. The jurors swear every morning they have steered clear of any journalistic accounts, but according to Marta and her dad, word almost always filters into the jury room.

Judge Yee says, "Enough that subject, I think."

Still facing his pad, Tommy nods curtly in satisfaction. I tolerate Tommy Molto, with his wilting face and hangdog manner, better than I expected to. It's his chief deputy, Jim Brand, who gets me cranked. He has this bad-ass thing going most of the time, except when it's worse and he comes on as too cool for the room.

Stern takes my dad through his progress in the very office that is now prosecuting him and his eventual arrival on the bench. In his account, the first indictment and trial are never mentioned, as the judge has ordered. This is the seamless chronicle of the courtroom, where history's speed bumps are leveled.

"Are you a married man, Rusty?"

"I was. I married Barbara more than thirty-eight years ago."

"Any children?"

"My son, Nat, is right there in the first row." Stern looks back with mock curiosity, as if he had not told me exactly where to sit. He is such a subtle courtroom actor that I find myself hoping now and then that his failing health is also for show, but I know better.

Around the courthouse, people will frequently draw me aside and ask in low tones how Stern is doing, assuming that somebody who has defended my father twice on murder charges must be a closer family friend than he really is. I tell everyone pretty much the same thing. Stern exhibits the courage of a cliff diver, but as for the true state of his health, I know very little. He is private about his condition. Marta is philosophical but equally closemouthed, even though the two of us have had a nearly instantaneous bond as the lawyer children of local legal eagles. Both Sterns are fiercely professional. Our relationship right now is about my father's troubles, not theirs.

But you don't need a medical degree to see that Sandy's condition is perilous. Last year, part of the left lobe of his lung was removed surgically, which seemed at the time to be a good sign that the disease had not spread. In the last four to five months though, he has endured at least two separate rounds of chemo and radiation. My high school pal Hal Marko, who is now a surgical resident, speculated that Stern must have had some kind of recurrence and added, in that incredibly cold-blooded tone I also hear from my law school friends, meant to show they have progressed from human being to professional, that Stern's median survival time should be less than a year. I have no idea if that's so, only that the treatments have left Stern a wreck. He has a persistent cough and shortness of breath, due not to his cancer, but as a side effect of the radiation. He claims to be regaining

his appetite, but he ate virtually nothing for the period
leading to the trial, and the man I grew up knowing as
chubby during his slimmest periods is positively thin.
He has not replaced his wardrobe, and his suits hang
like kaftans. Whenever he struggles to his feet, he is in
visible pain. To top it all off, the last drug he took, a
second-line chemo agent, left him with a bright rash all
over his body, including his face. From where the jury
sits, it must look as if he has had a large fuchsia tattooed
on one side. The inflammation crawls up his cheek and
around his eye, reaching in a single islet up above his
temple and pointing cruelly toward his bald head.

Judge Yee granted one continuance, but my dad and
Sandy decided not to seek another, despite the way he
looks. His mind remains strong, and if he husbands his
strength, he can withstand the physical rigors of trial.
But the meaning for Sandy of the decision to proceed
seems obvious: Now or never.

"Now, Rusty, you have been called as the first witness for the defense in this case."

"I have."

"You understand that the Constitution of the
United States protects you from being forced to testify
in your own trial."

"I understand that."

"You have chosen to testify nonetheless."

"I have."

"And you were here throughout the time that the
prosecution witnesses gave their testimony?"

"I was."

"And you heard all of them? Mr. Harnason? Dr.
Strack, the toxicologist. Dr. Gorvetich, the computer

expert? All fourteen of the persons whom the prosecutor called to the stand?"

"I heard each of them."

"And so, Rusty, you understand that you are here accused of murdering your wife, Barbara Bernstein Sabich?"

"I do."

"Did you do that, Rusty? Murder Mrs. Sabich?"

"No."

"Did you have any role of any kind in causing her death?"

"No."

The sheer oddity of a supreme court justice-elect indicted for murder a second time, and by the same prosecutor, no less, has garnered press around the globe. People stand in line outside the courtroom each day to get a seat, and two rows across the way are crowded with sketch artists and reporters. The accumulated attention of the world often seems to penetrate the courtroom, where there is a high-strung air brought on by so many people recalculating with every word. My father's 'No' lingers now, seemingly held aloft by the magnitude of the declaration. With all eyes on him, Stern looks around the large rococo courtroom and rears back slightly, as if he is only now discovering something that the better informed know he has always planned.

"No further questions," he says, and plunges with mortal weariness back to his seat.

My father's case is the first trial I've ever sat through end to end. The trial process has absorbed so much of my dad's life, as a prosecutor and a judge, that in spite of the indescribable heaviness of the whole business for me, I have found sitting here constantly informative. I finally have a clue what he was doing in the many hours he was gone from home and some sense of what he found so beguiling. And although the courtroom will never be the place for me, I have been fascinated by its little rituals and dramas, especially the moments too banal to be represented on TV or in the movies. The present instant, when the sides change, with one lawyer sitting and the opponent coming to his feet, is the law's equivalent of the time between innings, a moment of suspended animation. The court reporter's computer stops clicking. The jurors shift in their seats and scratch what itches, and the spectators clear their throats. Papers scrape across both tables as the lawyers gather their notes.

By whatever trick of fate, my dad's case is being heard in one of the four older courtrooms in this building, the Central Branch Courthouse, where the court of appeals is housed on the top floor. He arrives every day to stand trial for murder in a place where he remains, at least by title, the highest-ranking judicial official and next door to the courtroom where he was freed more than twenty years ago. All the old rooms, where serious felonies have been tried for seventy years now, are jewels of bygone architectural detail, with the jury boxes set off by these strings of walnut bubbles. The same kind of rail fronts the witness stand and the massive bench where Judge Yee looms over the courtroom. The spaces for the witness and the judge are each defined by red marble pillars that support a walnut canopy, decorated with more of those corny wooden balls.

Beneath that overhang, my dad sits impassively as he awaits the start of Tommy Molto's cross-examination. For the first time, he lets his blue eyes light on mine, and for a tiny instant, he squeezes them shut. Here we go, he seems to be saying. The wild rocket ship ride that has been life for both of us since my mother died nine months ago will end and allow us to parachute back to earth, where we will inhabit either some shrunken version of the life we had before or a new nightmare terrain, in which my weekly conversations with my father will be conducted for the rest of his life through a pane of bulletproof glass.

When a parent dies—everybody says this, so I know it isn't so totally original—but when you lose your mother or father, life is fundamentally different. One of the poles, north or south, has been wiped off the globe and will never rematerialize.

But my life was *really* different. I was sort of a kid for too long, and then suddenly I was where I was. I had fallen in love with Anna. My mom was dead. And my dad was indicted for killing her.

Because what happened to my parents was in each case so much worse for them than me, it sounds weak to say what I have gone through has been an ordeal. But it has. Of course, losing my mom so suddenly was the ultimate blow. But the charges against my dad have left me in a predicament few people can even begin to understand. My dad has been a public figure most of my life, meaning his shadow has frequently fallen across me. When I went to law school I knew I was only making that worse, that I was always going to be known as Rusty's kid and would be dragging his reputation and achievements along behind me like a bride trying to figure out how to get her train through a revolving door. But now he's infamous, not famous, an object of hatred and ridicule. When I see his picture on the Net or TV—or even on one national magazine cover— there's a way I feel he no longer quite belongs to me. And of course nobody knows how to treat me or what to say. It must be a little like being outed with HIV, where people know you haven't really done anything wrong but can't quite stifle an impulse to recoil.

But the worst part is what goes on inside of me, because from moment to moment I have no idea how I feel, or should feel for that matter. I guess parents are always moving objects. We grow up, and our perspectives constantly evolve. In this courtroom, there is just one question—did he or didn't he? But for me, for months now the issue has been far more complicated, trying to figure out what most kids get a lifetime to assess—namely, who my old man really is. Not who I thought. I've figured that much out already.

That process began on election day with an angry thumping on the door to Anna's condo. A small woman had her badge out.

'KCUPF.' Kindle County Unified Police Force. 'Do you have a second to talk?'

It was like TV and so I knew I was supposed to say, What is this about? But really, why would I care? She stepped into the apartment, strutted, really, without an invitation, a short, plump woman with her hat under her arm and her wiry, brass-colored hair drawn back in a pony tail.

'Debby Diaz.' Die As, she pronounced it. She offered

a small, rough hand and sat down on a hassock covered in retro blue shag, which Anna had bought largely as a gag a couple of weeks before. 'Known your dad forever. I was a bailiff when he started in the superior court. Actually, I remember you.'

'Me?'

'Yeah, I was assigned to that courtroom a couple times when you come down. You used to sit up on his chair on the bench during recesses. Couldn't really see you from down in the courtroom, but nobody told you that. Young man, you could really pound that gavel. Act of God you didn't break it.' She was quite merry with the memory, and I suddenly remembered what she was describing, including the musical echo when I slammed the gavel on the oak block. 'I was young and slim in those days,' she said. 'Waiting to get on the force.'

'I guess you made it.' I said that only because I couldn't think of anything else, but she took it for a joke and smiled a little.

'It was what I wanted. What I thought I wanted.' She shook her head briefly at the follies of youth. Then she focused on me with disturbingly sudden intensity. 'We're trying to clear on your mother's death.'

'Clear?'

'Get some questions answered. You know how it is. Not a damn thing happens for a month, then all of a sudden it's gotta be wrapped up in a week. Guys on the scene took a long statement from your father, but nobody thought to talk to you. When I heard your name, I figured I'd stroll over and do it myself.'

There are people you meet who you know are used

to not saying what they actually mean and Detective
Diaz was one of them for sure. I wondered for a second
how she'd found me, then realized I'd left this forward-
ing address when I finished at the court. All in all, I
was happier to be talking to her at home on election
day than I would have been if she'd shown up at school.
There are still plenty of people on the faculty who
remember my years at Nearing High and have a hard
time believing I can set much of an example.

'I still don't understand what you want to ask about,'
I told her, and she motioned as if it were all too vague,
too cop, too bureaucratic, to explain.

'Sit down,' she said, 'and you'll find out.' From the
seat on the hassock, she motioned me toward a chair in
my own place. What I really needed to do, I realized,
was call my father, or at least Anna. But the thought
seemed mostly useless against the reality of Detective
Diaz sitting there. Small as she was, there was an edge,
that cop-thing, like, I'm in charge here, don't mess
around.

'My mom died of heart failure,' I told her.

'True.'

'So. What is there to ask about?'

'Nat,' she said. 'I can call you "Nat," right? Somebody says we got to interview the kid to close this, so
I'm here to interview you. That's all.' She picked up
a magazine, a copy of *People* Anna had left there, and
turned a few pages. 'Could I care less about Brad and
Angie?' she asked before throwing it down. 'Things
cool between your mom and dad around the time she
passed?'

I couldn't help but smile. That's exactly the word for

how things were between my parents generally—cool. Not quite involved.

'Same as always,' I answered.

'But they weren't bitching at each other or to you?'

'Nothing different.'

'And how's your dad doing now? Pretty torn up, still?' She'd produced a little spiral notebook from somewhere and was writing in it.

'I mean, my dad—I never really know what's happening with him. He's pretty stoic. But I think we're both fairly much in shock. He kind of suspended most of his campaigning. If he'd asked me, I'd've told him to do more to take his mind off things.'

'Seeing anybody?'

'Hell, no.' The thought of my father with someone else, which several brain-damaged individuals had mentioned in the weeks after my mom's death, inevitably rattled me.

'You getting on okay with your dad?' she asked.

'Sure,' I said. 'Is that what this is about? My dad? Is somebody making trouble for him?'

When I was in the second grade, my father was tried for murder. In retrospect, it always amazes me how long it took for me to comprehend the full dimension of that simple statement. At the time, my parents told me that my father had had a bad fight with his friends at work, like bad fights I had with friends at school, that these former amigos were very mad at him and doing mean and unfair things. I naturally accepted that—I still do, actually. But I realized there was more to it, if for no other reason than that every adult I knew treated me more warily, as if I were suspected of something, too—the parents of my friends, the teachers and custodians at school, and, most conspicuously, my parents, who hovered in an intense protective way as if they feared I was coming down with something terrible. My dad stayed home from work. A bunch of policemen swarmed through the house one day. And eventually I learned, either by asking or by overhearing, that something very bad might happen to my father—that he might be gone for years and years and conceivably could never live with us again. He was petrified; I could sense that. So was my mother. And so I became terrified, too. They sent me to overnight camp for the summer, where I found myself more scared for being away. I would play ball and run with friends but wake up constantly to the reality that something awful might be happening at home. I cried like mad every night until they decided to ship me back. And when I got there, this thing they called a trial was over. Everybody knew my father had done nothing bad, that the bad things had been done by his former friends, just as my parents had been saying all along. But still it wasn't right. My dad wasn't working. And my parents seemed unable to recover a normal air with each other. It came as no surprise when my mom told me that just the two of us were moving away. I had known something cataclysmic had happened all along.

'You think your dad deserves trouble?' Detective Diaz asked.

'Well, of course not.'

'We don't make things up,' she said. I hadn't sat down yet, and she pointed to the chair again, this time with a pen. 'A guy like your dad, he's been around since they started telling time, everybody and his cat has got an opinion. Some people, you know, here and there, they got axes to grind. But that's how it goes, right? Judges, prosecutors, cops, they're always sand in somebody's ointment. But your dad's running for office. That's the main thing. Somebody looked at the file and said, We got to clear this before he takes the oath, answer all the questions.'

She asked me to tell her what happened the day my mom died. Or actually the day after.

'Is that the thing?' I asked. 'Did that seem strange—him sitting with the body for a day?'

She lifted a hand—back to that routine, just doing her job. 'I don't know. My mom, her people was Irish, they put the body in the living room with candles and sat around it all night. So, no, I mean. People lose someone, there ain't no manual for that. Everybody does it his own way. But you know, if somebody wants to make trouble, they'd say, "Now, that's strange. Putting everything away." You know how folks can be: What's he cleaning up? What's he hiding?'

I nodded. That made some sense, although those questions had never crossed my mind.

'One of the coppers has got a note that you said your father didn't want to call the police?'

'He was blanking. That's all. I mean, he's been around long enough to know somebody has to call the cops, right?'

'Seems like that to me,' said Detective Debby.

'Yeah, but it was the situation,' I said. 'I mean, this heart stuff ran in her family, but my mom was in great condition, worked out, stayed fit. Did you ever lose somebody you loved without warning? It's like there's no gravity all the sudden, like everything is just floating around. You don't know if you should stand up or sit down. You can't really think about doing anything. You just need to get a grip.'

'Anything look out of place when you got there?'

There was something out of place all right: My mother was lying dead in my parents' bed. How could this detective really think I'd remember anything else? My father had laid both of her hands out on the covers, and she had taken on a color, pale as water, that by itself left no question she was gone. I don't know how young a kid is when he figures out his mom and dad are headed to the exits before him. But age never seemed to have touched my mother. If one of them was going to just hit the floor, I would have expected it to be my father, who seems a little puffy with age and complains a lot about his back and his cholesterol.

'And when was the last time you were together with your mom?'

'The night before. We had dinner at the house. My girlfriend and me.'

'And how'd that go?'

'It was the first time the four of us had a meal together. Everybody seemed kind of nervous, which was weird because my girlfriend knew my parents before we started going out. But you know, sometimes that makes things harder, changing context with somebody? And, I think my parents have always been secretly worried that I'd end up alone, too moody and stuff, so this was kind of a big deal. Do you have kids?'

'Oh, yeah. All growed up, just like you.' That

sounded strange to me, the way she put it. I don't think either of my parents would have described me as all grown up. Truth, I might not have used those words myself. 'My son, he works for Ford, has two of his own, but my daughter, she ain't married and I don't know she ever will be. Like her mom, I guess, wants to go it alone. Her father? That man was an absolute rat, but now sometimes I wish I hadn't of told her so often. She's on the job. Tried to talk her out of it, too, but she just had to do it.' The way she tossed her head in wonder made us both laugh, but she went right back to asking about the night before my mom died.

'How'd your mom seem to you? Happy? Unhappy? Anything stick out in your mind?'

'I mean, my mom—you know, she's been treated for bipolar for years, sometimes, you can see she's struggling. Could see.' I grimaced over the tense. 'I guess that it all seemed pretty normal to me. My mom was a little high-strung, I'd say, and my dad was quieter than usual, and my girlfriend was nervous.'

'You say this was for dinner,' said Detective Diaz. 'Remember what you all ate?'

'Ate?'

She looked at her pad. 'Yeah, somebody wants to know what you ate.' She shrugged, like, Don't ask me, I just work here.

That was the last time I saw my mom, so the night had been on replay for weeks and the details remained incredibly fresh. I had no trouble answering the detective's questions about who cooked and what we ate, but it just made no sense to me, and somewhere along I began to realize I needed to shut up.

'And who poured the wine for your mom while you were eating dinner? Your dad again?'

I gave the detective a look.

'I'm just trying to think of every question somebody could possibly ask,' she said. 'I don't want to have to bother you again.'

'Who poured the wine at dinner?' I asked aloud, as if I didn't really recall. 'Maybe my dad. He has this Rabbit corkscrew my mom never could figure out. But I'm not really sure. It could even have been me.'

Debby Diaz asked another question or two, to which I gave similarly vague answers. She probably realized I was shining her on by then, but I really didn't care. Finally, she smacked her thighs and headed to the door. Once she had it open she snapped her fingers.

'Say, what's your girlfriend's name? Might be I need to talk to her.'

I had to keep from laughing. Some detective. Standing in the woman's condo and absolutely no clue. But I shook my head as if I didn't know the answer. Diaz gave me a really tough look then. We were both done pretending.

'Well, that can't be a secret,' she said. 'Don't make me have to find out.'

I told her to leave a card and said I'd get it to my girlfriend.

I had reached my dad on his inside line before the detective was through the lobby downstairs. He'd voted when the polls opened, then gone to work as if it were a normal day, even though there were no normal days for either of us just then.

He sounded so happy when he heard my voice. He

always is when I call. But I couldn't speak for a second. I hadn't fully realized what I was going to say until just then.

'Dad,' I said. 'Dad, I'm really scared you may be in trouble.'

Chapter 24

Tommy, June 22, 2009

Tommy Molto had always had mixed feelings about Sandy Stern. Sandy was good, there was no doubt about that. If you were a cobbler and took pride in your craft, then you had to admire somebody who found flawless leather and made shoes that wore like iron and felt like velvet on the foot. Sandy was a maestro in the courtroom. An Argentinian who'd come here in the late 1940s during the turmoil with Perón, he still played the polished Latin gentleman sixty years later, with a trace accent that enhanced his speech like some fancy seasoning—truffle oil or sea salt—and the manners of the staff in an expensive hotel. His routine went down better than ever these days, when an occasional aside *en español* could be interpreted for other jurors by at least two or three of their number.

But you had to watch Sandy. Because he appeared so elegant, so proper, he got away with more stuff than the average drug court hustler. Tommy knew that all the crap that rained down on him during Rusty Sabich's first trial, the subtle accusations of taking part in a frame-up, had been concocted by Sandy, who in the years since acted with Tommy as if nothing of consequence had happened, rather than putting a place holder on Tommy's life that was still there today.

At the moment, Sandy was tussling with cancer. From the look of it, things were not going well. He had the Daddy Warbucks haircut and had parted with a good sixty pounds, and the drugs had given him a rash that seemed to be literally burning through his face. Just a few minutes ago, before court resumed, Tommy asked Sandy how he was doing.

'Stable,' said Sandy. 'Holding my own. We'll know more in a few weeks. Some good signs with the latest round of treatment. Despite becoming the Scarlet Pimpernel.' He pointed to his cheek.

'In my prayers,' said Tommy. He never told someone that without carrying through.

But that was how it went with Sandy Stern. You prayed for his soul, and he mounted you from the rear. The defendant never testified first. The accused was always the last act in a trial, the star attraction, who went on at the final possible minute, so the wisdom of testifying could be evaluated in light of all the other evidence and so the defendant would make the biggest impression on the jury as they deliberated. Not that Tommy has been taken totally by surprise. He had figured all along Rusty might be coming, ever since Judge Yee's pretrial ruling, in chambers, out of earshot of the press, that nothing of the first trial—not the new DNA results nor Carolyn Polhemus's murder, nor any of the related legal proceedings—was ever going to be mentioned in this courtroom. But Tommy was planning to spend the next few nights preparing, getting Rusty's

cross sequenced, playing it through with Brand. Now
it was going to be like Tommy's days in drug court
thirty years ago, when there were so many cases that
you couldn't get completely ready for any of them and
had to cross from the seat of your pants. In those days,
when the rare defendant chose to testify, the first thing
you wanted to ask him was to remind you of his name.

Standing at the prosecution table, pretending to
examine his notes as if there were actually some order
to what he'd scribbled down, Tommy was visited by a
stillness that had been with him throughout the case.
Nobody would ever mark Tommy as relaxed in the
courtroom, not in this trial or any other, but at night,
when the trial process usually left him a mass of teeming anxieties, he had been more or less at ease, able to
sleep through the night beside Dominga, rather than
rising several times as had been his routine over the
years. The impact of this verdict on his future and his
family's, on the way he would forever be perceived,
was so large that he knew he simply must accept the
will of God. Ordinarily, he did not like to believe God
wasted His time worrying about a creature as unim-
portant as Tommy Molto. But how could Rusty have
come around again, against all the odds, if the outcome
in the first case didn't cross some rule of divine justice?

Tommy's mood had also been fortified by the fact
that the prosecution evidence turned out to make
a prettier package than he had foreseen. After trying
cases for thirty years, Tommy knew that at this stage of
the proceedings, you drank your own Kool-Aid. You
needed to believe you were going to win to have any
chance of convincing the jurors, even while you had

to remain in the grip of paranoia. And he was wary.
There was no telling yet what Stern was up to, but from
long experience with the man, Tommy expected the
unexpected.

The opening statement Sandy gave when the trial
began two weeks ago was a bland mantra of 'reasonable
doubt,' in which Stern invoked the term 'circumstantial proof' no fewer than eighteen times: 'The evidence
will not show a confession, an eyewitness. The evidence
instead will consist almost entirely of the conjecture
of various experts about what might have happened.
You will hear experts from the prosecution, and then
equally if not more qualified experts from the defense
who will tell you that the prosecution's experts are
quite likely wrong. And even the prosecution's experts,
ladies and gentlemen, will not be able to tell you with
any certainty that Mrs. Sabich was murdered, let alone
by who.' Before the jurors, Stern had paused with a
troubled frown, as if it had just occurred to him how
inappropriate it was to charge somebody with murder
on such a flimsy basis. He was gripping the rail of the
jury box for support—having come several feet closer
to them than any judge in this county would normally
permit. Despite the summer heat outside, Stern wore a
three-piece suit, undoubtedly from his stoutest period,
so it hung on him as shapelessly as—no coincidence—a
hospital gown. There was nothing that happened in life
that Sandy Stern would not contrive to use to advantage in the courtroom. His whole being was tilted that
way, he couldn't help himself, the same as some guys
who could not stop thinking of sex or money. Even
looking as repulsive as a figure from one of the *Friday*

the 13th movies was something he had figured out how to use for his client's benefit, Sandy's mere presence seeming to suggest that he had risen from his deathbed to prevent a savage injustice. Free Rusty, he seemed to say, and I can die in peace.

There was no telling if the jurors were buying that, but if they were paying attention at all to the State's evidence, they had to recognize that the prosecutors had a point. After some debate they had called Rusty's son, Nat, to start the case. That was risky, especially since Yee had already ruled that when Nat climbed down from the witness stand, he would be allowed to remain in the courtroom to support his father, notwithstanding the fact that he was going to testify again for the defense. Still, it was always a nice touch when you got your evidence from the other side, and Nat was a straight kid, who, sitting here day after day, often looked to have his own doubts. On the stand, the younger Sabich gave up what he had to—his father not wanting to call the cops after Barbara died, or the fact that the night before she bought it, Rusty had cooked the steaks and poured Barbara's wine, giving him ample opportunity to slip his wife a lethal dose of phenelzine.

The PAs put on Nenny Strack next. She was better than she'd been in Tommy's office, but even so, she took back almost everything on cross-examination. Still, they were stuck with her. If they'd called a different toxicologist, then Strack would be up there testifying for the defense, undercutting the other guy and saying she'd expressed all those doubts to the prosecutors. Instead, Brand cleaned up the mess with the coroner, who offered the opinion that Barbara had died of phenelzine poisoning. Dr. Russell had a lot to eat on cross, and Marta Stern had fed it to him piece by piece. She emphasized that Russell had believed initially that Barbara died by natural causes and, given postmortem redistribution, still could not definitively rule out that possibility.

From that valley, the prosecution had steadily climbed back into sunshine. Barbara's own pharmacologist got up there briefly to say he'd warned her repeatedly about the dangers of phenelzine and the foods she needed to avoid when taking it. Harnason was Harnason, sneaky-looking and strange, but he stayed on script. His sentence was going to drop from one hundred years to fifty in exchange for his testimony, but Harnason seemed to be the only person in the courtroom who didn't realize he was going to die in prison. He was the first witness Stern cross-examined rather than Marta, but it was an oddly understated performance. Sandy barely bothered flaying Harnason with the ugly facts he had already acknowledged during Brand's direct examination—that Harnason was a veteran liar and cheat, a fugitive who had already broken his oath to the court when he ran, and a murderer who had slept beside his lover night after night at the same time he knew he was poisoning him. Instead, Stern spent most of his time on Harnason's first prosecution thirty years ago, encouraging the man to rumble on about how unjustified his prison sentence was and how Rusty's decision had basically ruined his life. But Stern did not directly challenge Harnason's testimony that Rusty tipped him about the appellate court's decision or asked what it felt like to poison someone.

George Mason, the acting chief of the court of appeals, had followed Harnason with a lengthy dissection of the judicial canons, quite damaging to Sabich, even though on cross, Judge Mason, admittedly Rusty's longtime friend, reiterated his enduring high opinion of Sabich's integrity and credibility.

Slick but visibly nervous as a witness, Prima Dana Mann testified that his practice was limited to matrimonial matters and admitted consulting with Rusty twice, including once three weeks before Barbara died.

Then the case had ended with the best stuff the prosecution had: Rusty picking up the phenelzine, the fingerprint results from Barbara's medicine cabinet, Rusty's shopping trip the day Barbara died, and finally Milo Gorvetich, the computer expert, who laid out all the incriminating stuff they'd mined after seizing Rusty's home computer.

Once the prosecution rested, Marta had made an impassioned argument that the prosecution had failed to establish corpus delicti, meaning they had not offered evidence from which a jury could find beyond a reasonable doubt that there had been a murder. Judge Yee had reserved ruling. Usually that was a sign that the judge was considering flushing the case if the jury didn't, but Tommy tended to think it was just Basil Yee being himself, as aloof and cautious as certain house cats.

Now, as Tommy flipped through his yellow pad while he stood at the corner of the prosecution table, Jim Brand, still smelling of this morning's aftershave, scooted his chair over and leaned close.

"You going to ask about the girl?"

Tommy did not have much hope on this point, but he felt Yee was wrong to start. He stepped forward. Yee had been attending to other papers and finally looked down at Molto below the bench.

"Your Honor, may we be heard before I begin?"

The jury, into the third week of trial, knew what that meant and stirred in the box. Out of deference to Stern, who could not stand long at any of the whispered conferences beside the bench, the judge cleared the courtroom for sidebars. The jurors disliked the shuttling in and out, especially since it meant they were being treated like children who mustn't hear what the grownups were talking about.

Once they were gone, Molto took another step closer to the bench.

"Your Honor, since the defendant has chosen to testify, I'd like to be able to ask him about the affair he had the prior year."

Marta shot up at once to object. In a setback Tommy had not anticipated, Judge Yee had granted the defense motion to keep the prosecutors from showing that Rusty had been seeing another woman in the spring of 2007. Marta Stern had argued that even accepting the State's iffy evidence that Sabich had been unfaithful—the hotel sightings and the STD test—the behavior, particularly the chief judge's alleged pattern of pinching off cash from his paychecks to finance the affair, had ceased fifteen months before Barbara's death. In the absence of anything to show he had been seeing this woman when Mrs. Sabich died, the proof was irrelevant.

'Judge, it shows motive,' Tommy had protested.

'How?' asked Yee.

'Because he may have wanted to be with this woman, Your Honor.'

'"May"?' Judge Yee had moved his head from side to side. 'Proving Judge Sabich had affair sometime before—that not proof he a murderer, Mr. Molto. If that proof,' said the judge, 'lot of men are murderers.' The press, in the front row for the pretrial proceedings, had roared as if the quiet country judge were doing stand-up.

Now Marta, with her red ringlets like Shirley Temple and a brocaded jacket, came forward to oppose Tommy's efforts to ask the same questions the judge had disallowed prior to trial.

"Your Honor, that's obviously unacceptably prejudicial. It injects speculation that Judge Sabich had an affair, something which the Court has already recognized is irrelevant to these proceedings. And it's unfair to the defendant, who made his decision to testify based on the Court's prior rulings."

"Judge," said Tommy, "the whole point of your ruling was that there was no evidence whether the defendant was seeing this woman, whoever she is, at the time of the murder. Now that he's up there, aren't we at least entitled to ask about that very point?"

Judge Yee looked to the ceiling and touched his chin.

"Now," he said.

"I'm sorry," said Tommy. In his frugality with words, the judge was frequently Delphic.

"Ask now. Not with jury."

"Now?" said Tommy. Somehow he caught the eye of Rusty, who appeared as startled as Molto.

"You wanna ask," said the judge, "ask."

Tommy, who had expected to get nowhere, found himself briefly word-struck.

"Judge Sabich," he finally said, "did you have an affair in the spring of 2007?"

"No, no, no," said Yee. He shook his head in the schoolmarmish fashion he occasionally employed. The judge was a few pounds overweight, moon-faced, with heavy glasses and thin gray hair plastered over his scalp. Like Rusty, Tommy had been acquainted with Yee for decades. You couldn't say you knew the guy, because he was too accustomed to keeping to himself. He'd grown up in Ware as one of a kind, shunned by almost everybody, not only because he was by downstate standards so foreign in look and speech, but also because he was one of those schooltime brainiacs nobody could have understood, even if he could actually speak English. Why Yee had decided to become a trial lawyer, which was maybe the one job in the world anybody with common sense would have told him to stay away from, was a mystery. He'd had something in his head; people always do. But there was no way the prosecuting attorney's office down in Morgan County could refuse to hire him, a local guy whose law school performance— first in his class at State—outranked that of any applicant for at least twenty years. Against the odds, Yee had done well as a deputy PA, although he was at his best as an appellate lawyer. The PA eventually moved heaven and earth to get him on the bench, where Basil Yee had basically shined. He was known to let his hair down at judicial conferences. He drank a little too much and stayed up all night playing poker, one of those guys who didn't get away from his wife much and made the most of it when he did.

When Yee had been appointed to this case by the supreme court, Brand had been excited. Yee's record in bench trials, where he decided guilt or innocence himself, was astonishingly one-sided in favor of the prosecution, and thus they knew that Stern would be deprived of the option of allowing the judge, rather than a jury, to decide the case. But over the years, Tommy had learned that there were three interests at stake in every trial—those of the prosecution, the defense, and the court. And the judge's agenda frequently had nothing to do with the issues in the case. Yee was chosen for this assignment almost certainly on the basis of statistics, since he was the least-reversed trial judge in the state, a distinction of which he was fiercely proud. But he had not achieved that kind of record by accident. It meant he would take no chances. In the criminal world, solely the defendant had the right to appeal, and thus Judge Yee would rule against Sabich on evidentiary questions only if the precedents were unequivocally in Tommy's favor. Yee remained a prosecutor at heart. If they convicted Rusty, he was going to get life. But until then, Judge Yee was going to cut Sabich every break.

"Better I ask, Mr. Molto." The judge smiled. He was by nature a gentle man. "Will be faster," he said. "Judge Sabich, when your wife die, were you having an affair, romance, whatever"—Yee threw his small hands around to make the point—"any kind of being involved with another woman?"

Rusty had turned about fully in the witness chair to face the judge. "No, sir."

"And back, say, three month—any affair, romance?"

"No, sir."

The judge nodded with his whole upper body and lifted a hand toward Molto to invite further questions.

Tommy had retreated to the prosecution table beside Brand's seat. Jim whispered, "Ask if he hoped to see any woman romantically."

When Tommy did, Yee responded as he had before, with a steady head shake.

"No, no, Mr. Molto, not in America," said the judge. "No prison for what in man's head." Yee looked at Rusty. "Judge," said Yee, "any talk with another woman about romance? Anytime, say, three months before missus die?"

Rusty took no time and said, "No, sir," again.

"Same ruling, Mr. Molto," said the judge.

Tommy shrugged as he glanced back at Brand, who looked as though Yee had put a shiv through him. The whole deal made Tommy wonder a bit about Yee. As square as he appeared with his rayon shirts and out-of-date plastic glasses, he might have wandered. Still waters run deep. You could never tell with sex.

"Bring in jury," Judge Yee told the courtroom deputy.

Ready to start, Tommy felt suddenly at sea.

"How do I address him?" he whispered to Brand. "Stern said to call him 'Rusty.'"

"'Judge,'" Brand whispered tersely. That was right, of course. First names would play right into the vendetta stuff.

Tommy buttoned his coat. As always, it was just a bit too snug across the belly to really fit.

"Judge Sabich," he said.

"Mr. Molto."

From the witness stand, Rusty nonetheless managed a nod and a Mona Lisa smile that somehow reflected the decades of acquaintance. It was a subtle but purposeful gesture, the kind of little thing jurors never missed. Tommy suddenly remembered what he had pushed out of mind for months now. Tommy had come into the PA's office a year or two after Rusty, but they were close enough to being peers that over time they might have competed for the same trials, the same promotions. They never did. Tommy's best friend, Nico Della Guardia, was Rusty's main rival. Tommy didn't rank. It was obvious to all that he lacked Rusty's smarts, his savvy. Everybody had known that, Molto remembered. Including him.

CHAPTER 25

Nat, June 22, 2009

As soon as I hear what Tommy Molto wants to raise with Judge Yee, I move to the defense table and, crouching there, whisper to Stern that I'm taking a time-out. Alert to the proceedings, Sandy nonetheless nods soberly. I hustle to the doors before Molto can get very far.

Within a few hours after Debby Diaz's visit on election day, my dad had found out he was going to be indicted. In the weeks following my mom's death, he'd largely suspended his campaign. Koll followed suit briefly, but put his attack ads on the air in mid-October. My dad responded with his own tough commercials, but the only actual event he participated in was a broadcast debate for the League of Women Voters.

Election night, however, required a party, not for his sake, but for the campaign workers who'd knocked on doors for weeks. I showed up a little before ten p.m., because Ray Horgan had asked me to come down and pose for pictures with my dad. Knowing Ray would be there, I didn't push it when Anna asked me to go alone.

Ray had booked a big corner suite at the Dulcimer, and

when I arrived there were about twenty people watching TV as they hovered around the chafing dishes with the hors d'oeuvres. My dad was nowhere to be seen, and I was eventually directed to a room next door, where I found my father in sober conversation with Ray. They were the only people in the room, and as I would have figured, Ray beat it as soon as he saw me. My dad had his tie dragged down his shirtfront and looked even more vacant and worn out than he had in the weeks since my mom had died. My parents were never easy with each other, but her passing seemed to have depleted him to the core. He was sad in this total way I might not have foreseen.

I hugged him and congratulated him, but I was too nervous about Debby Diaz not to bring her up immediately.

'I did,' he said when I asked if he'd found out what all that had been about. He motioned for me to sit. I grabbed a piece of cheese from the tray that was on the coffee table between us. My father said, 'Tommy Molto plans to indict me for murdering your mother.' He held my eyes while the hard drive spun uselessly inside my brain for quite some time.

'That's crazy, right?'

'It's crazy,' he answered. 'I expect they're going to end up calling you as a witness. Sandy was over there late today. He got a little courtesy preview of their evidence.'

'Me? Why am I a witness?'

'You didn't do anything wrong, Nat, but I'll let Sandy explain. I shouldn't be discussing the evidence with you. But there *are* a few things I want you to hear from me.'

My dad got up to turn off the TV. Then he plunged

back into the overstuffed easy chair he'd been in. He looked the way elderly people do when they're struggling to find the thread, with the uncertainty spreading through their face and adding a tremble near the jaw. I was not any better. I knew the tears would be coming any instant. Somehow, I've always been embarrassed about crying in front of my father, because I know it's something he would never do.

'I'm sure it will be on the news tonight and in the papers tomorrow,' he said. 'They searched the house around six, as soon as the polls closed. Sandy was still at the PA's office. Nice touch,' my father said, and shook his head.

'What are they searching for?'

'I don't know, exactly. I know they took my computer. Which is a problem because there's so much internal material from the court. Sandy has already had several conversations with George Mason.' My dad looked off at the heavy drapes, which were made of some kind of paisley brocade, ugly stuff that was somebody's idea of what looked rich. He tossed his head around a little, because he knew he had wandered off point. 'Nat, when you talk to Sandy about the case, you're going to hear things I know will disappoint you.'

'What kind of things?'

He folded his hands in his lap. I have always loved my father's hands, big and thick, rough in any season.

'Last year I was seeing someone else, Nat.'

The words would not go through at first.

'You mean a woman? You were seeing another woman?' "Seeing someone else" made it sound almost innocuous.

'That's right.' I could tell my dad was trying to be courageous, refusing to look away.

'Did Mom know?'

'I never told her.'

'God, Dad.'

'I'm sorry, Nat. I won't even try to explain.'

'No, don't,' I said. My heart was banging and I was flushed, even while I thought, Why in the fuck am *I* embarrassed? 'Jesus, Dad. Who was it?'

'That really doesn't matter, does it? She's quite a bit younger. I'm sure a shrink would say I was chasing my youth. It was over and done for a long time before your mother died.'

'Anyone I know?'

He rotated his head emphatically.

'Jesus,' I said again. I've never been a quick study. I arrive at my views, whatever they are, only after things have boiled inside me for a long time, and I realized I was going to have to thrash around with this one for quite a while. All I knew for sure was that this was not cool at all, and I wanted to leave. I stood up and said the first thing in my head. 'I mean, Jesus Christ, Dad. Why didn't you buy a fucking sports car?'

His eyes rose to me and then went down. I could tell he was sort of counting to ten. My father and I have always had trouble about his disapproval. He thinks he is stoic and unreadable, but I inevitably see his brow shrink, if only by micrometers, and the way his pupils darken. And the effect on me is always as harsh as a lash. Even now, when I knew I had every right to be angry, I was abashed by what I had just said.

Finally, he spoke quietly.

'Because I guess I didn't want a fucking sports car,' he said.

I had a paper napkin balled in my fist and threw it on the table.

'One more thing, Nat.'

I was too messed up by now to talk.

'I didn't kill your mother. You'll have to wait to understand everything that's going on, but this case is old wine in new bottles. It's just a lot of rancid crap from a compulsive guy who never figured out how to give up.' My father, usually the soul of moderation, looked taken aback by permitting this blunt evaluation of the prosecutor. 'But I'm telling you this. I've never killed anyone. And God knows, not your mother. I didn't kill her, Nat.' His blue eyes had come back up to mine.

I stood over the table wanting nothing more than to get away, so I simply blurted out, 'I know,' before I left.

Marta Stern's head hangs outside the courtroom door. She has a kind of wind-sprung do of reddish curls and long arty earrings with colored glass, and the slightly dried-out look of a formerly fat person who got thin by exercising like mad. Throughout the trial, she's sort of been in charge of me, halfway between guardian angel and chaperone.

"They're ready." As I shuffle in beside her, she grips my arm and whispers, "Yee didn't change his ruling."

I shrug. As with so many other things, I'm not sure if I'm relieved I won't have to sit there pretending not to care while I listen in public to the details of my father's affair, or if instead I would have preferred to do the cross-examination myself. I say what I've felt so often since this whole stupid thing began.

"Let's just get it over with."

I take my seat in the front row at the same time the jurors are returning. Tommy Molto is already standing in front of my dad, a little like a boxer off his stool before the bell sounds. Beside my father, the projection screen the PAs have been using to show the jury computer slides of various documents admitted in evidence has been opened again.

"Proceed, Mr. Molto," Judge Yee says when the sixteen jurors—four alternates—are back in the fancy wooden armchairs in the jury box.

"Judge Sabich," says Molto.

"Mr. Molto." My dad gives this little nod as if he's known for a thousand years the two of them were going to find themselves here.

"Mr. Stern asked you on direct examination if you'd heard the testimony of the prosecution witnesses."

"I recall."

"And I want to ask you some more about the testimony you heard and the way you understood it."

"Certainly," says my dad. As a witness in this case, I can't be one of my dad's lawyers, but I help carry things back to the Sterns' office after court. Now that I've done my thing for the prosecution, I tend to hang around there until Anna is ready to meet me after work. The last three nights, my dad's legal team has practiced his cross-examination in a moot courtroom at Stern & Stern. Ray Horgan has been there to grill my dad, and Stern and Marta and Ray and the jury consultant they've employed, Mina Oberlander, have examined a videotape afterward, giving my dad pointers. For the most part, he's been directed to answer briefly and directly and to try to disagree, when he does, without appearing uncooperative. When it comes to cross-examination, especially of the defendant, apparently it's all about looking as though you have nothing to hide.

"You heard the testimony of John Harnason?"

"I did."

"And is it true, Judge, that in a conversation between just the two of you, you indicated to Mr. Harnason he was going to lose his appeal?"

"That is true," says my dad, with the kind of clipped, unhesitating response he has been practicing. I have known this fact since last November, but my father's confirmation is news in the courtroom and there is a stir, including in the jury box, where I'm sure many members took John Harnason as too weird to be believed. Across the way, Tommy Molto's thin lips are pursed in apparent surprise. With Mel Tooley as a witness in reserve, Molto must have expected to batter my dad when he denied telling Harnason.

"You heard Judge Mason's testimony in the prosecution case that doing that violated several rules of judicial behavior, didn't you?"

"I heard his testimony."

"Do you disagree with him?"

"I do not."

"It was improper, Judge, to engage in a private conversation with a defendant about his case while it was awaiting decision, wasn't it?"

"Surely."

"It violates a rule against what we call ex parte contact, right—without the other party?"

"Correct."

"Someone from my office was entitled to be there. True?"

"Absolutely."

"And as a judge of the court of appeals, were you free to reveal the court's decisions before they had been published?"

"There is not an explicit rule prohibiting that, Mr. Molto, but I would have been disappointed in any other member of the court who had done that, and I consider it a serious mistake in judgment on my part."

Responding to my father's characterization of this breach as 'a mistake in judgment,' Molto makes my dad agree that there are elaborate security procedures in the court of appeals to prevent word of decisions leaking out in advance, and that the law clerks and other employees are warned when they are hired never to reveal a decision beforehand.

"Now how many years, Judge, have you been on the bench?"

"Including the time I sat as a trial judge in the superior court?"

"Exactly."

"More than twenty years."

"And during the entire two decades you have been on the bench, Judge, how many times previously have you disclosed a decision that was not yet public to just one side?"

"I've never done that, Mr. Molto."

"So this was a serious violation not just of the rules, but also of the way you've always done business?"

"It was a terrible mistake in judgment."

"It was more than a mistake in judgment, Judge, wasn't it? It was improper."

"As I said, Mr. Molto, there is no specific rule, but I agree with Judge Mason that it was clearly wrong to tell Mr. Harnason about the outcome. It struck me as a formality at the moment because I knew the case was fully resolved. It didn't dawn on me that Mr. Harnason might flee as a result."

"You knew he was on bail?"

"Of course. I'd granted the motion."

"Exactly the point I was going to make," says Molto. Small, tight, with his bunchy form and timeworn face, Tommy smiles a little as he faces the jury. "You knew he would be in prison the rest of his life once his conviction was affirmed?"

"Naturally."

"But it didn't dawn on you he might run?"

"He hadn't run yet, Mr. Molto."

"But with your court's decision he was really out of chances, wasn't he? In any realistic sense? You believed the state supreme court wouldn't take the case, didn't you? You told Harnason he was at the end of the line, right?"

"That's right."

"And so you're telling us that after being a prosecutor for what—fifteen years?"

"Fifteen years."

"A prosecutor for fifteen years, and a judge for twenty more, it didn't occur to you that this man wanted to know the decision in advance so he could run away?"

"He appeared very upset, Mr. Molto. He told me, as he admitted when he testified, that he was overwhelmed by anxiety."

"He conned you?"

"I think Mr. Harnason said he decided to flee after learning about the outcome. I don't deny I shouldn't have told him, Mr. Molto. And I don't deny that one of many reasons that was wrong was because it ran the risk he would jump bail. But, no, at the time, it didn't occur to me that he would run."

"Because you were thinking of something else?"

"Probably."

"And what you were thinking about, Judge, was poisoning your wife, wasn't it?"

This is the artifice of the courtroom. Molto knows that my dad was probably worried about being nabbed with the girl he was screwing. And can't say that. He must be satisfied with answering, simply, "No."

"Would you say, Judge, you were doing Mr. Harnason a favor?"

"I don't know what I'd call it."

"Well, he was asking for something improper and you obliged him. Right?"

"Right."

"And in return, Judge—in return you asked him what it was like to poison someone, didn't you?"

The time-honored strategy on cross-examination is never to ask a question to which you don't know the answer. As my father has explained to me many times, that is not a rule of unlimited application. More properly put, the rule is never to ask a question to which you do not know the answer—if you care about the response. In this case Molto must feel he cannot really lose. If my father denies asking what it was like to poison someone, Molto will verify Harnason by going over the many other parts of the conversation my dad has already acknowledged.

"There was no 'in return,' Mr. Molto."

"Really? You're telling us that you violated all these rules in order to give Mr. Harnason a piece of information he desperately wanted—and you did that without thinking Mr. Harnason was going to do anything for you?"

"I did it because I felt sorry for Mr. Harnason and guilty about the fact that when you and I were both young prosecutors, I had sent him to the penitentiary for a crime that I now see didn't merit that punishment."

Caught, Tommy stares at my dad. He knows—and so does everybody in the courtroom—that my dad is trying to remind the jury not only about his past relationship with Tommy, but that prosecutors sometimes go too far.

"Now, you heard Mr. Harnason's testimony?"

"We've already agreed to that."

The response, slightly snippy, is the first time my dad has seemed in less than complete control. Stern sits back and looks straight at him, a cue to mind himself.

"And are you telling us he lied when he said that after revealing the decision in his case, you asked him what it was like to poison someone?"

"I do not remember the conversation exactly as Mr.

Harnason did, but I do remember that question being asked."

"Being asked by you?"

"Yes, I asked him that. I wanted—"

"Excuse me, Judge. I didn't ask what you wanted. How many trials have you taken part in or observed as a prosecutor or a trial judge or an appellate court judge?"

On the stand, my dad smiles ruefully about the long march of time.

"God knows. Thousands."

"And after thousands of trials, Judge, you understand that you're supposed to answer the questions I ask you, not the questions you wish I asked?"

"Objection," says Stern.

"Overruled," says Yee. Tommy might be hectoring a regular witness, but this is fair game with a judge on the stand.

"I understand that, Mr. Molto."

"I asked just this: Did you ask Mr. Harnason what it was like to poison someone?"

My father does not pause. He says, "I did," in a labored tone that suggests there is much more to it, but the answer nonetheless sets off one of those little courtroom murmurs I always thought were corny on shows like *Law & Order*, which I watched habitually as a kid, the next best thing to videotapes of my dad at work. Tommy Molto has scored.

In the interval, Brand motions Tommy to the prosecution table. The chief deputy whispers something, and Tommy nods.

"Yes, Mr. Brand just reminded me. To be clear,

Judge, Mr. Harnason had not been recaptured when your wife died, had he?"

"I think that's right."

"He'd been gone more than a year?"

"Yes."

"So when your wife died, Judge, you had no reason for serious concern that Mr. Harnason would be telling the police that you'd asked him what it was like to poison somebody?"

"Frankly, Mr. Molto, I never thought about that part of our conversation. I was much more concerned that I'd unwittingly given Harnason reason to flee." After a second, he adds, "My conversation with Mr. Harnason was more than fifteen months before my wife died, Mr. Molto."

"Before you poisoned her."

"I did not poison her, Mr. Molto."

"Well, let's consider that, Judge. Now, did you read the transcript of Mr. Harnason's trial in deciding his appeal?"

"Of course."

"Would it be fair to say you read the transcript carefully?"

"I hope that I read every trial transcript carefully in deciding an appeal."

"And what Mr. Harnason had done, Judge, was poison his lover with arsenic. Is that right?"

"That was what the State contended."

"And what Mr. Harnason told you he had done?"

"True enough, Mr. Molto. I thought we were talking about what was in the transcript."

Molto nods. "Correction accepted, Judge."

"That was why I asked Mr. Harnason what it was like to poison someone—because he'd admitted he'd done it."

Molto looks up, and Stern too places his pen down. The rest of the conversation between Harnason and my father, which concerned his first trial, is out of bounds under Judge Yee's order. My dad has recovered a little of the ground he lost to Molto before, but I can see that Sandy is worrying that my father will stray too close to the line and open the door to a far more dangerous subject. Molto seems to be considering that, but he chooses to go where he was headed.

"Well, one thing that was certainly in the transcript, Judge, was a very detailed description of which drugs American Medical, the reference laboratory under contract to the Kindle County coroner—the transcript recites which drugs American tests for in the course of a routine toxicology screen on blood samples from an autopsy. Do you recall reading that?"

"I take it for granted I read it, Mr. Molto."

"And it turns out, Judge, that arsenic is a drug that is not included in a routine tox screen. Is that right?"

"I remember that."

"And because of that, Mr. Harnason had nearly gotten away with murder, hadn't he?"

"As I recall, the coroner originally ruled Mr. Millan's death to be by natural causes."

"Which was how the coroner originally classified Mrs. Sabich's death as well. True?"

"Yes."

"Now, Judge, are you familiar with a class of drugs called 'MAO inhibitors'?"

"That was not a term I knew well formerly, but I'm certainly familiar with it now, Mr. Molto."

"And how about a drug called phenelzine. Are you familiar with that?"

"I certainly am."

"And how did you first hear about phenelzine?"

"Phenelzine is a kind of antidepressant that my wife took from time to time. It had been prescribed for her for several years."

"And phenelzine, Judge, is an MAO inhibitor, is it not?"

"I know that now, Mr. Molto."

"You knew it for some time, didn't you, Judge?"

"I really can't say that."

"Well, Judge, you heard the testimony during the prosecution case of Dr. Gorvetich, didn't you?"

"Yes."

"And you recall, I'm sure, that he described doing a forensic examination of your personal computer after it was removed from your house. Do you recall that?"

"I recall his testimony and I recall my home being searched at your order and my computer being seized." My dad does his best not to sound too bitter, but he has made the point purposefully about the intrusion.

"And you recall Dr. Gorvetich testifying that the cache on your Web browser shows that at some point in time, which he isolated as late September 2008, there were searches on your personal computer of two sites that describe phenelzine."

"I remember that testimony."

"And looking at the pages visited, Judge—" Tommy turns to a paralegal at the prosecution table and gives an exhibit number. The blank screen beside my dad fills up, and Tommy uses a laser pointer to highlight as he reads. "'Phenelzine is a monoamine oxidase (MAO) inhibitor.' Do you see that?"

"Of course."

"Do you recall reading that in late September 2008, Judge?"

"I do not, Mr. Molto, but I take your point."

"And page 463 of the Harnason transcript, which was previously introduced into evidence as People's Exhibit 47, which I believe you have just admitted you read—that page states, doesn't it, that MAO inhibitors are not tested for as part of a toxicology screen routinely performed on a postmortem examination of someone who has died unexpectedly?"

"Yes, it says that."

Molto then calls up to the screen Judge Hamlin's opinion for herself and Judge Mason in Harnason's case, which also says that arsenic and many other compounds, including MAO inhibitors, aren't tested for in connection with autopsies.

"And you read Judge Hamlin's opinion?"

"Yes, sir. Several drafts."

"So you know, Judge, that an overdose of phenelzine would not be detected by a routine tox screen, right? Just like the arsenic used to kill Mr. Harnason's lover?"

"Argumentative," says Stern by way of objection.

Judge Yee wags his head, as if it's no big deal, but says, "Sustained."

"Well, let me put it to you like this, Judge Sabich: Didn't you poison your wife with phenelzine, knowing it wasn't going to be detected by a routine toxicology screen and hoping to pass off her death as one by natural causes?"

"No, Mr. Molto, I did not."

Tommy pauses then and strolls a bit. The issue, as they like to say in very old court opinions, has been joined.

"Now, Judge, you heard the testimony of Officer Krilic about removing the contents of your wife's medicine cabinet from your house the day after she died?"

"I remember Officer Krilic asking me if he could do that rather than making a list of the drugs while he was at our house, and I recall giving him permission, Mr. Molto."

"It would have looked pretty suspicious if you'd refused, wouldn't it, Judge?"

"I told him to do whatever he needed to do, Mr. Molto. If I wanted to keep anyone from examining those pill bottles, I'm sure I could have thought of a reason to ask him to write down the names of the drugs while he was there."

At the prosecution table, Jim Brand feigns touching his chin while he rolls his fingers toward Molto. He's telling Molto to move on. My dad has just scored.

"Let's get to the point, Judge. Those are your fingerprints on the bottle of phenelzine from your wife's medicine cabinet, right?" Tommy calls out an exhibit number, and a paralegal from the PA's office puts up a series of slides, with several golden fingerprints displayed against an iridescent blue background. Etched in gold, the prints look like something from the Holy Ark.

"I heard Dr. Dickerman's testimony."

"We all heard him offer his opinion, Judge, that

those are your prints, but now in front of the jury"—
Tommy sweeps his hand toward the sixteen people
behind him—"I'm asking if you admit those in fact are
your fingerprints on your wife's phenelzine?"

"I regularly picked up Barbara's pills at the pharmacy and often put them on the shelves in her medicine cabinet. I have no reason to doubt those are my
prints. I do recall, Mr. Molto, that in the week before
her death, Barbara had been in the garden when I came
home, and her hands were dirty and she asked me to
show her a bottle I'd picked up and then to put it in her
medicine cabinet, but I can't tell you for certain that
was the phenelzine."

Molto stares a second with the barest smirk, enjoying the utter convenience of the explanation.

"So you're saying the prints came from showing
your wife the bottle you'd picked up?"

"I'm telling you that's possible."

"Well, let's look more carefully, Judge." Tommy
returns to the prosecution table and comes back with
the actual vial, now sealed in a glassine envelope.
"Referring to People's Exhibit 1, the phenelzine you
picked up at the pharmacy four days before your wife's
death—you're saying you showed it to her, something
like this, right?" Gripping the small bottle through the
plastic, he extends it toward my father.

"Again, yes, if it was the phenelzine I showed her."

"And I'm holding the bottle between my right
thumb and the side of my index finger, correct?"

"Right."

"And my right thumb, Judge, is pointing down
toward the label on the front of the vial, isn't it?"

"Yes."

"But calling your attention again to People's Exhibit 1A, the slide of the fingerprints Dr. Dickerman developed, three of the four prints, your right thumb, your right index finger, your right middle finger—they're all pointing up toward the label, Judge. Aren't they?"

My dad takes a second to look at the slide. He nods before being reminded by Judge Yee to speak for the record.

"I had to reach in the bag to get the bottle out, Mr. Molto."

"But the prints are on the bottom of the vial, aren't they, Judge?"

"It might have been upside down in the bag, Mr. Molto."

"In fact, Judge, Dr. Dickerman testified that the length and width of all of those impressions would suggest you gripped the bottle tightly so the childproof cap could be opened. Did you hear that testimony?"

"Yes. But I also could have been gripping it tightly to pull it out of the bag."

Molto stares with the inklings of another smile. My dad has handled all of that fairly well, ignoring the fact that my mom's prints appear nowhere on the bottle.

"Well, let's talk about the pharmacy, Judge Sabich. Ten phenelzine tablets were purchased at your pharmacy on September 25, 2008, four days before your wife's death."

"That was the evidence."

"And the signature on the credit card slip, Judge, People's Exhibit 42—that's yours, is it not?" The slide of the slip, which was passed among the jurors in another transparent envelope when it was admitted, pops up next on the screen beside the witness stand. My father does not bother to turn.

"Yes."

"You purchased the phenelzine, didn't you, Judge?"

"I do not remember doing that, Mr. Molto. I can only agree that it is plainly my signature and tell you that I often picked up the prescription when I was coming home, if Barbara asked me to do it. The pharmacy is across the street from the bus I rode to work every day."

Molto checks his exhibit list and whispers instructions for the next slide.

"And referring to People's 1B, a photograph, you heard Officer Krilic testify that the bottle of phenelzine portrayed there is in the same condition as when he removed it."

"Yes."

"And calling your attention to People's 1B, I think you can see that there are only six pills in the container, is that right?"

In the photo, taken looking down into the plastic vial, the six tablets, dead ringers for the burnt-orange ibuprofen I take for occasional headaches, rest on the bottom. It's hard to believe that pills so common-looking could kill anybody.

"Right."

"And do you know where the four missing pills went?"

"If you're asking, Mr. Molto, whether I had anything to do with removing those pills, the answer is no."

"But you heard Dr. Strack's testimony that four pills of phenelzine taken at once would constitute a lethal dose?"

"I heard that."

"Do you have any reason to disagree with that?"

"I understand that if taken at once, four tablets of phenelzine could constitute a lethal dose. But you pointed out that I picked up the prescription on September 25. And a single pill is the recommended daily dose. The twenty-fifth, the twenty-sixth, the twenty-seventh, the twenty-eighth." My father counts it out on the four fingers of his left hand.

"So are you contending, Judge, that your wife took the phenelzine daily prior to her death?"

"I'm not here to contend anything, Mr. Molto. I know that Dr. Strack, your expert, conceded that it's possible that a combination of a single dose of phenelzine taken in combination with certain food or drink could induce a fatal reaction."

"So your wife's death was an accident?"

"Mr. Molto, she was alive when I went to sleep and dead when I awoke. As you know, none of the experts can even tell for sure whether it was phenelzine that killed Barbara. Not one of them can say she didn't die of a hypertensive reaction like her father."

"Well, let's consider the possibility it was an accident, Judge, can we?"

"Whatever you like, Mr. Molto. I'm here to answer your questions." Again there is a little too much acid in my dad's response. Tommy and I—and now the jury—all know the same thing about my father. After twenty years on the bench and a dozen as chief judge, he is not accustomed to answering questions from anybody. The faint whiff of arrogance helps Molto because it implies that beneath it all, my dad may be a law unto himself.

"You mention there is a severe poisoning reaction when phenelzine is consumed with certain foods, right?"

"So I have learned."

"Speaking of what you've learned, did it surprise you, Judge, when Dr. Gorvetich testified, that information about the danger of phenelzine when it's taken along with any one of a number of foods containing tyramine—red wine and aged cheese and herring and dry sausage—did it surprise you to see that that information is freely available on the Internet?"

"I knew, Mr. Molto, that one of the drugs Barbara took from time to time could interact with certain foods. I knew that."

"Exactly my point. And we do know, Judge, don't we, because of Dr. Gorvetich's testimony, that the two websites you visited in late September specify those interactions, don't they?"

Molto nods, and the two pages from the Net, with yellow highlights drawn in on the slides, appear next to my father.

"I can see what's on the pages, Mr. Molto."

"Are you denying you visited those sites in late September last year?"

"I don't know exactly what happened, Mr. Molto. My wife took about twenty different drugs, and some were more dangerous than others. It was not completely unusual for me to check on the Internet after picking up Barbara's medications to remind myself of the properties of one or the other, so I could help her keep track of them. But if your question is whether I visited those websites on my home computer in the days before Barbara died—"

"That's exactly what I'm asking, Judge."

"My best recollection is that I didn't."

"You didn't?" Tommy is surprised. I am, too. My dad has already given a plausible explanation for going to those sites. It seems unnecessary to deny it. Stern has not stopped writing, but I can see from the way his lips have folded, he is not pleased.

"All right," says Tommy. He strolls a little bit, running his hand across the prosecution table, before he faces my dad again. "But we have no dispute, Judge, do we, that the night before your wife died, you in fact went out and purchased red wine, aged cheddar cheese, pickled herring, yogurt, and Genoa salami. Correct?"

"I remember doing that."

"That you do remember," says Tommy, one of those nice courtroom jabs meant to show the inconsistencies in my father's memory.

"I do. My wife had another prescription to pick up and she asked me to buy those items while I was at the store."

"You don't have the shopping list she handed you, Judge, do you?"

"Objection," says Stern, but my dad makes the point for him.

"I didn't say there was a shopping list, Mr. Molto. My wife asked me to buy a bottle of red wine that she liked, aged cheddar, Genoa salami, and multigrain crackers because our son who was coming to dinner enjoys those things, and to get some herring—which she liked—and yogurt to make a dip for the vegetables she already had."

It's true I love cheese and salami and have since I

was four or five. The family legend is that I wouldn't eat much else when I was that age, and I will say that when I'm called again to testify later this week. From the time Debby Diaz first visited, I have had a clear memory of my mom removing the items from the white cellophane bags my dad carried in that night, and of her inspecting each. Although I wonder at times about the desperate suggestibility of my memory, and how much my hope that my dad is innocent is influencing things, I'm nearly as sure I recall my father asking her, 'Is that what you wanted?' I will say that, too, when I get back up on the stand. But what I don't know is whether my mom requested those items or simply told him to get some wine and appetizers, or even whether he'd proposed getting hors d'oeuvres in the first place. Each alternative would be possible, although the truth is that my mom, being my mom, would have been most likely to name exactly what she liked and even told my dad the brands and what aisles they were in.

"Now, Judge. Who managed your wife's drug regimen for her manic-depression? Who selected the drugs on a day-to-day basis?"

"My wife. If she had questions, she called Dr. Vollman."

"Was she a bright woman?"

"Brilliant, in my opinion."

"And did you hear Dr. Vollman's testimony that he warned her repeatedly that when she was taking phenelzine, she had to be very careful about what she ate?"

"Yes, I heard him."

"In fact, Dr. Vollman testified that it would have

been his regular practice to warn you as well. Do you remember him warning you about phenelzine?"

My dad looks at the coffered courtroom ceiling with its crisscrossing decorated walnut beams.

"It's vague, Mr. Molto, but yes, I think I do remember that." This is another fact my dad has no need to admit. I wonder if the jurors will give him credit for his candor, or just take it as a sly device from someone who has spent most of his adult life around courtrooms.

"And so, Judge, you want us to believe that she asked you to get wine and cheese and salami and herring, knowing she was taking phenelzine? And more than that, that she drank the wine and ate the cheese and salami?"

"Excuse me, Mr. Molto, but I don't believe anyone has testified that my wife drank wine or ate cheese. I certainly didn't, because I have no memory of that happening."

"Your son, Judge, testified that your wife drank the wine, sir."

"My son testified that I poured a glass of wine for my wife. I didn't see Barbara drink it. Nat and I went outside then to grill the steaks, so I don't know who ate what."

Tommy stops. This is the first time my dad has really zinged him. My dad is right, too, about all of this. But searching my memory of that night, I seem to recall my mom with a wineglass in her hand, certainly at dinner.

"But let's be clear, Judge. Assume your wife was taking the phenelzine once a day as you've suggested. Does your own testimony make sense to you, sir, that she would send you to the store with a shopping list full of items that could kill her? That she would ask for herring, for instance, or yogurt, which you tell us she intended to eat?"

"You're asking me to guess, Mr. Molto, but I would bet that Barbara knew just how much she could 'cheat' without an adverse reaction. She'd probably started with a sip of wine, or half a piece of herring, and over the years figured out how much she could tolerate. She'd taken this medication from time to time for quite a while."

"Thank you, Judge." Molto's tone is suddenly triumphant as he stands there peering at my dad. "But if your wife didn't drink the wine and she didn't eat the salami and she didn't eat the cheese or the herring or the yogurt, Judge, then there's no chance, is there, that she died accidentally?"

There is just a second dropped before my dad answers. He—and I—realize something significant just occurred.

"Mr. Molto, you're asking me to speculate about things that happened when I was out of the room. It would have been odd for Barbara to eat or drink those things in any quantity. And I don't remember her doing it. But she was very excited about seeing my son and his girlfriend. She thought it was a great match. So I can't say she couldn't have forgotten herself. That's why they call it an accident."

"No, Judge, I'm not asking you to guess. I'm trying to confront you with the logic of your own testimony."

"Objection," says Stern. "Argumentative."

"Overruled," says the judge, who's pretty clearly saying my dad got himself into this mess.

"You told us your wife might have been taking a regular dose of phenelzine and died accidentally, didn't you?"

"I said that was a possibility raised by the testimony."

"You told us that it was your wife's decision to have you get all that stuff to eat that was dangerous to her, despite the fact that she was taking phenelzine. Right?"

"Yes."

"And then you told us that maybe she did that because she was not going to have any of it, or minuscule amounts that she knew wouldn't hurt her. Right?"

"I was speculating, Mr. Molto. It's only one possibility."

"And you told us you didn't see her eat or drink any of it. Right?"

"Not that I remember."

"And, Judge, if your wife didn't eat or drink anything containing tyramine, then she couldn't have died accidentally from a phenelzine reaction. Correct?"

"Objection," says Stern from his seat. "He's asking for an expert opinion from the witness."

Judge Yee looks up to think and sustains the objection. It doesn't matter, though. My dad cornered himself and has taken a pounding as a result. Molto is doing a great job of harping on the little pieces of evidence that have nagged at me all along. The PA lets what he's accomplished sink in as he shuffles through his notes.

"Now, Judge, one reason we are having this discussion about what your wife might have eaten and might have drunk is because the autopsy of the contents of her stomach didn't answer that question. Right?"

"I agree, Mr. Molto. The gastric contents were unrevealing."

"Didn't show if she ate cheese or steak. Right?"

"True."

"But normally, Judge, if an autopsy was performed within the first twenty-four hours after her death, we would have a better idea of what she'd eaten the night before, wouldn't we?"

"I heard the coroner's testimony, Mr. Molto, and without giving anything away, you know that our expert, Dr. Weicker from Los Angeles, disagrees with him, especially about how fast the salami or the herring would have broken down in the gastric fluids."

"But you and I, Judge, and the experts can agree on this much, can't we? The twenty-four hours you sat with your wife's body without notifying anybody of her death—that delay could only make it harder to identify what she ate."

My father waits. From the way his eyes move, you know he is trying to figure a way out.

"It made it harder, yes." This point, too, registers in the jury box. Molto is doing well.

"Now let me go back to what you told us only a moment ago, Judge. You said your wife was excited that night about seeing your son and his girlfriend."

"I did."

"She seemed happy?"

"'Happy' is a relative term, Mr. Molto, when we're talking about Barbara. She seemed very pleased."

"But you told the police, didn't you, Judge, that your wife did not seem clinically depressed at dinner, or in the days before? Is that what you said?"

"I did tell them that."

"And was that true?"

"That was my impression at the time."

"And the phenelzine, Judge—you heard the testimony of Dr. Vollman that she referred to that drug as the A-bomb, to be used for her darkest moods."

"I heard that."

"And after thirty-five-plus years with your wife, Judge, did you think you were good at gauging her moods?"

"Very often her serious depressions were obvious. But I can recall occasions when I had totally misread her state of mind."

"But again, Judge, accepting the fact that the phenelzine was reserved for her darkest days, you saw no sign that night as you four were having dinner that she was in that condition, did you?"

"I didn't."

"Or in the days before?"

"True."

I've already testified to the same thing. Thinking back to that night, I would have called my mom 'up,' frankly. She seemed to be looking forward to things.

"And so, Judge, based on what you observed and reported to the police—based on that, Judge, there was no reason for your wife to be taking a daily dose of phenelzine."

"Again, Mr. Molto, I never thought my estimates of her emotional state were perfect."

"But when you had picked up the phenelzine three days before, did you ask her if she was feeling depressed?"

"I don't remember such a conversation."

"Even though you'd picked up the A-bomb for her?"

"I don't recall taking particular note of what I'd picked up."

"Even though your fingerprints are on the bottle?"

"It was mechanical, Mr. Molto. I brought home the scrips. I put them on the shelf."

"And even though you visited websites and searched for information about the drug in late September, you're saying you didn't notice what you picked up?"

"Objection," says Stern. "Asked and answered. The judge already testified about what he remembers about those searches."

The pause, if nothing else, disturbs Molto's rhythm, which is why Stern has struggled to his feet. But everybody here knows that Tommy Molto is beating the crap out of my father. It doesn't make sense. That's the long and short. My father can have the rest of it his way. Maybe he missed her moods. There were times, especially when my mom was angry, that you didn't know it until the rage broke surface. And since I made those runs to the pharmacy myself when I was living at home, I can side with him about not noticing which of the dozens of medications she took he was picking up. But the Web searches—those are devastating. About the best thing to say, which I'm sure Stern will put out there in closing argument, is that it would be an odd thing for a judge and former prosecutor elaborately planning murder to use his own computer that way. To which Molto will respond in rebuttal with the obvious: He was not planning on getting caught, he was planning on passing this off as a death by natural causes.

But all of this depends on the screwy epistemology of the courtroom, where the million daily details of a life suddenly get elevated to evidence of murder. The truth is that my dad, and just about everybody else, could have noticed the phenelzine, taken a spin through those websites three days before just to remind himself this was in fact the A-bomb, and then just let it go, especially in the kind of marriage my parents had. There were oceans of stuff that went unspoken in my parents' house—the air there always seemed full of things struggling not to be said. And my mom never liked to be questioned about her medications. I heard her say a million times she could take care of herself.

Judge Yee overrules the objection, and my father repeats placidly that he has searched his memory and does not recall visiting those sites. The response rankles Tommy.

"Who else lived in your house, Judge, in late September 2008?"

"It was my wife and I."

"You're saying that your wife researched phenelzine on your computer?"

"It's a possibility if she had some question."

"Did she have her own computer?"

"She did."

"Did she routinely use your computer?"

"Not routinely. And not at length. But my computer was right outside our bedroom, so occasionally, she'd tell me and use it for a second."

I never heard about that happening, but it was possible with my mom. Overall, she probably would have preferred to have a computer strapped to her hip. Molto has proved those courtroom sayings about not gilding the lily. The last series of questions feels like it's helped my dad, and Molto, who is not especially poker-faced, seems to know it, frowning at himself as he strolls around. It's not hard to see why Tommy has been successful as a trial lawyer. He's sincere. Maybe misguided. But he comes across like somebody with nothing up his sleeve.

"To be clear, Judge, do you agree that your wife did not die accidentally?"

Because my dad has instructed Sandy to be frank with me about the evidence, I've known in advance about almost everything I've heard in court. My dad hasn't wanted me taken by surprise. And I've rolled it over, talked to Anna about it when she would listen, even made some notes now and then. But to think about your father killing your mother is even worse than thinking about your parents having sex. A part of your brain is just like, "No way, dude." So I've never seen as clearly how these things cascade backward in time. If my mom didn't die accidentally, then she also probably wasn't taking the phenelzine daily. And if she wasn't taking the phenelzine daily, she had no reason to renew the scrip. It means—or seems to mean—it was my dad who wanted the pills. And there's only one conceivable reason for that.

"Mr. Molto, again, I am not a pathologist or a toxicologist. I have my theories, you have your theories. All I know for sure is that your theory is wrong. I didn't kill her."

"So you still say it could have been an accident?"

"The experts say it could have been."

"So if your wife was possibly taking one pill every day, that would mean, wouldn't it, that she handled that pill bottle on four different occasions, right?"

"That's what it would mean."

"And yet, Judge, your wife left no fingerprints on that bottle, is that correct?"

"That's what Dr. Dickerman said."

"Now, Judge, there was a total of twenty-one pill bottles taken from your wife's medicine cabinet and inventoried by Officer Krilic."

"So he testified."

"And according to Dr. Dickerman, your wife's fingerprints appear on seventeen of those bottles. And on two others, there are smudged prints that cannot be positively identified, although he found points of comparisons on each that match your wife's. All true?"

"I remember the testimony the same way."

"Judge, how many times have you been involved as a prosecutor, a trial judge, and an appellate court judge in cases in which fingerprints were offered in evidence?"

"Certainly hundreds. Probably more."

"And so is it fair to say, sir, that over the course of the years, you have learned a great deal about fingerprints?"

"We can quibble about how much, but yes, I've learned a lot."

"For thirty-five years now you've been called upon in one capacity or another to make judgments about the quality or failings of fingerprint evidence. Right?"

"True enough."

"Could we call you an expert?"

"I'm not an expert like Dr. Dickerman."

"No one is," says Molto.

"Just ask him," says my father. This could come across as a cheap shot but the jurors saw Dickerman up there and several of them laugh out loud. In fact, the laughter grows in the courtroom. Even Judge Yee manages a quick chuckle. Molto too has enjoyed the remark. He shakes a finger at my dad in admiration.

"But you know, Judge, that some persons characteristically leave fingerprints on a receptive surface like these pill bottles, don't you?"

"I know, Mr. Molto, that it basically comes down to how much your hands sweat. Some people sweat more than others. But the amount that somebody sweats varies."

"Well, can you agree that somebody who printed on nineteen—or even seventeen other bottles—can you agree that it would be unusual for that person to handle this bottle of phenelzine four times"—and now Molto again holds up the actual bottle, in the plastic envelope sealed with evidence tape—"and leave no fingerprints?"

"I can't say that for sure, Mr. Molto. And frankly I don't recall hearing Dr. Dickerman say it, either."

On the stand, Dickerman had clearly given Jim Brand, who questioned him, less than Brand hoped for on this point. Back at the office, Stern and my dad had said that happened with Dickerman regularly. He took it as proof of his eminence that he was unpredictable.

"By the way, is Dr. Dickerman a friend of yours?" Molto asks.

"I would say yes. Just as he's a friend of yours. We've both known him for a long time."

Trying to insinuate that Dickerman might have been tilting his testimony toward my dad, Molto has come up on the short end of the exchange.

"Well, let's be clear, Judge. There are only two bottles in your wife's medicine cabinet on which we can say without doubt that her fingerprints don't appear. True?"

"Apparently."

"And one is the bottle of sleepers you picked up the day before she died, isn't it?"

"Yes."

"And that bottle is full, right?"

"Right."

"So leaving the unopened sleeping pills aside, the only bottle in your dead wife's medicine cabinet on which the experts can say definitively that her fingerprints are not present, Judge—the only container is the bottle of phenelzine, correct?"

"There are no identifiable prints of Barbara's on the bottle of phenelzine, and as you point out, on three others."

"Move to strike," says Molto, which means he thinks my dad didn't answer the question.

Judge Yee asks to have the question and answer read back.

"Answer may stand," says Yee, "but, Judge, only one opened bottle where expert can say for sure, no sign of your wife fingerprints. Yes?"

"That's fair enough, Your Honor."

"Okay." Yee nods for Molto to go on.

"But on the bottle of phenelzine—on that bottle the only prints which appear, Judge, are yours? Right?"

"My prints are on that bottle and on seven others, including the sleeping pills that were unopened."

"Move to strike," Molto says again.

"Sustained," Yee says somewhat darkly. He gave my dad a chance not to screw around and he didn't take it.

"So far as we can tell from the fingerprints, you are the only person who handled the phenelzine."

Already chastened by the judge, my dad answers more carefully.

"Considering only the fingerprints, that is true, Mr. Molto."

"Very well," says Tommy. He seems to realize only after he has spoken that he sounded as though he were imitating Stern. One of the jurors, a middle-aged black guy, picks up on that and smiles. He seems to love what Tommy is doing. Molto is back at the prosecution table, paging through his yellow legal pad, a sign that he is again changing subjects.

"Good time for a break?" the judge asks.

Molto nods. The judge knocks his gavel and calls a five-minute time-out. The spectators rise and buzz at once. My dad has been a big deal in Kindle County for decades now, especially in the kind of crowd that wants to come and watch a trial. Call it what you like, blood-lust or lurid curiosity, but many of them are here to see the mighty fall, to reconfirm that power corrupts and that overall, you're better off without it. I'm not sure there is anybody but me left out here in these seats who is still hoping my dad is innocent.

CHAPTER 26

Nat, June 22, 2009

While a witness is on the stand, no one is allowed to talk to him about his testimony, including his lawyers. Stern and Marta nod at my dad from the defense table, and Sandy makes a little fist to tell him to hang in, but neither approaches him. I feel bad about this. It comes too close to the reality of what's been going on to have him shunned by everybody in the room, so I go up just to ask if he needs another glass of water. He answers with another indifferent shrug.

"You okay?" I ask.

"Bloodied but still standing. He's kicking the shit out of me."

I'm not supposed to respond to that, and how could I, anyway? I say the same stupid thing he used to shout to me from the stands when my Little League team was down 12 to nothing in the second inning.

"Long way to go," I say.

"Whatever." He smiles a little. He has become so dourly fatalistic in the last several months, it often frightens me. Whoever my dad was, he will never be the same, even if Zeus hurled a thunderbolt that freed him right now. He won't ever fully plug himself back into life. He places his hand on my shoulder for a second and announces, "I'm going to pee."

Our conversation is largely typical of the recent past. I have not exactly stopped talking to my dad. I just say next to nothing to him of any consequence, even compared with the stilted conversations we had before. I'm sure he's noticed, but it's not as if the law really leaves us any choice. I'm a witness in the case and cannot talk to him about the evidence or the way the trial is going, and at this point, he really doesn't seem to think about anything else, not that I would, either. The silence serves me well. I don't know if my dad is guilty or not. There is a big part of me that will never accept it if he is. But I have known with a rock-hard intuition that my mother's death had some connection to my father's affair. Anna, who does not care for protracted discussions of this topic because she does not like getting between me and my father, asked me more than once what reason I have for thinking that. The short answer is I knew my mom. Anyway, at base I believe my dad really wants to know one thing from me, which is what I think of him and, more to the point, whether I still love him. Sometimes I feel I should hand him a Post-it note that says, "I'll let you know when I figure it out."

Understanding my dad has always been a chore. He seems to like being the man of mystery with me, a routine I've cared for less and less as I've gotten older. I know him, naturally, in the unsparing way kids know their parents, which is sort of the same way somebody knows a hurricane when they're standing at the eye. I know all his aggravating habits—the way he can just drift off in the middle of a conversation, as if what's crossed his mind is far more important than anybody in the room; or how he sits silent when people talk about anything a little bit personal, even if it's like how much their feet itch in wool socks; or the self-important air he's always assumed with me, as if being my father is a responsibility equal to carrying the signals for all of America's nukes. But the trial, the charges, the affair, have all gone to emphasize the fact that I don't really know my father on his own terms.

While I try to piece through that, I teeter between extremes. Sometimes I'm terrified the endless anxiety, which has left my father a kind of burned-out zombie, is going to kill him and that I will lose my second parent within a year. At other instants I'm so righteously honked off, I feel he's getting everything he deserves. But mostly, of course, I'm just angry about the many moments when I'm not sure one foot will go in front of the other, or that the cars going down the street will remain glued to the earth, because so much has changed so suddenly that I don't know what to believe in.

"Just a couple more subjects, Judge," says Molto when they resume.

"Whatever you like, Mr. Molto." My dad does a little better job of sounding like he's okay with that.

"All right, Judge. Now tell me this. Were you happy in your marriage to Mrs. Sabich?"

"It was like many marriages, Mr. Molto. We had our ups and downs."

"And at the time your wife died, Judge, were you up or were you down?"

"We were getting along, Mr. Molto, but I was not especially happy."

"And by getting along, you mean you weren't having marital spats?"

"I wouldn't say none, Mr. Molto, but there certainly hadn't been any big blowups that week."

"But you told us you were unhappy. Any particular reason for that, Judge?"

My dad takes quite a bit of time. I know he is weighing the fact that I am seated thirty feet away.

"It was an accumulation of things, Mr. Molto."

"Such as?"

"Well, one thing, Mr. Molto, was that my wife really hated my campaigning. She felt exposed by it in a way I thought was not entirely realistic."

"She was acting crazy?"

"In a colloquial sense."

"And you were sick of it?"

"I was."

"And was that one of the things that drove you to consult Dana Mann three weeks before your wife died?"

"I suppose."

"Is it true, Judge, you were thinking of ending your marriage?"

"Yes."

"Not for the first time, was it?"

"No."

"You'd seen Mr. Mann in July 2007?"

There is a delicate dance here on both sides. My father's conversations with Mann are shielded under the attorney-client privilege. As long as my dad steers clear of any discussion of what he told Dana, Molto can't ask, since forcing my dad or Stern to assert the privilege in front of the jury would risk a mistrial. But my dad, too, needs to be careful. If he were to lie about what he said to Mann, or even deliberately create a misleading impression on that score, the law might oblige Dana to come to court to correct him. It was pretty clear when Dana testified during the prosecution case that he is basically terrified of Molto and Jim Brand and the whole situation, even though he wasn't up there more than five minutes. He acknowledged a couple meetings with my dad and identified the bills he sent last September and in July the year before, and the cashier's checks my father returned in payment.

"And in fact, Judge, your conversation with Mr. Mann in the summer of 2007—that occurred not too long after you'd asked Mr. Harnason what it was like to poison someone, right?"

"Within a couple of months, give or take."

"And what happened then, Judge? Why did you not carry through on ending your marriage?"

"I was pondering my options, Mr. Molto. I got Mr. Mann's advice and decided not to seek a divorce."

The implication of all the evidence the jury won't hear, the stuff that Sandy and Marta have shown me— the STD tests and the witnesses' statements about my dad lurking around various hotels—is that instead of getting divorced, he recovered his sanity and ended the affair and stayed with my mom. I've never quite gotten around to asking my dad if I have it right. The one conversation we had on that subject is about all I can take. The weird part is that I never believed my parents had a wonderful marriage or that they were especially happy with each other, and I'd thought at least once a year that one of them was going to call it quits. But this—my dad doing some thirty-year-old on the sly in the middle of the afternoon? Sick.

"Now, you saw Mr. Mann again in the first week of September in 2008."

"I did."

"And was poisoning your wife among the options on your mind this time, just as it had been when you spoke to Mr. Harnason around the time of your first visit with Mann?"

I see Marta poke her father's arm, but Stern does not stir. I guess it's obvious the question is ridiculously argumentative and thus not worth an objection. In preparing me emotionally to see my father up there, Marta has explained that as a judge, my dad will look better fending for himself in court, without his lawyer trying too hard to protect him. And that's what my dad does now. He makes a small face and tells Tommy, "Of course not."

"Were you more determined to end your marriage this time when you saw Mr. Mann in September 2008?"

"I don't know, Mr. Molto. I was confused. Barbara and I had been together a long time."

"But you admit you'd already received advice from Mr. Mann in July 2007?"

"Yes."

"And so, Judge, it's a fair conclusion that you went back because you were ready to proceed on the advice and bring the marriage to an end."

Molto is going along as precisely as an ice-skater, avoiding the actual question of what my dad asked Dana.

"I suppose, Mr. Molto, for a brief period, I was more intent on terminating my marriage. I cooled off after that and reassessed."

"It wasn't the fact that you were at the height of your election campaign for the supreme court that made you hesitate, was it?"

"I certainly wouldn't have filed for divorce before November 4."

"Would have looked bad, wouldn't it?"

"I was much more concerned about the fact that I would have made news by filing then, whereas it would have been immaterial to anybody but my family after the election."

"But you concede, Judge, don't you, that some voters wouldn't be pleased to learn you were ending your marriage?"

"I imagine that's true."

"While they could be expected to be sympathetic if you suddenly found yourself a widower?"

My dad doesn't answer. He just shrugs and tosses up a hand.

"Did you tell your wife, Judge, that you were thinking of ending the marriage?"

"I didn't, no."

"Because—?"

"Because I was undecided. Because my mood changed again after I saw Mr. Mann. And because my wife was volatile. She could become very, very angry. There was no value in discussing it before I had made a final decision."

"You didn't look forward to talking about this with her, then, Judge?"

"Not at all. It would have been extremely unpleasant."

"So we can say, Judge, can't we, that the fact that your wife died when she did seemed to save you from confronting her or the voters?"

My dad makes the same face, part wince, part frown, as if this is all too stupid, trying to seem indifferent to the trap he's wandered into.

"You could say that if you wanted to, Mr. Molto."

"All in all, Judge, it was a very convenient time for Mrs. Sabich to die, wasn't it?"

"Objection," Stern says with vigor.

"Enough now," Judge Yee says quietly. "Time for other subject."

"Very well," Tommy says again, more deliberately than last time, and wanders back to his notes. He is preening just a little. Molto knows he is still knocking it out of the park. "Let's talk some more about your computer."

The night my father learned he was going to be indicted—November 4, 2008, a date I'm not likely to forget, the day his legal career was supposed to have reached its absolute zenith—the Kindle County Unified Police Force searched our house in Nearing. The police took both computers out of the house and, clearly looking for traces of phenelzine, seized all of my dad's clothing plus every implement from the kitchen—every plate, every glass, every open bottle or container in the refrigerator or the cabinets—and all my father's tools. Even after that, they weren't done. During the initial search, they had discovered some concrete patching my dad had done a few months before in the basement—my parents were always fighting seepage—and the cops returned and opened up the walls with jackhammers. Then they came back with another warrant and tore up the backyard, because one of the neighbors said he was sure my father had been out there digging around the time my mom died. He had been, too, planting that rhododendron for her the day the four of us had dinner. Furthermore, the prosecutors were not only jerks about ransacking the house, they also refused to release anything they seized, meaning my father basically had no wardrobe, no personal PC, and not so much as a pot to boil water in the kitchen for months.

The computer in particular was a point of warfare, because my dad, who worked a lot at night, regularly downloaded court documents to the home PC. There were dozens and dozens of draft opinions on there, many of them involving appeals in which the Kindle County Prosecuting Attorney's Office was a party, as well as lots of memorandums reflecting the internal workings of the court of appeals, in which the judges sort of dropped their shorts and shared candid thoughts about lawyers, arguments, and occasionally one another. The appellate judges were gonzo when they realized this had come into the prosecutors' hands.

George Mason, who became acting chief, didn't want the court of appeals to be seen as shielding my dad, but he would have had to go to court to calm his colleagues were it not for a twist I couldn't help finding amusing: There was no judge to settle the dispute. Everybody in the superior court had already declined to hear my dad's case, and even when a judge was appointed, there was going to be nowhere for the loser to appeal since the appellate court itself was one of the parties. Eventually Molto agreed with George that the PAs would image the hard drive, making an exact copy, and then examine the drive under the supervision of George or someone he appointed, so that no internal court documents were viewed. They made the same agreement about the computer that had been in my dad's chambers.

After my dad's personal PC was analyzed, the home computer was turned over to Judge Mason, and both computers, from home and court, remained in George's chambers side by side for the month it took before Judge Yee was appointed. During that period, my father was allowed to get what he needed off the hard drives to finish his pending opinions or keep his calendar, but only when George or his delegate could witness this and make an exact log of every keystroke. My dad went over there once and found his return to the realm he used to rule far too humiliating to repeat under these conditions. After that, the prosecutors agreed that any further copying from the PCs could be done by emissaries approved by Judge Mason and the PAs, who turned out to be me or, at Judge Mason's suggestion, Anna, whom he knew and trusted as my dad's former clerk and a minor tech guru. Once Yee was appointed, he sided with the prosecutors and ordered both computers turned over to them. The computer from my dad's chambers had nothing of value on it— just like my mom's. But my dad's PC was kind of a gold mine for the PAs and they haul it up to court each day in the same pink shrink-wrap in which it's remained ever since their expert, Dr. Gorvetich, came to the court of appeals to retrieve it in December.

"Now the day before your wife died, Judge, you shredded several e-mails on your home PC, didn't you?"

"I did not do that, Mr. Molto."

"All right," says Tommy. He nods as if he had expected the denial, and walks a little bit, with the grim air of a parent about to give a spanking. "Your Internet provider is ClearCast, is that right?"

"Yes."

"Now, just so we're all on the same page, when someone sends you an e-mail, it actually goes to ClearCast's server, and you then pull it down to your home PC through your e-mail client. Right?"

"I'm not a computer guy, Mr. Molto, but that sounds about right."

"And going back to Professor Gorvetich's testimony, you set up your account at ClearCast so that e-mails were deleted from the ClearCast server after thirty days, correct?"

"Not to be difficult, Mr. Molto, but it was my wife who dealt with that sort of thing. She was a PhD in math and knew a great, great deal more about computers than I did."

"But we can agree, Judge, that unlike your computer at the court of appeals, you actually downloaded e-mails from the ClearCast server to your e-mail client at home."

"If I understand what you're saying, you mean that when I was at work, I'd go to the ClearCast website to see my personal e-mail, but at home, those e-mails came right to the e-mail program on my PC and were stored there."

"Exactly what I'm saying. And after thirty days, that was the only place those e-mails remained, right?"

"I'd have to take your word for it. But it sounds right."

"Now, did you routinely delete the e-mail on your PC at home?"

"No. Sometimes I'd send documents from the court to my personal account, and I could never really tell what I was going to need, so I tended to just let e-mail accumulate."

"And by the way, Judge. You told us before that your wife sometimes used your PC."

"I said she sometimes used it for brief Web searches because it was right outside our bedroom."

"Mr. Brand reminded me during the break. Wasn't there a lot of confidential information from the court of appeals on your PC?"

"There was. Which was why we had two computers in our house, Mr. Molto. Barbara understood that she wasn't supposed to look at my documents or e-mails. But she didn't have to, if she was doing a quick Web search."

"I see," said Molto. He shows the same smug little smile that's appeared now and then when he's found my dad's explanation too tidy. "Now, you heard Dr. Gorvetich testify that after doing a forensic examination of your PC, he concluded that several messages had been deleted from your personal e-mail, and that based on dates in the registry, that had been done the day before your wife died. Did you hear that?"

"I did."

"And in fact he says they were not simply deleted, but that a shredding software called Evidence Eraser was downloaded and used to accomplish the task, so that there could be no forensic reconstruction of what had been on your computer. Did you hear that?"

"Yes."

"And you deny doing that?"

"I do."

"And who else lived at home with you, Judge?"

"My wife."

"And you said your wife and you had an understanding that she would not go near your e-mail."

"That's true."

"Your testimony doesn't make much sense, Judge, does it?"

"Mr. Molto, none of this makes sense, frankly. You say I carefully shredded the e-mail on my computer so it couldn't be reconstructed, and at the same time, I didn't bother to erase my searches about phenelzine, not to mention carelessly leaving my fingerprints on the pill bottle. So, yes, Mr. Molto, it all sounds ridiculous."

This cannot quite be classified as an outburst, because my dad has reeled all of this off in a fairly patient tone. And he's right. The contradictions in the prosecutors' theories are heartening. It is the first time my dad has really pinned Molto's ears back. Tommy stares at him as he says to Judge Yee, "Move to strike, Your Honor. The defendant will have an opportunity to give a closing argument."

"Read back, please," Yee tells the court reporter. This only makes it worse for the prosecution, since the jury gets to hear my dad's little rant again. And at the end, Yee shakes his head.

"He was answering, Mr. Molto. Better not to ask what makes sense. And Judge—" He addresses my dad with the same patience and courtesy he's shown throughout. "Please no arguments."

"I'm sorry, Your Honor."

Yee shakes his head to dismiss the apology. "Fair answer, bad question. Many good questions, but not that one."

"I agree, Your Honor," says Molto.

"Okay," says the judge, "everybody happy." The line, in the middle of a murder trial, strikes everybody in the courtroom as hysterical, and the judge, who is said to be a card in private, laughs hardest of all. "Okay," he says when the laughter has passed.

"Now, Judge, were there e-mails on your home computer you wouldn't want anyone else to see? That is, before they were deleted?"

"As I said, a lot of confidential court material."

"I meant personal material."

"Some," says my dad.

"What, exactly?"

The first thing that crosses my mind is his messages to the girl he was screwing. They were probably there, too, but there is clearer evidence from another source.

"For one thing, as he testified, Mr. Mann confirmed my appointments with him by e-mail."

"And Judge, were Mr. Mann's e-mails on your home PC when it was seized, to the best of your knowledge?"

"I know the testimony is that they were not."

"In fact, because he could place the time of those

messages, Dr. Gorvetich was able to determine that Evidence Eraser had been used on those messages."

"So he claimed."

"You doubt him?"

"I think our expert will question his conclusion that shredding software was used. Obviously, the message wasn't there."

"And you deny deleting it?"

"I don't recall deleting Mr. Mann's messages, but clearly I would have a reason to do that. I know I didn't download any shredding software or use it at any time on my computer."

"So without the use of Evidence Eraser, an investigator looking through your e-mail might realize you had been thinking of leaving your wife?"

I see now where Tommy is going. He will argue that my dad was employing a kind of belt and suspenders, sanitizing his computer in case the authorities recognized the phenelzine poisoning. But if things got to that point, it seems to me my dad would already have been in a lot of trouble.

"Possibly."

"Possibly," says Molto. He minces along again.

"Now, Judge, on September 29, if I understand what you told the police, you awoke to find your wife beside you dead. Correct?"

"Yes."

"And for the next day, close to twenty-four hours, actually, you called no one. Is that correct?"

"Yes."

"You didn't call paramedics to see if she could be revived?"

"She was cold to the touch, Mr. Molto. She had no pulse."

"You made the medical judgment yourself, and didn't call the paramedics. Right?"

"Yes."

"You did not let your son or any of your wife's relatives or friends know she'd passed, correct?"

"Not then."

"And according to what you told the police, you just sat around for a solid day thinking about your wife and your marriage. Right?"

"I straightened up a little so that she looked better when my son saw her. But yes, for the most part, I just sat there and thought."

"And finally, virtually a day later, you called your son?"

"Yes."

"And as he's testified, when you spoke to Nathaniel"—I quake a little at hearing my name from Molto's mouth—"you argued with him about whether to call the police."

"He didn't call it an argument and neither would I. It hadn't dawned on me that the police should be called, and frankly, at that point I wasn't looking forward to outsiders coming in."

"How many years were you a prosecutor, Judge?"

"Fifteen."

"And you're saying that you didn't realize that the police should be summoned in the case of any suspicious death?"

"It was not suspicious to me, Mr. Molto. She had high blood pressure and heart problems. Her father had died the same way."

"But you did not want to call the police?"

"I was confused, Mr. Molto, about what to do. I hadn't had a wife die lately." There is a snicker from the jury, which is a bit of a surprise. Stern's eyebrows are furrowed. He doesn't want my dad to be a smart guy.

"Now, you say you knew your wife had health problems. But she was in outstanding shape, wasn't she?"

"She was. But she worked out because she knew she was at risk genetically. Her father barely made it into his fifties."

"So not only did you make the medical judgment your wife was dead, without any qualified assistance, but you also decided the cause of death."

"I'm telling you what I was thinking. I'm explaining why I didn't consider calling the police."

"It wasn't, of course, Judge, to delay an autopsy?"

"It wasn't."

"It wasn't to allow the gastric juices to wash away all traces of the foods you'd fed her that would interact with the phenelzine you poured into the wine she drank?"

"It was not."

"And you say, Judge, that you straightened up a bit. Did your straightening up perhaps include washing out the glass in which you'd dissolved the phenelzine the night before?"

"No."

"Whose word do we have besides yours that you did not wash out the glass that contained the traces of the poison you gave your wife?"

"Is your point that it's only my word, Mr. Molto?"

"Whose word do we have, Judge, that you didn't

scrub the counter where'd you crushed the phenelzine, or the tools you used to do it?"

My dad doesn't bother to answer.

"Whose word, Judge, do we have that you didn't spend that twenty-four-hour period doing your best to hide every last little bit that would reveal how you'd poisoned your wife? Who, Judge? Who else's word do we have but yours?"

Tommy has crept close to my dad and stands now only a few feet from the witness stand, attempting to stare my father down.

"I understand, Mr. Molto. Only my word."

"Only yours," says Tommy Molto, and faces my father a bit longer before he goes back to the prosecution table, where he evens his notes before taking his seat.

Chapter 27

Tommy, June 22, 2009

In the umber light of the prosecuting attorney's office, where there seemed to be only two times of day, dusk and darkness, several members of Tommy's staff awaited him, eager to be the first to shake the boss's hand. As the brass elevator doors parted, Jim Brand exited initially, wheeling the trial cart. The open-topped buggy of stainless-steel wire, which looked like an elongated grocery basket, was employed to haul the trial files and Rusty's home computer across the street to court each day. The two women in court with the PAs each day, the detective, Rory Gissling, and their paralegal, Ruta Wisz, trailed a step behind Jim. As soon as they were all buzzed inside the office's steel-reinforced door, a round of applause broke out from a gauntlet of employees, many of whom had been in the courtroom pews to take in the cross-examination. Accepting handshakes and fist knocks, Tommy proceeded behind the cart down the dim hall toward the PA's corner office. It was a little like a scene in one of those old movies about Rome, where the conquerors entered a walled city behind a carriage bearing the remains of the former ruler.

The deputies hooted jokes comparing Rusty to butchered meat.

"He was turning like a chicken on a spit, Boss."

"Welcome to Benihana. Chef Tommy will slice and dice."

Even Judge Yee had caught Tommy's eye for a second when they recessed and nodded in respect. Truth told, Tommy was a bit at sea with all the acclaim. He had recognized long ago that he was the kind of man who did not really feel good when he succeeded. It was another of his embarrassing little secrets, tempered in the last few years by the realization that there were a lot more people like him than you might think. But when things went really well for Tommy Molto, he often felt guilty, convinced deep down he did not fully deserve it. Even Dominga's love was something he sometimes felt he was unworthy of. It was all too typical that even while he knew he was inflicting serious wounds on Sabich, Tommy had felt some worry begin to nag at him.

Yet with all that said, there was no taking away the fact he had been really good up there. He knew better than to give himself too much credit. You could prepare and prepare, but cross-examination was a tightrope act, and sometimes you ended up sure-footed and sometimes you fell on your head, and a lot of it was simply in the stars. Until Rusty tried to score by saying he didn't see Barbara eat the foods that had obviously killed her, Tommy had never completely realized how absurd it was to think she'd died by accident. That had been a great moment for him, and there were a few others—and he'd committed some miscues, too, opened the door too wide a couple of times, which always happened. But on balance, the rationale of the prosecution had seemed like a trumpet blast in the courtroom.

Even the mob of reporters outside the courthouse finally seemed impressed. Tommy had few total fans in the press. He tended to stiffen up in front of cameras, and the relentless personality that served him well in the courtroom didn't go down well with journalists, who hated being treated as the adversaries they often were. And these days, with that crowd, Tommy was playing with one hand behind his back anyway. As soon as Yee was appointed, Stern had filed a sealed motion about the DNA results from the first trial. Ruling in chambers, outside the open public record, Yee not only sequestered the DNA results, as Tommy had long predicted, but required the prosecution to identify anybody aware of them and placed each person under court order not to discuss the test until the verdict. It amounted to the judge announcing there would be contempt proceedings if the test results leaked. In the meantime, the papers—no doubt with Stern's encouragement—spun out the revenge theory every day, going through the first trial in detail, emphasizing the way the case had fallen apart and frequently mentioning that afterward, Tommy had been investigated for a year before returning to work. Tommy, who had long since stopped expecting fairness from the American press, could venture no response, except that the record would be clear by the time the case was over. But after his performance today, especially when the DNA results became public, Tommy knew that no lawyer or journalist would say anything except that Jim Brand and he had brought a case they had to prosecute.

Several deputies continued to accost them as they proceeded down the hall. When they reached Tommy's office, though, he stood in his door like a reluctant host. He allowed only his trial team to join him. He accepted a few more handshakes, then clapped several times to encourage everyone to return to work. The people in this office knew better than to declare victory at the midpoint in a trial, and the fact that so many of them wanted to celebrate the cross actually betrayed their own doubts about the case, the fact that it all sounded better than they might have expected. Many of the most experienced lawyers knew there was still a good chance they would not be in here drinking champagne after the verdict.

"A perfect ten," said Rory Gissling when Tommy returned from a quick call to Dominga. Tommy had gotten just one second on the phone with his wife. Talking and sometimes downright sassy, Tomaso was frequently a trial to his mother these days.

"Y'know," answered Tommy, but added nothing else for quite some time.

The four of them were around Tommy's big desk. Jim and he had dumped their coats and propped their feet up on the public property.

Rory said, "I think Yee should have let you get into the girl."

"Yee isn't going to let us get to the girl," said Tommy. "And I think I've figured out why."

"Because he doesn't want to get reversed," said Brand, employing the steady refrain whenever they talked about Judge Yee.

"It's because he knows we don't need it. You'll have

twelve people in the jury room. Between all of them, they'll have lived, say, at least five hundred years. And what's the first thing anybody says when you hear about a middle-aged guy dumping his college sweetheart?"

Rory laughed. She took the point. "He must have something going on the side."

"That's exactly what half the people in that room are going to say. And frankly, whatever the bunch of them make up is probably a ton better than anything we can prove."

Brand took his feet down and leaned forward. "So what are you worried about?"

Brand was the only person here who knew Tommy well enough to see it. Tommy took a second to search himself, but he still couldn't quite identify the answer.

"Sandy Stern is a counterpuncher," he said. "That's one thing." Stern had always understood that a trial is a war of expectations, where no one could always control the courtroom mood. Sandy knew he could survive the prosecutors having a good day, even a good week, as long as he could come back. In fact, it was clear now why Stern had put his client on first. Because he was going to rebuild Rusty's credibility from here. Tommy even suspected Stern had wanted Rusty to look bad at moments, so the jurors would end up somewhat shamed by their doubts when some of them were allayed. Tommy had long ago stopped trying to match chess moves with Stern in the courtroom. He would never prevail at Sandy's game. He played his own. Straight ahead every day. "You watch," Tommy said. "Stern always lives to fight another day."

"We'll handle it," said Brand.

"We will," said Tommy. "But you know, two weeks from now what the jury's going to remember about today is that they heard Rusty say he didn't do it. And that he didn't look bad. He was calm most of the time. He didn't get real evasive."

"He fought too much," said Rory. Ruta, the paralegal, was watching, but she was sure to add nothing. She was a chunky blonde, twenty-nine years old, about to start law school, and thrilled just to be in the PA's office to hear these conversations.

"He fought a little too much," said Tommy. "But he did a good job. A really good job given everything he has to answer for. But—" Tommy stopped. He suddenly knew what had been bothering him. He had pounded Sabich, but there had been a stubborn center to the man. There was not a minute when he looked as if he had killed anybody. Not that he would. Tommy had never spent a lot of time trying to figure out exactly what was wrong with Rusty, but it was something deep and complex, something Jekyll and Hyde. But he had his act down cold. No shifting eyes. Nothing apologetic. Reason was on the prosecutors' side. But the emotional content in the courtroom had been more complex. True, there was an insanely long list of things Rusty had to pass off as coincidental—Harnason, the fingerprints, picking up the phenelzine, going for the wine and cheese, the Web searches about the drug. But against his will, Tommy had experienced a second or two of intense frustration with the placid way Rusty explained it all. Sabich probably deserved his own chapter in the *DSM* to define his psychopathology, but after thirty years as a prosecutor, there was a lie detector in

Tommy's gut that he trusted better than even the best operator interpreting the box's fluttering styluses. And somebody on that jury, maybe most of them, must have seen the same thing Tommy saw. Even if Rusty was the only person in the room who fully believed it, he had somehow convinced himself he wasn't guilty.

"How did you like him blaming the wife for Googling phenelzine on his computer?" Brand asked. "That's nuts. Like she's taken this drug for twelve years and doesn't know everything about it."

"He had to go there," Rory said.

Tommy agreed. "He had to. Otherwise how can he explain just skipping off to the store and buying everything in the place that had a chance of killing her? You read those sites, you have to say, 'No, no, honey, we're gonna have tortilla chips and guacamole.' At least you would talk to her about it."

"But he blamed her for shredding the e-mail messages, too," said Brand.

Rory was shaking her head. "That was actually the one decent point he made," she said. "Why does he shred the e-mail but not the cached stuff for his Web browser?"

"Because he fucking forgot," said Brand. "Because he was getting ready to kill his wife, and that makes even somebody like him a little nervous and scattered. That's the same crappy argument you hear in every case. 'If I'm such a smart crook, why did I get caught?' I mean, he did. Besides, maybe he ran out of time."

"Before what?" asked Rory.

"Before she hit her expiration date. He's a sick fuck," said Brand. "He obviously decided he's gonna let the mama see her baby one last time before he sends her to the great beyond. I mean, that's a sick fuck's idea of kindness."

Listening to the byplay, Tommy sank a little further into himself. There was something about Brand calling Rusty a 'sick fuck' that troubled him. It was not as if calling Rusty names were unwarranted— what else could you say about a guy who elaborately planned the murder of a second woman after getting away with killing a first? But the truth was that in that entire courtroom, there was nobody who knew Rusty Sabich as roundly as Tommy himself. Not the judge's lawyer—not even Rusty's kid. Tommy had met Rusty thirty-five years ago when Tommy was still a law student and he'd worked on the Matuzek case, the bribery trial of a county commissioner where Rusty was the third trial chair for Ray Horgan. Since then, Tommy had observed the man from every angle—labored in the office next door to him, tried cases beside him, been supervised and bossed by him, watched Rusty as a defendant across the courtroom and then as a judge on the bench. In the early days, especially before Nat was born, they had actually been close. When Tommy was hired, Rusty and Tommy's high school bud Nico Della Guardia often hung on the weekends, and Tommy frequently joined them. They went to Trappers games, got slammed together more than once. The three of them sat around smoking three Cubans Nico had gotten hold of when Rusty came back into the office the day after Nathaniel was born. In time, Tommy had learned to like Rusty less. As Sabich advanced in the office, usually at Nico's expense, he had become aloof and impressed with himself. And after Carolyn's trial, when Tommy had returned here after being investigated for a year, he had seen Rusty's face as nothing but an ill-fitting mask that feigned unconvincing welcome whenever the two men met.

But still. Still. Tommy did not often bother asking himself why or how, in this job. You saw people go wrong: beloved priests who'd helped bring God into the lives of thousands of people, who ended up videotaping their tricks with naked six-year-olds; multizillionaires who owned football teams and shopping centers, and who'd cheat somebody out of fifteen grand because they always had to have an edge; pols elected as long-recognized reformers, who were barely sworn into office before they had their hands out for bribes. Tommy didn't try to understand why some people needed to defy themselves. That was above his pay grade. His duty was to follow the evidence, present it to twelve good people, and move on to the next case. But after three and a half decades, he knew one thing about Rusty Sabich: He was not a sick fuck. Wound tight? And how. Capable of obsessing on a woman like Carolyn so she became the only truth he knew or cared about? That could happen, too. He could have raged and killed her and then covered up. But the one thing Tommy always demanded of himself as he sat in the high-backed leather chair in which the PAs had been putting their butts for the last two decades was honesty. And confronting Rusty in the courtroom had ended up forcing Tommy to face off with questions he'd been pushing aside for close to a year. And this was what had most disturbed him: A crime as calculated as this one, planned for months and executed over the course of a week, didn't seem within the compass of the man Tommy had known so long.

Tommy realized nobody was meaner to him than Tomassino Molto III. He liked to make himself suffer, and he was doing that now. It was his Catholic martyr thing. In a minute, in an hour, he'd have his legs under him again. But there was no further point in battling. It was one of those thoughts you didn't want to have that you had anyway—like thinking about the instant you would die or what life would be like if something happened to Tomaso. Now, while Brand and Rory bantered, Tommy dwelled for a minute on an idea that had not visited him in months. It was against the odds, against the evidence and the course of pure reason, but he asked himself anyway. What if Rusty was innocent?

CHAPTER 28

Nat, June 22, 2009

We return as we have done each night to the fancy-schmancy offices of Stern & Stern. Sandy is one of those up-from-nothing guys who likes to be surrounded by the evidence of his success, and Marta, whose casualness seems like a deliberate contrast to her father, jokes behind his back that it all reminds her of an upscale steakhouse—lots of dark wood and low light through the stained-glass lamps, pleated leather furniture and crystal decanters on the conference room tables. There is also a tony quiet here compared with the atmosphere in most other law offices I've visited, as if Sandy is above routine disturbances. Here the phones blink rather than ring, and the computer keyboards are muted.

But a different silence has prevailed since we packed up to leave court. Stern is rigorous about discussing nothing within earshot of anyone who might be an unsuspected ally of Molto's or a relative of a juror's, and as a result I have learned that when we are in the courthouse, elevator talk is confined to current events, preferably uncontroversial ones, like sports. But tonight we rode down without a word being spoken, not even the usual harmless drivel. Although it's only a few blocks back to the LeSueur Building, Sandy must drive these days, and he asked me to join him and my dad in his Cadillac, because he wants to discuss my testimony for the defense, which is expected to start late in the day tomorrow. Sometimes on the way out of the courthouse, Sandy will make a remark to the immense press horde that awaits the lawyers on both sides each evening, but we struggled through tonight with Sandy limping along, muttering, 'No comment.'

Even in the privacy of the car, we said next to nothing. Everybody plainly wants some time to recharge and to assess how much damage Molto did. My dad looked out the window the whole time, and I could not keep from thinking of some dude on a prison bus, passing by the streets he will no longer stroll.

Upstairs, the usual après-court procedure is reversed. My dad goes off with Marta, while Stern takes me into his large office and closes the door. He orders up a soft drink for each of us from one of his assistants and we sit side by side in a couple of tall maroon leather chairs. Sandy's office has the precious feel of a museum, the walls full of pastel sketches of Stern in court, with many of the exhibits from his most famous trials in little plastic boxes on the tables. I am afraid even to put down my glass until he points out a cork-bottomed coaster.

As it turns out, my meeting with Stern is largely diplomatic. My initial interviews on the case, where I learned about the evidence, were with Sandy, who did his best at the time to point out the bright side, namely that Tommy had made no mention of the death penalty and had also agreed to allow my father to have bail. But usually when I'm in the office, I'm doing what I can to help Marta. As a result, Marta and he have decided it would be better if she presented my testimony. Stern wants to be sure that I have no objections.

"I love Marta," I tell him.

"Yes, you seem simpatico. I'm sure you'll make a good impression on the jurors together." He sips a moment. "So, what was the assessment from the spectators' seats? What did you make of today's proceedings?" Among Stern's many strengths, which I have observed in the last month, is utter fearlessness about feedback. I'm sure he also wants to take a seismic reading on the emotional state in which I'll testify.

"I thought Molto did a very good job."

"As did I." The unproductive cough comes then, as it often does, as punctuation. "Tommy has become a better lawyer with age, with the flame turned down on his jets. But that was as good as I have seen him."

I've wondered why Marta and he decided to put my father on first, and I ask. "Anna says defendants almost always testify last."

"True. But it seemed better here to alter the normal course."

"To screw up Tommy?" That was Anna's guess.

"Admittedly, I was hoping to catch Tommy unaware, but that was not the principal goal." Stern looks off in space for a second, trying to measure how much he can say, given the fact that I will be on the stand again tomorrow. In the light of the table lamp beside us, the rash on the right side of his face seems to have receded just a tad today. "Frankly, Nat, I wanted to make sure we had time to recover if your father's testimony ended up in catastrophe."

There is a lot in that one sentence.

"Does that mean you didn't want him up there?"

In the intervals when Stern used to get time to think with his cigar, he now draws a finger across his lips.

"Generally speaking, a defendant is better off if he testifies. About seventy percent of acquittals, Nat, come in cases in which the defendant takes the stand in his own defense. The jury wants to hear what he has to say about all of this, and that's especially true in a case like this one, where the defendant is a law-trained individual, familiar with the courts and accustomed to speaking in public."

"I hear a 'but' in there."

Sandy smiles. I have the sense both the Sterns really like me. I know they feel for me, which is true of a lot of people these days. Mom dead. Dad on trial. There has been no end to folks telling me I'll remember this period the rest of my life, which offers not the remotest clue how to get through it.

"In a circumstantial case like this one, Nat, where the evidence is so diffuse, you take the risk of allowing the prosecutor to make his closing argument in cross-examination. It's hard for a jury to see how all the pieces fit together, and you'd rather not allow the PAs to demonstrate that twice. It was a very close question, but all in all, I thought your father was better off not testifying. It was certainly not as risky. But your father chose otherwise."

"So are you disappointed now?"

"Hardly. No, no. Tommy was better organized than I

might have hoped, and for the most part he didn't allow himself to become distracted, even when your father goaded him a bit. The chemistry between the two of them is a bit mystical, don't you think? They have been antagonists for decades, but they seem to hold attitudes toward one another that are too complex to be called raw hatred. But all in all, everything that occurred today was within the zone of expectations. Your father was an A minus and Tommy was an A plus, but that's tolerable. If I had known in advance it would have turned out with that kind of marginal loss, I would have been in favor of your father's testimony. The jury heard him say he is innocent. And he looked composed at all times."

"So what were you worried about?"

A phone call comes in then, and Stern struggles to his feet. He speaks only a minute but takes the opportunity once he is done to hang his coat behind the door along the way. It is a jarring sight to see him so slender, half the man I remember. He is using suspenders to support his trousers, and the pants gap on him so much that he looks almost like a circus clown. His knee is virtually paralyzed by the arthritis, and he collapses backward when he resumes the chair. But despite his discomforts, he still has my question in mind.

"There is no end of things that can go wrong when a defendant testifies. One of the possibilities that most concerned me was that Molto would make the very motion to Judge Yee he did at the start of cross-examination." Sandy is referring to Molto's attempt to question my dad in front of the jury about his affair. "I was fairly confident Judge Yee would not change his mind now, but the issue was hardly free from doubt. Many judges would have yielded to the prosecutors' arguments that these events were part of the whole story."

I actually grunt considering the prospect. Stern has told me that it's paramount for the jury to see I'm supporting my dad, but it would have been horrible for me to sit through that. When I say that to Stern, he frowns a bit.

"I don't think your father would have allowed that to occur, Nat. I never pressed the point, but I believe he was determined not to answer any questions about that young woman, whoever she is, even if Judge Yee held him in contempt before the jury or struck his testimony. Either of those events, needless to mention, would have been disastrous."

I struggle with this news, as Stern watches.

"You are unsettled," he says.

"I'm pissed that he'd fuck up his chances to go free to protect that girl. He doesn't owe her that."

"Just so," he responds. "Which is why I suspect it was you more than this young woman he was seeking to spare."

This is the advocate as artist. A trial is sometimes like a great play, where the air of the entire theater fills up with the currents of emotion and each line resounds in the present tense from a hundred different angles. And Stern is like one of those amazing actors who seem to be holding the hand of everybody in the place. His unspoken sympathies are magical, but I'm not really buying it now.

"I still don't understand what he was doing up there if he was ready to throw it all away. Did he think he didn't stand a chance without testifying?"

"Your father never shared his reasoning with me. He heard my advice and made his decision. But it did not seem tactical."

"What was it, then?"

Stern assumes one of his complicated expressions, as if to suggest that language cannot fully capture what he feels.

"Lonely, if I had to choose one word."

Naturally, I'm puzzled.

"I have known your father well for thirty years, and I would call our relationship intimate. But only in a professional sense. He says very little about himself. Always."

"Welcome to the club."

"I mean only to acknowledge that I am relying on my own estimates, rather than anything he has told me. But we have interesting evenings, your father and I. I would say his chances of survival are better than mine." Stern's smile is rueful, and his hand creeps along a few inches for the missing cigar. One of the thoughts my dad and I have shared is that there really is no need to ask about Sandy's prospects of recovery. We'll know there's no hope the first time he lights up. "But I feel myself far more involved in this world than he is."

I nod. "He sometimes seems like he thinks he's out of body and just watching all of this happen to somebody else."

"Just so," answers Stern. "And very much the point. He had very little concern whether his testimony would help or hurt his case. He wanted to tell what actually happened. The piece of it he knew."

My reaction to Stern surprises even me. "He'll never tell anybody everything."

Stern smiles again, wistful, wise. One thing is clear: Sandy Stern is enjoying this conversation. He has obviously spent nearly as many nights as I have up late and preoccupied by my father's many riddles.

"But he wanted to tell you, Nat, as much as he could."

"Me?"

"Oh, I have no doubt he testified almost exclusively so he could enhance your confidence in him."

"I don't lack confidence." This is, at some level, a lie. The logic of my father's case is actually against him, even with me. But it is so contrary to my being to think of my father as a murderer that I can never cross that river of belief. If I had not already spent so many frigging years talking to shrinks, I'd probably be talking to one now, but nobody can really help you answer the kinds of questions I'm dealing with. Even if my father were guilty, it wouldn't mean he gave me an instant's less love and attention. But most of the other lessons in life I've taken from him would come to nothing. It would mean I'd been raised by someone in disguise, that I had loved a costume, not him.

"He thinks you do."

I shrug. "There's some bad stuff."

"Of course," answers Stern. We are quiet together.

"Do you think he's guilty, Mr. Stern?" He has told me repeatedly to call him Sandy, but after a year at the supreme court, where every lawyer was Mr. or Ms. and the bosses all had the same first name—Justice—I can't bring myself to do it. Instead, I watch Stern labor with my question. I know it's neither fair nor proper to put this to a lawyer trying to captain a defense. I expect Sandy to sidestep. But we have gotten far outside the legal chalk lines by now. Sandy is a father talking to a good friend's child.

"In this line of endeavor, one learns never to assume too much. But I was thoroughly convinced that your father was innocent in the first case. The recent DNA results were a terrible shock to me, I admit that, but just so, there are still several compelling hypotheses of his innocence then."

"Such as?"

"Frankly, Nat, the specimen was subject to enormous question in your father's first trial, and there are no better answers today."

Anna has said the same thing to me, that the whole thing was totally sketchy.

"But even if the specimen was genuine," says Stern, "it would prove merely that your father was the lover of the woman who was killed. You will forgive me for being forthright about that, but the evidence at trial was quite clear that your father was not the only man who fell in that category at the time of the murder. A very credible surmise is that someone else saw your father with her that night and killed her in a jealous rage after he left."

Anna had admitted to a fascination like a Trekkie's with my dad's first case, which she's been interested in since she was a kid. She recently went back and read Stern's copy of the transcript, mostly because I couldn't stand to do it myself. After that, she offered exactly the same theory as Stern. The notion has seemed utterly plausible all along, but it's even more persuasive coming from Sandy.

"So now, Nat, while I should be in doubt, my heart

remains on your father's side. Certainly, I have never been impressed with the evidence in this case. The State, so far as I am concerned, cannot even prove beyond a reasonable doubt that your mother died of poisoning. If Judge Yee was unpolluted by the DNA results, I think there is a fair chance he would have granted our motion for acquittal at the end of the prosecution case. Nor do many of the other details add up to what Molto and Brand think."

"Tommy did a good job of weaving it all together."

"But that weaving metaphor is employed frequently in circumstantial cases, and it can fit for both sides. Pull one thread and the whole cloth falls apart. And we shall be tugging at it quite a bit."

"Can I ask how?"

He smiles again, a man who's always enjoyed his secrets.

"More," he says, "after you have testified."

"Will you be able to answer that stuff about his computer? It was pretty damaging."

"It's well you've raised that." He lifts a finger. "Marta will discuss this further with you, but we have been hoping you might help a bit on that score."

"Me?"

"We were thinking about asking you a little about computers. Are you knowledgeable?"

"I'm okay. I'm not like Anna or a lot of other people I know."

"And your father? Is he sophisticated?"

"If you call turning the computer on sophisticated. He's somewhere between a useless dweeb and a total ignoramus."

Stern laughs out loud. "So you don't imagine that he downloaded shredding software and removed e-mail messages?"

I giggle at the notion. Admittedly, I want to believe my dad is innocent. But I know with the kind of preternatural faith I have in things like gravity, he could not have done something like that on his own.

"We have been thinking that we should do some demonstrations with your father's computer, just to show the jurors how unlikely the prosecution's theory is. You might be the right witness for various reasons."

"Whatever," I answer.

Stern looks at his watch, a golden Cartier that seems to reflect all of Stern's elegant precision. Marta is waiting.

At the door, I say, "Thanks for talking, Mr. Stern."

"Sandy," he answers.

Chapter 29

Nat, June 22, 2009

When I leave my meeting with Marta, my dad is waiting for me, the sleeves rolled on his white shirt and his rep tie wrenched down from his collar. He has said he is not sleeping much, and after the long day on the stand he looks totally blasted. The flesh around his eyes seems to have gone pruny, and he's lost a lot of color. It's about the worst emotional combination imaginable, I guess, feeling both hopeless and scared.

"Tough afternoon," I say.

He shrugs. These days, my dad frequently takes on the bleary look of a bag man.

"There will be something tomorrow, Nat," he says. I wait for more, but he is silent and simply frowns. "I can't talk about it yet. I'm sorry." He stands there uselessly, knowing the rules leave him with no more to say or do but somehow unable to accept that fact. I'm sure that's where his brain has been stuck for months, looking for the keystrokes that will undo the entire situation.

"Do you need anything, Dad? Anything from home?"

He takes a second to focus on my question. "I'd really love another tie," he says as if he were asking for an ice cream, something he's been craving at the bottom of his brain. "I've been wearing the same two ties for three weeks now. Would you mind going? Bring me four or five, if you would, Nat. I'd really like the violet one your mom bought me for Christmas the year before last." I remember my mom saying that it would improve his usual low-rent style.

One of the few useful services I have performed for my father, given everything else, is to shuttle back and forth to the house to get personal possessions he needs. About a month before the trial began, my father moved into a residency hotel in Center City for the duration of the proceedings. He didn't want to waste time commuting before and after the long days in court. More to the point, he was sick of the creeps with cameras who jumped out of the bushes every time he went in and out his front door.

The Miramar, where he is staying, is nowhere near any body of water, despite its name, and is one of those places that chose to change its signs and client mix instead of remodeling. The colonial furnishings in the lobby look as if they were there when George Washington spent the night, and the wallpaper in two different corners of his room hangs down like the tongue of a slobbering dog. None of that seems to matter to my father, who returns to the efficiency only to sleep when Stern and he have finished preparing for the next day. Now and then he'll make lame jokes about getting accustomed to smaller spaces.

The truth is that right now he is living only in his

head, and his head is crowded almost exclusively with the details of the case. When he is not in the court-room, he likes doing legal and factual research in Stern's office. It's baffling, since he seems to have no hope about the outcome, but I guess it's his only way to cope. It would be better if there were some friends to distract him, but my dad has found himself remark-ably alone. These kinds of charges, especially for a sec-ond time, don't fetch party invitations, and he is too much of a loner to have ever had much of a social life anyway, especially because my mom was pretty much phobic about leaving home. Even his former colleagues are rarely in touch. He was a fairly remote figure on the court, and his only really good friend there, George Mason, is, like me, a witness who has to keep his dis-tance right now. The idea that riled me months ago, of my dad dating, would probably make some sense right now, even if it was just to have company for dinner or a movie; but he seems totally uninterested in any-thing outside his case and prefers to spend his few free moments by himself.

He does not even seem to enjoy spending time with Anna and me. We've tried a couple of evenings, but it's all been somehow stilted. Despite how much he loved Anna as a clerk, he does not seem comfortable speaking in front of her in this time of distress, and the three of us often descend to silence. Now and then, when Anna is working late or out of town, I'll have a quick dinner with him, which is permissible as long as we steer clear of the case. He reminds me a lot of my law school friend Mike Pepi, whose wife left him for her boss at River National and who talks obsessively about his divorce.

After a half-hour rant about LeeAnn and the lawyers, Pepi will abruptly say, 'Let's discuss something else,' and then go back to the subject immediately, seeming to find a segue in subjects as unlikely as quilting exhibits or the latest astronomical status of Pluto.

My dad's pretty much the same way. He would probably like to dissect every Q&A from court, but since he really can't talk to me about that stuff, he rambles about his own state of mind. Again and again, he has said that this experience is nothing like the first time twenty-plus years ago. Then, he says, he really couldn't believe it and constantly wished his life could be the same as it was before. Now he takes a tectonic shift for granted. He refers offhandedly to going to prison. But even if he is acquitted, the DNA results from the first trial will be released to the press after the jury returns its verdict. Sophisticates may grasp the arguments about specimen contamination or the victim's other lovers, but the nuances won't find their way into the headlines. If my dad walks away again, he will be shirked by virtually everyone who recognizes his name.

Now, outside Marta's office, I hug my dad, something I do every night before I leave, and tell him I'll have the ties for him in the morning. The little blue Prius Anna bought herself last year is at the curb.

"Would you mind a trip to Nearing?" I ask after I've kissed her. "He wants some ties."

Would you want to wear a tie that came from the hand of a woman you killed? Or is my father sinister and subtle enough to foresee that I'd ask myself that very question? It's this kind of cloud chamber, where the questions ricochet in all directions leaving their skinny vapor trails, in which I've lived for months. For the last hour, I've thought a lot about Stern's remark that my father took the stand to enhance my confidence in him. I know my dad is desperate not to lose me. As parents, he and my mom were always so eager for my love that it seemed to pain all of us. But to disconnect from me now, especially, would bring my dad to an end too much like that of his own father, who died alone in one of those tin can trailers out west.

"How did he do?" Anna asks after we have been driving quite some time. She is accustomed to my lengthy silences, especially after court.

"God," I answer, and just worry my head as we stutter through the Center City traffic toward the Nearing Bridge. On the street, some messenger is traveling along on a unicycle and a full-body rabbit's suit, the ears bobbing as he pedals. I guess that's what they mean when they say, All the world's a stage. "Did you read anything?" I ask.

"Frain," she answers. "He's already posted." Michael Frain writes a national column, with oddball observations on culture and events, called "The Survivor's Guide." He is married to a federal judge here, and to keep from traveling, he gravitates toward local stories that can entertain people coast to coast. He's been writing a lot about my father's case and seems to think my dad literally got away with murder.

"Bad?"

"'Like a bombing raid on a small village.'"

"I'm not sure it was that awful. My dad got some licks in here and there. And Sandy has something up his sleeve they didn't want to talk about before I go on the stand again." Nonetheless, the words resound. 'A bombing raid.' I think about what I heard this afternoon. It seemed worse moment by moment, watching him getting pecked at like Prometheus tied to that rock. But after talking to Sandy, it feels as if my dad had a really rough plane ride, on which he somehow landed safely, more scared than injured.

"Do you remember whether my mom drank the wine that night?" I ask Anna as I am rethinking my father's testimony. Long ago, I violated the rules about not discussing the case with Anna. I have to talk to someone, and there is no realistic chance she will get called to the stand herself.

Debby Diaz located Anna two days after the detective had come to see me, but I had warned her, and she knows how to play the game far better than I do. She had Diaz meet her at her office, and one of the senior partners sat in as her lawyer. When Diaz asked about who did what the night before my mom died, Anna said she had been too nervous about showing up as my girlfriend for the first time to remember anything clearly. She kept adding, 'I'm not sure,' and, 'It might have been the other way,' and, 'I really don't recall,' whenever she answered a question. Diaz gave up about halfway through the interview. The prosecutors put Anna's name on their witness list anyway, just like everyone else the cops talked to during their investigation, including my dad's dry cleaner. It's an old trick so they can conceal who they will actually call. As a result, she's obliged to stay out of the courtroom, but always eager to hear what took place.

Now, in reply to my question about the wine, Anna reminds me that when we sat down to dinner, my mother insisted my dad open the nice bottle Anna had brought and that he poured some for each of us. Neither of us, though, seems to recall clearly whether my mom lifted that glass or the one she'd been served in the kitchen.

"What about the appetizers. Did she eat any?"

"God, Nat. I don't know. I mean, the veggies and dip, probably. I remember your father offering her the whole tray, but I sort of thought he finally took it out with you guys while you were cooking. Who knows?" She wriggles up her nose at the uncertainty of all of it. "How are you feeling, anyway, after all of that?"

I flap my hands around uselessly. I'm always amazed how flattened and listless I feel when I leave my dad. Being around him requires everything I've got.

"You know," I say. "I heard it all laid out, and it's not like I can tell myself these guys, Molto and Brand, have just lost the thread, because it makes sense, what they're saying. But I still don't believe it," I tell her.

"You shouldn't." Always my dad's number one fan, Anna has been stalwart in his defense. "It's impossible."

"'Impossible'? Well, it's not like it would violate the rules of the physical world." Anna's green eyes slide my way. I never make points with her when I play philosopher.

"That's not your father."

I weigh that for a second. "I realize you worked for him, but up close and personal, my dad has actually got the cork in pretty tight." Anna and I have moments like this routinely, when I ventilate my doubts and she helps me see around them. "You know, once when I was a kid—I must have been twelve, because we'd moved back from Detroit and my dad was still sitting as a trial judge—me and him were driving somewhere. There was this big-publicity case he was presiding over. The wife of a local minister at one of these megachurches had murdered her husband. It turned out the minister was gay. She had no clue, and then she found out and she killed him by slicing off his you-know-what while he was asleep. He ended up bleeding to death."

"I guess that made the point," says Anna, and laughs a little. Girls always find that kind of thing more amusing than guys.

"Or unmade it," I answer. "Anyway, there was not much for the defense lawyers to do except claim she was insane. They called lots of witnesses to say this was completely unlike her. And I asked my dad what he thought. That was always sweet, because I knew he'd never answer those questions for anybody else, and I said, 'Do you believe she was insane?' and he just looked at me and said, 'Nat, you can never tell what can happen in this life, what people can do.' And don't ask me why, but I knew for sure he was talking about what had happened to him a couple years before."

"He wasn't saying he was a murderer."

"I don't know what he was saying. It was pretty strange. He seemed to be warning me about something."

We are stopped at the foot of the Nearing Bridge, where three lanes go to two and rush-hour traffic stands still every night. Years ago, I had a friend who claimed to know about the theory of relativity and who said that every living thing constantly sheds an image. If we could ever figure out how to get ahead of light, we could wind time back and witness any moment in the past, like viewing a three-dimensional silent movie. I often wonder how much I'd give to do that, to just watch what unfolded in my parents' house in the thirty-six hours after Anna and I left. I try to conjure it now and then, but the only thing that comes to me is the figure of him sitting on that bed.

"Sandy still thinks my dad is innocent," I tell her now.

"That's good. How do you know?"

"I asked him. We were prepping for my testimony and I asked what he thought. Of course, what else do you tell the client's son?"

"You don't tell him that if you don't believe it," she says. "You mush-mouth and avoid the question." Anna has been a practicing lawyer barely over two years, but I accept her authority on these matters as absolute. "It has to mean something to you that the people who know the evidence best still have faith in your father."

I shrug. "Sandy's got the same ideas as you about the DNA in the first case." I know from what I've heard previously that Ray Horgan, who was single at the time, was dating the woman who was killed. He has to be the logical suspect, if it's not my dad, especially when you consider that he turned on my father and testified for Molto back then. But you would think my dad would have realized that. Instead he patched it up with Ray, who's pretty much been my dad's bitch ever since, trying to make it up.

I keep all this to myself, though. It's never good when I mention Ray or what went on between Anna and him. Now and then I consider the fact that my dad was having his own fling during the same period. Along with all the other half-baked crap that floats through my brain, the timing has actually made me wonder once or twice if I missed the boat and it was my father Anna was seeing, until I sort of come to and realize Anna and I wouldn't be together, headed over this bridge or anywhere else, if that was what had happened. Instead, I simply try to fathom what happens to men in middle age. Apparently, their brains give out at the same time as their backs and prostates.

"Thanks for doing this," I tell Anna when we've arrived at the door of my parents' house.

In reply, she gives me a little hug. She has joined me on a number of these visits. Being here tends to creep me out totally—the scene of the alleged crime, where all the truth is somehow buried in the walls. The shades are drawn to hinder the prying cameras, and the air, once we are inside, smells like something was fried a few hours ago.

For Anna and me, the trial has been hard. In fact, everything has been hard in the last nine months, and sometimes I'm a little amazed we're still together. I drift off to never-never land with regularity and go through evenings when I can't or won't talk, and our frequent conversations about my dad and the trial often put us at odds. She is generally quicker to defend him, which means I sometimes end up pissed with her.

Not to mention the routine hindrances of life. Things are still slow at the firm, but she remains in high demand among the partners for what work there is. There are spells when days pass without my seeing her and I know she has been home only because I can see her form pressed into the bed and remember bumping up against her in the middle of the night. But she loves all that and tells me constantly that because of me, she is even clearer that she is doing what she wants. And you can tell. I cherish the moments when I'm going to meet her and catch sight of her before she sees me. She strides down the Center City streets with so much purpose, looking beautiful and brilliant and fully in charge.

I, on the other hand, am totally at sea. I don't know from one day to the next whether I will be working. I still sub now and then at Nearing High, but not while the trial is going, and I have been able to put off a number of decisions about my legal career, since I am a lot richer than I ever thought I'd be, with the bucks my Bernstein grandparents left behind having passed to me after my mom's death.

We mount the stairs and linger outside my parents' room, at the door to the little study where my dad's computer sat before it was captured by Tommy Molto.

"That sounded really bad today," I tell her, nodding inside. As happens frequently, I have been far too elliptical for her to get it, and I have to explain how the browser searches about phenelzine and the deleted e-mails played in the courtroom.

"I thought Hans and Franz are going to testify that maybe there weren't any e-mails deleted," she says.

'Hans and Franz' is our nickname for the two computer experts Stern hired to counter Dr. Gorvetich, the computer science prof who is working for the prosecution. Hans and Franz are Polish guys in their late twenties, one tall, one short, and both with hedgehog hairdos. They speak unbelievably fast and still have pretty strong accents and sometimes remind me of twins who are the only people on earth who can understand each other. They think Dr. Gorvetich, their former professor, is a total tool and take some relish in mocking his conclusions, which is apparently not hard to do. Nonetheless, from their offhand comments I get the feeling that Gorvetich is probably right that shredding software was downloaded to remove certain messages.

Anna shakes her head while I explain.

"I don't really believe any tests that come out of Molto's office," she says. "You know, it was pretty well established that he messed with the evidence in the first trial."

"I can't believe they'd do that."

Anna laughs. "One of the few worthwhile things my mother-in-law ever said to me was, 'Never be surprised when people don't change.'"

In the bedroom, we have some chuckles looking through the ties in my dad's closet. There must be fifty of them, all basically the same, red or blue, with little patterns or stripes. The violet tie he asked for stands out like Rudolph the Red-Nosed Reindeer. I find some tissue paper and a bag downstairs and we fold them on my parents' bed.

"Want to hear something that will weird you out totally?" I ask Anna. One thing about my girlfriend: There is no chance she would say no to a question like that. "When Paloma and I were in high school, we'd sneak home to do it while her folks were working, and for whatever reason, she thought it was a total turn-on to do it in her parents' bed."

Anna smiles a little and wags her head. Apparently it doesn't sound so bad to her.

"Well, it freaks me out now just to think about it," I say, "but you know, you're seventeen, it's like you want to do it everywhere. But of course one day we ended up over here and she had this notion to get it on in this bed. That was too much. I mean, I couldn't perform. It was zero."

"Is that a challenge?" Anna asks, and comes close to me and goes right for it. I feel mini-Me stirring at once, but I pull away.

"You are a freaky, freaky girl," I tell her.

She laughs but comes back toward me. "Should I say I double-dare you?"

My mom's death ended that blissful period when we were fucking all the time and began the blissful period when we are fucking most of the time in spite of everything else. There is a connection and oblivion in sex that has sustained us. In January, we both got the flu and were home from work for three days. We were each pretty wretched, both with high temps and a lot of annoying symptoms, and we slept most of the time, but every few hours, we'd find each other and go at it, the two overheated bodies sticking to each other like plastic wrap and the intensity and pleasure seeming to be part of the fevered delirium. That trance state somehow has never quite ended.

Whatever Anna's off-center desires, making love in the bed where my mother died is more than I can handle, but I pull her down the hall into the room I slept in for twenty-five years. That bed is kind of home field for me as far as sex is concerned, the place where I had my first orgasm, in my own company at the age of thirteen, and where I first got laid—actually with Mike Pepi's older sister, who was nearly twenty—and we have a great time there. I am considering round two when Anna sits up abruptly.

"Jesus, I'm hungry," she says. "Let's go." We agree on sushi. There's a decent place on the way back into town.

We grab the ties and are out the door in a few minutes. Back in the car, I feel the weight of everything settling on me again. That's the problem with sex. No matter how long you make it last, there is still an afterward.

"I wish you could come for my testimony," I tell her. "Stern could ask the prosecutors, right?"

She thinks about it only a second before shaking her head.

"That's not a good idea. If I'm there and you end up talking about what happened that night, somebody's bound to bop over from the prosecution table and ask me what I remember."

From the start, Anna has dreaded saying something that would make things worse for my dad, and the truth is almost anything could do it. Just the little bit that came back to her tonight about my dad pouring the wine at the dinner table or offering my mom the tray of appetizers loaded with tyramine would be greeted by Brand and Molto with an entire brass band. Everybody—Stern, Marta, my father, Anna, and me—has agreed that we're better off if she remains one of those witnesses both sides fear calling, unable to predict who will come off better for it.

"One thing Sandy told me tonight is that he didn't want my dad to testify."

"Really?"

"He was afraid it would help Molto connect the dots in front of the jury. And he thought there was an outside chance that Yee might change his ruling about the affair and let Molto get into it. Which he tried to do."

"You're *kid*ding!"

"I couldn't even sit there and listen to the argument. You know, I'm still like 'Fuck him'—my dad?—every time it comes up."

She takes her time, treading carefully. Generally, we see this subject differently, because, in a few words, he's not her dad.

"It's not my place," she says, "and it's not like I haven't told you this before, but sooner or later you have to get past that."

This is an old discussion by now. It always comes back to my stubborn conviction that the affair had something to do with my mom's death.

"It was just so fucking stupid," I say. "And so fucking selfish. Don't you think?"

"It was," she says. "But here's what I *really* think. The guy I met and fell in love with. That guy?"

"A super-awesome dude," I say.

"Totally," she answers. "Well, that super-awesome dude was a law clerk on the state supreme court. Which just happened to be an office his father was running for. And that super-awesome dude used to show up for work in the supreme court with weed in his pocket. Even though if he got caught, it would have been on page one. Even though he would have lost his job. And his law license for a while. And maybe the election for his father."

"Okay, but I was feeling really fucked up for a while."

"So was your father, probably. So was the girl, for all you know. And I understand your dad disappointed you. But we all do weird, unbelievable stuff once in a while and hurt the people we think we love. If someone does that kind of crap all the time, then you have every right to hate their guts, but we all have our moments. You don't want to hear about all the stupid sexual stuff I've done."

"That's for sure." A couple of Anna's stories have been enough. She spent too much time looking for love in all the wrong places. "There's still a difference between the fucked-up stuff you do when you're young, and the fucked-up stuff you do when you really know better."

"That's pretty convenient, don't you think?"

"I don't know what I think," I answer. I've had enough by now. The lights, twinkling on the Nearing Bridge, blear. I am going to cry. I get to this point every day, when it all overwhelms me and I'd give anything just to be able to hit fast forward and deal with a certain future. "I hate this. I hate this whole fucked-up situation."

"I know, baby."

"I hate it all."

"I know."

"Let's just go home," I say then. "I want to go home."

CHAPTER 30

Tommy, June 23, 2009

Another day in the courtroom. The defense was clearly mobilized. Despite the pasting Rusty took yesterday, he arrived looking well composed, even wearing a new tie, a sporty violet number that seemed to boast that his spirit was undimmed. Sandy was issuing instructions from his chair, as if it were a throne, and Marta and the rest of the Sterns' staff were hustling about.

Marta stopped over at the prosecution table. Age favored some people, and it had clearly done well by her. When Marta Stern started practicing with Sandy, she was like a teapot on the boil, shrill and constantly stirred up. But something about becoming a wife and mom had calmed her. She could still get in your face, but usually with a reason. After the last baby, she dropped about thirty pounds, which she had managed to keep off. Despite being a dead ringer for a not-so-good-looking father, she was actually kind of attractive. And a hell of a lawyer. She was not the same showman as her old man, but she was smart and steady, with a lot of Sandy's instinctive judgment.

"We're going to want to use Rusty's computer," she told Tommy. "Probably this afternoon."

Tommy waved his hand nobly, like it was nothing to him, as if the defense and their shenanigans were annoying, but only in the trivial way of gnats. When she turned away, though, he made a note on his pad, "Computer???" and underscored it several times. Given how devastating the evidence of the deleted messages and the Web searches was, the prosecutors made a point of bringing Rusty's PC to court every day in the pink shrink-wrap in which it had been encased since being recaptured from Judge Mason last December. It sat on the prosecution table all day, right in front of the jury.

Jangling like a passing train, Brand arrived with the trial cart, Rory and Ruta, the paralegal, behind him.

"Who the fuck is she?" Brand whispered when he got to the defense table.

Tommy had no clue what Jim meant.

"There's some dumpy Latina out in the hall. I thought maybe you'd seen her." Brand motioned Rory over and asked her to find out what she could. As Gissling departed, Tommy mentioned the computer.

"They want to turn it on?" Brand asked.

"She said 'use it.'"

"We need to talk to Gorvetich. My impression is turning it on messes everything up."

Tommy shook his head in disagreement, but Brand wasn't happy.

"Boss, it's not supposed to be done that way. Even pushing the on switch makes changes on the hard drive."

"Jimmy, that doesn't matter. It's his computer. And

we put it in issue. Yee would never listen if we told him they should have to do a simulation. If they want to show the jury something on the machine, we can't stop them from making a demonstration with the actual evidence."

"To demonstrate what?"

"I didn't get that memo," said Tommy.

Gissling was back with a card, and the four of them huddled over it. Rosa Belanquez was the customer service manager at the First Kindle branch in Nearing.

"What's she gonna say?" asked Brand.

"She claims she's only here to testify about records," answered Rory. That made no sense to any of them. Almost all of the records from the bank, which Rory dug up last fall, had been excluded from evidence because they related to Rusty's affair. The one exception was the cashier's checks Rusty sent to Prima Dana. Brand looked at Tommy. It was just like Tommy said last night. Stern was up to something.

"How about we try to scare her off?" Brand asked. "Tell her that testifying violates the ninety-day letter."

"Jimmy!" Tommy couldn't dial down the volume quite enough, and across the courtroom, Stern and Marta and Rusty's son all stared. But Brand's idea was dangerous and stupid. The first thing Rosa would do was come ask Stern, who would then go to the judge and accuse the prosecutors of obstruction. With some point. Testifying had nothing to do with the ninety-day letter.

As the trial wore on, Brand had gotten more intense. Victory was in sight, and the fact that they might win a case that seemed like a bad bet to start had revved

Jimmy up in an unhealthy way. It was Tommy's future, Tommy's legacy, that was at stake. But Jimmy was a samurai who regarded Tommy's interests as more important than his own. That part was touching. Yet Brand's greatest weakness as a lawyer was his temper, and it always had been. Tommy waited until Brand, as ever, came back to himself.

"Sorry," he said now, and repeated the word a couple of times. "I just don't know what Stern is up to."

The bailiff yelled out, "All rise," and Yee came charging out the door behind the bench.

Tommy patted Brand's hand. "You're about to find out," he said.

CHAPTER 31

Nat, June 23, 2009

My dad picks out the violet tie and knots it, looking in the men's room mirror, then faces me for approval.

"Perfect," I tell him.

"Thanks again for making the trip." For a second we stare at each other, as unspoken misery floats through his face. "What a fucking mess," he says.

"You see the Traps last night?" I ask.

He moans. "When are they going to get a closer?" That's an eternal question. He considers himself in the mirror another second. "Time to rock and roll," he says.

Ever the formalist in court, my father waits until Judge Yee has asked him to resume the stand before he takes his seat beneath the walnut canopy, so the jurors can watch him do it. Stern and Marta and Mina, the jury consultant, all thought they'd gotten a pretty good group. They wanted black guys from the city and suburban men who'd identify with my father, and nine of the first twelve seats are occupied by males of the two categories. I watch to see if any of them are willing to look at my dad after the beat-down he took yesterday. That is supposed to be an indication of their sympathies, and I'm heartened to notice that two of the African-Americans, who live within a block of each other in the North End, smile and nod at him minutely as he is settling in.

In the meantime, Sandy uses the table and a boost from Marta to get slowly to his feet. The rash today is definitely not quite as red.

"Now, Rusty, yesterday when you were answering Mr. Molto's questions, you pointed out to him a number of times that he was asking you to guess about different things, especially the cause of your wife's death. Do you recall those questions?"

"Objection," Molto says. He doesn't like the summary, but Judge Yee overrules him.

"Rusty, do you know for certain how your wife died?" Stern asks.

"I know I didn't kill her. That's all."

"You have listened to the testimony?"

"Of course."

"You know the coroner first ruled that she died of natural causes."

"I do."

"And you and Mr. Molto discussed the possibility that in her excitement about having your son and his new girlfriend to dinner, your wife accidentally took an overdose of phenelzine."

"I remember."

"And you also talked about the possibility she took a standard dose of phenelzine and died accidentally because of a fatal interaction with something she ate or drank?"

"I recall."

"And Rusty, since Mr. Molto asked, do any of these other theories about the mode of your wife's death—natural causes, or accidental overdose, or drug interaction—do any seem incompatible with the evidence?"

"Not really. They all seem plausible."

"But do you, sir, have a surmise based on the evidence about how your wife died, a theory that, given all the proof, seems most likely to you?"

"Objection," says Molto. "That calls for an opinion the witness is not qualified to offer."

The judge taps a pencil on the bench while he thinks.

"This theory of the defense?" he asks.

"As framed, Your Honor, yes," answers Stern. "Without excluding other possibilities, this is the theory of the defense about how Mrs. Sabich died."

Defendants are granted special latitude in offering hypotheses of their innocence, a way to explain the proof that leaves them blameless.

"Very well," says Yee. "Objection overruled. Proceed."

"Do you recall the question, Rusty?" Stern asks.

"Of course," says my father. He takes a second more to adjust himself in his seat and looks straight at the jury, something he has not done often before. "I believe my wife killed herself by means of a deliberate overdose of phenelzine."

In court, I've noticed, you measure shock value by sound. Sometimes a particular answer produces the swarming buzz of a hive. At other moments, like this one, the consequence of a response is reflected by the absolute silence that follows it. Everyone here must think. But in me, this answer unearths a fear long entombed in the darkest part of my heart. The effect ripples outward, chest to lung to limbs. And I know with a sense of unspeakable relief that it is the absolute truth.

"You surely did not tell the police that," Sandy says.

"I knew a fraction then, Mr. Stern, of what I know now."

"Just so," Stern answers. He is holding on to the corner of the defense table with one hand and pivots a step or two around his grip. "There was no note, Rusty."

"No," he says, "I believe Barbara's hope was to make her death appear to have been from natural causes."

"Just as the coroner first ruled," says Stern.

"Objection," says Molto. Yee sustains the objection, but he smiles in a private way at Sandy's art.

"And why would Mrs. Sabich want to obscure the fact she had taken her own life, in your view?"

"For my son's sake, I believe."

"And by your son, are you referring to this handsome lad in the front row?"

"I am." My father smiles at me for the benefit of the jury. It is not a moment when I feel much like being exposed, and I struggle even to smile back.

"And why would your wife want your son not to know she had died at her own hand?"

"Nat is an only child. I think my son would be the first to say he had a hard time growing up. He's a fine man with a fine life now. But his mother was always very protective of him. I'm sure Barbara would want to limit the anguish and injury to Nat if she ended her life that way."

Stern says nothing but nods slightly, as if it all makes sense to him. As it does to me. It's the kind of unspoken lore that accumulates in a family that my own depression descends from my mother's. Because of that, my mom would not have wanted me to know she'd been unable to tame the savage god. It would have been too bleak a prophecy for me.

"And Rusty, to the best of your knowledge, did your wife have any history of suicide attempts?"

"Because of the depth of Barbara's depressions, Dr. Vollman had always advised me to keep my eyes open. And yes, I was aware of one attempt that had taken place in the late eighties when Barbara and I were separated."

"Move to strike," says Molto. "If it took place while they were separated, Judge Sabich cannot be testifying from personal knowledge."

"Sustained," says Yee.

Stern nods agreeably and says, "Then we shall have to call another witness."

Molto stands again. "Same motion, Your Honor. That was not a question. It was stage directions."

"Was that an objection, Your Honor, or a review?" responds Stern.

Yee, who has a sense of humor, is smiling broadly, revealing his small teeth. "Boys, boys," he says.

"Question withdrawn," says Stern.

During this byplay, my father's eyes have again found mine. I know now why he was apologizing yesterday. The move to Detroit when I was ten did not make my mother any happier, whatever she might have anticipated. As kids always do, I knew something was desperately wrong. I had frequent nightmares and would awaken with the covers in turmoil and a screaming heart and would shout out for my mom. Sometimes, she came. Sometimes I had to get up to find her. She was almost always sitting in her bedroom in the dark, so lost to herself that it took her several seconds to see me standing right in front of her. More and more often, I would simply wake up to check on her. One night I couldn't find her. I went from room to room, screaming her name, until I thought about the bathroom. She was there, in a full tub. It was an amazing moment. I was not accustomed any longer to seeing my mother naked. But that mattered far less than the fact that she had a small lamp in her hand, which had been plugged in across the room with an extension cord.

I want to say I stood there for a minute. I'm sure it was actually far less than that, only seconds, but she waited far too long before turning back to me, and life.

'It's okay,' she said then. 'I was going to read.'

'No it isn't,' I said.

'It's okay,' she said. 'I was going to read, Nat.'

I cried, wild with despair. She stood up in the nude to hug me, but I had the good sense to go straight for the phone to call my father. My mom was diagnosed as bipolar within a few days. The road back to my dad, to our family, to our former life, began then. But that moment, like a specter, was never fully banished from the times my mom and I were together for the rest of her life.

"Did you and your wife ever discuss the fact that she had been suicidal?"

"Objection," says Molto. "Hearsay."

"Did you and your wife ever discuss whether she would commit suicide?"

Across the courtroom, Tommy frowns. But he is finally stuck. For reasons I could never understand in law school, what my mother said about the past is hearsay and what she said about the future is not.

"When we began living together again in the late 1980s, she assured me repeatedly that she would never do that again to Nat—that he would never walk into a room to confront that." I know this is true, because she made the same promise hundreds of times to me.

"Was Nat living at home last year when Barbara died?"

"No."

"And does your wife's promise concerning Nat also inform your belief about why she would prefer to make her suicide appear to be a death by natural causes?"

"It does."

"To the best of your knowledge, Rusty, did Barbara make any attempt at suicide while you were living together?"

"No."

"And so, you had no experience with the outward behavior your wife might exhibit if she were intent on taking her life?"

"I did not."

"But if she had made it apparent that she were bent on such a course, what would you have done?"

"Objection. Speculation," says Molto.

"Would you have attempted to stop her?"

"Of course."

The second question and answer are interjected quickly before Judge Yee can rule on the initial objection.

"Sustained, sustained," says Yee.

"And so if Barbara was intent on killing herself, Rusty, she would have had to hide that fact from your son and you?"

"Judge!" Molto says sharply.

On the stand, my father's head shoots around in Molto's direction and he answers, "Yes?" He draws back at once, flabbergasted by his own mistake. "Oh, my God," he says.

Yee, that merry fellow, is wildly amused, and the entire courtroom chortles along with him. It's comic relief in a grim discussion, and the laughter goes on for a while. At the end, Yee shakes a finger at Stern.

"Enough, Mr. Stern. We all have point."

Stern responds by declining his head, a hobbled effort at a humble bow, before he goes on.

"Was your wife familiar, if you know, with John Harnason's case?"

"We talked about the matter when it was before me and afterwards. She was interested because she'd read about the case in the papers, and also because I'd described the way Mr. Harnason had accosted me after the oral argument. And of course in the weeks before Barbara died, Mr. Harnason was the subject of television ads being aired by my opponent in the election for the state supreme court. My wife complained to me often about the ads, so I know she saw them."

"Did Mrs. Sabich read the Court's decision in the *Harnason* case?"

"Yes. I dissented very rarely. Barbara didn't take great interest in my work, but, as I said, she'd followed the case and she asked me to bring home a copy of the decision."

"And to review what is already in evidence, the decision discusses the fact that certain drugs, including MAO inhibitors, are not covered in a routine toxicology screen?"

"It does."

Stern then turns to other subjects. My dad explains at some length that he and my mom ended their separation in 1988 with an agreement that she would stay on her meds for bipolar disease, and that was why he was so involved in picking up her pills and even putting them away. All this is clearly meant to explain why his prints are on the bottle of phenelzine. Stern then whispers to Marta, who steps across the courtroom to speak to Jim Brand. She returns with an exhibit in its glassine envelope.

"Now, Rusty, Mr. Molto asked you about your visits to Dana Mann. Do you recall that?"

"Of course."

"And was your wife acquainted with Mr. Mann?"

"Yes. Dana and his wife, Paula Kerr, were both law school classmates of mine. We had socialized a lot as couples, especially then."

"And did she know Mr. Mann's specialty in practice?"

"Certainly. Just one example, but five or six years ago, while Dana was president of the Matrimonial Bar Association, he'd asked me to give a speech to the organization. Paula came, and so Barbara had also attended the dinner."

"Now, Mr. Molto asked you on cross-examination about your two visits with Mr. Mann. And I believe you indicated that the second time you saw him, September

4, 2008, you briefly thought you were going to file for divorce. Correct?"

"Yes."

"And Mr. Mann sent you bills for his services."

"At my request. I didn't want him to make a gift of his services, for many reasons."

"You get what you pay for?" Sandy asks.

My father smiles and nods. The judge reminds him to answer aloud, and my dad says yes.

"And calling your attention to People's Exhibit 22, is that the latter invoice he sent you September 2008?" It comes up on the screen at that moment.

"Yes."

"And it's addressed to you at your home address in Nearing, correct?"

"It is."

"Is that how you received that bill—at home?"

"No, what I received was an e-mailed copy. I'd asked that all correspondence be by e-mail to my personal account."

"But you paid that invoice, People's 22, is that right?"

"Yes. I made two ATM withdrawals and bought a cashier's check at the bank."

"What bank was that?"

"First Kindle in Nearing."

"And this is the cashier's check you sent, People's 23, correct?"

"Correct." It comes up on the screen. In the memo section is the invoice number and the words "9/4/08 Consultation."

"And again, Rusty, you sent a cashier's check, rather than a personal check, for what reason?"

"So I didn't have to tell Barbara that I'd seen Dana, or why."

"Very well," says Stern. He shoots just a tiny glance toward Tommy, to let him know that he'd picked up on yesterday's intimations.

"And finally, calling your attention to People's Exhibit 24, which was also admitted during Mr. Mann's testimony. What is that?"

"That's a receipt for my payment."

"And again, it's addressed to your home in Nearing. Is that how you received it?"

"No, I received it by e-mail."

"Now, Rusty, all of these exhibits that you received by e-mail—People's 22, 23, 24, and two confirmations of your appointments—all those records were deleted from your personal computer. Is that right?"

"I heard Dr. Gorvetich's testimony to that effect."

"Did you delete those e-mails?"

"It makes sense, Mr. Stern, that I would have done that, because, as I testified, I did not want Barbara to know about my visits with Dana until I was sure I was going to proceed with a divorce. But my best recollection is that I didn't do that. And I know for certain that I never downloaded any shredding software to my computer."

"And you never discussed with Mrs. Sabich those visits to Mr. Mann or the fact that you were contemplating divorce?"

"No."

Stern leans down to speak to Marta. Finally, he tells the judge, "Nothing further."

Yee nods to Molto, who springs up like a jack-in-the-box.

"Judge, as to your theory that your wife killed herself by taking an overdose of phenelzine. Are there any fingerprints of hers on the bottle of phenelzine that was in her medicine cabinet?"

"No."

"Whose fingerprints are on that vial, Judge?"

"Mine," my father says.

"Only yours, correct?"

"Correct."

"And the websites about phenelzine—they were visited on whose computer in late September 2008?"

"Mine."

"Was your wife's computer also forensically examined?"

"As Dr. Gorvetich testified."

"Any searches about phenelzine on her computer?"

"None that were identified."

"And about this idea that your wife killed herself, Judge. For twenty years, from 1988 to 2008, she made no attempts on her life, right?"

"To the best of my knowledge."

"And in late September 2008, had anything with Mrs. Sabich changed, so far as you know?"

My dad looks hard at Tommy Molto. I don't know exactly what's happened, but this is clearly a moment my father has been waiting for.

"Yes, Mr. Molto," says my father, "there had been a significant change."

Tommy looks as though he's been slapped. He asked a question he thought was safe and walked off a cliff instead. Molto glances at Brand, who below the prosecution table opens his palm and lowers his hand an inch. Sit down, he's telling Tommy. Don't make it worse.

That's what Tommy does. He says, "Nothing further," and Judge Yee tells my father to step down. My dad closes his coat and slowly descends the three stairs from the witness stand. He looks like a proud soldier, shoulders back, head high, eyes forward. However impossible it might have seemed late yesterday, my dad suddenly seems to have won.

CHAPTER 32

Nat, June 23, 2009

J udge Yee tells Sandy to call his next witness, and
Marta springs up and calls Rosa Belanquez, who
proves to be a customer service representative at my
parents' bank.

Mrs. Belanquez is a pretty woman in her thirties, a
little round and nicely put together for her moment in
the big time. There is a small cross at her throat and
a tiny diamond on her ring finger. She is America,
the good America, a woman who probably came here
or whose parents did, who worked hard and for whom
the right things happened, a solid job in the bank,
some success, a little money, enough to help her family, whom she raises the way she was raised, to work
hard, to do the right things, to love God and one
another. She is a real nice lady. You can see it just in
the way she settles herself on the stand and smiles at
Marta.

"Calling your attention to September 23, 2008,
did you have any occasion to have a conversation with
a woman who identified herself to you as Barbara
Sabich?"

I do the math. September 23, 2008, was the Tuesday before my mother died.

"I did."

"And what did Mrs. Sabich say and what did you say?"

Jim Brand, big and solid, wearing a heavy plaid suit in the dead of summer, stands up and objects, "Hearsay."

"Judge," says Marta, "none of this will be for the truth. Only to show knowledge."

Judge Yee nods. Marta is claiming that the defense is not attempting to use my mom's statements to prove that anything she said is actually true, just that she said them.

"One answer at a time," he says. He means he'll rule on the hearsay objection with each answer, an advantage for the defense, who will get to trot all of this out for the jury, even if the judge ultimately decides it shouldn't have been heard.

"First of all," says Marta, "did Mrs. Sabich have anything with her?"

"Mrs. Sabich had a receipt from a lawyer's office."

"Calling your attention to what has been marked and admitted as People's Exhibit 24, do you recognize that document?" The receipt from Dana Mann's office, which was on the screen a few minutes ago at the end of my dad's testimony, reappears there.

"That was the receipt that Mrs. Sabich had."

"And did Mrs. Sabich tell you how she had received it?"

"Objection, hearsay," says Brand.

Marta gives him a simpering frown but withdraws the question.

"All right," she says. "Do you recall how Mrs. Sabich produced the receipt?"

"She had it in an envelope."

"What kind of envelope?"

"Standard commercial window envelope."

"Do you remember if there was a stamp on it?"

"Pitney Bowes, I think."

"Did you see any return address on the envelope?"

"How it was," says Mrs. Belanquez, "was she handed me the envelope and I took out the receipt. It was from the mail. You could see."

Brand stands up to object again. Molto puts his hand on his sleeve, and Brand sits down without a word. Tommy doesn't want it to look as though the prosecutors are hiding something. More than his boss, Brand is inclined to fight even the facts that are obvious. Prima Dana's office fucked up and mailed a receipt to my parents' home for the invoice my dad had paid, and my mom, who ordinarily handled all the bills, opened the envelope and went to the bank, trying to figure out what was going on.

"Now tell us, please, about the conversation you had with Mrs. Sabich."

"There's a cashier's check number on the receipt." Mrs. Belanquez has revolved in the chair and is pointing at the screen beside her. "She wanted to know if that was our number. I said I thought so, but I had to see. I went and looked at the record, and then I told her that I needed to talk to the manager."

Marta takes a plastic envelope off the defense table and goes over to Brand. He studies it and comes to his feet.

"Judge, we haven't seen this."

"Your Honor, that document was produced to the defense by the prosecution last November during initial discovery."

That must be true, because Detective Gissling is motioning to Brand and nodding. Marta whispers to Brand, he throws out a hand, and the paper is received in evidence, and a slide of it is lit up on the screen for the jury by Sandy's paralegal. It's the requisition for a cashier's check. I saw the document last fall. It really didn't count for much compared with the check to the outfit that tested for STDs.

"Calling your attention to Defendant's Exhibit 1, what is that?"

"It's the record I looked at. The backup on our bank check."

"Now, you say you had a discussion with your manager."

"Yes."

"And after you spoke to the manager, did you speak further to Mrs. Sabich?"

"Yes, sure."

"And what did you tell her?"

"I told her—" Mrs. Belanquez smiles and licks her lips and apologizes for being nervous. "I told her what the manager said."

"Which was what?"

Brand objects that this is hearsay.

"I'll hear it," says Judge Yee.

"Well, see. The judge bought the bank check with cash he had in hand and a three-hundred-dollar ATM withdrawal that he made right there. I mean, you could tell from the time of the ATM record. So it was basically a withdrawal from the account. And we didn't charge him to issue the cashier's check because he was an account holder. So the question was, well, Is this an account record, and what can she see and what can't she see, because she, Mrs. Sabich, was on that account, too. And the manager just said, Well, if we gave him a free cashier's check because he had an account, and she's on the account, then it's an account record and show her whatever she wants to see.

"So I told her that. And I showed her the purchase invoice for the bank check and the actual check."

"And calling your attention to People's Exhibit 23, is that the bank check you showed Mrs. Sabich?"

Made payable to "Mann and Rapini," the check reads in the memo section, "Payment—Invoice 645332."

Mrs. Belanquez says, "Yes," and Marta says she has nothing further. The courtroom is silent. Everyone knows something just happened, something huge. My dad said my mom committed suicide, and now there's a reason why. Because she knew he'd been to see Dana the divorce lawyer, that he was getting ready to leave her.

Across the courtroom, Jim Brand is not happy. Prosecutors rarely are when the defense turns out to know something they don't. He sits in his chair with his legs splayed and actually tosses his pen in the air and catches it before he gets out of his seat with the air of a cowpoke about to get after unruly livestock.

"So was that the full extent of your conversation with Mrs. Sabich?" he asks.

"No, hardly."

"Well, tell us what else happened," says Brand, as if that's the most natural question in the world, as if he just can't understand why Marta wouldn't ask herself. The art of the courtroom continues to impress me, the theatrical improvisations and the backhanded ways of communicating with the jury.

In response, Marta in her printed silk jacket comes to her feet but says nothing as Mrs. Belanquez answers.

"Well, after she saw the cashier's check, she wanted to know if there were others and how they got paid for, and whatnot. And so we got to going back and forth with other checks and statements and withdrawal slips and deposit slips. Lots of transactions. We were there most of the day."

"Judge," says Marta, "I think we're pretty far beyond the scope of the direct. We're now talking about documents Your Honor has ruled several times have nothing to do with this case."

"Anything else, Mr. Brand?" Judge Yee asks.

"Guess not," says Brand. But he's regained a little ground, let the jury know that something else was going on. Mrs. Belanquez is excused and clacks out of the courtroom in her tall high heels, casting a small smile at Marta, whom she must like. Her heavy perfume lingers behind her as she passes me on the front pew.

I'm not sure any of the spectators besides me, including the jurors, have absorbed the full impact of Mrs. Belanquez's testimony. But I have that feeling again that my heart is pumping hot lead. I'm not supposed to be surprised. I have said all along my mom knew. And yet it is unbearable, particularly as I add in the contents of those documents the jury will never really know about. I see it all—Mrs. Belanquez's desk in the bank, with the usual phony colonial furnishings, and customers and employees streaming by on every side, and there is my mom, who sometimes needed half a Xanax before she went out in public, who despised feeling observed or exposed. And now she is sitting in front of nice Mrs. Belanquez as she pieces together what was going on, first that my dad has been to see Dana Mann, a divorce lawyer, for professional advice, only a few weeks earlier, and then fifteen months before, he had been cleverly bootlegging money from his paycheck and spending it on things like a payment to a clinic to test for sexually transmitted diseases. She knows right then he's been unfaithful, that he's lied to her nonstop in half a dozen ways, including, worst of all, about whether he is going to continue to be her husband, and she has to take in all of that with a stone face and a breaking heart as she sits across from Mrs. Belanquez, knowing Rosa Belanquez can see the wedding ring on her finger and, therefore, the magnitude of her humiliation.

By now, I am in the corridor outside the courtroom, crying. It's all clear now, that she returned home that Tuesday and sooner or later went through my dad's e-mail and learned whatever else there was to discover about who he had been fucking the year before. Did they fight that week before she died? Did they scream and shout and knock over the furniture and just put on a good face the night Anna and I arrived? Or did my mom take all that with her? It had to be the latter way, I think. She'd known for close to a week by the time we came to dinner and obviously had kept it to herself. She'd been smiling and scheming, considering her alternatives and, I am sure now, planning her death. My dad had picked up the phenelzine for her two days after my mom had been to the bank.

Marta Stern has come out in the hall to find me. She's not within six inches of my height as she reaches up to my shoulder. She's wearing a heavy necklace of hammered gold I haven't noticed before.

"It was so wrong," I tell Marta. I doubt she knows exactly what I mean, because until I speak I'm not sure I know myself. My dad didn't kill my mother in the meaning of the law. But it doesn't change what happened. He deserves to walk out of the courtroom, but when he does, somewhere in my heart, he will always be to blame.

CHAPTER 33

Tommy, June 23, 2009

Marta wanted a recess to set up Rusty's computer for the next witness, and Yee did not look pleased. In the last couple of days, it had become clear that the judge's patience was wearing out. He was living out of a suitcase several hundred miles from home and was still trying to manage his docket of pending cases back in Ware by phone. It would take him months to clear up the backlog once he returned. Rather than consume an hour to remove the shrink-wrap and seals now, Yee instructed the lawyers to have the computer ready in the morning. He would send the jury home and spend the balance of the day on the phone with his chambers, trying to deal with two emergency motions downstate.

That was just as well. Tommy and his team needed a break. Brand and Marta reached an agreement that the PA's techs would remove the shrink-wrap, and the experts from both sides would cut off the last of the evidence tape and set up the machine before court tomorrow morning. With that, the prosecution team and their trial cart rattled back across the street to the office. Once they were by themselves in the elevator in the County Building, Rory Gissling started apologizing.

"I should have fucking known," she said.

"Bullshit," Tommy told her.

"I should have smelled it out," said Rory, "asked around. When the bank got all those documents together in a nanosecond, I should have guessed they'd already done it for somebody else."

"You're a detective," said Tommy, "not a mind reader."

It wasn't bad in and of itself, what the Sterns had proved, the fact that Barbara had known her husband was planning to leave her—not to mention screwing around, which the jury was never going to hear squat about. It was all so-what, really. So she knew. That opened the door to a million possibilities that worked for the prosecution. Rusty and Barbara fought like minks, and he ended up cooling her. She threatened to go to the kid. Or the *Trib*. God knows what. It was a trial; they'd find a theory to fit the facts if they noodled for a day or two.

But the defense had proved something far more consequential: The prosecution didn't know everything. Those nice men across the room were ignorant about a major piece of evidence in a circumstantial case. It was as if the PAs had drawn a map of the world and missed most of North America. The prosecutors said Rusty killed Barbara, and the defense came back and said, See, these guys don't have the entire picture. Barbara got some sad news, and that's why she quietly ended her life.

The four of them, Brand and Tommy and Rory and Ruta, sat in Tommy's office with the door closed. Tommy looked through the message slips on his desk, just to pretend he wasn't that upset, but all he really wanted to do was think about the case and try to figure out how bad the damage was.

Brand went out to get a pop and came back.

"How can soda from that fucking machine be eighty-five cents?" he asked. "Can't we talk to Central Services? Jody gets it at Safeway for twenty cents a can. People in business, really. They're just fucking thieves."

Tommy reached in his pocket and handed Brand a quarter. "Tell Jody I want a Diet Coke, extra ice, and keep the change."

"He makes that call, Tommy," said Rory, "and you'll finish trying this case yourself."

Jody had been a deputy PA when Brand met her and had her picture in the dictionary next to the phrase "Tough cookie."

"I can't get Central Services to paint the walls or fix the heat," Tommy said when the four of them had passed through the momentary laugh.

The group reverted to silence.

"So Harnason is a coincidence?" Brand finally asked. He was trying to figure out what Sandy was going to argue to the jury in closing.

"They covered that," said Rory. "Barbara knew about that case."

"Right," said Tommy. "They covered that. Harnason's case is what gave her the idea she could kill herself with a drug that would look like natural causes and wouldn't show up on a tox screen. So she could slip off to the great beyond without shaking up the kid even worse. That's what he's going to be saying up there, Nat? How protective his mom was. He's going to back up this whole story."

It was bad, Tommy was realizing. The suicide thing was going to take Rusty out.

"What are his fingerprints doing on the phenelzine?" asked Brand.

"Well, now he's got one bad fact to explain instead of six. Everything else fits. They're going to have her on his computer. You know that, right? That's what they want to set it up for. They're going to show she could have gotten into his e-mail. You're basically going to ask this jury for a guilty when our own expert admits she could have handled the bottle without leaving prints, and Rusty was always picking up her meds."

Brand sat there looking at the wall. Tommy had never quite finished furnishing in here. He was the acting PA, and it seemed presumptuous to fill the walls with his own plaques and pictures. He had hung up a few nice shots of Dominga and Tomaso and an old photo of his mom and dad with him at law school graduation. But there were several chalky spots where hunks of paint and plaster had been pulled off when Muriel Wynn vacated four years ago that Central Services, despite regular calls, had never come around to fix. Brand seemed to be focusing on one of them.

"We're not going to lose this fucking case," he said suddenly.

"It was rough sledding from the start," Tommy told him.

"It's gone in beautifully. We are *not* going to lose."

"Come on, Jimmy. Let's take a night off. Think it over."

"There's a flaw," said Brand, referring to the new theory of defense.

"Probably more than one, if you really want to know," the PA answered.

"Why does she wipe his computer?" Brand asked. "Okay, she reads what's on there. But why ax the messages?"

"Right," said Tommy. They would think of a lot of questions like that over the next day. They needed time to adjust. And, being honest, to catch up. Because Sandy and Marta had been thinking of those questions and making up answers for months now. Wanting to feel better, Jim pressed now.

"If she's planning to kill herself quietly," said Brand, "no note, et cetera, why does she leave tracks behind by deleting his e-mails?"

It was Rory who first realized what the defense was going to say.

"So Rusty will know," she said. "The messages he'd kept, he'd kept for a reason. Maybe he liked to reread his love notes from his little girlfriend. But whatever it was, when he goes back, he'll see that all of those messages are gone. He'll know that Barbara shredded them one by one. And that's how he'll know the missus found out about everything and snuffed herself. That's maybe why she searched around about phenelzine on his computer, so he'll realize just how she did it. But he'll be the only one. The kid, the rest of the world, they'll think she died of her bumpy heartbeat. But Rusty will rot with guilt."

Brand was staring, just staring, at Rory, his mouth parted slightly in that oh-fuck-me way.

"Shit," he said then, and threw his empty soda can at the wall. He was not the first ever to do that. There was a triangle of damaged plaster Tommy and his deputies had been creating for years now when they acted out, mashing fists and paper balls there and tossing objects. But Brand's aim was better. The can hit right in the center and dropped into the trash can positioned below to catch what was flung from time to time.

They all watched in silence. In the morning, Tommy told himself, he would take a look to see if there was something else down there in the garbage can. What he would be looking for was their case.

CHAPTER 34

Nat, June 24, 2009

It is seven thirty a.m., and the streets of Center City are beginning to fill with the morning's pedestrians and drivers, urgent to get on to the business of the day. Anna brings the silent Prius to the curb and drops me in front of the LeSueur Building.

"I hope it goes well." She reaches out to take my hand. "Text me as soon as you're done." I lean over to receive a quick embrace and then depart. I have not yet managed to give up the student look and mash my nice suit under the straps of my rucksack, swinging it on before I head inside.

It was a bad night. Anna was mortified to hear about the banker's testimony and seemed to take it every bit as hard as I did. She kept saying how sorry she was, which ended up irritating me because it felt like she was expecting me to comfort her. Perhaps she was trapped in the same place as I was, thinking about my mom laying the table for the four of us on the porch that night and knowing that her life was all but over.

With all the drama, I was in no condition yesterday

to go over my expected testimony with Marta, so she has come in early this morning instead. With three kids at home, that isn't easy for her and her husband, Solomon, but she brushes off my thanks as she leads me through the office to the coffeepot.

Watching Marta in court over the weeks, I've realized she will never quite have the career of her father. She has the same intellect as her dad, but not the same magic. She is warm and approachable, whereas her father gains from being formal and remote, but it doesn't seem to matter to her. She is one of those people who likes who she is and what has happened in her life. I tell her all the time she is my role model.

"Was it weird when you decided to practice with your father?" I ask her as we are watching the carafe fill. It's a question that's lingered with me for a couple of weeks now, but in the rush of trial there hasn't been much time to ask.

She laughs and admits she never quite made a decision. There was a family crisis years ago after her mother died—she does not mention it, but I am pretty sure that Clara, Marta's mom and Sandy's first wife, was a suicide, a weird thought this morning. Sandy, in her words, was "at sixes and sevens," and Marta slid into the role of her father's sidekick without a lot of thought.

"It's what people mean, though, when they say that things turn out for the best," she says. "I've loved practicing with my dad, and the truth is that if my mom hadn't died, it might not have happened. He's the best lawyer I've ever met, and we have this harmony in the office that we can't find anywhere else. I don't think we've ever raised our voices here. But if I bring him home for dinner when Helen is traveling, I'm screaming at him by the time he's through the door. He breaks *every* rule I have for the kids. I love my father," Marta adds then as a sudden afterthought, and flushes so quickly that I don't realize at first what's happened. It's the clearest declaration anybody has made yet that Sandy Stern is dying. She stares down into her coffee.

"I haven't recovered from my mother yet," she says, "and that's nearly twenty years."

"Really? I keep waiting to feel normal again."

"It's just a new normal," she says.

Whatever professional distance there is supposed to be between Marta and me has largely vanished. We just have too much in common. Both attorneys. With moms who met untimely deaths and these lawyer dads who seem big enough to block the sun but are each currently imperiled. We have, figuratively speaking, made it through this case holding hands, and I actually put my arm on her shoulder for a minute as we are walking back to the office. She is going to be one of those people I ask for advice the rest of my life.

We go over my testimony quickly. A lot of it is tender stuff after yesterday, but there is no debating the necessity.

"What's the deal with the computer?" I ask her.

"We're taking a little flyer. It was your dad's idea. He says there's no risk. We'll see. But I want you to be able to say in front of the jury that we didn't discuss that part in advance. So just follow my instructions. It won't be complicated."

The point is obvious anyway, to show how easy it would have been for my mom to have signed herself on to his machine.

When I head out to use the john before we go to court, I bump into my dad. He stayed clear of me yesterday, and even now there is, as usual, not a lot for either of us to say.

"I'm sorry, Nat."

My mom was short, so it seemed to surprise everyone, especially me, that I grew a couple inches taller than my father. For the longest time, I felt crazy weird about the fact that I was looking down at him, if just a bit. He grabs my shoulders and I stumble into some kind of hug, and then he goes off in his direction and I go in mine.

The first time I testified, I was an absolute mess. I had never seen a trial before, and here I was, the first witness in the case, called by the prosecution to give evidence against my father for murdering my mother. I just sat up there like a lump and answered as quickly as I could. Judge Yee kept telling me to keep my voice up. When Brand was done, Marta asked me a couple of questions designed to show that my dad seemed to be in a state of shock when he argued with me about calling the police. Then she told Yee she'd reserve any remaining examination until I was recalled in the defense case.

When I ascend this time to the chair under the walnut canopy, it's easier. I'll be seeing this courtroom in my dreams the rest of my life, but I am, in a very strange way, at home.

"Please state your name and spell the last name for the record."

"Nathaniel Sabich, S, A, B, I, C, H."

"You are the same Nathaniel Sabich who testified during the People's case?"

"Same guy." A young Latina in the front row of the jury smiles. She seemed to think I was cool when I was up here the first time.

"And since you testified, you have been present here in court each day, is that right?"

"I have. I'm the only family my dad has got, and Judge Yee said I could be in here to support him."

"But to be clear, Nat, have you discussed the evidence in this case with your father, or your testimony here today?"

"No. You know, he's told me he didn't do it and I've told him I believe him, but no, we don't talk about what the witnesses have said or what I'm going to say."

These last answers, which stray beyond the strict bounds of the rules of evidence, were worked out with Marta in advance. She would have been just as happy to see Brand object when I said I believed my dad, only to reemphasize that fact for the jurors, but I could see Molto touch Brand's wrist as he was about to spring up. By all accounts, Molto was kind of a hothead as a young guy, but time and responsibility have apparently chilled him out. He knows the jurors have seen me here day after day and have to realize whose side I'm on. The dude's my dad, after all. What else am I going to believe?

"And you are a licensed attorney?"

"That's right."

"And so you understand the consequence of being under oath."

"Of course."

"Nat, let me ask you first, about the case of John Harnason. Did you ever discuss that case with your mother?"

"My mom?"

"Well, were you ever present when your mother or your mother and father discussed the case?"

So I tell what happened during my dad's sixtieth birthday dinner, when it became clear that my mom had read about the case on her own. Then we go on to my dad's shopping trip the night my mom died. I explain how I've had this thing for salami and cheese since I was a kid, and yeah, my mom was like everybody's mom and liked to feed me the stuff I'd always craved, and yeah, my mom always sent my dad, or in earlier years me, to do those kinds of errands because she didn't like to leave the house and even did her weekly grocery shopping online. Then I tell the jury that it's true, my dad always picked up my mom's medications, and took them upstairs when he changed out of his suit, and very often put the bottles up on the shelf. Tap, tap, tap. My dad says that Sandy works like a jeweler with his little hammer. And so it's going now. I stand behind my dad's story, link by link.

It's all calm and easy until we get to my mom's suicide attempt when I was ten. The prosecutors raise hell before I can get into it, and the jury has to leave, which is pretty much ridiculous, because it all goes to back up what my dad said yesterday. But once the jury comes back, we don't get very far into what happened before I lose it. Prior to today, there may have been four people on earth I've told that story—even Anna didn't hear it until last night—and now I'm sitting here with reporters and sketch artists in the front row of this immense courtroom, confessing for the five o'clock news that my mom was totally out of control.

"And I walked into the bathroom," I say once I think I've regained composure, and start sobbing again immediately.

I try two or three more times but can't get through it.

"Was she trying to electrocute herself?" Marta finally asks.

I just nod.

Judge Yee intervenes then. "Record reflect witness nodded to mean yes. Think we all understand, Ms. Stern," he says, calling a halt on this subject. He recesses for ten minutes to give me a chance to pull myself together.

"I'm sorry," I tell him and then the jury before we adjourn.

"No 'sorry' needed," says Judge Yee.

I leave the courtroom and stand by myself at the end of the corridor, looking out the window at the highway. The truth is that talking about my mom has never been easy for me. I loved my mom, love her now, and always will. My dad was always floating at a distance, coming in and out, big and brilliant, sort of like the moon, but the gravity that held me to the earth was my mother, even though I seem to have struggled with her love all my life. There was a way I knew she loved me too much—that it wasn't good for me, that too much came with it—and as a result, I was always straining to escape the burden of her attention. When I was little, she was forever whispering to me—I'll eternally feel her breath on my neck as she spoke, and the hairs standing back there. She didn't want anyone else to hear what she was saying. And there was a message implicit in that: Only us. There was only us. She told me flat out, 'You are the world to me, you are the whole world, little boy.'

I was thrilled to hear it, of course. But something heavy and dark came with the words. From the time I was a little kid, I sort of felt responsible for her. Maybe all children feel like that. I wouldn't know, since I've only been me. But I realized I was more than important to her. I was her lifeline. I knew that the only time my mom felt completely right was with me, tending to me, talking to me, thinking about me. The only time she was balanced in the world was then.

Looking back, I think it's obvious that my biggest issue once I reached my teens was about the consequence of leaving her. As I watch the cars course down I-843, I suddenly realize something I haven't faced before. I blame my dad for her death, because I don't want to blame myself. But I always knew that when I left home, something like this might happen. I knew it and went anyway. I had to. Nobody, least of all my mom, wanted me to give up my life for hers. But still. My dad acted like an asshole. Yet I also need to forgive myself. When I do, maybe I'll be able to start forgiving him.

"Now let's turn to the subject of computers," says Marta when the trial resumes. My dad's PC has been set up on a table in the middle of the courtroom, and Marta points to it. "Over the years, Nat, have you seen your father use a computer?"

"Sure."

"Where?"

"At home. Or when I visited him in his chambers."

"How often?"

"Countless times."

"And have you talked with him about his computer?"

"Often."

"Have you helped him use his computer?"

"Naturally. For people my age, that's sort of the reverse of having your parents help you ride a bicycle. We *all* help our parents with computers."

The jurors love this. So does Judge Yee, who more and more I am beginning to see is kind of a cool guy.

"And is your father computer literate?"

"If knowing the difference between on and off makes you literate, then yes. Otherwise, not so much."

There is loud laughter from the jury box. Everybody in this room feels sorry for me, so I am Mr. Popularity.

"And what about you? Are you computer literate?"

"Compared to my father? Yes. I know a lot more than him."

"What about your mother?"

"She was like a genius. She was a PhD in math. Until my friends started doing PhDs in computer science, she knew more than anyone I knew. And even those guys sometimes would call her up with questions. She was way inside the machine."

"Did you know the password on your father's computer?"

"I think I did. My father used the same password on everything."

"Which was?"

"Let me explain. His proper name. Rozat. It has that little mark over the 'z' when he writes it correctly, so in English sometimes he'd spell it R, O, Z, H, A, T. That was the password on our voice mail at home. On the burglar alarm system. The ATM. On bank accounts. Always 'Rozhat.' He was like everybody else. How can you have sixteen different passwords and remember what they are?"

"And did you ever discuss this fact—that your father used only one password—with your mother?"

"A zillion times."

"Do you specifically recall any occasions?"

"I can remember two years ago, I was visiting my folks, and my dad got a new credit card in the mail and he had to call in to activate it, and they asked him for the password on his account and he actually covered the phone and asked my mom, 'What's my password?' And she rolled her eyes and was like, 'Oh, for God's sake,' and she just turned to me, you know, this kind of hopeless look, and I about fell off my chair, and my dad still was bewildered, and then we both said to him at the same time, 'Rozhat,' and he was like, 'Oh, shit.' And when he put down the phone, he was just shaking his head at himself and we were all hysterical."

Across the courtroom, my dad is actually laughing. He smiles now and then, but this may be the first outright laughter I've seen since the trial started. The jury too is enjoying the story, and so I say to them, "Excuse me, you know, for using that word."

"Now, Nat," says Marta. "Are you aware that I am going to ask you to do a demonstration with your father's computer?"

"Yes."

"And do you know what I am going to ask you to demonstrate?"

"No."

"Now you've heard some testimony about shredding software, is that right?"

"Sure."

"Have you ever downloaded shredding software?"

"No."

"Have you ever known your father to download shredding software?"

"It's impossible."

Brand objects, and my answer is stricken.

"Sorry," I tell the judge.

He raises a hand obligingly. "Just answer question," he says.

"All right, Nat," says Marta, "I'm going to ask you to come down from the witness stand to start your father's computer. I'll ask you to enter the password, Rozhat, and if it works, to download the shredding software mentioned by the prosecution to see if you can use it."

"Objection," Brand says.

The jury has to leave again. Brand argues that because I know the password doesn't mean that my mom did, and even if I have difficulty using the shredding software, that doesn't mean that my father couldn't have practiced.

Judge Yee rules for Marta. "First, let's see if password

is right password, because Mrs. Sabich knew that password. And since prosecutors say the judge use this
shredding software, defense has right to show what
it takes to do that. If young Mr. Sabich got problems
doing that, defense can't argue that proves judge would
have problems. But defense can argue this is too hard
for the judge. Prosecutor can argue otherwise. Okay,
bring in jury."

I am standing in front of the computer by the time
they're all back in their seats. Judge Yee has come down
from the bench to see, and everybody from the prosecution table is standing around me as well. Marta
asks the judge if she can turn the monitor toward the
jury, which he allows, although it is also projected on
the screen beside the witness stand. Then I push the
on switch on the tower, and the machine purrs to
life and cycles through. The sunny screen comes on
and prompts for the password, at which point Marta
speaks.

"Judge, if I may, I'm going to ask Mr. Sabich to type
in the letters R, O, Z, H, A, T, for the password, with
the Court's permission."

"Proceed," says the judge.

It works, of course. There is that canned musical
tone, and then, to my amazement, a Christmas card
appears, addressed to my dad. I become aware of how
quiet the courtroom has suddenly become.

The card says, "Seasons Greetings 2008," and
within the borders an animated script becomes visible
line by line, the murmur growing among the spectators
with each word.

Roses are red

Violets are blue

You're in trouble again

And I did it to you.

    Love, You Know Who.

CHAPTER 35

Tommy, June 24, 2009

I n the moment, Tommy's first sensation was like realizing a pipe has burst inside the wall or that the guy on the other end of the phone has had a heart attack. It isn't working; that's all you know for a second. Regular life has stopped cold.

As Tommy read the message on the screen, he felt a flurry of motion beside him. The jurors, already leaning forward to view the computer, had left their seats to get closer, and once they did, several of the reporters edged across the imaginary boundary line to the well of the court so they could see, too. That in turn led a number of spectators to crowd ahead to find out what had occurred. The bailiffs rushed toward everyone, yelling for them to get back. Only when the sound of Judge Yee's gavel snapped through the courtroom did Tommy realize that Yee, who had come down to witness the demonstration, had resumed the bench.

"Everybody sit," proclaimed the judge. "Everybody in seats." He smacked the block again and repeated his order.

All retreated except Rusty's son, who stood bewildered

and by himself in the center of the courtroom, as use-less as a naked mannequin in a store window. In time, Marta pointed him back up to the witness stand. The judge gaveled for order yet again.

"Quiet, please, quiet." The stir continued, and Judge Yee, rarely forceful, banged harder and said, "Quiet or I ask bailiff to remove you. Quiet!"

Like a grade-school class, the courtroom finally settled.

"Okay, first," said the judge. "Mr. Sabich, I want you go back down and read what is on computer for the court reporter, so we got a clear record. Okay?"

Nat marched back down and described what was on the screen in a monotone:

"There is a Christmas card with a black border and some black wreaths, like from Halloween, on the screen. It says, 'Seasons Greetings, 2008,' and below it, there is some script." He read out the little poem.

"Okay," said Judge Yee. "Okay. Ms. Stern, how you want to proceed?"

After conferring with her father, she suggested a brief recess.

"Good idea," said the judge. "Lawyers, please come back to chambers."

The four attorneys followed Yee out the door beside the bench and down to the other end of the internal corridor that separated the courtrooms from the judges' office space. Stern was struggling along, and Tommy and Jim ended up twenty feet in front of them. Full of rage, Brand kept muttering, "This is complete bullshit," as they walked.

For the trial, Judge Yee had been using the chambers

of Malcolm Marsh, who was on leave to teach trial practice for a year in Australia. Judge Marsh was a serious violinist, who arranged to play with the symphony to celebrate his sixty-fifth birthday, and he decorated his chambers with framed recordings and signed sheet music. Judge Yee removed his robe and motioned the lawyers to their seats, while he remained standing behind Marsh's desk.

"Okay," said Yee, "anybody here can tell me what happened?"

There was a lengthy silence before Marta spoke.

"Your Honor, it appears that someone planted a message on Judge Sabich's computer before it was impounded, and the message seems to say that whoever wrote it set Judge Sabich up on these charges."

"That's crap," said Brand.

Judge Yee lifted a finger sternly. "Please, Brand," he said, and Jim apologized repeatedly.

"That was completely stupid," he said several times.

"What to do?" asked the judge.

Eventually, Marta said, "I think we should examine the computer. We should let the experts from both sides come in and in each other's presence do whatever diagnostic tests they can without changing the data and tell us when the message was put on the computer and whether or not it appears legitimate."

"Good," said Yee. He liked the plan. The Sterns would summon their two whiz kids on an emergency basis, while the prosecutors did the same with Professor Gorvetich. Brand and Marta stood up to make the calls. Marta reached their guys on her cell, but it turned out that Brand had Gorvetich's number back across the

street, so he departed. In the meantime, Yee asked the
bailiff to send the jurors home, and the lawyers agreed
to head back to their offices to await the experts' conclusion. The computer would remain in the courtroom
under the eye of the court security officers.

On the way out, Stern gave Tommy one of his mysterious little smiles. Sandy was actually looking better, his face a little fuller and the rash clearly starting
to fade. Just in time, Tommy thought. Just in fucking
time for Sandy to smile for the cameras when he won.

"Interesting case," Stern said.

Out in the courtroom, Tommy and Rory and Ruta put
the trial cart back together. Brand was fussy about the
order in which he stored the exhibits, and the three
of them kept trying to remind themselves what Jim
wanted, each of them unwilling at the moment to see
Brand go off, as he would, if it wasn't all as he liked.

Milo Gorvetich arrived just as Tommy was about to
return to the office across the street. Milo was a little
guy, shorter than Tommy or Stern, with wild white
hair and a goatee stained yellow from his pipe. It had
been Brand's idea to hire him in the first place, because
Brand had taken a programming class from Milo two
decades ago. As the first member of the U football
team ever to appear in Gorvetich's classroom, Brand
had gotten enough attention from the professor to
make some form of gentlemen's C. But Gorvetich was
an old man now. He rambled and had lost his edge.
Sandy's hotshot kids had run rings around him, and at
this stage Tommy was no longer sure he fully trusted
him. He told Milo what had occurred, and the old

guy's eyes widened. Tommy feared he was going to be pretty much clueless.

With the two women, Tommy crossed the street. He found Brand in his office, stewing, his feet on his desk while he chewed on a straw. Brand had many of the physical blessings that Tommy had envied in other trial lawyers for years. Big and solid and handsome, he had that aura of iron strength jurors loved in prosecutors especially. But Tommy exceeded Jim in one physical trait that was nearly essential to trying lawsuits—the ability to do well without sleep. Jim needed eight hours, and when he didn't get it, he got cranky like a little kid. He'd plainly had a long night here yesterday, working with the techs and trying to think his way through the defense's new suicide theory. The cellophane wrappings from the dinner he'd had out of the vending machine were mixed in the wastebasket beside his desk with the rose-colored filaments of the shrink-wrap they'd stripped off of Sabich's computer, before the seals were removed in the courtroom this morning.

"So is this just too fucking convenient or what?" Brand asked. "The victim comes back from the dead to announce she framed the defendant. I mean, give me a fucking break. Really. This is just crap. Day one they say it's suicide. Day two she says, Yeah, and I did it to screw him."

Tommy sat down in the wooden chair beside Brand's desk. There was a new picture of Jody and the girls, and Tommy studied it for a second.

"Good-looking women," said Tommy.

Brand smiled a little. Tommy told him Gorvetich had arrived.

"What did he say?" Brand asked.

"He said they should be able to look at the calendaring client and see right away when the object was created. I didn't quite understand, but I figured you would. 'Object' means the card?"

"Right." Brand thought for a second as he chewed on his straw. "I think the calendar program stores the date the object was created as part of the object. I think he even said that to me on the phone."

"But we've had that thing—Rusty's computer—under lock and key since last November, right?"

"Pretty much. Early December, actually. It was over at the appellate court for a month with George Mason while we hassled about what we could look at. You remember."

Tommy remembered. He'd thought the court of appeals judges were going to cross the street and picket the County Building. When you started looking into their business, judges were about as entitled as sultans.

"Okay, but if the card is real—"

Brand interrupted. "It's not real."

"Okay," said Tommy. "Okay. But just playing along for a second—"

"It's not real," Brand said again. His nostrils were flared like a bull's. He could not abide the fact that the boss was even willing to consider the possibility. But that said it all. Either the card was going to turn out to be a plant, in which case Sabich was slabbed, or it would be legitimate and they would have little choice but to dismiss the case. It was that simple.

Tommy and Brand sat another minute with nothing to say. Malvern, Tommy's assistant, had seen him come in and knocked to tell him Dominga was on the phone. She'd probably heard the news about a "dramatic development" in the Sabich case.

"Let me know when Gorvetich reports back," Tommy said as he stood.

Brand's phone was ringing, and he nodded as he picked up. Tommy didn't get to the door.

"Gorvetich," Brand said behind him. He had a finger raised when Molto looked back.

Tommy watched Jim listen. His dark eyes weren't moving, and his face was set in a solemn frown. Tommy was not sure Brand was breathing. "Okay," said Brand. Then he repeated, "I understand," several times. At the end, Jimmy slammed down the handset and sat there with his eyes shut.

"What?" Molto asked.

"They've finished an initial examination."

"And?"

"And the object was created the day before Barbara Sabich died." Jim took a second to think. "It's real," said Brand. He kicked the trash can beside his desk, and the contents went flying. "It's fucking real."

CHAPTER 36

Nat, June 24, 2009

After Judge Yee dismisses the lawyers from his chambers, Marta and my dad and Sandy and I return to the LeSueur Building and end up together in Stern's large office. For weeks the dead man walking, Sandy is now trying to contain his exuberance, for my dad's sake. But there is something in him that would make you say he is his old self. His phone keeps lighting up with calls from reporters, and he tells them that the defense will have no comment for the present. Finally, he buzzes his secretary and tells her to put no one else through.

"They're all asking the same question," says Sandy. "If we think Molto will dismiss."

"Will he?" I ask.

"One never knows with Tommy. Brand might tie him to his chair rather than let that occur."

"Molto isn't going to give up," Marta says. "When push comes to shove, they'll gin up some screwy theory about how Rusty planted this on the computer."

"Rusty has not had his hands on the computer since prior to his indictment," says Stern.

He looks at my father, who is hunched in an armchair, listening but with little to say. For an hour and a
half, he has seemed the most shocked and withdrawn of
all of us. In psych class years ago, I visited a mental hospital and saw several people who had been lobotomized
in the 1950s. With part of their brains gone, their eyes
sank back into their heads by several inches. My dad
looks a little like that now.

"Any such theory will be an embarrassment to
them," Stern says.

"I'm just saying," says Marta. "And the reporters are
assuming it's Barbara?"

"Who else?" asks Sandy.

For the last ninety minutes, I have been asking
myself that question. I gave up thinking I fully understood my parents—either one of them—a long time
ago. Who they were to each other, or in the parts of
their lives that never touched mine, is something I
won't ever completely comprehend. It's a little like trying to figure out who actors really are beyond the roles
they play on-screen. How much is typecasting? How
much is pretend? Anna insists it's pretty much the same
with her mom.

But the brutal fact when I ask myself if I can
really believe that my mother killed herself and set
my father up to take the fall for her death—the fact
is that some deeply internal apparatus registers that
prospect as entirely credible. My mother's rages were
lethal and took her to a place where she was largely
unrecognizable.

And it all fits. That's why it's only my dad's prints on
the bottle of phenelzine. That's why she sent him out

for wine and cheese. That's why the searches for phenelzine weren't shredded on his computer.

"But why poison herself with something that could have been mistaken for natural causes?" asks my father. It's his first real contribution to the conversations.

"Well, I believe," says Sandy—he stops for his little sawing cough—"it's far more incriminating that way. And of course, that implicates the *Harnason* case, which was in front of you and which Barbara knew a great deal about."

"It's incriminating," my father answers, "only if it's discovered."

"Enter Tommy Molto," answers Stern. "Given the history, would Tommy really allow an untimely death of another female who is close to you to pass without a thorough investigation? Barbara surely took Tommy as your pledged enemy."

My father shakes his head once. Unlike his lawyers, he is not completely sold.

"Why not sign her name?" he asks.

"It's just as obvious, isn't it?"

"And if she's going to frame me, why bother bailing me out that way?"

Sandy looks at me at that point, not to see how I'm reacting, but as a demonstration.

"Putting you in the dock again, Rusty, was a fine repayment for your infidelity. But leaving you in prison for the rest of your life went too far, especially when one considers Nat."

My father thinks it through. His mind is clearly moving more slowly than usual.

"It's a trick," my father says then. "If it's Barbara,

then there's a trick. It's going to be like invisible ink. As soon as we rely on this, there will be something we don't see."

"Well, Matteus and Ryzard," says Sandy, who alone refuses to refer to the two computer experts as Hans and Franz, "should recognize that."

"They won't be better than her," my father answers definitively.

My dad soothed my mom by paying her limitless compliments. Her cooking. Her appearance. I think he meant all of it, even though he probably resented the fact that the praise was required. But one thing he always said with complete sincerity was, 'Barbara Bernstein is the smartest human being I know.' He is confident now that she will prove to have out-thought everybody in the room. I would find that touching if it didn't imply that in the end, my mom's intentions were ultimately nowhere as benign as Stern just suggested. She didn't mean merely to scare him, my dad is saying. She is fucking with him big-time from the grave.

About ten minutes later, Sandy's secretary announces that Hans is on the phone. The experts have finished examining the computer. Even Gorvetich agrees that the card appears legitimate. It was composed the afternoon before my mom died, apparently just minutes before Anna and I arrived for dinner. Stern informs the judge's chambers, and all the lawyers are ordered to court so that the three computer scientists can report to Judge Yee. We head down to the garage and pile into Sandy's Cadillac for the short trip back.

"Bad hair day for Tommy," says Marta. "I'd like to

have been there to see the look on their face when Gorvetich told him the card is real."

Everyone in Stern's office had simply assumed that
would be the verdict. We all knew my dad never had
the time or the technical skill to pull off anything like
that.

The courtroom seems like a ghost town when we get
there. The place has been jammed for weeks, with not
an inch to spare on the spectator pews, but apparently
neither the reporters nor the court buffs who roam the
halls looking for free entertainment have gotten word
about proceedings now. Marta and Sandy go off to
meet for a second with Hans and Franz, but they're
interrupted when Judge Yee returns to the bench.

Professor Gorvetich is about five feet four, with a
froth of white hair arising from various spots on his
scalp, a bedraggled goatee, and a belly too big to fit
inside his cheap sport coat. He has shown up wearing
sneakers, for which I guess you can't blame him given
the short notice. Hans and Franz are casual, too. Matteus is older and taller, but they are both thin and fit
and stylish, with their shirts out of their designer jeans
and their hair spiked. The lawyers have agreed that
Gorvetich should speak to the judge—it's his client's ox
getting gored. He stands next to the computer down in
the center of the courtroom.

The card, he says, is a standard graphics file that
opens in association with a reminder that was meant to
pop up on New Year's Day 2009. The dating explains
why none of the experts detected the card when all the
various forensics exams on the computer were run by
the prosecution and the defense in early December.

The fact that the message was intended for the holiday season speaks volumes to me, since it was always a weird time in my house. My mom was raised Jewish and lit Hanukkah candles with me every year, but that was largely in self-defense. My mom did not like religious holidays in general and for whatever reason, she loathed Christmas especially. For my dad, on the other hand, Christmas was one of the few bright spots in the year when he was a kid, and he continued to look forward to it. Maybe the worst part from my mom's perspective was that the Serbs celebrate Christmas January 7, which meant that for her, the season seemed to drag on forever. She particularly hated the traditional Christmas dinners to which we were regularly invited by my dad's crazy Serbian cousins because they always served pork roast, the occasions often fell on school nights for me, and everybody got drunk on plum brandy. It was usually February before my dad and her were speaking again.

"We examined the registry files on the computer and paid particular attention to the .pst file, which contains the calendar objects," says Gorvetich. "The creation date for an object is contained in the object itself. The .pst file itself also shows a date that reflects the last time the calendar program was used in any way, even if it was no more than opening it. The object in question shows a creation date of September 28, 2008, at 5:37 p.m.

"So at this stage, I can tell the Court that this has every appearance of a legitimate object. Unfortunately, because the file was opened in court this morning, which I would have discouraged, the .pst file now bears today's date. But we have all checked our notes, and when the computer was examined and imaged by both sides last fall, the .pst date was October 30, 2008, several days before the computer was seized. As I noted when I testified, there is debris in the registry from the use of shredding software, but that debris was identified when the computer image was examined by both sides last December."

Tommy Molto stands up. "Judge, can I ask something?"

Yee lifts his hand.

"What if somebody got hold of the computer after October and rolled the clock back and then added this card?" Molto asked.

Brand clearly knows this isn't possible and is reaching after his boss. Hans and Franz are shaking their heads, too. Gorvetich says as much.

"The program doesn't work like that. In order to create proper calendaring, the clock can't be rolled back within the program."

Judge Yee is tapping his pencil against the blotter in front of him on the bench.

"Mr. Molto," he says finally, "what you gonna do?"

Tommy stands up. "Your Honor, if we may, we're going to think about it overnight."

"Okay," says the judge. "Nine a.m. for status. Jury on standby." He bangs his gavel.

I come to my feet and wait to head out with my father. Although he is probably going to go free tomorrow, my dad, the eternal enigma, is still not smiling.

CHAPTER 37

Tommy, June 25, 2009

*E*stoy *embarazada*.' As he walked toward the office on Thursday morning from the parking structure, the words and the shy pride with which his wife had spoken them were still cascading through Tommy. '*Estoy embarazada*,' Dominga had said when Tommy had picked up the phone yesterday after he'd left Brand's office. Her periods had always been flaky, and Tommy and she had been trying for a while, believing Tomaso shouldn't be an only child. But it hadn't seemed to be taking. Which was fine. Tommy had been blessed beyond imagining already. But now she was *embarazada*, six weeks along, with life again within her.

So this was how Tommy had always known there was a God. You could call it a coincidence that his wife would find out she was pregnant at the very moment he learned his long pursuit of Rusty Sabich had failed again. But did that really make sense, that things just fall out like that, with joy enough to offset any sorrow?

He had gone home early yesterday, in relative peace, and celebrated by sharing the company of his wife and son until they went to sleep, then he awoke at three a.m.

to ponder. Sitting in the dark in their house, which was probably going to be too small now, he was swarmed by the doubts he had pushed aside when the prospect of the new baby remained remote. Should a man his age really be having another child—a girl, Tommy hoped for his wife's sake—who was likely to bury her father in her teens, or her twenties at the latest? Tommy did not know. He loved Dominga, he had fallen desperately in love, and all the rest of this followed, inevitably, even if the life he ended up living bore scant resemblance to anything he had expected for the nearly sixty years before. You follow your heart toward goodness and accept what comes.

With Rusty, too, he had done the right thing. Given nearly a day to reflect, Tommy realized that ending the case now was going to suit everybody. The PAs had been duped, by the victim, no less. No one could ever point any fingers at them. Rusty would walk away, but what he'd gone through was a consequence not of any bad faith by Tommy, but of the fucked-up mess Rusty had made in his own fucked-up house. If you really thought about it, Sabich was the one who should be apologizing. Not that he would.

The problem was going to be Brand, who had begun making a case after court. Even though the card was real, he said, there was no way to prove Rusty wasn't the one who had created it last September. It was on his computer, after all. He had planned to kill Barbara, hoping it would be taken as a death by natural causes, but if anybody saw through that, Sabich would haul out this suicide/frame-up stuff in stages.

And given the realities, Jimmy might even be right.

After all, who killed herself to set up somebody else? But Tommy had made the essential point to Brand a long time ago: Rusty Sabich was too smart, and too wary of Tommy, to kill his wife, except in a way that would virtually prohibit conviction. Even if Sabich had orchestrated it all this way, he had the better argument. Could he have planted that card and left his prints on the phenelzine or the Web searches on his computer? Tommy and Brand were screwed. If they tried to account for the new evidence, they would be stuck trying to add a third floor to their theory, when they'd already built the house and taken the jury on a tour. Sure, if they had been allowed to prove that Rusty already got away with killing one woman, then the jurors might believe he'd schemed so elaborately to murder another. But Yee was not going back on those rulings at this stage. And as far as the record was concerned, it was Barbara, not Rusty, who was the computer geek and knew how to seed that card in September to bloom at year end.

If the PAs hung tough on their case, then Yee would probably dismiss them out. You could see that on the judge's face yesterday. They could try now to persuade him to let the case go to verdict, arguing that it was the jury's right exclusively to decide what witnesses to believe. But Yee would never buy that. The issue wasn't credibility. The prosecutors' evidence provided no way to conclude beyond a reasonable doubt that this was murder rather than suicide. It was a null set, as the math guys say—the proof came to nothing.

So they were where they were. If they stood down on the case now, they would be good guys who just did

their jobs and followed the evidence where it seemed
to lead. If they pressed on, as Brand would want, they
would be embittered crusaders who couldn't face the
truth.

By now, having again thought through everything
he had pondered the night before, Tommy had arrived
in the marble lobby of the old County Building,
acknowledging the familiar faces arriving to start the
workday. Nobody came over to chat, which was a sign
of how deeply the news coverage last night had cut.
Goldy, the elevator operator, who'd looked old when
Tommy started here thirty years ago, took him up and
he passed through the office door.

Down the long dim hall, Tommy could see Brand
waiting for him. It was going to be a hard conversation,
and as Molto approached he was looking for words,
wishing he had spent some time thinking about what
to tell a man who was not simply his most loyal deputy,
but also his best friend. When Tommy was about fifty
feet away, Brand started dancing.

Too astonished to move any farther, Tommy
watched as Jim did the kind of hip-hop juke that NFL
players performed in the end zone. He knew Brand
well enough to realize that Jim, who'd run back several interceptions for TDs in his time, had practiced
these steps in front of the bathroom mirror, wishing he
hadn't been born a generation too soon.

Brand's gyrations were taking him Tommy's way,
and when he got closer, Molto could hear him singing,
although you wouldn't call it much of a tune. He belted
out a word or two each time he hopped from one foot
to the other.

"Rus-ty.

"Gone down.

"Rus-ty.

"Gone down.

"Rus-ty.

"Gone away.

"Rus-ty.

"Gone away.

"Rus-ty.

"Gone to the Big House."

Despite being well off meter, he sang the last line like a Broadway performer with his arms thrown wide and at booming volume. Several secretaries and cops and other deputies had stopped to witness the performance.

"You go, girl," one of them remarked, which filled the hallway with laughter.

"What?" Molto asked.

Brand was too exultant to talk. Smiling hugely, he came up to Tommy and bent down to clutch the boss, a good eight inches shorter, in a fierce embrace. Then he walked the PA into his own office, where someone was waiting. It turned out to be Gorvetich, who resembled a scraggly version of Edward G. Robinson in his latter days.

"Tell him," said Brand. "Milo had an amazing idea last night."

Gorvetich scratched for a second at his yellowish goatee. "It was really Jim's idea," he said.

"Not even close," said Brand.

"Whoever," said Tommy. "You can share the Nobel Prize. What's the scoop?"

Gorvetich shrugged. "You remember when I met

you, Tom, you were catching hell from the appellate judges."

Tommy nodded. "They didn't want us looking at the internal court documents on Rusty's computer."

"Right. And so we imaged the hard drive—"

"Made a copy," said Molto.

"An exact copy. And we turned the actual computer over to the chief judge there."

"Mason."

"Judge Mason. Well, Jim and I were talking last night, and we decided that just to be sure about this Christmas card, we should go back and look at the image of Sabich's hard drive we made last November, when you first seized the computer. And we did. And that object, the card? It's not there."

Tommy sat down in his big chair and looked at both of them. His first reaction was to distrust Gorvetich. The old man was no match for Brand and must have been pushed into a critical mistake by his former student.

"I thought the card was made up last September before Barbara died?" Molto asked.

"As did I," said Gorvetich. "It gives every appearance. But it wasn't. Because it's not on the image. It was placed on the computer after we first seized it."

"When?"

"Well, I don't know. Because the .pst file now bears yesterday's date."

"Because the defense opened that file in court when they turned on the computer," Brand said. He was too happy right now to remind Tommy that he'd warned against letting the Sterns do that.

"Exactly," said Gorvetich. "But the card had to have been added during the month the PC was over at Judge Mason's. It was shrink-wrapped and sealed right in Judge Mason's chambers the day Judge Yee ordered it returned to our custody."

Tommy thought. Somehow it was Stern's words yesterday that came back to him: 'Interesting case.'

"Where was the image?"

"The imaged copy of the hard drive was preserved on an external drive in your evidence room. Jim got it out and burned a copy for me last night."

Tommy didn't like that at all. "Sandy's guys weren't with you?"

Brand broke in. "If you're worried that they'll claim we screwed with the image, we gave them a copy when we made it. They can look at this themselves on their copy. The card won't be there."

Gorvetich explained that the image had been made with a program called Evidence Tool Kit. The software's algorithms were proprietary and the image could be deciphered only with the same software, which by design was read-only to ensure that no one could attempt to alter an image after it was made.

"I guarantee you, Tommy," Gorvetich said, "Rusty found a way to put this on there."

Molto asked how Rusty could have done that. Gorvetich was not positive, but after thinking on it all night, he had a working theory. There was a piece of software called Office Spy, a hacker's invention now available as Internet shareware, that allowed someone to go into a calendar program and recast the objects stored there. You could roll back the date on a reminder, erase an incriminating entry from the calendar, or omit—or add—the names of people who had been at a critical meeting. Once the new object—the Christmas card, in this case—had been inserted on Sabich's computer, Office Spy had to be removed from the hard drive with shredding software, and then that software itself also had to be deleted, which required manual changes to registry files. Not only was the object—the card— missing on the image from last fall, but now that Gorvetich had made the comparison, he'd noticed subtle differences in the debris remnants of the shredding software held in various empty sectors of the drive. The implication was that shredding software had been added and removed from the computer twice, once before Barbara's death and once after the computer had first been seized.

"I thought Mason had the computer completely secure."

"He did. Or he thought he did," said Gorvetich.

"I mean, Jesus, Boss. Rusty ran that court for thirteen years. You think he didn't have the keys to everything? It would have been better to examine the fucking drive again when we got it back, but Mason said he made a log of everything Rusty's people looked at, and Yee just ordered the computer sealed as a condition of returning it to our custody. We couldn't start arguing with him about that."

Tommy explained it to himself again. Barbara didn't create the Christmas card, because Barbara was dead when that happened. And the only person who had anything to gain from placing the card on the calendar was Rusty Sabich. So much for the crap that Rusty didn't know about computers.

Tommy finally laughed out loud. It wasn't glee he felt so much as amazement.

"Boy, am I going to enjoy my conversation with that arrogant little Argentinian," said Molto. "Boy," he repeated.

Across the room, Brand, who'd never sat down, lifted his hands.

"Wanna dance?" he asked.

CHAPTER 38

Nat, June 25, 2009

Just as Marta had foreseen, the prosecutors arrive in court this morning with a new theory about why my dad is guilty. Jim Brand stands up and tells Judge Yee that the prosecutors have decided overnight the Christmas card is a fraud.

"Your Honor!" protests Sandy from his chair. He paws like a cartoon character in his labored efforts to rise. Marta finally helps haul him to his feet. "The prosecution's own expert acknowledged yesterday that this so-called object was genuine."

"That was before we examined the image," Brand answers. He calls on pompous little Professor Gorvetich to explain his new conclusions. Before Gorvetich has stopped speaking, Marta gropes in her purse for her cell phone and is charging out of the courtroom to call Hans and Franz.

Judge Yee is clearly losing patience. The pencil started going about halfway through Gorvetich's lecture.

"People," he says finally, "what we doing here? Young Mr. Sabich supposed to be on witness stand.

Jurors are by their phones. We trying this lawsuit or what?"

"Your Honor," says Stern, "I had hoped the prosecutors would terminate this proceeding today. I can hardly believe this. May I ask if they actually intend to offer evidence to support their new theory about the card?"

"You bet your life," answers Brand. "This was a fraud on the Court."

Stern shakes his head sadly. "The defense obviously cannot proceed, Your Honor, until we have conducted our own examination."

We all head back to Stern's to await word from Hans and Franz, who have their own copy of the imaged hard drive in storage at their office. I call Anna in the interval to tell her what has transpired. She has believed all along that when push came to shove, Tommy Molto would cheat to win, and she's certain he's trying to do it again.

"The leopard doesn't change his spots," Anna says now. Last night, she made the same prediction as Marta that Molto would figure out some excuse to avoid dismissing.

Hans and Franz are in the office in an hour, dressed pretty much as they were yesterday, in their designer jeans and gelled hair. It seems the boys are in the clubs every night until closing, and they look like Marta got them out of bed.

"Even a broken clock is right twice a day," says Hans, the taller of the two. "Gorvetich is correct."

"The card isn't on the image?" Marta asks. She had taken off her heels, perching her squat feet in her hose on one of her father's coffee tables, and nearly falls over.

I groan out loud. I am sick of not knowing what to believe. The last to react is my father, who emits a shrill laugh.

"It's Barbara," he says. He puts his fingers on the bridge of his nose and pivots his head back and forth in utter amazement. It seems like a bizarre idea, but even so, I feel instantly he may be right. "She figured out a way to do this so it wouldn't show up on the image."

"Could that be?" Marta asks the two experts. "Could she have used something like invisible ink and created this object so it wouldn't copy?"

Hans shakes his head but looks at Franz for confirmation. He also shakes his head emphatically.

"No way," says Ryzard. "This software, the Evidence Tool Kit, that's like the bomb, man. Industry standard. Makes exact copy. Been used thousands of times in thousands of cases, with no variation reported."

"You didn't know Barbara," my father says.

"Judge," says Franz, "I got an ex-wife. Sometimes I think she got superpowers, too, especially when I get some extra money. She's like in court for more alimony before the check clears."

"You didn't know Barbara," my father says again.

"Judge, listen to me," says Franz. "She would have to have known exactly what software was going to be used—"

"You just said it's the industry standard."

"Sixty percent of the market. But not one hundred. Then she would have had to penetrate the algorithms. And create a whole program to run counter to the software, which would launch on start-up. And which wouldn't show anywhere on the image. Or on the drive when we looked at it yesterday. I mean, dude, you can take every geek in the Silicon Valley and put them together, they couldn't do that. You're talkin every kind of impossible."

My father studies Franz with that stupefied, still-eyed look I see on my dad so often these days.

"So when could the card have been added?" Marta asks.

Franz looks to Hans, who shrugs.

"Had to be when it was over in the other judge's office."

"Judge Mason? Why? Why not after that?"

"Dude, the whole computer was sealed and shrink-wrapped and initialed until yesterday. You saw it. Gorvetich even made us look at the seals before they took them off in court so I would agree they were the originals. And Matteus and Gorvetich and I peeled off the last of the evidence tape and connected the monitor and CPU in the courtroom together."

"Couldn't they have taken off the wrappings and the seals and put them back on?"

Hans and Franz are trying to explain why that is not possible—the evidence tape says "Violated" in blue once it's peeled away—when Sandy interrupts.

"Prosecutors don't generally tamper with evidence in order to add proof that supports a defendant's innocence. If the card is a fraud, we will not get very far with the judge or the jury by arguing that this is the prosecutors' handiwork. Either we pursue Rusty's theory about Barbara, or we find another way to explain why the imaged hard drive did not capture what was actually there."

"Didn't happen," Hans answers definitively.

"Then we had better see if we can counter what the PAs are bound to say."

In the last couple of days, Stern has begun using a cane. With it, he gets around a good deal more nimbly than in the courtroom. Now he poles his way behind his desk and dials the telephone.

"Who are you calling, Dad?" Marta asks.

"George," Sandy answers.

Judge Mason, still the acting chief, is not available but calls back in twenty minutes. When he comes on, Stern and he have an exchange, obviously about Sandy's health, because Stern keeps answering, "All according to plan," and, "Better than expected." Finally, Stern asks if he can put the judge on the speakerphone so the rest of the trial team can hear. I probably should not be here, but I have no thought of leaving. I was one of the people, along with Anna and my dad, who used that computer while it was in Judge Mason's chambers.

"I've already had a conversation this morning with Tommy Molto," says the judge. "As you remember, Sandy, when we received the computer, we all agreed that no one would have access to it alone, and that I would keep a log of every document that was examined. Tom asked me for a copy of the log, and I e-mailed it to him. I'd be happy to do the same for you."

"Please," answers Stern.

Judge Mason and he agree that it makes more sense to talk after we've seen the log. While we are waiting for the document to cross the Net, Stern and Marta question Hans and Franz about what would have been required to pull this off. The two have already been engaged in rapid speculation, notions whizzing and pinging like bullets in a shooting gallery, and have pretty much agreed with Gorvetich that this was done with a piece of shareware called Office Spy, which would then have to be shredded.

"And how long would it take to do all that?" Sandy asks. "Install the software, add the object, delete the software, and clean up the registry?"

"An hour?" answers Hans, looking to Franz.

"Maybe me, I could do it in forty-five minutes, if I'd practiced some," says Franz. "Let's imagine I've already got Spy and the object on a flash drive, so I can save a little download time. And I've done the same operation with another PC, so I know exactly where to look to clean up the deletion of Evidence Eraser. But you know, somebody who doesn't have an extensive background? Has to be twice as long. At least."

"At least," says Hans. "More like several hours."

When the log shows up, it records four separate visits. My father went to the private chambers where George had my dad's PC set up on November 12, a week after the election. It was a dismal experience that caused my dad to vow no more. George witnessed this himself. My dad was there for twenty-eight minutes. He copied four documents to a flash drive, three draft opinions and one research memo from one of his clerks, and opened up his calendar and wrote down his remaining appointments for the balance of the year.

I came a week later to copy three more draft opinions and returned the next day for one more about which I'd misunderstood my dad's instructions. Riley, one of Judge Mason's law clerks, was with me on both occasions. And I was there for twenty-two minutes the first time and six minutes the day after.

Finally, right before Thanksgiving, Anna went over, standing in for me at the last minute. My dad was desperate to get a look at an earlier draft of an opinion he was working on at home that was already late. He was also starting, in optimistic moments, to book appointments in 2009 and wanted to review his calendar. I had gotten called to sub that morning and didn't want to say no, but the assignment was going to last at least two weeks. Anna had volunteered earlier to do the copying for my father, since she was normally in Center City, and Judge Mason had approved her enthusiastically. The log says she was there for about an hour, but that was because she had gotten a call from the office and was on her cell most of the time.

"Was Riley with her throughout that visit?" Sandy asks Judge Mason.

Judge Mason summons Riley Moran. She has known Anna for two years, since Riley's clerkship began before Anna's ended. Riley remembers things pretty much the same way I heard them from Anna at the time. Peter Berglan, one of the most demanding assholes Anna has to work for, had reached out for her on her cell and basically told her she had to participate in a conference call. Riley says that Anna got up from the computer and went to a chair across the room. Riley stepped out, because it was clearly a client matter she shouldn't overhear, but she peeked back in at least three times in the next forty minutes to see if Anna was done. Anna was in the chair and nowhere near the computer on each occasion. Eventually, Anna came next door to tell Riley she was ready, and Riley watched when Anna returned to the computer to finish downloading and making notes about my dad's upcoming appointments. The log reflects that the calendar was open to the same date it had been when Anna got up.

"Is that it?" George asks when Riley is gone.

Sandy thanks Judge Mason, then we all sit in the office in silence.

"What will Molto say?" asks Sandy out loud. "It does not seem possible anyone could have tampered with the computer."

"An hour," says Marta. She's talking about Anna.

"An hour is not enough time," Sandy says. "Rusty, even Rusty's son, might have anticipated a defense and done this, but Anna is clearly the least likely. If worse comes to worse, we can get her cell phone records and talk to Peter Berglan."

I have come to the same conclusions. My dad lacked the technical expertise even to try this. So do I, frankly, and obviously I know I wasn't responsible. Anna, as Stern says, would have had no reason to risk her entire career. None of us really makes a credible culprit.

Stern tilts his hand toward my father. "Rusty, did you have keys to the courthouse?"

"To my chambers," answers my dad. "That's all."

"Do you still have them?"

"No one has asked for them back."

"Did you ever visit after hours?"

"Before or after I went on leave?"

"After."

"Never."

"And before?"

"Once or twice, when I'd forgotten something I needed over a long weekend. It was a pain, frankly. There was one security guard. You'd have to stand there pounding on the doors until you got the guy's attention. It took me twenty minutes to get in one time."

"And whose chambers was the computer in?"

"George's."

"As acting chief, had he moved into your chambers?"

"He still hasn't, so far as I know."

"And what about the security guard. Would the security guard have keys to all the chambers?"

My father thinks. "Well, he carried one hell of a key ring. You could hear him coming. And there were times when people locked themselves out of their chambers and security was called to let them back in. But whether night security had the keys—I just don't know."

"That's their theory," says Marta. "Right? Inside job. Maybe Rusty came in there with a computer whiz in the middle of the night."

"Talk to the security guard," my father suggests.

"You can bet Tommy is keeping company with him right now," Marta says. "And you know how this will go, Rusty. Either they'll accuse the security guard of being your best friend, or find he has a felony he didn't disclose when he applied for his job and they'll threaten him with prosecution until he remembers letting you in. Or they'll find a day the regular guard was off and Jim Brand will badger the substitute into saying, Well, she can't remember which judge, but there was a night one of those judges came in. They'll patch together something."

"*Res ipsa loquitur*," says Sandy. The thing speaks for itself. "No one but Rusty really had the motive to do this. No one else in November could have known what the evidence would show or what defense might work. We didn't even have complete discovery yet."

"It's weak," says Marta. "And we'll end up with a trial within a trial. All these witnesses? Judge Mason and Riley. And the security guard. And Nat and Anna. Rusty again. The PAs'll be lucky if the jury even remembers what the case is about by the time all that's over."

Sandy is pondering. His hand goes up to his face unconsciously to pat around the edges of the rash. From the looks, it must still hurt.

"All true," he says. "But overall, we should not fool ourselves. This is still not a fortunate development for the defense."

With that judgment spoken, we each end up looking at my father to see how he has reacted to the discussion. Slumped in a club chair, worn and pale and sleepless, he has lost track of all of us and is startled by the attention when he finally glances up. He smiles faintly at me, a bit sheepish, then looks back down to his hands folded in his lap.

At four p.m., we are summoned by Judge Yee, who wants an update so he can set a schedule. Several report-ers have heard about this session, and Yee agrees to meet in open court. A number of the deputy PAs have also followed their bosses across the street to savor what all of them are sure is going to be a sweet moment. I sit in the front pew, only a few feet behind my dad. He is saying next to nothing to anybody, folded in upon him-self like a piece of empty luggage.

Yee asks simply, "What is going on?" and Stern comes up to the podium. He has brought his cane to court for the first time.

"Your Honor, our experts have reviewed the image made late last November, and they agree that the object does not appear there. They will need at least twenty-four hours to determine why."

Brand again stands to answer for the prosecution. "'Why'?" he asks with his voice rising sarcastically. "With all due respect to Mr. Stern, Judge, there's an obvious answer. This was a fraud. Pure and simple. This object was clearly added to Judge Sabich's computer after it was seized last November and before it was returned to the prosecution's custody after Your Honor's appointment. There is no other explanation."

"Judge Yee," answers Stern, "that is hardly as clear as Mr. Brand wishes it were. Neither Judge Sabich nor any of his agents had access to that machine for longer than fifty-eight minutes. We have been advised by experts that the kind of alterations they are talking about could never have been accomplished in that time frame, probably not even by professionals, which none of those persons were."

"I don't know about that, Judge. We would need to test that," says Brand. The hedged way he responds makes me think that Gorvetich gave him a longer time estimate than we received from Hans and Franz. They will need another theory, but they have one, just as Stern supposed. "And besides, Your Honor," says Brand, "did Judge Sabich ever surrender his keys to the courthouse?"

"Judge Sabich had no keys to the chambers of Judge Mason, where the computer was housed," says Sandy.

"Are we saying that Judge Sabich never in his life entered the courthouse after hours? Are we saying he doesn't know the security staff members who had the keys to all the chambers?"

Judge Yee watches the back-and-forth with his hand across his mouth, but the pencil starts wagging in his hand. It's like a dog's tail in reverse, a measure of when he is displeased.

"Your Honor," says Stern, "the prosecution is very quick to accuse Judge Sabich. But without any compelling evidence."

"Who else benefited from this fraud?" Brand answers.

"Judge, I confess that what keeps going through my mind is that twenty years ago Mr. Molto admitted and was sanctioned by the prosecuting attorney's office for deliberately mishandling evidence."

This produces another of those courthouse moments when I am entirely lost. Sandy said nothing about this in his office, and the effect on Brand is volcanic. He has a temper anyway, and he stands at the podium screaming, with his face crimson and the veins throbbing at his temple. At the prosecution table, Tommy Molto also has come to his feet.

"Judge," he shouts, but he can barely be heard over Brand.

"Outrage" and "outrageous" are the words Brand keeps yelling. He turns his back to the judge for a second to say a wrathful word to Stern, then resumes his screaming.

Judge Yee has finally had enough.

"Wait, wait, wait," he says. "Wait. Enough. All lawyers. Sit, please. Sit." He allows a second for the baying hounds to retreat. "Nothing in this trial about twenty years ago. Twenty years ago is twenty years ago. That one thing. And second, this trial, this trial about who murdered Mrs. Sabich, not about whether someone fooled with judge's computer. Let me tell you, ladies and gentlemen, what I think. I think none of this ought to be in evidence. Keys and spy programs and how many hours to do this and that? The jury will be told to disregard the message they saw. And we finish trying this lawsuit. Young Mr. Sabich, he goes back on the stand tomorrow morning. That what I am thinking is the best."

Brand stands up at the prosecution table. "Judge," he says. "Judge. May we be heard? Please." Yee allows Brand to reapproach the podium, which he does only after a talking-to from Molto, who has grabbed his sleeve on the way. I am sure he told Brand to settle down. Brand is far more measured.

"Judge, I understand that the Court wishes we didn't have to get sidetracked this way, but if the Court would consider this, Your Honor. Think how unfair your suggestion is to the prosecution. The jury has already seen that message. The defense will be able to argue that Mrs. Sabich killed herself. They will be able to argue that she went into her husband's computer. And they will even be able to insinuate she may have intended to frame him. They will say all of that, and when they do, the jurors have to think about that message, while the evidence that goes to show that whole theory is a fraud doesn't come in? Judge, you can't deny us that opportunity."

Yee has his hand over his mouth again. Even I can understand Brand's point.

"Judge, this can be proved quickly," says Brand. "A few witnesses at most."

Stern, always quick to seize an advantage, answers from his chair.

"A few witnesses from the prosecution, perhaps, Your Honor. But the defense will have no choice about refuting this allegation fully. We are basically going to have a trial on unindicted charges of obstruction of justice."

"What about that?" asks Judge Yee of Brand. "Indict Judge Sabich for obstruction of justice. Have that trial later." Judge Yee is clearly ready to go home and would like to hand this problem to someone else.

"Judge," says Brand, "you are asking us to finish this trial with both hands tied behind our backs."

"Okay," says the judge. "I going to think overnight. Tomorrow morning, young Mr. Sabich testifies. After that, we argue about what other evidence. But tomorrow, we try this lawsuit. No decision yet who can prove what. But we gonna have testimony. Everybody understand?"

The lawyers all nod. The judge bangs his gavel. Court is over for the day.

CHAPTER 39

Tommy, June 25, 2009

Tommy's problem, if you wanted to call it that, always was being too sensitive. The older he got, the more he knew that pretty much everybody had their tender spots. And over time, he had gotten better at absorbing the customary hard knocks—nasty editorials, or sniping defense lawyers, or neighborhood groups blaming him for every bad cop. But still. He had his stuff. And once a spear got through the armor, it went in pretty deep.

When Stern stood before Judge Yee and reminded the world that Tommy had admitted to mishandling evidence in Rusty's first trial, his heart went flat. Tommy's admission was never a secret. People who knew stuff knew that, too. But everybody understood it was just something Tommy had to say to get his job back, and it had never hit the press back then. And because reporters, generally speaking, only reprinted what they'd printed before, there had been no mention that Tommy had acknowledged any wrongdoing in the frequent stories that had run recently about Rusty's first trial. Tommy had worked his whole career to protect the public and what was right, and he didn't care to be known as someone who had once sailed too close to the wind. The first word in his head when he began to calm down was 'Dominga.' He had never explained all this to his wife.

As soon as Yee banged his gavel, the reporters gathered around Tommy, five or six of them.

"This is ancient history," Tommy said, "which Judge Yee just ruled has nothing to do with this case. I'll have no further comment until this matter is concluded." He had to repeat that six or seven times, and when the pack finally turned away to file their stories, he asked the paralegal and Rory to get the evidence cart back across the street. Then he motioned Brand over to the corner of the empty jury box, where they could sit and talk. He didn't want to go downstairs now, because the cameras would be there and the reporters would pull their standard stunt, sticking a microphone in Tommy's face so they could get some footage of him refusing to deny he broke the rules the first time Rusty was tried. Sandy Stern, packing up to leave, looked over for a second, then gimped their way with his cane. Tommy shook his head at him when Stern was still twenty feet away.

"Don't," he said.

"Tom, I was caught in the moment."

"Fuck you, Sandy. You knew what you were doing, and so do I." In his thirty-some years as a PA, Tommy had spoken those words to another lawyer only a handful of times. Stern had his hands raised, but Tommy kept shaking his head.

When Stern at last turned away, Brand yelled after

him, "You're just a drug court scumbag in a better suit."

Tommy grabbed Brand's sleeve.

"There are whale turds in the bottom of the ocean that aren't that low," Brand whispered to Molto.

But you could never take one thing away from Stern—he always came up with something to rescue his client. He didn't want the jury reading about the fact that the Christmas card was a fraud on the front page of tomorrow's *Tribune*. So he fed them a better headline: MOLTO ADMITTED MISCONDUCT. For all Tommy knew, the way it would play in the jurors' heads, half of them would figure out some theory about why the Christmas card was the PA's fault.

"We should leak the DNA," Brand murmured.

Tommy actually considered that for an instant, then shook his head no. They would end up with a mistrial. Basil Yee was ready to head home. Any reason to quit the case and he'd take it, pack and go. And Tommy wasn't about to lie under oath or let anybody else do it, either, in the investigation of the leak that would result. It was a fit revenge on Stern and Sabich. But the news would be out in a couple of weeks anyway, and letting it go now would only screw all this up worse.

"If Yee actually keeps all the fraud evidence out, we have to appeal," said Brand.

A midtrial appeal was rare but permissible for the prosecution in a criminal trial, because the PAs could not appeal after an acquittal. Brand was right—they would have to do that, because they stood little chance with the jury otherwise. And maybe once they raised that prospect, Yee would relent. Avoiding the court of appeals was the best way to assure he would maintain his treasured record on reversals. And the judge would detest the idea of keeping the jury—and himself—on ice for the two to three weeks the appellate proceedings would require.

"How did this get so screwed up in just a couple of days?" Tommy asked.

"We get that evidence in, we'll be fine. Rory's got a couple of dicks talking to the night staff at the court-house now. Somebody saw something, heard something, about Rusty sneaking in. When we come up with a hard witness, we can turn Yee around."

Maybe Jim was right. But shame was settling on Tommy hard. He could never cut himself a break. He hadn't tampered with anything, just leaked some information. But it was wrong. He'd done wrong. And Sandy Stern wanted to remind everybody of that.

"I need to pee," he told Brand.

In the men's room, Rusty Sabich was already at one of the urinals. There was no privacy panel between the ice white fixtures, and Tommy fixed his eyes on the tiles in front of him. He could hear the trouble Rusty had, the slow stream and the piddling beginning. In that department, Tommy was still a youngster. The advantage somehow emboldened him.

"That was low, Rusty." He repeated Brand's line about whales.

Rusty made no answer. Molto felt Sabich's shoulders shift as he hitched himself back into his trousers before his zipper scraped on ascent. The water ran in the sink a second later. When Tommy turned, Rusty was still there, drying his hands on a brown paper towel, his slackening face set inscrutably and his fair eyes unmoving.

"It was low, Tommy. And it was unlike Sandy, frankly. But the guy is sick. I'm sorry. I had no idea he was going down that road. If he had spoken to me first, I would have said no. I swear."

The apology, the acknowledgment that Stern was out of line, actually made Tommy feel worse. What bothered him the most was what he was going to see in the faces of his deputies and the judges. He would need to issue a statement as soon as the trial was over, probably make the file public. And say, I broke the rules, it was a small infraction, but I paid the price, and I've never forgotten the lesson. Sabich watched him wrestle through all of that. Trials are like this, Tommy thought. You open arteries on both sides. Physicians said it was better to be the doctor than the patient, and it was better to be the prosecutor than the defendant. But that didn't mean nobody else got hurt. He should have learned his lesson the first time he tangled with this guy. Going after Rusty meant trying to crawl through barbed wire.

"Tommy," said Rusty, "did you ever consider the possibility I'm not as bad a guy as you think, and you're not as bad a guy as I think?"

"That just amounts to a way of saying you're a sweetheart."

"I'm not a sweetheart. But I'm not a murderer. Barbara killed herself, Tommy."

"So you say. Did Carolyn rape and bludgeon herself, too?"

"I didn't do that, either. You'll have to take it up with the guy who did."

"It's just a pity, Rusty, the way these women keep dying around you."

"I'm not a killer, Tommy. You know that. In your heart of hearts you know that."

Tommy started to dry his own hands. "So what are you, Rusty?"

Sabich snorted a little, laughing for just a second at his own expense. "I'm a fool, Tommy. I've made a lot of mistakes, and it will be a long time before I can tell you which of them was the worst. Vanity. Lust. Pride to think I could change what couldn't be changed. I'm not telling you I didn't go looking for this. But she killed herself."

"And framed you for it?"

He shrugged. "I haven't figured that out yet. Maybe. Probably not."

"So what should I do, Rusty. Send the jury a thank-you note and tell them to go home?"

Sabich eyed Tommy a second. "Us girls?" he asked.

"Whatever."

Rusty went back to look under the stalls to be sure there were no unseen occupants, then returned to Molto.

"How about we end the whole thing? You and I both know there is absolutely no way to tell where this bastard is going. It's a runaway train now. I'll plead to obstruction for messing with the computer. Other charges are dismissed."

Sabich was in his unflinching hard-guy mode. But he wasn't kidding. Tommy's heart was skipping around in response.

"You walk on murder?"

"Which I didn't commit. Take what you can get, Tommy."

"How much time?"

"A year."

"Two," said Tommy. He negotiated out of instinct.

Sabich shrugged again. "Two."

"I'll talk to Brand."

Tommy stared at Sabich another second, trying to figure out what had just happened, but he stopped at the door. It was an odd moment, yet they ended up shaking hands.

"You ready?" Tommy asked when he sat next to Brand in the same chair in the back of the jury box. The courtroom was not quite empty yet. Stern's people were out in the hall, but the court personnel were still walking in and out. In a minuscule whisper, he told Brand what Sabich had offered. Jim just stared, his dark eyes hard as flints.

"Say what?"

Tommy repeated the deal.

"He can't do that," said Brand.

"He can if we let him."

Brand was almost never flustered. He lost track of himself in anger. But he rarely seemed stuck for words, yet he could not get hold of this one.

"He walks on murder?"

"He just told me something that's completely true. This trial is a runaway. Nobody knows what happens next."

"He walks on two murders?"

"He's got a good chance of doing that anyway.

Better, frankly, than we have of convicting him of anything else."

"You're not going to do this, Boss. You can't. The guy's a double fucking murderer."

"Let's go across the street. The coast is probably clear by now."

It was a hot day outside. The sun was strong this week, and as usual in this part of the country, it was turning to summer abruptly, as if somebody had thrown a switch. It had been a bad spring, with unprecedented amounts of rain. Great thing about global warming. You didn't know where you were living from one day to the next. For a month, Kindle County had been the Amazon.

When they got to the office, they took five minutes for messages. Tommy must have had ten calls from reporters. He would need to spend some time with Jan DeGrazia, the press deputy, later this afternoon, just to hear her advice. Finally, he went next door to Brand's smaller office.

They sat on either side of the room. There was a football, signed by some ancient star, which was regarded as a permanent part of the chief deputy's furnishings. It had been here as long as Tommy could recall, going back to John White, who had been chief deputy when he—and Rusty—had arrived as new prosecutors. Very often the ball was tossed around during discussions. Brand, whose hands fit the thing as if they were part of the cover, was usually the first to go for it, and even if no one else was in the mood to play, he would spin it in a perfect spiral toward the ceiling and grab it in descent without ever moving. Seeing it on Brand's desk, Tommy flipped it softly at Jim as Molto sat down. For the only time he could remember, Brand dropped it. He swore when he picked it up.

"You know this only makes sense one way," Brand said. "Rusty pleading?"

"What do you mean?"

"I mean he'd only plead to obstruction if he killed his wife."

"What if he didn't kill his wife, but messed with the computer?"

"He only messed with the computer if he killed her," Brand answered.

That was the traditional logic of the law. The law said that if a man ran away or covered up or lied, it proved he was guilty. But to Tom, that never made sense. Why should somebody falsely accused follow the rules? Why wouldn't somebody who saw the legal machinery clank and grind and screw itself stupid say, "I'm not trusting this broken contraption"? Lying to dispel a false accusation was probably better justified than lying in the face of a truthful one. That was how Tommy saw it. And always had.

When he explained his view to Jim, Brand actually seemed to consider it. It was rare to see Brand as pensive as he was now. But there was a lot at stake, and neither one of them had ever anticipated being at this moment.

Brand picked up the football from between his feet and tossed it to himself a couple of times. He was coming to something. Tommy could tell.

"I think we should take the deal," he said.

Tommy didn't answer. He was a little frightened

when Brand said it, even though he knew he was right.

"I think we should take the deal," Brand repeated. "And I'll tell you why."

"Why?"

"Because you deserve it."

"I do?"

"You do. Sandy took a great big dump on your head today. And it's only a preview. If Rusty walks on this case, you're going to hear a boatload of the same crap about what you admitted back in the day, so they can explain away the DNA in the first case. They'll say, 'That's only because Molto screwed with the evidence back then.'"

Tommy nodded. He'd realized that by now. God knows why he didn't see it all along. Probably because he hadn't screwed with the evidence.

"Okay, but if Sabich pleads to obstruction—a supreme court justice-elect standing up in open court and admitting he tampered with the evidence to try to get himself off—if he does that, people will know what he is. They'll say he got away with murder. Twice. They may criticize you for taking the plea. But Yee will cover you on that, almost for sure. You know, Basil's going to give one of those speeches judges always give when they're relieved to get rid of a case—he'll talk about what a wise resolution this is. Overall, people will know you chased a really bad bird for a really long time and finally got him in the joint where he belongs. You'll strip him of all his feathers. And you deserve that."

"I can't do this job thinking about what I deserve."

"You can do the job so that public confidence in the

administration of justice is maintained. You certainly fucking can. And you should."

Brand was putting Tommy's ego in wrapping paper and tying it in a bow.

"You deserve this," Brand said. "You take the deal and the monkey is off your back. You can run for PA next year, if you like."

That again. Tommy thought for a second. He had never actually been able to consider running, except as the kind of fantasy that lasts as long as your shower. He told Brand what he'd told him before, that if he could run for anything, it would be for judge.

"I have a twenty-one-month-old," Tommy said. "I need a job I can keep for fifteen years."

"And another one on the way," said Brand.

Tommy smiled. He felt his heart open. He had a good life. He had worked hard and done right. He would never say it out loud, but what Brand said was true. He deserved it. He deserved to be known as someone who had followed his conscience.

"And another on the way," Tommy said.

CHAPTER 40

Nat, June 26, 2009

Something is wrong.

When I arrive at the Sterns' offices on Friday morning, my dad is in a do not disturb conference with Marta and Sandy in Stern's office. After I spend forty-five minutes in the reception area among the steak-house furnishings, Sandy's assistant emerges to suggest I go over to the courthouse, where the defense team will join me shortly.

When I get there, the PAs have not arrived either. I send a text to Anna from my seat in the front row: "Something is wrong. Sandy sicker????? Very mysterious."

Marta finally comes in but bustles straight through the courtroom to go back to Judge Yee's chambers. When she reemerges, she stops with me for just a second.

"We're talking to the prosecutors down the hall," she says.

"What's up?"

Her expression is too confused to connote anything very clear.

A few minutes later, Judge Yee peeks into the courtroom to check on things. Without his robe on, he's like a child at the door, hoping not to be observed, and when he catches sight of me, he motions me in his direction.

"Coffee?" he asks when I arrive in the rear corridor.

"Sure," I say.

We go back to the chambers, where I spend a few moments inspecting the framed sheet music on the walls. One, I realize, is signed by Vivaldi.

"We gotta wait for these guys," the judge tells me without further explanation. I am locked in witness land, where I cannot ask any questions, of the judge least of all. "So what you think?" he asks when he has brought in coffee for each of us. The judge has pulled out a drawer on the big desk and is using it as a footrest. "You think you gonna be a trial lawyer like Dad?"

"I don't think so, Judge. I don't think I have the nerves for it."

"Oh yeah," he says. "Hard on the nerves for everybody. Lotsa drunks. Court make lotsa drunks."

"I suppose I should worry about that, but I meant I don't really have the personality for it. I don't actually like it very much when people are paying attention to me. I'm not cut out for it."

"You can never tell," he says. "Me? How I talk? Everybody like, That no job for you. They all laugh—even my mama. And she don't speak three words English."

"So what happened?"

"I got an idea. You know? I was boy. Watchin *Perry Mason*, on TV. Oh, love *Perry Mason*. In high school, I got a job with newspaper. Not a reporter. Sell the paper. *Tribune* from here. *Tribune* want more subscriber downstate. So I go knock on door. Most people, very nice, but all them, every one hate the city. Don't want city newspaper. All very nice to me. 'No, Basil. Like you but not that paper.' Except this one guy. Big guy. Six three. Three hundred pound. White hair. Crazy, crazy eyes. And he see me and he come out the door like he gonna kill me. 'Get off my property. Japs kill three my buddies. Get off.' And I try to explain. Japanese kill my grandfather, too. But he not listenin. Don't wanna listen.

"So I go home. My mama, my daddy, they like, 'Man like that. He won't listen. How people are.' But I think, No, I can make him understand. If he have to listen, I can make him understand. So I remember *Perry Mason*. And the jury. They gotta listen. That their job. To listen. And okay, I don't speak English good. Tried and tried. I write like professor. Straight A in English all through school. But when I talk, I cannot think. Really. Like machine get stuck. But I say to myself, People can understand. If they have to listen. PA at home—Morris Loomis—I know him since grade school. His son, Mike, and me, good friend. So after law school, Morris say, 'Okay, Basil. I let you try. But you lose, then you write briefs.' And first case, I stand up, I say, 'I don't talk English good. Very sorry. I speak slow so you understand. But case not about me. About witnesses. About victim. Them you must understand.' And the jury, they all nod. Okay. And you know, two day, three day, they all understand. Every word. And I win. Won that case. Won ten jury in a row before I lost. Sometime in jury box, one whisper to the other, 'What he say?' But I always tell them, 'Case about the witnesses. Not about me. Not about defense lawyer, even though he talk a lot better. About witnesses. About the proof. Listen to them and make up your mind.' Jury always think, That guy, he not hiding nothing. I win all the time.

"So you can never tell. Court very mysterious, what jury understand, don't understand. You know?"

I laugh out loud. I love Judge Yee.

We talk about classical music for a while. Judge Yee knows his stuff. It turns out he plays the oboe and is still in the regional orchestra downstate and frequently uses his lunch hour to practice. He has an oboe that has been muted so you can hear the notes only from a few feet, and he actually plays through a Vivaldi piece for me, in honor of the sheet music on the walls. I am pretty much a musical ignoramus, even though I am interested in it as a language. But like most kids, I chafed at piano lessons for years until my mom let me quit. Serious music is one of those things I have on the list for "When I Grow Up."

There is a knock as the judge is about to begin another piece. Marta is there.

"Judge," she says, "we need a few more minutes. My father would like to talk to Nat."

"To me?" I ask.

I follow her down the corridor to what is called the visiting attorneys' room. It's not much bigger than a closet, with no windows and a beaten desk and a couple of old wooden armchairs. Sandy is in one of them. He does not look particularly well this morning. The rash is better, but he looks more depleted.

"Nat," he says, but does not bother to try to get up to greet me. I come around to shake his hand, then he motions for me to sit. "Nat, your father has asked me to speak to you. We have reached a plea bargain with the prosecution."

I keep thinking with this case, Well, I'll never have a shock like that again. And then there is something else that knocks me flat.

"I know this comes as a surprise," says Stern. "The murder charges against your father will be dismissed. And he will plead guilty to an information the prosecutors will file in a few minutes, charging him with obstruction of justice. We have had quite a bit of back-and-forth this morning with Molto and Brand. I wanted them to accept a plea to contempt of court instead, which would give your father a chance to keep his pension, but they insist it must be a felony. The bottom line is the same. Your father will be in custody for two years. And can then go on with his life."

"'Custody'?" I say. "You mean jail?"

"Yes. We've agreed that it will be the state work farm. Minimum security. He won't be far away."

"'Obstruction'? What did he do?"

Stern smiles. "Well, that was one of the morning's problems. He will admit he is guilty, that he willfully and knowingly obstructed justice in this case. But he will not go into details. I take it there is someone else he does not want to implicate, but candidly, he won't even say that much. Molto was not satisfied, but in the end, he knows this plea is as good as he is likely to do. So we have an agreement. Your father wanted me to tell you."

I don't hesitate. "I need to talk to my dad."

"Nat—"

"I need to talk to him."

"You know, Nat, when I first began in this line, I swore to myself I would never let an innocent man plead guilty. That resolve did not get me through my first year in practice. I represented a young man. A fine young man. Poor. But he was twenty years old with never so much as an arrest after growing up in the bleakest part of Kehwahnee. That fact speaks volumes about his character. But he was in a car with childhood friends, they were sharing a few bottles of malt liquor, and one of them saw a man who had two-timed his mother, and this young man had a gun in his pocket and shot this two-timer through the window of the car with no more reflection than it took to say the word 'dead.' My client had nothing to do with that murder. Nothing. But you know how things go in this process. The killer said his friends had been together in the car to help him hunt the decedent down. He told that tale to avoid the death penalty, which was being freely applied in this county in those days. And so my client was charged with murder. Better sense told the prosecutors my client was not involved. But they had a witness. And they offered my client probation for a lesser plea. He wanted to be a police officer, that young man. And would have made a fine one. But he pleaded guilty. And went on with a different life. And clearly that was the right decision. He became a tile layer, he has a business, three children, all through college. One of them is a lawyer only a little older than you."

"What are you saying, Sandy?"

"I'm saying that I have learned to trust my client's judgment on these matters. No one is better equipped to decide whether it is worth brooking the risks."

"So you don't think he's guilty?"

"I don't know, Nat. He is adamant this is the proper outcome."

"I need to see my father."

I take it that he has been down the hall in the witness room with Marta, and Stern wants to speak to him before I do. I help Sandy to his feet. I am alone only a few minutes, but I have started crying by the time my dad walks in. The startling part is that he looks better this morning than he has in many months. A self-possessed look has returned.

"Tell me the truth," I say as soon as I see him. He smiles at that. He leans down to embrace me, then sits opposite me, where Stern sat before.

"The truth," he says, "is that I did not kill your mother. I have never killed anyone. But I did obstruct justice."

"How? I don't believe you could have done that with the computer. I don't believe it."

"Nat, I'm three times seven. I know what I did."

"You lose everything," I say.

"Not my son, I hope."

"How will you support yourself afterwards? This is a felony, Dad."

"I'm well aware."

"You'll give up your judgeship, your law license. You won't even have your pension."

"I'll try not to land on your doorstep." He actually smiles. "Nat, this is a compromise. I plead guilty to something I did and serve the sentence, without risking conviction for something I'm completely innocent of. Is that a bad deal? After Judge Yee rules about whether all the computer evidence can come in, one side will have the upper hand and this kind of resolution won't be possible. It's time we get this over with and move on to the rest of life. You need to forgive me for all the stupid things I did in the last two years. But I did them, and it's not wrong that I pay this price. I can live with this outcome and you should, too."

We stand in unison and I hug my father, blubbering foolishly. When we break apart, the man who never cries is weeping, too.

Court is convened in a few minutes. Word of what is about to transpire has hit the courthouse, and the buffs and PAs stream into the courtroom, along with at least a dozen reporters. I do not have the heart to go in at first. I stand at the door, through the grace of the courtroom deputies, who allow me to watch the proceedings through the tiny window in the door. There is so much misery in this building, which is full of the anguish of the victims and the defendants and their loved ones, that I actually think the people who work here every day go out of their way to be especially kind to the people like me who, through no will of their own, are caught in the thresher called justice. One of them, an older Hispanic man, actually keeps his hand on my back for a second when the session begins and my father rises to stand between Marta and Sandy before Judge Yee. Brand and Molto are on Stern's other side. My dad nods and speaks. The prosecutors hand up papers, probably a formal plea agreement and the new charges, and the judge begins questioning my dad, an elaborate process that has been going several minutes already when I catch sight of Anna. I sent her a simple text— "My dad is going to plead guilty to obstruction to end the case"—only a few minutes ago. Now she is tearing down the hall, dashing in her high heels, with one hand at the V of her blouse, because her go-to-work underwear is not meant for running.

"I don't believe this," she says.

I explain what I can, and then we enter the courtroom arm in arm and proceed to the front-row seats still reserved for my father's dwindling family. Judge Yee's eyes flick up to see me, and he emits the minutest smile of reassurance. He then looks back down to the form book in front of him, which contains the required questions a judge must ask before accepting a guilty plea. Notably, Judge Yee reads the printed text without any of the grammatical errors that emerge when he is speaking on his own, although his accent remains strong.

"And Judge Sabich, you are pleading guilty to this one-count information because you are in fact guilty of the crime charged there, correct?"

"Yes, Your Honor."

"All right, prosecutors. Please state the factual basis for the offense."

Jim Brand speaks. He describes all the technical details concerning the computers, the "object" now present on my dad's hard drive that was not there when it was imaged in early November 2008. Then he adds that a night custodian in the courthouse, Anthony

Potts, is prepared to testify that he recalls seeing my father in the corridors there one night last fall and that my father seemed to speed away when Potts observed him.

"All right," says Judge Yee, and looks down to his primer. "And, Mr. Stern, is the defense satisfied that the factual basis offered constitutes sufficient competent evidence to prove Judge Sabich guilty were the matter submitted to trial?"

"We are, Your Honor."

"Judge Sabich, do you agree with Mr. Stern about that?"

"Yes, Judge Yee."

"All right," says Yee. He closes the book. He is back on his own. "The Court wish to compliment all party on a very good resolution for this case. This case very, very complex. This outcome that defense and prosecution agree to is fair to the People and the defendant in judgment of the Court." He nods several times, as if to enforce that opinion on the reporters across from me on the other side of the front row.

"Okay," he says. "Court find there is sufficient basis for guilty plea and accept the plea of defendant Roz—" He stumbles with the name, which comes out something akin to "Rosy"—"Sabich to information 09–0872. Indictment 08–2456 is dismissed on all count with prejudice. Judge Sabich, you remanded to custody of Kindle County sheriff for a period of two year. Court adjourned." He smacks the gavel.

My father shakes hands with Sandy and kisses Marta's cheek, then turns to me. He starts when he does. It takes me a second to realize it is Anna he is reacting to. It's her first time in court, and she is plainly unexpected. Like me, she has spent the last ten minutes crying quietly, and her makeup is all over her face. He gives her this complicated little smile and then looks at me and nods. Then he turns away and without a word from anyone places his hands behind his back. He is fully prepared for this moment. It occurs to me he has probably been through it a hundred times in his dreams.

Manny, the deputy sheriff, fastens the cuffs on my dad and whispers to him, probably trying to be sure they are not too tight, then pushes my dad toward the courtroom's side door, where there is a small lockup in which he will be held until he is transported to the jail with the rest of the defendants who have appeared in court this morning.

My father leaves the courtroom without ever looking back.

IV.

Chapter 41

Tommy, August 3, 2009

Summer in all its sweet indulgence. It was five p.m. and Tommy was one of the squad of fathers following their children around the tot lot, relieving beleaguered moms in the hour before dinner. The playground was, without doubt, Tomaso's favorite place on earth. When Tommy's son arrived, he ran from one piece of equipment to another, touching the little merry-go-round, climbing onto the spiderweb and off. Dashing a step behind, Tommy always felt the anguish of his two-year-old that he could not do everything at once.

Dominga was having a harder time with this pregnancy than with Tomaso's. There was more morning nausea and constant fatigue, and she complained of feeling swollen in the heat, like something ripening on the vine. Now officially a lame duck, Tommy was finding it easier to get out of the office and tried to be home no later than four thirty to give her a break. Tomaso and he often returned from the playground to find her sound asleep. Tomaso would crawl across his mother's recumbent body, trying to squeeze his way into her arms. Dominga smiled before she stirred and clutched her little boy to her, grimy and beloved.

Life was good. Tommy was going to be sixty any minute, and his life was better than at any time he could recall. Just as the first Sabich trial and its dismal aftermath had darkened his existence decades before, so the second trial was proving to be the start of a life as an esteemed figure. Public perceptions had formed very much as Brand had foreseen the night they decided to take Rusty's plea. Sabich's conviction verified Tommy on everything. The DNA from the first trial was regarded as controversial, because of doubts about the specimen, but the common comparison was to O.J., who'd also gotten away with murder because of bad labwork. The consensus on the editorial pages was that prosecutor Molto had made the best of it and had convicted a man whose conviction was long overdue. In fact, in the last six weeks, the papers had dropped the word "Acting" when they referred to him as PA. And the county executive had let it be known that Tommy was welcome on the ticket next year if he wanted to run for the job.

He had actually pondered that possibility for a few days. But it was time to accept his blessings. He was ten times luckier than all his peers in the PA's office who'd had to struggle to make their careers while their kids were young. Tommy could leap onto the bench now, a worthy job that would leave him time to savor his boys and to be more than a rumor in their lives. Two weeks ago, he had announced he was running for superior court judge and endorsed Jim Brand to succeed him. Ramon Beroja, a former deputy PA now on the county board, was going to run against Jim in the primary, but the party preferred Brand, largely because of the broad suspicions that Ramon would take on the county executive next. Jim would spend the next six months running hard, but he was expected to win.

Across the tot lot, a man was eyeing Tommy, an old bushy-looking fellow with a stretch of appallingly white legs revealed between the ends of his cargo shorts and his calf-high tube socks. This was not uncommon. Tommy was a familiar figure on TV, and people were always trying to place him, often mistaking him for someone they'd known at an earlier time. But this man was more intent than the usual curious neighbors with their puzzled glances. When the kids he was trailing moved in Tomaso's direction, the man approached Tommy and had actually shaken his hand before Molto finally placed Milo Gorvetich, the computer expert from the Sabich trial.

"Aren't grandchildren life's greatest blessing?" he asked, nodding toward two little girls, both wearing glasses. The girls were on the slide while Tomaso followed them there and stood on the bottom rung, looking up longingly but afraid to venture any farther. This drama played itself out daily. Eventually, Tomaso would cry and his father would lift him to the top. There Tomaso would linger again until he finally found his courage and plunged to the bottom, where Tommy would be waiting to catch him.

"He's my son," said Tommy. "I got a late start."

"Oh, dear," answered Gorvetich, but Tommy laughed. He kept telling Dominga he was going to have a T-shirt made for Tomaso that read, 'That old man over there is actually my father.' Usually by the time Tommy explained himself to the other parents here, they had placed him as PA. From the comments that followed, he could tell that many assumed he was a county power broker looking after the child born of his second or third marriage to a trophy wife. Nobody really ever understood anybody else's life.

"A beautiful boy," said Gorvetich.

"The light of my life," Tommy answered.

It turned out that Gorvetich's youngest daughter was a neighbor of Tommy's, living one street behind him closer to the river. She was a professor of physics married to an engineer. Gorvetich, a widower, was here often at this hour to look after the girls until their parents were home from work.

"So are you preparing for your next big trial?" Gorvetich asked by way of small talk.

"Not yet," said Tommy. The norm, in fact, was for the PA to be solely an administrator. Most of Tommy's predecessors never saw the inside of a courtroom, and Tommy was already testing the idea that the Sabich case would be the last trial of his life.

"Standard fare for you," said Gorvetich, "but I must say I have been preoccupied by that case since it ended. One thinks of trials as emphatic and conclusive, and this was anything but."

Sometimes it was like that, Tommy answered. A few tight little categories—guilty, not guilty, of this or that—to hold a universe of complicated facts.

"We do a little justice, rather than none at all," answered Tommy.

"To an outsider it's confounding, but you boys are

accustomed enough to the murkiness of all of it to find some grim humor, I suppose."

"I don't think I found much to laugh at in that case."

"There's the difference between Brand and you, then," said Gorvetich.

Tommy had his eye on Tomaso, who was yet to move off the ladder, even though a line had formed behind him. Tommy tried to wrest the boy from the first rung, but he squawked in objection and uttered his favorite syllable: "No." In time, Tommy persuaded Tomaso to let the other children climb, but as soon as they had started up, Tomaso went right back to the first rung like a hawk on a perch. His father stood immediately behind him, within arm's reach.

"Persistent," said Gorvetich, laughing.

"Stubborn like his father. Genes are amazing things." He drew his mind back to the conversation before. "What were you saying about Brand?"

"Only that I was struck by a remark he made when we had dinner the week after. It was a little celebration. I believe you were invited."

Tommy remembered. After a month of working round the clock for the trial, he did not want another night away from his family. He explained now that his wife was newly pregnant at the time of the dinner. Tommy accepted Gorvetich's congratulations, before the old professor went back to his story.

"It was the end of the evening. We were out on the walk in front of the Matchbook, and we were both well in our cups, and I made a remark to Jim about how unsettling it must be to be part of a system that sometimes comes to such an unsatisfying outcome. Jim laughed and said that as time went on, he was finding more and more perverse humor in this case, seeing somebody who had contrived to commit the perfect murder end up punished for a crime in which he had no role."

"What did that mean?" Tommy asked.

"I don't know. I asked at the time, but Jim brushed it off. I thought you might understand."

"Hardly," said Tommy.

"I've rolled it over in my mind. When Sabich pled guilty, I took it for granted he had a collaborator in tampering with his PC. It would have been an exceptional technical feat for a man who demonstrated such limited knowledge of his computer to do that himself. Remember, he hadn't even realized that his Web searches would be cached in the browser."

"Right," said Tommy.

"I've wondered if Jim had concluded that the accomplice wasn't an accomplice at all, but somebody who acted entirely on his own without any direction from Sabich."

Tommy shrugged. He had no idea what this was about. They had tried to consider every possibility the day they'd discovered that the card wasn't on the image. Half expecting the defense to accuse them of something, they had reviewed the chain of evidence carefully to be sure it was secure. Back in December when Yee ordered the PC returned, Gorvetich and Orestes Mauro, an evidence tech from the PA's office, covered the screen, the keyboard, the power button on the tower, and even the mouse in evidence tape, which they'd initialed before shrink-wrapping all the components. The day Nat Sabich testified, the shrink-wrap had been sliced off in the PA's office with the consent of the defense, but the tape seals were removed only in the courtroom in the presence of Sabich's two hot-shot experts, who verified that none of them showed the word "Violated" that appeared in blue if the tape was ever disturbed.

So the only possibility was that the tampering had taken place while the machine was in George Mason's chambers. Gorvetich had looked at Mason's log and was of the opinion that no one had access to the computer long enough to make all the changes, especially the registry deletions, which he said would be time-consuming even for him. The only plausible explanation seemed to be that Sabich and some techie they were yet to discover had snuck into the building after hours. But apparently another explanation had occurred to Brand in the ensuing weeks.

"Brand was probably spitballing," said Molto.

"Perhaps so," said Gorvetich. "Or I misunderstood. We'd had quite a bit to drink."

"Probably that. I'll have to ask him."

"Or let it go," said Gorvetich.

The old man seemed woolly-headed and self-involved at all times, but there was a shrewd light in his eyes for a second. Tommy did not quite understand what he was thinking, but Milo's granddaughters had wandered to the other side of the play area and he departed quickly. That was just as well, since Tommy heard the cry he recognized as Tomaso's at the same instant. When Tom looked up, he saw that his son had ascended the ladder. The two-year-old now stood at the top, utterly terrified by what he had achieved.

CHAPTER 42

Rusty, August 4, 2009

'Prison holds no fear for him.' We said that all the time decades ago when I was a deputy PA. We were usually talking about hardened crooks—con men, gangbangers, professional thieves—who committed crimes as a way of life and were undeterred by the prospect of confinement, either because they never considered the future or because a stop in the penitentiary had long been accepted as part of what passed for a career plan.

The saying circulates in my head all the time, because it is a nearly constant preoccupation to tell myself that prison is not so bad. I survived yesterday. I will survive today, then go on to tomorrow. The things you think would matter—the dread of other inmates and the fabled dangers of the shower—occupy their share of psychic space, but they count far less than what seemed to be trivial matters on the outside. You have no way to know how much you enjoy the company of other human beings or the warmth of natural daylight until you live without them. Nor can you fully comprehend the preciousness of liberty until matters of daily

whim—when to get up, where to go, what to wear—
are rigidly prescribed by someone else. Ironically, stu-
pendously, the worst part of being in the joint is the
most obvious—you cannot leave.

Because my safety in the general population is
regarded as a high-risk proposition, I am held in what is
called administrative detention, which is better known
as seg. I routinely debate whether I would be better off taking my chances in genpop, which would at
least allow me to work eight hours a day. The inmates
here are mostly young, Latin and black gang members
who were picked up on drug offenses and do not have
a long record of violence. Whether any of them would
care to do me harm is a matter of pure speculation. I
have already heard through the COs, who are the institution's Internet, that there are two men here whose
convictions I affirmed, and by pure addition and sub-
traction, I can figure that there are probably a few more
whose fathers or grandfathers I prosecuted decades
ago. Overall, I accept the view of the assistant warden,
who encouraged me to volunteer for seg, that I am too
famous not to be a symbol to some depressed and furious young man, a trophy fish whom he'd enjoy feeling
on his hook.

So I am held in an eight-by-eight cell with cement
walls, a short steel-reinforced door through which my
meals are delivered, and a single bulb. There is also a
six-inch-by-twenty-four-inch window, which barely
admits any light. In here, I am free to spend my time
as I like. I read a book every day or two. Stern suggested I may be able to find a market for my memoirs
when I am released, and I write a little every day, but

I'll probably burn the pages as soon as I am out. The newspaper comes by mail, two days late, with the occasional articles relating to the state prisons scissored out. I have started to study Spanish—I practice with a couple of the COs willing to answer back. And, like a man of leisure at the end of the nineteenth century, I attend to my correspondence. I write a letter to Nat every day and hear often from several figures from my former life whose loyalty I value immensely, particularly George Mason and Ray Horgan and one of my neighbors. There are also a good two dozen nut-jobs, mostly female, who have written to me in the last month to proclaim their faith in my innocence and to share their own tales of injustice, usually involving a corrupt judge who presided over their divorce.

When the four prisoners who are being held in administrative detention are released together in the yard for our one hour of exercise, I have an instant impulse to embrace each of them, which does not take long to stifle. Rocky Toranto is a transvestite, HIV-positive, who would not stop turning tricks in genpop. The other two who eye me as I trot around the yard and do my jumping jacks and push-ups are criminally insane. Manuel Rodegas has a face like a bug that was crushed. He is about five feet three, and his head seems to grow straight out of his shoulders. His conversation, while occasionally lucid, veers into gibberish much of the time. Harold Kumbeela is everyone's bad dream, six feet six, three hundred pounds, who crippled one man and nearly killed another while he was housed downstairs. He is far too violent to have been assigned to the state work farm and is here only because of a paid arrangement with Homeland Security, which rents half a dozen cells for immigration detainees who are awaiting deportation, which in Harold's case cannot come too soon. Unfortunately for me, Harold has learned that I was a judge and regularly seeks my advice about his case. Telling him I know nothing about immigration law was a feint that bought me only a couple of weeks. 'Yeah, bra,' he told me a few days ago, 'but maybe, dude, you could be studying up, you know. Do a bra a favor, you know?' I have asked the COs to keep an eye on Harold, which they do anyway.

Nat comes down to see me every Sunday, bringing a basket of books, which the staff inspects, and the fourteen dollars I am allowed each week in the commissary. I spend the entire sum on candy, since no matter how much I exercise, the food rarely seems to be worth eating. Nat and I sit at a little whitewashed version of a picnic table. Because it is minimum security, I am allowed to reach over and touch his hand for a second and to hug him when he arrives and departs. We get only an hour. He cried the first two times he saw me here, but we have started to enjoy our visits, where he does most of the talking, generally bringing me news of the world, of work, and of the family, as well as the week's best offering of Internet jokes. We spend much of the hour laughing, although there is always a moment of anguish when we discuss the Trappers, mired in yet another hopeless season.

Thus far, Nat has been my only visitor. It would be imprudent for Anna to join him for many reasons, and she keeps the same distance she has for most of the last two years. Besides, I am not really eager for anybody else to see me in here. On Sundays, when Nat arrives, I am walked through the nesting gatehouses by a CO named Gregg, literally progressing toward daylight.

I am therefore completely startled when the door to my cell swings wide open and Torrez, one of the COs who helps me with my Spanish, says, "*Su amigo.*" He stands aside and Tommy Molto ducks his head to come through the door. I have been lying on my bunk, reading a novel. I sit up suddenly, but I have no idea what to say. Nor does Tom, who stands inside the door, seeming to wonder only now why he is here.

"Rusty." Tommy offers his hand, which I take. "Like the whiskers," he says.

I have grown a beard here, largely because the light in my cell makes shaving hazardous and because the safety razors that we are allowed are famously dull.

"How you doing here?" Molto asks.

I open my hands. "I don't care much for the health club, but at least there's room service."

He smiles. I use the line all the time in my letters.

"I didn't come to gloat, if that's what you're afraid of," says Molto. "There was a meeting here of state prison officials and PAs from around the state."

"Strange place for a get-together."

"No reporters."

"Ah."

"The Corrections Department wants the prosecutors to okay a plan to release some inmates over sixty-five."

"Because they're no longer risks?"

"To save money. The state can't really afford to pay for their health care."

I smile. What a world. No one in the criminal justice system ever talks about the cost of punishment. Everybody there thinks there's no price to morality.

"Maybe Harnason made a better deal than he thought," I tell Tommy.

Tommy likes that but shrugs. "I thought he told the truth."

"So did I. Pretty much."

Tommy nods. The cell door is still open, and Torrez is right outside. To make himself comfy, Tommy in his suit has leaned back against the wall. I have decided not to tell him that moisture often collects there.

"Anyway," says Tommy, "there are some people who think you also ought to be a candidate for early release."

"Me? Anyone outside my family?"

"There seems to be a theory in my office that you pled guilty to a crime you didn't commit."

"That's about as good as the other theories you guys had about me. They were all wrong, and so is this one."

"Well, as long as I was around, I thought I'd look in on you and see what you had to say. Kind of a coincidence, but maybe that means I'm supposed to be here."

Tommy always was a little bit of a Catholic mystic. I ponder what he's said. I don't know whether to be heartened or infuriated when it strikes me that Tommy still seems willing to trust my word. It's hard to imagine what he thinks of me. Probably nothing consistent. That's his problem.

"You've heard it now, Tom. Where'd this theory in your office come from, anyway?"

"I ran into Milo Gorvetich yesterday, and he repeated something people had been saying. I didn't quite understand at first, but it came to me in the middle of the night and it bothered me."

Tommy looks about, then sticks his head outside the door to ask Torrez for a chair. It takes a minute, and the best they can come up with is a plastic crate. I was thinking of offering Molto the seatless stainless-steel commode, but Tommy is too proper to find that amusing. Nor is it much for comfort.

"You were bothered in the middle of the night," I remind him when he is situated.

"What bothers me is that I have a son. In fact, I'm about six months from having another one."

I offer my good wishes. "You give me hope, Tommy."

"How's that?"

"Starting again at a late age? Seems to be working for you. Maybe something good will happen to me once I get out of here."

"I hope so, Rusty. Everything is possible with faith, if you don't mind me saying so."

I'm not sure that's the solution for me, but I take the advice as well-intended, and I tell Tommy as much. There is silence then.

"Anyway," Molto says eventually, "if someone told me I needed to spend two years in the hole to save my boys' lives, I'd do it in a heartbeat."

"Good for you."

"So if I was convinced that somebody I loved had monkeyed with that computer, even with no say-so from me, I might have fallen on my sword and pled guilty, just to end the whole thing."

"Right. But I'd be innocent that way, and I've said to you that I'm guilty."

"So you claim."

"Don't you find this a little ironic? I've told you for more than twenty years I'm not a murderer, and you won't believe me. You finally find a crime I actually committed, and when I say I did that, you won't accept that, either."

Molto smiles. "I'll tell you what. Since you're such a truthful guy. You explain to me exactly how you managed to mess around with that computer. Just me and you. You have my word that no one else will ever be prosecuted. In fact, whatever you say will never leave this cell. Just let me hear it."

"Sorry, Tom. We already made a deal. I said I wasn't going to answer questions, if you accepted the plea. And I'm sticking to it."

"You want me to put it in writing? You have a pen? I'll write it down now. Tear a blank page out of one of your books." He points to the stack on my single slender shelf. 'I, Tommy Molto, Prosecuting Attorney for Kindle County, promise no further prosecutions of any kind related in any way to Rusty Sabich's PC and to keep any information relayed strictly confidential.' You think that's a promise I can't keep?"

"Probably not, to be honest. But that's not the point, anyway."

"Just you and me, Rusty. Tell me what happened. And I can let this whole thing go."

"And you think you'd believe me, Tom?"

"God knows why, but yes. I don't know if you're a sociopath or not, but I wouldn't be surprised, Rusty, if you haven't lied yet. At least as you understand the truth."

"You've got that part right. Okay," I say, "here's the truth. Once and for all. You and me." I get up off the bed so I can look straight at him. "I obstructed justice. Now leave it be."

"That's what you want?"

"That's what I want."

Molto shakes his head again and in the process notices the wet spot on the shoulder of his suit. He rubs at it a few times, and when he looks up I can't quite banish a smile. His eyes harden. I have touched the old nerve between us, Rusty up, Tommy down. I've made him Mr. Truth-and-Justice in town, but when it comes to the two of us, I can still push his buttons.

"Screw you, Rusty," he says then. He heads out the door, then comes back, but only to grab the crate.

CHAPTER 43

Tommy, August 4–5, 2009

Tommy always wondered what would become of kids like Orestes Mauro, the PA office's evidence specialist, who dealt with digital equipment. Having lived this long, Tommy felt he should have some idea, but he really didn't think there was anybody like Orestes when he was young. The kid was smart enough and got his work done, albeit his own way. But Orestes lived a life of play. The buds to his iPod were in his ears at all times, except when he removed one to speak to somebody else. Whenever Tommy overheard Orestes talking in the hall, it was about online games and the latest releases for his Xbox. And most of his interest in computers treated the machine and the software as a multi-level puzzle, so the task at hand, whatever it was, was largely secondary to the beguiling enigma of how everything inside the box functioned. Work, as a boring necessity, was something Orestes acknowledged, as long as it did not last too long. He was a sweet, friendly kid. If he noticed you were there.

Orestes was visible in the evidence section, work-ing over several cardboard boxes on which he was tapping out rhythms, when Tommy came through the door to the PA's office. It was close to seven p.m. He had been stuck in traffic far too long on his way back in from Morrisroe and the state work farm, and he'd finally pulled off to take surface streets the rest of the way home, which brought him past the County Building. He had already missed dinner with Dominga and Tomaso, so he decided to stop and pick up the files for his meeting at the court of appeals in the morning. He could take an extra half hour at home in the a.m. and give Dominga a little more time to sleep.

Catching sight of Orestes, he veered into the evidence room, a converted warehouse space behind the freight elevator. Evidence gathered by grand jury subpoena was required by law to remain in control of the PA's office, rather than the police, and it was boxed and cataloged here. When O saw Tommy coming, he turned a full circle on his toe, a little bit of Michael Jackson.

"Boss man!" He was always too loud with the buds in.

"Hey, O." Tommy motioned to his ears, and Orestes pulled one out. Tommy tapped his other side, too. Orestes complied but clearly expected something grave.

"T's up?"

"The Sabich case," Tommy answered.

Orestes groaned in response. "That the judge?"

"The judge," answered Tommy.

"Oh, man, that whole thing, that's just too fucked up," he said.

A fair analysis. Tommy had been thinking about Rusty all the way back. It had been completely unsettling to see him in that cell, but more to Tommy than

Sabich from the appearances. Tom had anticipated that Rusty might have been depressed or goofy, like most of the guys in seg, but there was something about him that seemed freed. His hair was long and he had a prison beard, whiter than Tommy might have expected, so he looked like an island castaway. And he had the same air—you can't touch me. The worst has happened. Now you can't touch me. Even so, Sabich had remained himself. He probably hadn't lied to Tommy, but he'd spoken in his own way, careful, even cagey, about the words he was using, so he could tell himself he was being honest, but typical of Rusty, making sure only he really knew the truth. Which left Tommy in the same bind he'd been in with Rusty for decades now. What was the fucking truth, anyway?

"I'm still trying to figure out how they screwed around with the computer."

"Oh, man," said Orestes. "Can't figure that. Wasn't me, man. I know that." He laughed.

"Me neither. But I keep thinking there's something we missed. I'm wondering if maybe Sabich copped to the obstruction to protect his kid. Does that make any sense to you?"

"Okay," said Orestes. He took the extraordinary step of turning off his iPod and sat on a metal stool. "Nobody asked me, but remember that big meet we had after you all had been in court, once you knew the card was phony? And Milo was trippin about how nobody who was on the computer in Judge Mason's chambers—not Sabich or the kid or the former clerk—not any one of them had time to mess around and to do all the stuff it took to get the card on there. Remember?"

"Sure."

"And Jimmy B., he went off then about how Sabich must have snuck into the courthouse?"

"Right."

"But here's the thing. What if it was all of them? What if they were in this together, planting that card? One of them downloaded from a flash drive, and another ran Spy, and another edited the directory. Together all of them, even a couple of them, had the time."

Tommy grabbed his forehead. Of course. Maybe Orestes had a better future than he thought.

"So is that what you think happened?" Molto asked.

Orestes laughed out loud. "Dude," he said, "I don't have a clue. Computers, man, are always a trip. Ain't no one person who knows everything. That's why they're so cool."

Tommy contemplated this bit of philosophy. It was pretty sci-fi. Computers, O was saying, were already like people in the sense that you could never fully understand them.

"But if you were planting that card, is that how you would have done it?"

"Me?" O laughed again, a high-pitched musical sound. "Oh, I could have done it for sure. But that's me."

Orestes's casual confidence was slightly alarming. His job was to set up systems to ensure the evidence in his control was tamper-proof. Naturally, Tommy asked what he meant.

"Well, that's just how it rolled out. Like the night I was up there with Jimmy B. to take the wrapping off—"

"I thought that was in the morning, right before court?"

"Hey, man. Twelve p.m. to eight." Orestes laid a thumb on one of the vivid stripes in his shirt. "Gotta go to school in the a.m. Get an education. Make something of myself." Orestes did a rim shot on one of the cardboard boxes to reemphasize the point. "So I went down to Brand's office, because the PC was on the trial cart, and together we pulled off all the wrapping, which took like forever because we had initialed three or four layers, and then I get down to the components and when I looked at it all, it's like, Fuck me, this is messed up."

"Meaning?"

"Cause, you know, the evidence tape on the tower, it was across the power button. But the power button is recessed, like down? So there's like this itty-bitty space under the tape, and I tell Brand, like, 'Bad job, we done a bad job, you could power that baby up.' He's like, 'No way,' so I had one of my tools—" From his breast pocket Orestes produced a tiny driver, small enough to fix the screws in eyeglasses. "And I just run it up in there. Brand, man, he's my peeps, but he just about choked me. He's thinking I was gonna violate the tape. That was the day the *chiquita* showed up from the bank, and Brand was like, 'Whoa, coolio, it's way bad enough already.' I didn't do nothing. Just scared him. Gorvetich and them got all the tape off in the morning, no problem.

"But that's what I'm sayin. If I was going to mess with the computer, I'd have messed with it then."

"So you could have turned the computer on?"

"I didn't."

"I know you didn't, O. But you could have? The other components, like the keyboard and the monitor—they were still sealed, weren't they?"

"Totally, man. But the ports on the tower weren't taped. You coulda used another mouse or monitor that was compatible. There're only about a billion. That's why I was tripped out about it. But that's not what happened or nothin. It had all been wrapped up for months, anyway. The initials were there and everything, I'm just saying, since you ask, that's how I coulda done it. But I didn't, and Sabich and them—they did. But I don't know how. Rule one, man. What you don't know, you don't know. You just don't."

O had a great smile under the little fuzz that passed for a 'stache. He was a really smart kid, Tommy thought again. And as the years went on, he'd begin to realize what it was he didn't know.

Brand was in his office in the morning, moving files around on his desk, when Tommy returned about eleven a.m. from his conference at the court of appeals. The substance of the meeting had been largely the same as the meeting at the prison yesterday. Nobody had enough money. What do they cut?

Brand had taken the day off yesterday to interview political consultants. His opponent, Beroja, had the advantage of an existing organization. Brand would have a lot of help from the party, but he had to get his own people in place.

Molto asked what he made of the consultants he'd met.

"I liked the two women. O'Bannon and Meyers? Pretty sharp. Only guess what their last local campaign was."

"Sabich?"

"Exactly." Brand laughed. "Talk about hired guns."

"I saw him yesterday, by the way."

"Who?"

"Rusty."

That stopped Brand, who'd continued rearranging the piles on his desk. The trial cart from the Sabich case remained in the corner of Brand's office, still holding all of Jim and Tommy's files, as well as the exhibits, which Judge Yee had returned when the proceedings were over. To try a case, you ignored everything in the universe—family occasions, the news, other cases—and once it ended, all the stuff that had been pushed aside became more pressing than something as trivial as cleaning up. You could walk into the offices of half the deputy PAs and see trial boxes that had sat around untouched for months in the aftermath of verdicts. When you finally found the time to put that stuff away, it was as poignant as surveying the relics of a former love affair, these documents and pill bottles that once seemed as momentous as pieces of the True Cross and were now entirely beside the point in the flow of daily life. In a few months, Tommy would not be able to tell you how most of those objects fit into the intricate labyrinth of inference and conclusion that had been the state's case. Now it was only the outcome that mattered. Rusty Sabich was a felon in prison.

"I was out in Morrisroe," said Tommy. He briefed Brand on the meeting. Letting convicts loose was going to be a campaign issue once it hit the press, but Brand was more interested in Sabich.

"You just dropped in on him? No lawyer, no nothing?"

"Kind of like old friends," said Tommy. It hadn't even occurred to him that Sabich might have refused to speak to him. Or seemingly to Sabich, for that matter. They were both much too engaged by the long-running contest between them to want to involve anyone else. It was like fighting with your ex-wife.

"How's he look?" Brand asked.

"Better than I thought he would."

"Shit," said Brand.

"I wanted to ask him face-to-face how he screwed with the computer."

"Again?"

"He wouldn't answer. I think he's protecting his kid."

"That's about what I figured."

"I know. I ran into Gorvetich a couple of days ago. He said you got blasted together after the trial and you said you think Rusty copped to something he didn't do. I couldn't imagine what the hell you were talking about at first. And then it came to me that you thought he was fronting for his son."

Brand shrugged. "Who knows what I was thinking? I was on my ass. So was Milo."

"But I still don't see what would have given you the idea Rusty was taking the kid's weight?"

Brand pulled a mouth and stared back down at his desk. The piles were organized with military precision, edges even and spaced exact distances apart, like the beds in a barracks. He picked up a stack of manila folders and looked around for someplace to put them.

"Just a feeling," he said.

"But why?"

Brand dropped the files on an open corner on the desk where they clearly didn't belong.

"Who cares, Boss? Rusty's in the can. Where he should be. At least for a little while. What are you afraid of?"

Afraid. That was the right word. Tommy had woken up at three, and most of the time he'd been flat-out nightmare scared. He tried to believe he was just torturing himself the way he sometimes did, unable or unwilling to absorb his own success. But he knew he was going to have to find out in order to be able to live with himself.

"What I'm afraid of, Jimmy, is that you *know* Rusty didn't put the card on the computer."

Brand finally sat down in his desk chair. "Why would you think that, Tom?"

"I've just been putting together a lot of pieces in the last couple of days. What you said to Gorvetich. The fact that you were sitting here all night after the PC had been unwrapped. And that Orestes had showed you how it could be powered up without removing the evidence tape. That was after the banker came in and it looked all of a sudden like our case was circling the drain. And you know computers. You took programming from Gorvetich. So I gotta ask, right, Jim? We still don't have anything else that would pass as an explanation. You didn't put that card on there, did you?"

"How could I have done that?" asked Brand with disarming calm. "I couldn't have turned that computer on and messed with it without the program directory showing it had been opened. Remember?"

"Right. Except the PC was going to be turned on the next day in court, and it would be that date and time that would show up in the directory." He had Brand's attention now. Jim was watching Tommy with care.

"It's brilliant," said Tommy. "Create a defense, which explains all the evidence, so Stern has to embrace it. And then when he has, you blow it completely out of the water. And blame the defendant for the fraud. It's just absolutely brilliant."

Brand looked across the desk for quite some time with a dead expression. And then slowly, he began to smile, until he was grinning at Molto in the familiar way he so often did, as the two of them appreciated the clowning, the irony, the flat-out comedy, of human misbehavior and the law's futile efforts to curb it.

"It woulda been pretty fuckin brilliant," he said.

Inside Tommy, something broke, probably his heart. He sat in a wooden chair across the office. All Brand had needed to tell him was no. In the meantime, Jim's smile had slackened as he registered Tommy's mood.

"That man killed somebody, Boss. Two somebodies. He's guilty."

"Except of what we convicted him of."

"Who cares?"

"I do," said Tommy. For all the years he'd worked in this office, he'd listened to one PA after another lecture his deputies about a prosecutor's duty to strike hard blows but fair. Some of them meant it; some of them said it with a wink and a nod, knowing how hard it was to play redcoats and Indians, to march in straight lines down the center of the road while the bad guys hid in the bushes and attacked. Tommy had probably wavered on all of that before Tomaso was born. But you had a different stake in the future with a child. You had to teach him right from wrong. Without quibbling or qualification. The murky truth would always be on the street. But there was no hope at all if the prosecutor didn't draw hard lines and stand behind them.

"The man stood up in court and admitted he was guilty," said Brand.

"Would you do that to protect your son? He knew he didn't do it, Jim, and his kid would be the only other person with a motive to try to take him out that way. So he pled to put an end to all of it."

"He's a murderer."

"You know," said Tommy, "I'm not even completely sure about that anymore. Tell me why that woman, who was already struggling, didn't just give up the ghost when she found out about her husband's affair and kill herself?"

"His fingerprints are on the pill bottle. He searched about phenelzine."

"That's our whole case? You really telling me we wouldn't have thought twice about proceeding if we knew Barbara had been to the bank?"

"He didn't deserve to walk away again. Not to mention you. You've been wearing Rusty as lead ankle weights for twenty years."

He didn't want what Brand had done. It was no gift

to him. But even as he'd sat there in the dark in the middle of the night, hearing the sobbing, sleeping breaths now and then of his son, and occasionally his wife, often in an inexplicably close rhythm, he'd understood this much: that if Brand had done it, he'd done it for him.

"It works out for you, too, Jim. You're the guy who's running to become the next PA."

Bluff but quick-eyed and defensive up until now, Brand sat forward in true anger. His big hands were closed hard.

"I've been sucking hind tit for you for years, Tommy, because I owe you that. Because you're entitled to that. You've been better to me than my own brothers were. I've never put myself ahead of you. I love your ass and you know it."

He did know that. Brand loved him. And he loved Brand. He loved Brand the way warriors learned to love the men and women who stood beside them in the trenches, who watched their backs and were among the few who actually understood the fear and bloodshed and turmoil of war. You became like Siamese twins that way, joined at the heart or some other vital organ. Brand was loyal. And Brand was smart. But he hung on tight to Tommy for his own reasons. Because he needed a conscience.

"Look," said Brand. "Shit happens. It's the middle of the fucking night and you're fried and angry, and you get this half-ass idea, mostly because you know you could do it, and you get started and it takes on a life of its own. To tell you the truth, I was laughing out loud the whole three hours it took me. It seemed pretty comical at the time."

Tommy considered that. That was probably true, too. Not that it did any good.

"I'm not going to let that guy sit in the can for something he didn't do, Jim."

"You're crazy."

"No, I'm not. I'm going to call Judge Yee. We're going to file a motion in arrest of judgment this afternoon. Sabich will be out by tomorrow morning. I just need to figure out what to say. And what to do with you."

"With me?" Brand stiffened. "Me? I didn't do anything. I didn't testify falsely. I didn't offer any false evidence. I'm not the one who turned on the computer. Read the record, Tom. You won't find a word in the transcript where I did anything other than tell the court that the card was a fraud. And I brought evidence forward to prove that and prevent the court from being misled. What crime is that?"

Tommy considered Brand sadly. These days, crime made him sad. When he was younger, crime made him angry. Now he knew it was just an indelible part of life. The wheel turned, people seethed with impulse and held themselves back most of the time. And when they didn't, it was Tommy's job to see them punished, not so much because what they had done was incomprehensible—not when you were really honest about how people could be—but because the other folks, the ones trying to contain themselves every day, needed the warning and, more important, the vindication of knowing bad guys got what they deserved. The regular people had to see the point of the bit and bridle they put on themselves.

"You can't prosecute me," said Brand. "And if you ever did, Tom, you know exactly how it would end up. People will just blame you."

With Brand's last words, Tommy felt his heart wince and he made a pained sound. But before answering, he sat thinking all of it through. Brand was quicker than he was, and he'd had many weeks to analyze the situation. So how would this actually unfold? Molto asked himself.

A special prosecutor would have to be appointed. The argument Brand had made a second ago, that he had done nothing to defraud the court, would cut no ice with the special. Tampering with the evidence in the middle of a trial was a crime of one kind or another.

Proving that, however, was a different matter. There were just the two of them in this room. Even if Tommy's account of the conversation was accepted, Brand hadn't really made a detailed admission yet.

But the most important point was what Brand had said last, the artful threat he'd posed. Because Brand was right. Once Tommy fired the bullet, it was sure to ricochet and go right through him. If a prosecutor ever got close to indicting Brand, Jim would bargain his way out by saying Tommy knew, that whatever Brand did, he'd done at Tommy's behest. If Molto turned on him, as Jim saw it, he'd repay the favor by turning on Tommy. If Brand lied well enough, Tommy could even end up convicted. And even if it didn't get quite that far, he'd be back in the same purgatory he was in twenty years ago. People would believe it, because he'd admitted messing around then. Life, Tommy thought not for the first time, was not particularly fair.

"Okay," Molto said after he'd weighed things out for several minutes more, "here's what's going to happen. I'm going to tell Judge Yee that we've discovered that the chain of evidence on the PC had been corrupted: The computer sat unwrapped in your office the night before it was turned on, and contrary to what we always understood, we've learned that the tape seals were not secure and that the computer could have been tampered with by anyone who was in the PA's office that night or early the following morning. We're not saying that happened. But since Sabich would never have pled if he knew we couldn't prove a proper chain of evidence, we're moving to void the conviction and to dismiss those charges as well.

"And you're going to resign from the office in the next thirty days. Because there will be a big stink when Rusty walks away again. And it was your fault that the computer was not properly secured. You're going to take the blame for Sabich skating. Because it is your fault, Jim."

"Which will fuck my candidacy," said Brand.

"Which will fuck your candidacy," said Molto.

"Am I supposed to say, Thank you?" said Brand.

"You could. I think you will when you get some time."

"It sucks," said Brand.

Tommy shrugged. "It's kind of a sucky world, Jimmy," he said. "At least sometimes." He stood up. "I'm going to call Sandy Stern."

Cornered and embittered, Brand was nibbling unconsciously on one of his thumbnails. "Isn't he dead yet?"

"Not from what I hear. They say he's actually rally-
ing. It just goes to show you, Jimmy."

"What's that?"

"It's why we get up in the morning. Because there's
never any telling." He looked at Brand, whom he'd
once loved, and shook his head. "Never," he repeated.

Chapter 44

Anna, August 5–6, 2009

Y ou won't believe this," Nat tells me first thing when I pick up my cell in my office. He repeats the words. Each time I think Nat and I have crashed the last wave, that it cannot get any crazier, that we are finally on the downslide toward a regular life, something else comes up. "I just got off the phone with Sandy. They're letting my father out. Can you believe this? They're dismissing the charges."

"Oh, Nat."

"Can you believe this? Apparently Molto found out from the evidence tech that the computer wasn't secured the night before I turned it on. So there's no chain of evidence, and without a good chain there's no provable offense."

"I don't understand."

"I don't either. Not really. Neither does Sandy. But Yee already entered the order. Sandy still hasn't reached my father, because guys in seg can't get unscheduled phone calls. How's that for catch-22? Stern is waiting for the warden to call him back." A second later, Nat's phone beeps with an incoming call, and he lets me go so he can talk to Marta.

I sit in my little office, looking at the picture of Nat on my desk, full of relief for him, with joy for his joy. And even then, there is a cold corner on my heart. Although I would never wish it this way, the ugly truth is that for me it has been easier to have Rusty gone, to have no more of those confused moments when we have been together, with the signals jammed on both sides by mutual will and each of us seemingly counting the seconds until we can get away. Since Barbara died, we have said next to nothing to one another and have barely even lifted our eyes in each other's direction. The only real exception came in that moment right after his guilty plea, when Rusty turned and saw with clear surprise that I was seated beside Nat in the courtroom. "Complex" is not word enough for that look. Longing. Disapproval. Incomprehension. Everything he has probably ever felt about me was contained there. Then he turned away and held his hands behind himself.

I sit at my desk for the next forty minutes and do absolutely nothing except wait for the phone to ring again. When it does, the Sterns have finally come up with a plan. Rusty will be released from the state work farm at Morrisroe at three a.m. The timing is Sandy's idea. He is unsure whether word of Rusty's departure will leak, but he is confident that these days none of the news organizations can easily afford the overtime involved in sending out reporters and photographers in the middle of the night.

"Can you come with?" Nat asks me.

"Isn't this a time for just your dad and you?"

"No," he says. "Marta and Sandy are going to be there. We're the only family my dad has now. You should come, too."

It is a long night waiting to leave. The glum, visibly withdrawn man I have lived with for close to a year now is gone, at least for a while. Nat cannot sit down. He walks circles around the condo, checks the Web for the latest commentary about his father, and turns on the TV to read the crawl on the all-news cable stations. Apparently, a cadre of reporters arrived downstate to catch footage of Judge Yee leaving his chambers at five thirty p.m. today. He said nothing but smiled and waved at the cameras, amused as always by the amazing turns in life and thus the law. The reporters all use the word "stunning" to describe today's events. Stern has released a statement that the reporters read verbatim, praising the integrity of the prosecuting attorney and saying Sandy expects his client to be released tomorrow.

Around nine p.m., I suggest to Nat that we go out to grab some groceries for his father. It makes a good diversion, since Nat takes pleasure in gathering the things he knows his dad likes. Back home, we decide to go to bed—something good will happen there, a nap, at least—and we actually have to scramble to reach the Sabich family house in Nearing on time at one a.m., where we have agreed to meet to be sure there is not a press vigil already. Assuming all goes well at the institution, Rusty should be back here by four a.m. and will depart at once, before the press horde stakes out the place, for the family cabin in Skageon. It seems bizarre that a man would emerge from seg and choose to spend more time alone, but according to Stern, Rusty pointed out that being able to go down to town to buy a paper or watch a movie will make all the difference.

The Sterns arrive a few minutes after us in Marta's Navigator. Marta and Nat embrace at length in the driveway. When he releases her, he goes to the passenger side, where he leans in to hug Stern, more briefly. I met both of the Sterns a few months ago, when they were preparing for the trial, but Nat reintroduces me. I shake hands with Sandy. Under the dome light, he looks far more robust than the last time I saw him in court. The startling rash that covered a large part of his face is nothing but a faint blotch, and he has lost the starved, hollow look of a prisoner of war. It is not clear to Nat, or perhaps even to Sandy, whether this recovery is only a brief reprieve or something more lasting. For whatever significance it may hold, he does remark, as he is apologizing for not standing to greet me, that he is going to do something about "this damnable knee" as soon as he can face the hospital again.

On the ride, Nat peppers Sandy with questions about his father's future. Will Rusty get his pension? Can he go back on the bench? Nat alone seems unable to recognize what is patent to everybody else in the car, that Rusty's release on these terms, the ultimate in technicalities, will only go to make him more of a pariah. Since the DNA results became public in late June, the media talkers have often painted Rusty as a vicious schemer who committed two murders and manipulated a system he knew intimately to escape with minimal punishment. Now they will howl that he has escaped with no punishment at all.

Stern, however, is patient with Nat, explaining that

his father will regain his pension, but that his status on the bench is far more complicated.

"The conviction is void, Nat, and since your father was automatically removed from office when he pleaded guilty, he will be reinstated. But Rusty admitted in open court that he obstructed justice, and he can hardly take that back. Not to mention everything he acknowledged at trial—improperly disclosing a decision of his court to Mr. Harnason, engaging in ex parte contact. The Courts Commission would be hard-pressed to ignore all of that. So they are bound to try to remove him.

"Overall, Nat, subject to your father's wishes, I would regard it as a very satisfactory outcome if we can barter your father's hasty resignation from the bench for an agreement that Bar Admissions and Discipline will take no action—or very limited action—against him. I would like to make sure that he will be able to return to practicing law eventually." For a second, the difficulties of Rusty's future, with no job, few friends, and next to nothing in the way of public respect, confound all of us and bring silence to the car.

We are at the institution nearly an hour early and spend time in an all-night truck stop, coffeeing ourselves to stay awake and lingering over the pictures of Marta's kids that she has stored on her phone. Finally, at two forty-five, we drive through the tiny town to approach the institution. The work farm stands on the formerly empty portion of the grounds of the state's lone maximum-security prison for women. The camp itself is a series of Quonset-like barracks and a central administration building of brick, where Rusty is

housed on the top floor. The only substantial structure, it is surrounded by barns and two vast fields full
of ripe beans and corn plants, which are high enough
in August to look like graceful figures when their leaves
bob on the breeze. Although the camp is a minimum-
security facility, the neighboring institution requires
a chain-link fence topped in whorls of razor wire and,
within, brick walls nearly twenty feet high, with guard
towers rising every couple hundred yards.

To further confuse the press, Stern and the warden
agreed that Rusty will be released through the transport gate on the west side of the institution, where
inmates are bused in and out. We park there in the
gravel drive, outside the massive steel doors.

A few minutes before three, we hear voices in the
still night, and then, without ceremony, one of the
huge doors squeals and parts no more than a yard.
Rusty Sabich steps into the beam of Marta's headlights,
shielding his eyes with a manila envelope. He is wearing
the same blue suit he had on when he was sentenced,
with no tie, and his hair has grown amazingly long,
more of a surprise to me than the whitish beard Nat has
described after his visits. He is also quite a bit thinner.
Nat and he walk toward each other and finally fall into
each other's arms. Although we all stand at least twenty
feet away, in the still night, you can hear the sounds of
both men weeping.

Finally, they break apart, dabbing their eyes, and
walk arm in arm toward the rest of us. Stern has used
his cane to come to his feet, and Rusty embraces both
his lawyers at length, then gives me a quick hug. In the
drama of the moment, I have not noticed that another

car has pulled up behind us, and I am briefly alarmed
until Sandy explains that this is a photographer, Felix
Lugon, formerly of the *Trib*, whom Stern notified. He
wanted a picture for his walls, he says, but will also be
able to use the photo as a way to bargain for a page-one
story spinning Rusty's side of things in the next couple
of days, if that proves advisable. The Sterns and Nat and
Rusty link arms and pose for a couple of shots, then
Lugon snaps away as Rusty gets into the front seat of
Marta's SUV. Marta has already triggered the ignition
when another figure emerges from the gate and trots
toward us. It turns out to be a guard in uniform. Rusty
opens the window and shakes hands with him, jabber-
ing in Spanish, then after a final wave, the window is
raised and we drive off through the heavy dust that
Lugon's car raised, finally on the way to bring Rusty
Sabich home.

The trip back always seems faster. Marta cruises along at
more than eighty, eager to get Rusty on his way. After
seeing Rusty, Sandy has scotched the idea of publishing his photo. Rusty's appearance is so different that he
will have virtual anonymity, assuming we can avoid the
press outside his house.

The former prisoner is quiet for some time, watching the landscape whiz past from the passenger's seat
and grunting faintly now and then, as if to say, Oh,
yes, I forgot open space, what it looks and feels like. He
unseals the envelope he was carrying, which contains
his belongings. He takes all the cards out of his wallet
and looks them over one by one, as if to remind himself
what they are for. And he seems inexpressibly delighted

to find that his cell phone still works, although it blinks out after a second, in need of a charge.

"Can you explain this to me?" Rusty finally says when we have been on the road some time.

"Explain what?" asks Stern, to whom the question was directed, from the backseat.

"Why Tommy did this."

"I've already told you what he said, Rusty. The computer was not secured the night before it was turned on in court. Game, set, match. They cannot establish a chain."

"But they must know more than that. Don't you think? Why would Tommy admit that at this stage?"

"Because he is supposed to. Tommy is not the old Tommy. Everyone in the Tri-Cities will tell you that. Besides, what else could they know?"

Rusty does not answer, but after a minute he describes a visit that Tommy Molto made to him two days ago in the prison, where Tommy told him that some people in his office believe Rusty pleaded guilty to a crime he did not commit. Even the famously unflappable Sandy Stern cannot keep from jolting visibly.

"Forgive me," Stern says, "I am only the poor lawyer, but it might have been wise to let us know that."

"I'm sorry, Sandy. I realize this sounds ridiculous, but I took it as a private conversation."

"I see," says Stern. Rusty has turned to see Sandy in the rear seat, and behind his back Marta soundlessly mimes banging the heel of her palm against her forehead. In the rear seat between Nat and Sandy, I feel Nat's grip tighten on my hand, as he silently ticks his head back and forth. None of us is ever going to understand.

We are in Nearing a few minutes after four. The neighborhood is quiet. In the driveway, there is another round of hugs. Nat and I transfer the groceries from my car to Rusty's in the garage, and we stand aside to wave him on his way to Skageon. Instead, the ignition on Rusty's Camry gives one polite cough, a little like the sound Sandy keeps making, and goes utterly silent. Dead.

"The best laid plans," says Rusty as he climbs out. I offer my car, but Nat reminds me that I have a dep tomorrow in Greenwood County. For a second, the five of us debate alternatives. Marta is eager to get her father home in order not to deplete him further, but she has a set of jumper cables at her house, which is nearby. Male bulk will be required to move the two seventy-pound bags of fertilizer that are blocking the cabinet. If the car won't start after the jump, then we'll try to figure a way for Rusty to rent or borrow a ride.

I get into my car to drive Nat over, but he comes around to my side and whispers through the open window, "Don't leave him alone, not now."

I stare at him for just a second, then hand over the keys. Nat is already behind the wheel when he leans out to whisper again.

"See if he wants breakfast, maybe? Do you mind?"

Rusty has already gone inside the house alone when I follow through the garage with two bags of groceries. He has plugged in his cell phone and is at the kitchen window, peeking through the curtains.

"Reporters?" I ask.

"No, no. I thought I might have seen a light next door. The Gregoriuses always have a car or two nobody is driving."

The truth is that he seems far better than I would have hoped. During the trial and the months leading up to it, he had become a man as different in a short space of time as anybody I have ever known. Stern seemed less depleted by mortal illness. Rusty was ruined and empty, a sunken ship. Sometimes when we were with him, I watched him greet people he knew on the street. He still remembered what to say. He would stick out his hand at the right moment, but it was almost as if he were afraid to occupy his space on earth. I was never sure Nat noticed any of this. He was so busy trying to come to terms with his father, he did not seem to realize that the guy he'd known had largely fled. But now he's back. And it is not freedom to thank. I know that instantly. It is having been punished, paying a price.

"Nat thought you might want some breakfast," I say.

He takes a step closer to peek into the bags. "Is there any fresh fruit in there? I never thought the first thing I'd long for after prison is a strawberry."

A close observer always of both his parents, Nat had bought blueberries and strawberries, and I start to wash and cut.

As the tap runs, Rusty says behind me, "Barbara always wanted to redo this kitchen. She just hated the idea of having workmen in here all the time."

I look around. He's right. The place is dated and small. The cherry cabinets are still beautiful, but everything else is out of style. Still, the mention of Barbara is odd. As occurs often, the ghostly way Barbara haunted this household moves through me, the intensity of the passion she felt for her son and the persisting depths of her unhappiness. She was one of those people who needed courage to live.

"I didn't kill her," he says. I glance back very briefly to see him seated at the cherry kitchen table, with its old-fashioned scalloped edge, staring to observe my reaction.

"I know," I say. "Were you afraid I doubted that?"

My response is honest, but it ignores the months it took for me to feel comfortable with that conclusion. My problem, much as I have never wanted to judge the proof, is my own preloaded software. I stitch together evidence like some lady who quilts obsessively. It's why I was destined for the legal profession, the canny girl who was looking out for her mother and herself from an early age, searching the world for signs and putting them together. So there was no way for me not to ponder the most uncomfortable things I knew—that Rusty went to consult Prima Dana forty-eight hours after I told him I was going to start seeing Nat or the savage look with which he left the Dulcimer that day, a man smelting in the heat of his own rage. Worst of all, I remembered the read receipts that seemed to indicate that Barbara had gone through my e-mails to Rusty. She had betrayed nothing the night Nat and I had come to Nearing, but I often imagined that there had finally been a shattering scene between Rusty and her after we left.

Yet I could never make myself envision murder. My time with Rusty is far behind me. Yet I saw enough of his essence in those few months to be sure he is not a killer.

"At moments," he answers now.

"Is that why you thought I'd fiddled with your computer? I mean, Tommy's right, isn't he? You pleaded guilty to something you didn't do." I have thought of this before, but the exchange with Stern in the SUV clinched it for me.

"I didn't know what to think, Anna. I knew I didn't do it. I was never completely confident in the so-called experts, but they kept insisting that the computer was fully sealed when it was brought to court, so that ruled out someone in Molto's office—which by the way has got to be the answer. Don't you think? Tommy can say whatever he wants for public consumption. He knows somebody who works for him got around the seals and added the card in order to sucker-punch us."

That point has not been quite as clear in my mind until he says it, but I realize he is right. I have never forgotten Molto fooled around with the evidence decades ago, and I feel a little embarrassed I did not recognize this before. We will never know what turned the PA around now. Probably fear of exposure, for some reason.

"Anyway," he says, "back in June, I thought the only people who could have done it were Nat or you. Or the two of you together. The experts never seemed to focus on that, the possibility the two of you could have worked in concert to put the card on there. The last thing I wanted was for the whole inquiry to go on long enough for that thought to finally dawn on Tommy and Gorvetich.

"But I couldn't ever make sense of why either of you would have done something like that. A thousand things went through my mind. And made sense for a couple of seconds. But one of them was that you believed I was guilty and tried to get me out of it because you blamed yourself for me killing Barbara, thinking I did it so I could get you back."

I am sweeping the last of the berries into a bowl, and I avoid turning to him for a second. The very worst moment I had in the last two years was when those read receipts turned up on my computer, and next worst was the day Nat called me from the courthouse to say, 'She knew. My mom knew.' The banker had just testified, and Nat had taken one of his familiar breaks to cry. I love the fact that he cries. I have realized in the last year that I have waited all my life for a man who never claims to be immune to the pain of life, unlike that great fake I have for a mother.

'Knew?' I asked. 'What did she know?' Because of everything that emerged in court I realize that Barbara was putting on an act for Nat's sake the night before she died, but in the moment she had been convincing, and there were times in the last year when I harbored a faint hope that the read receipts were triggered by something else, like the scrubbing program run on Rusty's PC, and that Barbara had died unknowing. Now I crashed into my own despair. I have been stabbed at so often by guilt and apprehension that it was hard to believe they could cut sharper or deeper, yet I felt then as if I were being dissected. Generally speaking, I have been good throughout my life at faking my way along, especially when I am suffering. But my difficulty in understanding myself sometimes paralyzes me. Why did I ever want Rusty? And what seems like the greatest mystery of all—why didn't I ever give a fig about Barbara? In the past two months, there has been a parade of moments when I have nearly been knocked cold by the recognition of the monumental pain I caused her in the last week of her life. Why didn't I see the stakes for her when I was throwing myself at her husband? Who was I? It's like trying to understand why I once jumped off a rock forty feet above the Kindle while I was in high school and nearly killed myself when I lost consciousness for a second with the impact. Why did I think that was fun?

In my own defense, I really didn't know how edgy Barbara was. Before we became intimate, Rusty always presented her as difficult rather than crazy, speaking of Barbara much the way the Indians do the Pakistanis, or the Greeks talk about the Turks, traditional enemies at peace along an uneasy border. At the time, I took that only as an opening, an opportunity. I never considered the harm to her. Because, as is always true of people who do the wrong thing, I was certain we would never be caught.

I place the berries on the table in front of him and hand over a fork.

"You having any?" he asks.

"No appetite." I smile weakly. "Did you?"

"What?"

"Still want me back when Barbara died?"

"No. Not really. Not by then."

I have a dozen excuses for what went on with Rusty. The law seemed such a grand point of arrival for me, a destiny I was so long headed toward. I wanted to absorb everything, do everything. It was like standing before a temple. And I knew how much longing rested unexpressed inside him. You could almost hear it from him, like a brake grinding on a drum. I believed, stupidly, I would be good for him. And I knew that whatever the open sesame was with men, I hadn't found it yet, and this was another key to try. But in the end, I was using him, and I realized that. I desperately wanted somebody like him, somebody important, to want me, as if I would somehow possess everything the world had poured on him, if he was willing to forsake it all for me. It made sense. That's all I can say. In the irrational internal way the heart and mind can mesh. It made sense then and makes no sense now. At moments, I feel like begging, Take me back, put me back there so I can figure out who that girl was two years ago. It would not matter, anyway. I will always have to live with the regret.

"I didn't think so," I say. "That night Nat and I were here, the night before she died? You seemed to have let go of it. It's one more reason I never thought you killed her. I just didn't know why you'd gotten to that point so quickly."

"Because it turned out I wanted my son more than I wanted you. Is that too blunt?"

"No."

"It helped me put things in perspective. Not that it wasn't an awful situation. It still is, I suppose."

I don't think he means to accuse me, but of course, I am guilty enough to feel accused anyway.

"You are in love with him, right?" Rusty asks.

"Madly. Insanely. Do you mind my saying that?"

"It's what I want to hear."

Just uttering this little about Nat, I feel my heart swell, and tears forcing themselves to my eyes.

"He is the sweetest man in the world. Brilliant and funny. But so sweet. So kind." Why did it take me so long to see that was what I needed, someone who wants my care and can return it?

"A lot more than I am," Rusty says.

We both know that's true. "He had nicer parents," I answer.

Rusty looks away. "And he still has no clue?"

I shrug. How do we ever know what's in someone else's heart or mind? If we are always a mystery to ourselves, then what is the chance of fully understanding anybody else? None, really.

"I don't think so. I've started to tell him a thousand times, but I always stop myself."

"I think that's right," Rusty says. "Nothing to gain."

"Nothing," I say.

I have returned to see my therapist several times, but Dennis has no answers to the insane opera in which I found myself enmeshed after Barbara died, in part because he told me not to see Nat in the first place. But there's one thing Dennis and I always agree on, and that's that telling Nat the truth now would be impossibly destructive—not only of us, but of him. Most of what he assumed about his life on earth has shifted already in the last year. I can't ask him to pay another price just to relieve my overwhelming guilt. For me, this was always going to be a relationship built across the crater of a volcano. I have to walk those dangerous heights alone.

But people get used to things. Rusty got used to prison, amputees learn to live without limbs. If I can stay with Nat, the present will overwhelm the past. I can see us in a house, with kids, frantic with two jobs and figuring out who is going to be able to get home in time to pick up from the soccer games, can envision us anchored in a world entirely of our own making and still thrilled to the core by who we are to each other. I can see that. But I am not sure how to get from here to there. I kept thinking that if we could hold it together until the trial ended, we would be able to go on, a day at a time, and I still believe that now.

"I'm going to leave you two in peace," he says. "I can't really live here. Not now," he says. "Maybe I can come back eventually." He's quiet a second. "Can I ask something really personal?"

I am instantly afraid, until he says, "Do I have any hope of grandchildren?"

I just turn to him and smile.

"Wild horses," he tells me.

Outside, the garage door creaks and clatters. Nat is back. We both look in that direction. I stand up and Rusty gets up, too. I hug him quickly, but in earnest this time, with the sincerity and appreciation people always owe somebody they loved.

Then I head to the garage door to greet my sweet, sweet man. But before I get there, I turn back.

"You know, there's another reason I love him," I say.

"Which is?"

"There are ways he's a lot like you."

The Camry starts. With the long drive north, the battery will recharge. Nat gives Rusty the cables just in case, then we stand on the driveway, waving. The car backs down the drive, then Rusty stops and gets out, and he and Nat hug each other yet again. I think one of the hardest things in a relationship is dealing with the way your partner sees his parents. I learned that in my marriage to Paul, the fact he didn't understand how his mom tended to boss him, and I've witnessed similar things a number of times since. It's like watching someone struggle with Chinese handcuffs. You keep thinking, No, in, push in, don't pull back, they just get tighter, and the poor sap, this guy you love or hope to love, struggles anyway. I am glad for Rusty and for Nat, glad for this night, but I know they still have oceans left to swim across.

Then Nat and I start home. When you love someone, he is your life. The first principle of existence. And because of that, he has the power to change you and everything you know. It is like suddenly turning a map over so that south is at the top. It's still correct, still able to get you to anyplace you want to go. But it could not seem more different.

As an intellectual matter, I remember that I clerked for Nat's father and was once mad for him. I remember that I actually knew Rusty long before I first met Nat. But Nat was someone else then, a stick figure compared with the person who now dominates my life, while Rusty's chief significance today lies in the inevitable ways he can affect his son. My life is Nat. With Rusty gone, I feel the utter solidity of that fact.

We are both quiet, humming with our stuff. It has been quite a night.

"I need to tell you something," I say suddenly as we are crossing the Nearing Bridge. There is pink light leaking up from the horizon, but the buildings in Center City are still blazing, reflecting gorgeously on the water.

"What?" he asks.

"It's upsetting, but I want you to hear this now. Okay?"

When I glance over, he nods, looking darkly pensive beneath those thick eyebrows.

"When I moved in with Dede Wirklich after my divorce, I was working at Masterston Buff, writing ad copy, and still trying to finish college at night. And I was taking this advanced macroeconomics class in the U Business School. I'd gotten an A plus in Intro Econ, and I thought I was good at math and could sail through. The prof was Garth Morse. Remember that name? He was one of Clinton's economic advisers, and he's still on TV all the time, because he's really smooth and good-looking, and I thought it would be totally cool to take a class from somebody like that. But it was way, way over my head, with all these out-there equations that the B students understood instantly. I was upset anyway about leaving Paul and having a hard time concentrating, and I got back the midterm and there was this big fat F. So I went to see Morse. And I was in his office about ten minutes, and he gives me this long, long look, like he's seen too many old movies, and says, 'This is too complicated, we need to talk about it over dinner.' And okay, I wasn't totally surprised. He had a reputation. He thought he was God's gift. And Dede was like, 'Are you crazy, go ahead, you want to stay in college forever?' He really was good-looking and a pretty exciting, interesting guy, totally charismatic. But still. His wife was pregnant. I don't remember how I knew that—maybe he mentioned it in class—but that part really bothered me. But Dede had a point, I needed to graduate and move on, and I really couldn't stand just then, right after my marriage ended, to fail at anything else. And so—"

Nat hits the brakes so hard that I clutch and think about the air bag, when I can think at all. I look out the windshield to see what we hit. We are on the shoulder, right at the foot of the bridge.

"Are you okay?" I ask.

He has released his seat belt so he can bring his face close to mine.

"Why are you telling me this?" he asks. "Why now? Tonight?"

I shrug. "Because I'm sleep-deprived?"

"Do you love me?" he asks me then.

"Of course. Of course. Like I've never loved anybody else." I so mean that. He knows. I know he knows.

"Do you think I love you?"

"Yes."

"I love you," he says. "I love you. I don't need to know the worst things you've ever done. I know you had a rough time getting to me. And I had a rough time getting to you. But we're together. And together we're better people than we've ever been. I really believe that. That's all." He leans over to kiss me softly, looks in my eyes another second, then checks the mirrors before pulling the car back onto the road.

When you are twenty, you come to your boy-friends fresh. You are still hoping to find The One, and everybody who went before is really just a stepping-stone to that place and doesn't really matter. But at thirty-six—thirty-six!—that's no longer the case. You have been to the summit, believed in somebody's love forever, had the greatest sex you think you'll ever know—and somehow moved on to find something else. You have come to whoever is with you now along a rope line of experiences. You both know it. You cannot pretend what's in the past didn't happen. But it's the past, the way Sodom and Gomorrah lay in ash behind Lot's wife, who should have known better than to look back. Everybody understands when you get to this age that you carry history along, a person, a time whose effects cannot be fully forgotten. Nat has Kat, who I know still e-mails now and then and manages to upset him. And that is how it will be with Rusty and what happened with him. I see that now. He will be like the telltale heart still beating every now and then in the wall. But gone. It will be the past I lived, crazy but over, the past that somehow brought me to the life I really, really want that I will live every day with Nat.

CHAPTER 45

Rusty, August 25, 2009

I was in my teens before I realized my parents were not a physical match. Their marriage had been arranged in the old-country manner. He was a penniless refugee, piercingly handsome, and she was a dowdy old maid—twenty-three—from a family with property, meaning the three-flat in which my mother lived until the day she died. I am sure she was thrilled with him at first, while I doubt he ever tried to pretend he was enamored and grew ever more surly.

Every Friday night when I was a boy, my father disappeared after dinner. I looked forward to that, truth be told, since it meant I would not have to sleep on the floor in my mother's bedroom, locked in there, which was how we hid out from his frequent drunken rages. When I was in grade school, I assumed my father was spending his Friday nights in a tavern or playing pinochle, both routine pastimes for him, but he seldom came home from his carousing and instead went directly to the bakery to begin preparing for Saturday morning. But one Friday night when I was thirteen, my mother started a small kitchen fire. Most of the damage was to her—she was high-strung and fretful by nature—and the parade of firemen who stormed into her house reduced her to a state in which all she could do was shriek for my father.

I went to the tavern first, where one of my father's acquaintances—he really did not have friends—took mercy on me and my obvious agitation and said, as I was leaving, 'Hey, kid. Try the Hotel Delaney over on Western.' When I told the desk clerk there that I had to find Ivan Sabich, he gave me a watery, unhappy look but finally grunted out a number. It was not the kind of place where there were phones in the rooms in those days. I would say that even as I thumped up the filthy stairs, with the carpet worn to its backing and the halls reeking of some naphthalike agent used to control the infestation of pests, I was actually in some doubt about what I would find. But when I knocked, I recognized the woman, Ruth Plynk, a widow a good decade older than my father, who peered through the crack in the door in her slip.

I don't know why she came to the door. Maybe because my father was in the john. Probably because he was afraid the desk clerk had come up for more money. 'Tell him the house is on fire,' I said, and left. I did not know exactly what I felt—shame and anger. But mostly disbelief. The world was different, my world. After that, I sat enraged at dinner every Friday night, because my father hummed during the meals, the only time during the week that any sound came from him that bore even a remote resemblance to music.

Of course, I never thought once about staring at Ruth Plynk through the small space in that parted door when I was in the several hotel rooms I visited with Anna. It was only when I had to tell my son I'd had an affair that the moment returned to me, but it has not gone away in all the months since, whenever I see Nat's evident confusion in my presence.

That look is on his face now as he stands on my back doorstep. He told me last night, when I called to say I was finally headed back to sign the agreements Sandy has worked out, that he wanted to visit, but he has arrived earlier than expected. The first fall air has brought intermittent storms today. He wears a hooded sweatshirt, and his dark hair tosses in the high wind.

I am happy in the most fundamental way to see my son, although the sight of him is also accompanied by faint distress. We mean well by our children, but so much rests beyond our control. There is a nervous distraction to Nat, a looking here and there that I suspect will be permanent, and an ingrained frown that I realize I have seen for more than sixty years in the mirror. I pull open the door, we hug briefly, and he steps past me, stamping the rain off his shoes.

"Coffee?" I ask.

"Sure." He takes a seat at the kitchen table and looks about. This is surely hard for him, to return to this house where so many charged moments have passed in the last year. The silence lingers until he asks how I enjoyed Skageon.

"It was fine." I debate saying more but decide for many reasons that candor may be best. "I actually saw a bit of Lorna Murphy. The next-door neighbor?" The Murphys' vast summer house sprawls over several lots next to our little cottage.

"Really?" Despite all that has gone on in the last two years, he seems more amazed than troubled.

"She wrote to me last fall after your mom died, and we sort of stayed in touch."

"Ah. Grief counseling," says the permanent wise guy.

There is actually something to that. Lorna lost Matt, some kind of construction king, four years ago. A lithe blonde, an inch or two taller than I am, she has expressed a stubborn faith in me. I thought that was because she had been so long getting to the point of thinking about another guy, she simply couldn't change her mind after I was indicted. She wrote to me every week I was in prison and was my first call as I drove to Skageon on the morning of my release. I had no clue if I had the courage to suggest meeting up there, and in the event, I didn't have to. She said she would come up as soon as I told her I was headed that way. It was time for each of us to be with someone else.

She is a dear woman, quiet, warm but contained. I suspect she is not my future. Time will tell. But I learned one thing with her. If I don't fall in love with Lorna, I will fall in love with someone else. I will do it again. That is my nature.

"I was going to ask if you fished while you were up there."

"Oh, I fished. I fished from the canoe. I caught two nice walleye. Great meals."

"Really? I'd love to fish with you one weekend this fall."

"It's a date."

The coffee is done. I pour for each of us, and I sit

down at the cherry kitchen table, with its wavy edge. It has been here throughout Nat's life, the story of our family written there in the stains and gouges. I can remember the origin of many of them—misfired art projects, temper tantrums, pans too hot for bare wood I stupidly set down.

Nat is looking away, lost in something. I stir my coffee and wait for him.

"How's all your work coming?" I ask eventually. Nat will continue subbing here in Nearing this fall, but he was also hired at Easton Law School to teach a jurisprudence course in the winter term, filling in for one of his former professors who will be on leave. He has been spending much of his time preparing for that. And he is back to work on his law review article, comparing the law's model of knowing conduct with what's suggested by the latest neuroscience research. It could be a pathbreaking piece.

"Dad," he says without looking at me, "I want you to tell me the truth."

"Okay," I say. I feel a stitch draw in my heart.

"About Mom," he says.

"She killed herself, Nat."

He closes his eyes. "Not the party line. What actually happened."

"That's what actually happened."

"Dad." He shows again some of that perpetual agitation, the birdlike glancing about. "Dad, one of the things I really hated about growing up in this house was that everybody had secrets. Mom had her secrets, and you had your secrets, and you and Mom had secrets together, so I had to have secrets, and I always wished everybody would just fucking talk. You know?"

This is one complaint I fully understand and would probably be powerless to change.

"I want to know what really happened to Mom. What you know."

"Nat, your mother committed suicide. I don't kid myself to think that my behavior had no role in it, but I didn't kill her."

"Dad, I know that. You think I don't know that? But I'm your son. I get you, okay? And I've thought about this. And I know two things. Number one. You didn't sit here for twenty-four hours after she died to handle your grief, because frankly, that's not you. You've always pushed emotions down like somebody sticking wadding into a cannon. Maybe it'll blow later. But you go on. You always go on. You'd have cried or frowned or shaken your head for a while, but you would have gotten on the phone. You were sitting here trying to figure something out. That's one thing I know. And here's the other. I watched you when you pled guilty to obstruction of justice. And you were serene. You said you were guilty with absolute conviction. But since I *know* you didn't screw with that computer—because you told Anna that—that means that whatever lying and messing around you did, you did a long time ago. And I say it was when Mom died. Am I right?"

Smart kid. His mother's son. Always a very, very smart boy. I manage a small smile, a bit proud, when I nod.

"So I want to know everything," he says.

"Nat, your mother was your mother. What I was to her or she to me doesn't change any of that. I wasn't trying to treat you as a child. The truth is that I asked myself if I'd want to know the things I never told you, and I really believe I wouldn't. And I hope you'll take a minute to consider that."

Nat never really gets angry at anyone the way he does with me. Anger at his mother was too dangerous. I am a safer target, and the fashion in which I have always eluded him, or tried to, as he sees it, infuriates him. But the rage that closes his brow, that darkens his blue eyes, is, of course, Barbara's.

"Okay," I say. "Okay. The truth, Nat, is your mother killed herself. And that I didn't want you, or anybody else, to know that. I didn't want you to be upset, or to have to shoulder the weight the children of suicides always carry. And I didn't want you to ask why. Or to know what I'd done to provoke her."

"The affair?"

"The affair."

"Okay. But how did she die?"

I raise a hand. "I'm going to tell you. I'm going to tell you everything." I take a breath. Sixty-two years old, I have the vulnerabilities of the Serbian kid who was never considered cool in school. I was smart and, as a young boy, no one to mess with on the schoolyard— I was vicious when provoked. But I was not cool—not someone anybody cared to hang with on the weekends, to invite to parties, or to joke with in the hall. I have always been alone and feared the meaning of my isolation. Although I have lived in Kindle County my entire life, attended grade school, high school, college, and law school here, practiced in this place for more than thirty-five years, I lack a best friend, especially since rheumatoid arthritis drove Dan Lipranzer, the detective

I preferred to work with as a prosecutor, to Arizona. Not to say I don't have good times or enjoy the company of close professional acquaintances, like George Mason. But I lack a figure of essential connection. That was something I think Anna knew about me and seized upon. But my greatest hopes somehow have always been pinned to my son. Which is not a fair assignment for a child. Yet as a result I've always had a special fear of being rejected by Nat. I need to steel myself now.

"The day you and Anna came for dinner, I'd been working in the garden."

"Planting the rhodie."

"Planting the rhododendron for your mother, right. And my back was killing me. And she brought me my four Advil as we were making dinner."

"I remember that."

"I didn't take them. I was distracted by the whole situation—you and Anna together. I forgot. And so after you were gone, as I was getting ready to go to sleep, your mom brought the pills upstairs to me again. She put them down on the night table. She told me I should take them or I wouldn't be able to get out of bed in the morning, and she went into the bathroom to get me a glass of water. And I don't know, Nat. The phenelzine tablets—they look just like the ibuprofen. Same size. Same color. Somebody even said that out loud at one point during the trial. But no matter how close the resemblance, there was a difference of some kind, something minute, but a difference. I never put the pills down side by side to see what it was I'd noticed, but I picked them up and stared at them in my hand for the longest time, and when I looked back up, your mother was there, with the glass of water, and you know, Nat, that was quite a moment."

"Because?"

"Because for just a second, a few seconds, she was really happy. Gleeful. Victorious. She was happy I knew."

"Knew what?" he asks.

I stare at my son. Accepting the truth is often the hardest task human beings face.

"That she was trying to kill you?" he asks at last.

"Yes."

"Mom was trying to kill you?"

"She'd been to the bank. She'd been in my e-mail. She knew what she knew. And she was lethally angry."

"And she'd decided to kill you?"

"Yes."

"My mother was a murderer?"

"Call it what you want."

Now that he has heard it, he is finding it hard to speak. I can just about see his pulse twitching in his fingertips. It is a bad moment for both of us.

"Jesus," says my son. "You're telling me my mother was a killer." He snorts and says out loud, the cat-quick logician, "Well, one parent must be, right?"

I get it after a second. Either I'm lying because I murdered her or this is the truth.

"Right," I say.

He takes another instant to himself, staring at the refrigerator. The Christmas pictures from more than a year and a half ago have still not come down. The babies born, the happy families.

"She knew who it was. The girl?"

"As I said, she'd been in my e-mail."

"I'm not going to ask you to tell me—"

"Good. Because I'm not going to."

"But it must have really pissed her off."

"I'm sure she was enraged. And not only for her sake. She was trying to spare other people, too."

"So it was somebody's daughter. One of your friends? It had to be someone she was close to."

"No more, Nat. I can't sacrifice somebody else's privacy."

"Was it Denise? That's what I've always figured—that you got involved with Denise."

Denise is Nat's cousin, a couple years older than him, the daughter of Barbara's youngest uncle. A stunning young woman, she's had more than her share of trouble and is currently struggling in her marriage to a state trooper for the sake of their two-year-old.

"There's no point, Nat. I behaved like an absolute jerk. That's all."

"I already knew that, Dad."

Touché. He sits at the table, looking away again, dealing once more with all his disappointment. I suspect what he is thinking: Mom was right. It all would have been easier without me. If one of us had to go, if I had created a situation where he could have only one parent, better it be Barbara. That was exactly what Barbara concluded, particularly because I had no right to imperil Nat's happiness with Anna.

In the meantime, Nat heaves a labored sigh and takes a second to finally remove his jacket.

"Okay. So you looked at Mom. And she's got this mad gleam in her eye."

"I wouldn't quite put it like that. But I looked at the pills and at her, back and forth, and it was one of those moments. 'Zero at the bone.' And I think I said something stupid and obvious like, 'Is this Advil?' and she said, 'Some generic.' And I stared at the pills again. Nat, I don't know what I was going to do then. Something didn't seem right, but I don't know if I was going to swallow them or say, 'Show me the bottle,' and I never found out, because she came over and snatched them from my hand and downed all four of them. One motion. 'Fine,' she said, and walked away in a typical huff. I thought it was your mother being your mother."

"She preferred to die rather than get caught?"

"I don't know. I'll never know. I think in the moment, she couldn't enjoy watching me kill myself as much as she thought she would. She had to be feeling a lot right then, including a good deal of shame."

"She saved you from her?"

I nod. I'm not sure that's right, but it will do for a son thinking about his mother.

"The phenelzine," he says. "That was just because it happened to look exactly like a pill you regularly took?"

"It does. Which she'd probably realized years ago. And that provided an opportunity. But I think the larger point was to make it appear like I died of natural causes. So no one would ever guess."

"Like Harnason tried to do."

"Just like Harnason. I'm sure she took some satisfaction in finding the primer in how to kill me in one of my own cases."

He smiles a little ruefully, which I take as an unvanquished appreciation for his mother.

"But there was a fail-safe," I say. "If the phenelzine overdose was detected somehow, she would say I'd committed suicide. That was why she'd made sure I picked up that prescription—and handled the bottle when I came in so I'd leave prints. That's why she'd sent me to the store to get the sausage and the cheese and the wine. One of the searches about phenelzine and its effects had already been done on my computer. She had a belt and suspenders."

He nods. He's followed all of that.

"Okay, but what was she going to say was your motive to kill yourself right before the election? You were about to hit the peak of your professional life, Dad."

"That's sometimes hard for people, Nat. And there was the divorce, my visits with Dana. I hadn't carried through the year before, so she could say I just couldn't face it."

"Wouldn't it look bad for her to come up with all of that after the fact?"

"She'd cry a little. Who wouldn't believe that a despairing widow would be eager to spare the reputation of her prominent husband, not to mention her sensitive son? She'd say the bottle of phenelzine had been out on my sink when she found me, and when they identified only my prints on the vial, it would corroborate her story. But no one would ask questions. Especially with Tommy Molto sitting in the PA's office saying good riddance to me. Besides, they could have torn the house apart. There was none of the stuff here they were looking for—mortar and pestle, dust from the phenelzine. They could have exhumed my body. They would never find anything that wasn't consistent with me voluntarily taking an overdose of phenelzine. Because of course that was exactly how I would have died."

He fingers his coffee cup while he considers it all. And then, as I would have expected a while ago, he begins to cry.

"Jesus Christ, Dad. You know. This lawyer thing in you. You can be like Mr. Spock. That's what I was saying before. You couldn't have sat around mourning. It's just not in you. Your way is to go completely cold. Like you're a million miles off. You talk about her as if she was a serial killer, or a hit man—you know, somebody who knew how to do this, to kill people. Instead of a super-angry, super-hurt person."

"Nat," I say, and say no more. That is how it has gone forever, my displeasure with him expressed in no more than his name. There is no point in reminding him that this is the truth he demanded. He goes to the sink for a paper towel to wipe his eyes and blow his nose.

"And how did you figure all of this out, Dad?"

"Slowly. That's what took a day."

"Ah." He sits again. Then runs his hand forward for me to go on.

"When I woke up, the sheets were wet with her perspiration. And your mom was dead. My first thought was that it was heart failure. I did CPR, and then when I went for the phone on her nightstand, I saw a stack of papers which she'd left under the water glass she'd brought for me to take the pills."

"What kind of papers?"

"The ones she'd gotten from the bank. The receipt from Dana's firm. Copies of the cashier's checks that paid my legal bills and the STD clinic. Monthly statements with the deposit amounts circled. She'd obviously put them there after I went to sleep."

"Because?"

"It was the equivalent of a note. She wanted me to know she knew."

"Ah," says my son.

"I was shocked, of course. And not especially happy with myself. But I realized how angry she must have been. And that this clearly wasn't an accident. It didn't take me long to think about the pills and to wonder what she'd taken that she'd intended to give me. So I went to her medicine cabinet. And the bottle of phenelzine was right inside in front. I picked it up and opened it, looked down to be certain those were the tablets. That's where the rest of my fingerprints came from.

"Then I went to my computer to find out about the stuff. And you know how the browser finishes your search term if you've used it before? 'Phenelzine' came right up. That's when I realized she'd been on the PC. I was scared immediately that she had been through my e-mail. When I looked, she'd gone in there and deleted those messages."

"From that woman? Pretty stupid to have left them there, Dad."

I shrug. "I never thought your mother would nose around like that. She would have gone postal if I'd ever glanced at *her* e-mail."

The truth, of course, is that I knew I was taking some chance, but that I could not bear to erase those messages, the lone memento I had of a time I still often longed for. But I cannot say that to my son.

"Why would she bother deleting them? Or the e-mails from Dana?"

"Because of you."

"Me?"

"That's my best guess. If things worked out as she intended, if my death was taken as one by natural causes, there was still a good chance you'd want to look through my e-mail, not to investigate, but just to remember your father, the same way mourners like to look through old letters. By sanitizing the account, she'd leave your memory of me in peace.

"But on the rare chance there was an investigation, it would have suited her purposes for those e-mails to be gone."

"Because?"

"Because it ensured there would be nobody to contradict whatever story your mother was going to tell. She'd have to account for the papers from the bank and acknowledge knowing I'd had an affair the year before. But she could say she never knew with who. It would have come off that I was thinking of divorce, but couldn't face it for unclear reasons. Maybe the girl dumped me when I told her I was going to leave my marriage. With all the corroboration of my suicide, there would never have been any further investigation."

He takes his time again.

"Where did those papers go, anyway? The ones from the bank on the nightstand?"

I laugh. "You're smarter than Tommy and Brand. Once we put the banker on to testify she gave your mother those documents, I kept waiting for the prosecutors to ask where the hell her copies went. They searched the house several times. But things were happening too fast, and besides, it was just as reasonable for them to think that she had destroyed them."

"But you did, right?"

"I did. Tore them into bits and flushed them down the toilet. That day. Once I figured it all out."

"Thereby committing obstruction of justice."

"Thereby," I reply. "My testimony in the trial was not a model of candor. There was a lot I didn't say I should have said if I was telling the whole truth. But I don't think I committed perjury. I certainly didn't want to—it would have rendered my whole professional life a joke. But the day your mother died? I destroyed evidence. I misled the police. I committed obstruction of justice."

"Because?"

"I already told you. I didn't want you to know how your mother died, or what role my own stupid behavior had played in that. Once I read about phenelzine, I thought the odds were overwhelming that the coroner would just take it as heart failure. I knew that Molto would be the biggest hurdle, so I would have been happiest if we could have avoided the police and the coroner, but you wouldn't let me. The funeral home probably wouldn't have, either, but I was going to try."

Nat looks at length into his coffee cup, then gets up without a word to refill it. He adds milk, then sits again and assumes the same pose. I know what he is weighing. Whether to believe me.

"I'm sorry, Nat. I'm sorry to tell you this. I wish there were some other conclusion to be drawn. It is what it is. You can never really anticipate what's going to happen once things start to go wrong."

"Why didn't you say all this stuff at trial, Dad?"

"It still wasn't a story I was eager for you to hear about your mother, Nat. But the biggest problem would have been admitting that I messed with the police and destroyed your mother's papers. As the law says, 'False in one thing, false in all.' The jury wouldn't have had much sympathy for a judge screwing around that way. I told as much of the truth as I could, Nat. And I didn't lie."

He looks at me at length, the same question still circulating, and I say to him, "I got myself into quite a mess, Nat."

"I'd say." He closes his eyes and works his neck for a second. "What are you going to do, Dad? With yourself?"

"Sandy has the agreements for me to sign this afternoon."

"How is he?"

I rap my knuckles on the wooden table.

"And what's the deal he cut?" Nat asks.

"I resign from the bench, because of what I did with Harnason. But I get to keep my pension. It's ninety percent of my three best years, so I'll be fine financially. Your mother left a decent bequest for me, too. There's already talk about who will replace me on the court of appeals, by the way. Want to guess the name Sandy is hearing most often?"

"N. J. Koll?"

"Tommy Molto."

He smiles but doesn't laugh. "And what happens with BAD?" Bar Admissions and Discipline. "What happens with your law license?"

"Nothing. I keep it. The obstruction conviction is a nullity. Purely judicial misbehavior is not in their baili-wick traditionally."

"And what will you do?"

"I had some talk with the state defender's office up in Skageon. They always need an extra pair of hands. I thought that would be interesting after being a prosecutor and a judge. I don't know if I'll stay up there permanently, or try to come back eventually. I'll let things cool down for a year or two. Give people time to forget the details."

My son looks at me and turns it all over again. His eyes well.

"I just feel so bad for Mom. I mean, think about this, Dad. She scarfs down those pills, and knows what she's done to herself. And instead of going to the emer-gency room, she takes a sleeping pill and crawls into bed next to you to die."

"I know," I answer.

Nat blows his nose again, then rises and heads to the back door. I stand three steps above, watching him with his fingers on the knob.

"I hope you don't mind me saying this, but I still don't think you've told me everything, Dad."

I lift my hands as if to say, What more? He stares, then comes back up and raises his arms to me. We cling to each other a second.

"I love you, Nat," I tell him, with my face close to his ear.

"I love you, too," he answers.

"Hi to Anna," I say.

He nods and goes. From the kitchen window, I watch him walking down the driveway to Anna's little car. We filled him with our troubles, Barbara and I, but he will be okay. He is a good man. He is with a good person. He will be okay. We did our best for him, both of us, even if we tried too hard at times, like lots of parents of our generation.

But along the way I've made more mistakes than that one. Probably the biggest of them was not accepting the inevitability of change more than twenty years ago. Rather than imagine a new life, I pretended about the old one. And for that I have surely paid a price. In my darker moods, I feel the cost has been too high, that fate has exacted an unfair revenge. But most of the time, when I think of how much worse it all could have turned out, I realize I have been lucky. It does not matter, though. I am going on. I have never doubted that.

My initial days out of confinement weren't easy. I was not accustomed to other people or much stimulation. I was jumpy around Lorna and for the first week never slept through the night. But I came back to myself. The weather was remarkable, day after sparkling day. I was up before her, and in order not to wake her, I would sit outside in my fleece, looking at the water and feeling the full thrill of life, knowing I still have the chance to make something better for myself.

I go now into the living room, where the forest of framed family pictures decorates the shelves: my parents and Barbara's, all of them gone; our wedding photo; the pictures of Barbara and me with Nat as he grew. A life. I look longest at a portrait of Barbara taken up in Skageon not long after Nat was born. She is uncommonly beautiful, facing the camera with a small smile and a look of elusive serenity.

I have thought often about Barbara's last hours, and on much the same terms as my son, who was always so quick to feel her pain. I'm sure she took some time to foresee how all of this would play out. When that message popped up on the computer during the trial, I wondered if she'd died hoping it would look as if I'd murdered her, that she'd somehow seeded the card as a final revenge. But now I am sure Nat has it right. Barbara's ultimate moments were totally despairing, particularly that she hadn't gotten more from me. Bad marriages are even more complex than good ones, but always full of the same lament: You don't love me enough.

In the months I awaited trial, I thought of Barbara far more than Anna, whom I'd finally left behind. I would come look at these photographs and mourn my wife, occasionally miss her, and far more often try to fathom who she was at her worst. I wish I could say I did my best by her, but that would not be true. Nearly four decades on, I still have no clear idea what it was I wanted from her so deeply, so intensely, that it bound me to her against all reason. But whatever it may be belongs to the past.

In the living room, I stand. I pat the pockets of my shirt, my pants, to be sure I have everything, that I am, in a sense, still all here. I am. In a minute, I will head into Center City to Stern's office to sign away my career on the bench in final settlement for all my folly in recent years. And that's okay. I'm ready to find out what happens next.

Evanston
11/20/09

Acknowledgments

I am indebted to many persons for their help with this book. A number of physicians provided essential assistance on medical issues: Dr. Carl Boyar, medical director of Clearbrook Center in Arlington Heights, Illinois; Dr. Michael W. Kaufman of NorthShore University HealthSystem in Evanston, Illinois, a pathologist; Dr. Jerrold Leikin of NorthShore University HealthSystem in Glenview, Illinois, a toxicologist; Dr. Nina Paleologos of NorthShore University HealthSystem in Evanston, a neurologist; and Dr. Sydney Wright of Northwestern University Hospital, Chicago, Illinois, a psychopharmacologist. My law partner Marc J. Zwillinger, in the D.C. office of Sonnenschein Nath & Rosenthal, and Russ Shumway, our technical director of E-Discovery and Forensic Services, greatly enhanced my understanding of computer forensics. I am immensely grateful to all of these experts for their aid. The mistakes I made, notwithstanding their efforts, are clearly my fault, not theirs.

I had three incisive advance readings from close friends, James McManus, Julian Solotorovsky, and

Jeffrey Toobin. I am very, very grateful to each of them for helping me shape the manuscript. My daughter, Rachel Turow, and her husband, Ben Schiffrin, were also important sounding boards, and I owe Rachel special thanks for helping me avoid several embarrassing errors.

To my editor at Grand Central, Deb Futter; my agent, Gail Hochman; and, most especially, Nina, who all stayed with me, draft by draft, thanks is not really word enough.

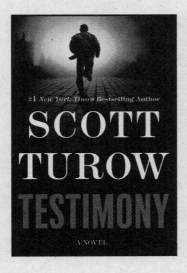

Prologue

5 March 2015

*T*here were men," said the witness. He was lean and dark, the color of an acorn, and seated beside his lawyer at the small table reserved for testimony, he appeared as tense as a sprinter on the starting line.

"How many men?" I said.

"Eighteen?" he asked himself. "More. Twenty? Twenty," he agreed.

The witness's name was Ferko Rincic, but in the records of the International Criminal Court, he would be identified solely as Witness 1. To protect him, a shade closed off the spectators' section in the large courtroom, and electronically distorted versions of Ferko's voice and image were being transmitted to the few onlookers, as well as over the Internet. Standing several feet away at the prosecutor's table, I had just commenced my examination with the customary preliminaries: Ferko's age—thirty-eight, he said, although he looked far older—and where he lived on April 27, 2004, which was the place they called Barupra in Bosnia.

"And about Barupra," I said. "Did anyone share your house with you?"

Ferko was still turning to the right at the sound of the translator's voice in his headphones.

"My woman. Three daughters. And my son."

"How many children in all did you have?"

"Six. But two daughters, they already had men and lived with their families."

I picked up a tiny photo, creased and forlorn with wear.

"And did you provide me with an old photograph of your family when you arrived this morning?"

Rincic agreed. I announced that the photo would be marked as Exhibit P38.

"Thirty-eight?" asked Judge Gautam, who was presiding. She was one of three judges on the bench, all watching impassively in their black robes, resplendent with cuffs and sashes of royal blue. Following the Continental custom, the same odd white linen cravat I also wore, called a 'jabot,' was tied beneath their chins.

"Now let me call your attention to the computer screen in front of you. Is that photo there, P38, a fair resemblance to how your family looked on April 27, 2004?"

"Daughter third, she was already much taller. Taller still than her mother."

"But is that generally how you all appeared back then, you and your wife and those of your children still at home?"

He peered at the monitor again, his expression shrinking in stages to some form of resignation before at last saying yes.

I began another question, but Rincic suddenly stood up behind the witness table and waved at me, remonstrating in Romany, words the translator was too surprised to bother with. It took me an instant, therefore, to realize he was concerned about his photo. Esma Czarni, the English barrister who had initially brought Ferko's complaint

*here to the International Criminal Court, rose beside
him, drawing her torrents of dark hair close enough to
briefly obscure Ferko while she sought to calm him. In the
meantime, I asked the deputy registrar to return the old
snapshot. When she had, Ferko studied it another second,
holding it in both hands, before sliding the picture into his
shirt pocket and resuming his place next to Esma.*

"And in P38, is that your house directly behind you?"

*He nodded, and Judge Gautam asked him to answer
out loud, so the court reporter could record his response.*

*"And what about these other structures in the back-
ground?" I asked. "Who lived in those houses?" 'House'
was generous. The dwellings shown were no better than
lean-tos, each jerry-rigged from whatever the residents of
Barupra had salvaged. Timbers or old iron posts had been
forced into the ground and then draped most commonly
with blue canvas tarpaulins or plastic sheeting. There
were also chunks of building materials, especially pieces
of old roofs, which had been scavenged from the wreckage
of nearby houses destroyed in the Bosnian War. That war
had been over for nine years in 2004, but there was still
no shortage of debris, because no one knew which sites had
been booby-trapped or mined.*

"The People," answered Ferko, about his neighbors.

*"And is the word in Romany for 'the People' 'Roma'?"
He nodded again.*

*"And to be clear for the record, a more vulgar word in
English for the Roma is 'Gypsies'?"*

*" 'Gypsy,' " Ferko repeated with a decisive nod. That
might well have been the only word of English he knew.*

*"Well, we'll say 'Roma.' Was it only Roma who lived
in Barupra?"*

"*Yes, all Roma.*"

"*How many persons approximately?*"

"*Four hundred about.*"

"*And now let me ask you to look again at the computer screen. This will be Exhibit P46, Your Honors. Is that roughly how the village of Barupra appeared during the time you lived there?*"

Esma had secured a couple of photos of Barupra and the surrounding area, taken in 2000 by one of the international aid agencies. The picture I was displaying showed the camp from a distance, a collection of ragged dwellings clinging together at the edge of a forbidding drop-off.

"*And how long had you and the other Roma lived there?*"

Ferko seesawed his head. "*Five years?*"

"*And where had you and your family and the other people in Barupra—where had you been before that, if you can say?*"

"*Kosovo. We ran from there, 1999.*"

"*Because of the Kosovo War?*"

"*Because of the Albanians,*" he answered with another dismal wobble of his head.

"*So let us return then to the late hours of 27 April, 2004. About twenty men appeared in the Roma refugee camp at Barupra in Bosnia, correct?*" We waited again for the laborious process of translation to unfold a floor above the courtroom, where the interpreters were positioned behind a window. My questions were transformed first from English to French—the International Criminal Court's other official language—and then by a second translator into Romany, the Roma's own tongue. The answer came back the same way, like a wave rippling off the shore, finally *reaching me in the female translator's plummy British accent. This time, though, the process was short-circuited.*

"Va," answered Rincic in Romany as soon as he heard the question in his language, adding an emphatic nod. We all understood that.

"And what nature of men were they?" I asked. "Did they appear to have any profession?"

"Chetniks."

"And please describe to the Court what you mean by that word."

I leaned down to Goos, the tall red-faced investigator assigned to the case, who was seated next to me at the foremost prosecutor's desk.

"What the hell is a Chetnik?" I whispered. Up until that moment I had thought I was doing fairly well, having been on the job all of three days. There was nothing here I was familiar with—the courtroom, my colleagues, or the rigmarole of the International Criminal Court with its air of grave formality. The black robe I wore and the little doily of a tie beneath my chin made me feel as if I were in a high school play. This was also the first time in my life I had examined my own witness without the opportunity to speak to him in advance. I had first met Ferko Rincic in the corridor, only seconds before Esma escorted him into the courtroom. He had gripped the hand I offered merely by the fingertips in a mood of obvious distrust. I did not need anyone to tell me he would rather not have been here.

"They are supposed to be soldiers," said Ferko of the Chetniks. "Mostly they are just killers."

By now, Goos had inscribed his own note concerning the Chetniks in his uneven script on the pad between us: "Serb paramilitaries."

"*And how were these Chetniks dressed?*" At the witness table, Rincic himself wore weathered twill trousers, a collarless white shirt, a dark vest, and a yellowish porkpie hat, which none of us had thought to tell him to remove in the courtroom. All of it—his long crooked nose that appeared to have been broken several times, his hat, and his thick black mustache, which might have been a smear of greasepaint—made Ferko resemble a lost child of the Marx brothers.

"*Army uniform. Fatigues. Flak jackets.*"

"*Were there any insignia or other identification on their uniforms?*"

"*Not so I remember.*"

"*Were you able to see their faces?*"

"*No, no. They were masked. Chetniks.*"

"*What kind of masks? Could you make out any of their features?*"

"*Balaclavas. Black. For skiing. You saw only the eyes.*"

"*Were they armed?*"

Again Rincic nodded. This time, to reemphasize the need to answer aloud, Judge Gautam created a broadcast thump by tapping on the silver microphone stalk that rose in front of her, as well before Rincic and me, and at forty other seats in the rows of desks ringing the bench. Those spots were normally reserved for defense lawyers and victims' representatives, but they had no occupants for today's pretrial proceeding, in which the prosecutor was the lone party.

The large courtroom was a pristine exercise in Dutch Modern, perhaps a hundred feet wide, with a bamboo floor, and furnishings and wainscoting in yellowish birch, the color of spicy mustard. The design impulse had favored the basic over the grand. Decorative elements were no more elaborate than wooden screens on the closed fronts of the desks and on the wall behind the judges, where the round white seal of the International Criminal Court also appeared.

Once Ferko had said yes, I asked, "Did you recognize the weapons they carried?"

"AKs," he answered. "Zastavas."

"Would that be the Zastava M70?" It was the Yugoslav Army version of the AK-47.

"And how is it that you can recognize a Zastava, sir?"

Ferko raised his hands futilely, while his face once more swam through a series of bereft expressions.

"We lived in those times," he said.

Goos called up a photo of the weapon on the computer screens, which rose around the courtroom, beside the microphones. It was a Kalashnikov-style assault rifle with a folding stock and a long wooden handguard above the curved ammunition magazine that projected with phallic menace. I had first seen Zastavas years ago in Kindle County, when I was prosecuting street gangs who were frequently better armed than the police.

"Now when the Chetniks arrived, where were you situated? Were you in your house?"

"No. I was in the privy." I already suspected the translator, with her upper-class accent, was significantly enhancing Ferko's grammar and word choice. Based on my very brief impression of him, I was fairly certain he had not said anything remotely like 'privy.'

"And why were you in the privy?"

When this question finally reached Ferko, he jolted back in surprise and slowly lifted his palms. Laughter followed throughout the courtroom—from the bench, the registry staff seated below the judges, and my new colleagues from *the Office of the Prosecutor, a dozen of whom were at the desks behind me to watch this unprecedented hearing.*

"Let me withdraw that silly question, Your Honors."

Goos, with his ruddy round face, was smiling up at me in good fellowship. The moment of comedy seemed to have suited everyone well.

"If I may lead Your Honors: Had a need awakened you, Mr. Witness, and brought you to the privy in the middle of the night?"

"Va," said Rincic and patted his tummy.

"Now, if you were in the privy, sir, how were you able to see these Chetniks?"

"At the top of the door, there is a space. For air. There is a footstool in the privy. When I first heard the commotion as they came into the village, I opened the door a slice. But once I saw it was Chetniks, I locked the door and stood on the stool to watch."

"Was there any light in the area?"

"On the privy, yes, there was a small light with a battery. But there was some moon that night, too."

"And were you alone in the privy throughout the time you saw or heard the Chetniks?"

Several people around the courtroom giggled again, thinking I had once more stubbed my toe on the obvious.

"At first," Ferko said. "When the running and screaming started, I saw my son wander by. He was lost and crying, and I opened the door very quick and brought him in there with me."

"And how old was your son?"

"Three years."

"And once you had grabbed your son, what did you do?"

"I covered his mouth to keep him quiet, but once he knew he couldn't talk, I stood again on the stool."

"I want to ask you about that point in time when the screaming started. But before I do, let me turn to other things you might have heard. First of all, these Chetnik soldiers, did they speak at all?"

"Va."

"To the People or to themselves or both?"

"Both."

"All right. Now how did they speak to the People?"

"One had an electronic horn." He meant a power bullhorn.

"And what language did that soldier speak?"

"Bosnian."

"Do you speak Bosnian?"

He shrugged. "I understand. It is somewhat like they speak in Kosovo. Not the same. But I understand mostly."

"And did he sound like other Bosnians you had heard speaking?"

"Not completely. Right words. Like a schoolteacher. But still, on my ear, it was not right."

"Are you saying he had a foreign accent?"

"Va."

"And did the Chetniks speak to one another?"

"Very little. Mostly it was with the hands." Ferko raised his own slim fingers and beckoned in the air to demonstrate.

"They used hand signals?" There was a pause overhead. The term 'hand signal' apparently did not have an obvious equivalent in Romany. Eventually, though, Ferko again said yes.

"Did you hear the soldiers say anything to one another?"

"A few whispers when they were near the privy."

"And these words—what language was that?"

"I don't know."

"Was it any dialect of Serbo-Croatian? Croatian, Bosnian, Serbian? Do you understand those dialects?"

"Enough."

"And were the words you heard in any of those tongues?"

"No, no, I don't think so. To me, I thought it was foreign. Something foreign. I didn't recognize. But it was very few words."

"And the man with the horn. What did he say first in Bosnian?"

"He said, 'Come out of your houses. Dress quick and assemble here. You are returning to Kosovo. Gather the valuables you can carry. Do not worry about other personal possessions. We will collect them all and transport them to Kosovo with you.' He repeated that many times."

"Now, you say screaming started. Tell us about that, please."

"The soldier continued yelling into the horn, but the other Chetniks went from house to house with their rifles and electric torches, waking everyone. They were very well organized. Two would enter, while other Chetniks made a circle outside with their rifles pointed."

Judge Gautam interrupted. She was about fifty, with a pleasant settled affect and long black hair in a contemporary flip. I had been warned, however, that she was not nearly as mild as she appeared.

"Excuse me, Mr. Ten Boom," she said to me.

"Your Honor?"

"The witness has just testified that the soldiers were speaking a foreign language and that it was not Croatian,

Bosnian, or Serbian. That surely does not sound like Chet-niks, does it?"

"I wouldn't know, Your Honor. I never heard the word before today."

Again the sounds of hilarity cascaded through the courtroom, most heartily behind me from the prosecutors. Both of the other judges laughed. Gautam herself man-aged a bare smile.

"May I ask the witness a question or two to clarify?" she said.

I swept a hand out grandly. There was not a court-room in the world where a lawyer could tell a judge to keep her thoughts to herself.

"You testified, Mr. Witness, that the soldiers were in fatigues. Was that camouflage garb?"

"Va."

"The same for each soldier or different?"

Ferko looked up to reflect. "The same, probably."

"And over the years in Kosovo and Bosnia, had you seen many soldiers in camouflage fatigues?"

"Many."

"And had you noticed that different armies and dif-ferent military branches each had their own fatigues, with distinctive camouflage patterns and coloring?"

Ferko nodded.

"And on that night in 2004, when you saw these sol-diers in fatigues, could you recognize the army or mili-tary branch they belonged to?"

Ferko again lifted his palms haplessly. "Yugoslav maybe?"

"But over the years had you noticed the fatigues of dif-ferent countries sometimes resembled each other? Had you seen, for example, the similarity in the camouflage outfits

of the Yugoslav National Army and the United States Air Force?"

Ferko gazed at the ceiling for a second, then waved his hands around vaguely.

"But in the dark, could you say whether these soldiers wore the Yugoslav uniforms or the American uniforms?"

Once the question reached him, Ferko shook his head and made a face.

"No," he said simply.

Judge Gautam nodded sagely. "Now Mr. Ten Boom," she said to me, "would you care to follow up in any way on my questions?"

On my notepad, Goos, who'd worked throughout the Balkans a decade ago, had written, 'NO USAF in Bosnia then.' Olivier Cayat, the law school friend who'd recruited me for the ICC, had briefed me on Judge Gautam. A former UN official in Palestine who had never actually practiced law, she was known to be part of the clique within the ICC disturbed that an American prosecutor had been assigned this case. But her insinuation that I might have been covering up for my countrymen was insulting—and unwarranted. She had just heard me go to considerable lengths to make sure Ferko mentioned that the gunmen were speaking a language he didn't know.

Having resumed my seat during the judge's questions, I took a second to adjust my robe as I again stood, preparing to ask Ferko if he'd seen even one member of the US Air Force on the ground in Bosnia at that time. From behind, Olivier discreetly pushed a folded note in front of me, which I opened below the level of the desk. 'IGNORE her,' it read. 'A trap.'

The attention of the courtroom was already focused on me, and I stood in silence before I understood. If I asked that question, Judge Gautam, who was guaranteed to have the last word, would add some public comment branding me as an apologist for the US. I ticked my chin down slightly to let Olivier know I'd gotten the point. The formal air of the ICC felt genteel as velvet, but the currents below were treacherous.

"No follow-up," I said.

"Well," the judge said, "given the witness's answers, and without objection from my colleagues, we will ask him to refrain from describing these men as 'Chetniks' and to refer to them simply as 'soldiers.' And would you do the same, please, Mr. Ten Boom?"

She attempted to smile pleasantly, but there was a lethal glimmer from her black eyes.

In the meantime, Esma slid her chair from the end of the desk and leaned close to Ferko again to explain the judge's direction. I had first met Esma last night, when we'd conferred about what I could expect Ferko to say. At one point, I had asked her to limit her conferences with Rincic in front of the court. His testimony would count for little if it looked like he was merely the mouthpiece for an experienced barrister. She had reassured me with a tart little smirk, amused that I thought I needed to school her about the dynamics of the courtroom. She'd proven her savvy by leaving behind the designer attire she'd worn yesterday, coming to court in a simple blue jumper and only a bit of makeup and jewelry.

I turned again to Ferko.

"Now you said, sir, there was screaming?"

"The women were yelling and carrying on to have strange men see them when they were not dressed. The children began crying. The men were angry. They rushed *from the houses, sometimes wearing only shoes and underwear, cursing at the soldiers."*

"And do you remember anything the people in Barupra said to these soldiers?"

"Sometimes the women cried out, 'Dear God, where would we be moving? We have no other home. This is our home now. We cannot move.' And some of the soldiers yelled, 'Poslusaj!'"

With Goos's help, I had Ferko explain that the term meant 'Do as we say.'

"In each house," he said then, "the soldiers gave the People only a minute to leave. Then two or three soldiers would go in with their assault rifles pointed to check that the place was empty. Often they just tore the house down as they swung the light of their torches this way and that."

I asked, "Now, had you ever heard before about any plans to move the residents of Barupra back to Kosovo?"

"When we came first, yes. But then, no more. Not for years."

"Did you yourself—did you want to go back to Kosovo?"

"No."

"Why?"

"Because the Albanians would kill the People. They had tried already. That was why we had come all the way to Bosnia. To be near the US base. We thought that close to the Americans we would be safe." He stopped for a second to reflect on that expectation.

"And by that you mean Eagle Base, established near Tuzla by the US Army, as part of NATO's peacekeeping efforts?"

A bridge too far. When the translation reached him, Ferko again stared comically and once more raised his palms, short of words.

"American soldiers. NATO. I know only that."

"Now, as the soldiers cleared the houses and the residents gathered in various collection points, what happened?"

"There were trucks that drove up from below."

"How many trucks?"

"Fifteen?"

"What kind of trucks?"

"For cargo. With metal sides. And the canvas over."

"Did you recognize the make?"

"Yugoslav, I thought. From the shape of the cab. But I didn't see for sure. They were military trucks."

"Now, as the vehicles arrived, did anything else unusual occur?"

"You mean the shooting?"

"Was there a shooting, Mr.—" I stopped. I had been about to use his name. *"Please tell these judges of this Pre-Trial Chamber about the shooting."*

With that, I turned to face the bench, the first time I had nakedly surveyed the court. Judge watching is usually a furtive exercise, since jurists, at least in the US, resent being studied for signs of their impressions. The three judges, all intent, occupied a bench raised only a couple of steps, a longer version of the Bauhausy yellow closed-panel desks in the well of the court. Beside Judge Gautam on her right sat Judge Agata Hallstrom, a lean sixtyish blonde who had been a civil court judge in Sweden, and on the left, Judge Nikolus Goodenough from Trinidad, the former chief justice of their Supreme Court. He never stopped scribbling notes.

"As they went from house to house, the People would argue. They would shout, 'I'm not moving.' The women especially. The soldiers grabbed them and forced them out,

and if they resisted, the soldiers struck them with their rifles, the butts or the barrels. Twice, the soldiers fired their guns in the air in warning. Once, a soldier shot his rifle and a woman would still not move, and I then heard her scream as she rushed out: 'He burned me with his gun. He put the muzzle on me while it was still hot. I am marked for life.' There was much screaming and running about. But the soldiers, especially those in the outer circle, they remained—" Again a pause ensued as the translator searched for a word. *"Stoic,"* she came up with at last, probably a million miles from what Ferko had actually said. *"They stayed in position with their weapons pointed. But near the privy, one man, Boldo, when they got to his house, he stormed out with an AK of his own."*

"Do you know why Boldo owned an AK?"

"Because he had the money to buy one," Ferko said, which produced another ripple of laughter in the courtroom. Bosnia, even in 2004, was not a place where a person could be entirely sanguine about being unarmed.

"And did Boldo say anything?"

"Oh yes. He was shouting, 'We are not going. You cannot make us and we are not going.' The two soldiers who had been clearing his house fell to the ground. They yelled in Bosnian, 'Spusti! Spusti!' "

There was another silence as the translator came to a dead end facing the Bosnian. Below me, Goos muttered, *"Put it down."* For all his amiability, speaking Serbo-Croatian was, so far as I could tell, the only visible talent Goos brought to the job.

"Were they yelling 'Put it down' in Bosnian?"

"Va."

"And did he put it down?"

"*No, no. He kept waving the AK around. The soldier in charge, who had the horn, he yelled again.*"

"*In what language?*"

"*Bosnian. Then he counted, one, two, three, and fired. Boom boom boom. Boldo exploded with blood and fell like he had been chopped down. Then his son came running out of the house. The soldiers yelled again, 'Stani!'*"

"*Stay back,*" whispered Goos.

"*The soldiers kept telling him to stay away from the body and the gun, but of course it was his father, and when the son went forward there was gunfire from the other side. Two or three shots. The son fell, too.*"

"*And how old was Boldo's son?*"

"*Fourteen? A boy.*" Again, Ferko worried his head about in mournful wonder. "*Finally, Boldo's brother ran up from his house. He was screaming and cursing. 'How could you shoot my family? What did they do?' He was weeping and carrying on. He fell to the ground, near the bodies. And he picked up Boldo's AK. After the two shootings, the soldier who seemed to be in charge, the one who killed Boldo, he ran up and waved and gave orders. He pushed the soldier who had shot Boldo's son away. And he ordered other soldiers forward to grab Boldo's brother. They wrestled with him quite a while. The brother was screaming and he would not let go of the AK. They hit him with their rifle butts a few times, but on the last occasion, the blow hit one of the other soldiers instead of Boldo's brother and that soldier fell. At that point, the commander ordered the soldiers back and he said to Boldo's brother, like Boldo, that if he did not drop the AK before the count of three, he would be shot. Instead, Boldo's brother raised the AK, and the commander shot him, too.*"

Just once. In the side. The brother fell down and held his side and made terrible sounds."

"Did they administer medical treatment to him?"

"No, he was there moaning the whole time."

"And what became of Boldo's brother?"

"He died. He was still there in a large circle of blood in the dirt when I came out of the privy later."

"And about the words the commander yelled to his troops—did you understand them?"

"No, no. But there was much shouting. The People were screaming to get back. And take cover."

"And after the gunfire stopped, what was the mood in the camp, if you can say?"

"Quiet. Like in church. The People went to the trucks. They didn't yell. They didn't want to get killed. The soldiers helped them up. As the houses were cleared, the trucks drove off. The camp was empty in perhaps twenty minutes after the last shots."

"Now when the trucks drove off, in what direction were they going?"

"They went west, down toward the mine below."

I had a topographical map, which I doubted Ferko would understand. It depicted the valley adjacent to Barupra and the switchback gravel road that descended to where a large pit had been excavated.

"And what kind of mine was in the valley?"

"Coal, they said. It closed because of the war."

"And what variety of coal mine was it? With shafts or open pit?"

"They dug for coal. Scraped up the earth. It was the brown coal."

"And how far from the village was the mining area?"

"A kilometer perhaps, down the road."

"Now, once the trucks left, did you ever hear the horn again?"

"Yes, I heard the horn again. It echoed back off the hill."

"What was said?"

"'Get out of the trucks. You will wait here in the Cave for the buses that will take you to Kosovo. We will go pick up your belongings now and they will follow you in the trucks.'"

"And by 'the Cave,' what did you understand the bull-horn to be referring to?"

"The Cave," said Ferko.

"What cave was that?"

"The cave he was talking about."

Beside me, Goos pinched his mouth to keep from laughing.

"Part of the mine was an area the People called the Cave?"

"Va."

"Now, calling your attention again to the computer screen at your desk—this will be P76, Your Honors—does that photograph depict the Cave more or less as it was in April 2004?"

This was another photo that Esma had turned up, in this case from the New York Times. The picture had been snapped from a distance in January 2002. It showed dozens of people scavenging coal in the harsh winter with their bare hands, many of them stout older women in headscarves, crawling along the incline below Barupra. We had enlarged and cropped the photograph to better depict the landscape. Apparently, years before a vein of coal had been discovered in the hillside, and heavy equip-ment had gouged out a deep oblong opening. That was the

Cave. With its huge overhang, the site did not look especially stable, and in fact there were yellow signs in Bosnian telling people to keep out: ZABRANJEN ULAZ.

"How large was the Cave? Can you estimate its measurements?"

"Several hundred meters across."

"And how deep into the hill did it go?"

"Fifty meters. At least."

"Was it large enough that everyone from Barupra could stand inside the Cave?"

"More or less."

"Now, did you hear anything further from the horn?"

"Yes. Eventually, he started repeating, 'Step back. Crowd in. Everyone into the Cave. Everyone. No exceptions. We need to count you and take your names. We will let you out one by one to do a census. Stay put. Stay put. You will be there only a few minutes.'"

"Now when these instructions were given, where were you?"

"Once the trucks and the People were all gone, I came out of the privy. My son and I hid in what remained of one house where I could look down into the valley."

"And could you see the Cave?"

"Not so much. I could see the headlamps of the trucks better. In that light, I saw them pushing the People back."

"And what happened with the vehicles?"

"The trucks? After several minutes, they started to move again. I thought they were going to come back up to collect everyone's belongings, as the horn had said. I picked up my son and was ready to run back to the privy, but I saw the lights going off in the other direction, *further down to the valley floor, and then across it to the other road."*

"West?" I asked.

He simply threw his hand out to indicate the direction.

"And did you hear the horn at all after the trucks moved?"

"Yes, but it seemed fainter."

"What was the horn saying?"

"The same. 'Stay put. Stay put.'" This time Ferko repeated the words in Bosnian. "'Ostanite na svojim mjestima.'"

"And what did you observe next?"

"Next?" He waited. For the first time, a tremble of emotion moved through Ferko's long face. He grabbed the bridge of his nose before starting again. "Next, I saw flashes on the hill above the Cave and heard the explosions. Six or seven. And I could hear the hill tumbling down." Without being asked, Ferko waved his hands over his head and imitated the sound, like a motorcycle's rumble. "The earth and the rock rushing down were almost as loud as the explosions. It went in waves. The roar lasted a full minute."

"Did you believe that the explosions had started a landslide?"

"Va."

"And what did you do next?"

"What could I do? I was terrified and I had my son. I hid with him under a tarp in case the soldiers came back. Half an hour perhaps I waited. It was suddenly so still. Every now and then there was the sound of wind. Under the tarp, I could feel the dust still settling out of the sky."

"Now after that half an hour, what did you do?"

"I told my son to remain under the plastic. Then I ran down into the valley."

"Did you go to the Cave?"

"Of course. But it was gone. The hill above it had tumbled down. The Cave was almost completely filled in and rocks now blocked the road."

"And what did you do then?"

"What could I do?" He shook his head miserably. He was weeping now, in spite of himself. He wiped his nose and eyes against his sleeve. "I called my woman's name and my children's names. I called for my brother and his children. I called and called and scrambled over the rocks, climbing and calling and pulling at the rocks. God himself only knows how long. But there was no point. I knew there was no point. I could claw at the rock the rest of my life and get no closer. I knew the truth."

"And what truth was that, sir?"

"They were dead. My woman. My children. All the People. They were dead. Buried alive. All four hundred of them."

Although virtually everyone in the courtroom—the judges, the rows of prosecutors, the court personnel, the spectators behind the glass, and the few reporters with them—although almost all of us knew what the answer to that question was going to be, there was nonetheless a terrible drama to hearing the facts spoken aloud. Silence enshrouded the room as if a warning finger had been raised, and all of us, every person, seemed to sink into ourselves, into the crater of fear and loneliness where the face of evil inevitably casts us.

So here you are, I thought suddenly, as the moment lingered. Now you are here.